CW00542303

SECRETS ANI
ROSIE LEE'S

Born in London, JANE LACEY-CRANE's writing
career began in cable TV, writing true crime
documentaries. More recently, Jane has
contributed to an anthology of short stories and
written two weekly crime serials. When she's not
writing, Jane loves to read good books, binge
watch TV boxsets and drink tea. And wine.

SECRETS AND TEA AT ROSIE LEE'S

Jane Lacey-Crane

www.ariafiction.com

First published in the United Kingdom in 2018 by Aria, an imprint of Head of Zeus Ltd

Copyright © Jane Lacey-Crane, 2018

The moral right of Jane Lacey-Crane to be identified as the author of this work has been asserted in accordance with the Copyright, Designs and Patents Act of 1988.

All rights reserved. No part of this publication may be reproduced, stored in a retrieval system, or transmitted, in any form or by any means, electronic, mechanical, photocopying, recording, or otherwise, without the prior permission of both the copyright owner and the above publisher of this book.

This is a work of fiction. All characters, organizations, and events portrayed in this novel are either products of the author's imagination or are used fictitiously.

9 7 5 3 1 2 4 6 8

A CIP catalogue record for this book is available from the British Library.

ISBN (E) 9781788546010

Aria
c/o Head of Zeus
First Floor East
5–8 Hardwick Street London EC1R 4RG
www.ariafiction.com

About *Secrets and Tea at Rosie Lee's*

Welcome to Rosie Lee's cafe in the heart of the East End - where there's not an avocado, slice of sour dough or double-shot no-foam soy milk caramel latte on the menu!

Rosie-Lee's owner Abby is a woman without a plan... and her beloved little cafe is a business with a serious lack of customers. The Rosie Lee's fry-up is legendary, but cooked breakfasts alone – however perfectly sizzled the bacon – aren't going to pay the bills.

Fast approaching forty and fighting a serious case of empty nest syndrome, Abby realises it's not just her menu that needs a makeover. And when Jack Chance, her The One That Got Away, saunters through the cafe doors and back into her life things definitely look set to change...

Abby has always believed a cup of strong builders tea makes everything better, but Jack's reappearance is a complication even the trusty sausage sarnie can't resolve....

For Grace & Sam – Mummy did it!

For Jason – thank you for those twelve-ish months!

Chapter 1

Rosie Lee's Café is a typical example of what a good café can be like – as long as it's 1988. That's probably the last time the décor or the menu was updated. This reviewer suspects that the owner may be waiting until its particular interior design style comes back into fashion. They may be in for a long wait.

'Bollocks!' I exclaimed. The positive review I'd been hoping for obviously wasn't about to materialise. I forced myself to read on.

Despite it being located just a stone's throw from Old Spitalfields Market, a newly regenerated hub of all things creative and on trend, the tide of urban regeneration seems to have passed Rosie Lee's by. I ordered the traditional breakfast fry-up and, I will say, the food didn't disappoint. The breakfast was cooked to perfection and my cup of good old 'Rosie Lee' (tea) was hot and freshly brewed. And the toast, although not sourdough, was crisp and very tasty. I should mention, though, that there is no gluten-free option.

I winced at the memory of the day this reviewer had visited us. He'd asked Flo for gluten-free bread and she'd told him that if he wanted anything fancy he could take his hipster beard and bugger off somewhere else.

All in all, Rosie Lee's Café is fairly uninspiring, but it won't give you food poisoning. Just for that this reviewer is giving it one teapot out of a potential five. Now, on to more interesting territory. Bare Naked Coffee is an artisanal bakery and coffee house...

I closed the newspaper. I didn't need to read about how fabulous their unleavened hemp bread was, or how their primo coffee blend 'was to die for!'

'Bollocks,' I repeated.

'Abby! The coffee machine's not working! Come and do that thing you do with it, would you, love?'

'What's up with it now, Flo?' Her cries for help brought me out of the kitchen and into the café. A frazzled and sweaty-looking Flo stood in front of the offending machine.

'The steam's not working. I'm not getting any froth!'

'Brilliant,' I said, reaching for the spanner under the counter. This was the fourth time in the last week that the bloody machine had died on us, so I'd taken to keeping tools handy. There was a small queue of people all waiting for their orders, and I brandished my spanner at them, like some demented warrior queen.

'Sorry for the wait, folks, let me just try and get this sorted for you.' They looked at me and then at the spanner, undoubtedly expecting me to do something highly technical with it. Instead I lifted it up high and brought it down heavily onto the top of the machine. Once, twice, three times. It hissed and wheezed for a few seconds and I held my breath.

'I think you might have killed it completely this time,' said Flo from her new, safer position on the other side of the counter.

'Just wait for a minute, hold on.' Taking a metal jug full of milk from beside the machine, I dipped the end of the steam nozzle into it. With one eye closed, I turned the handle that forced the steam into the milk and prayed that it wouldn't explode in my face. From somewhere inside I heard gurgling, then the machine let out a high-pitched whistle as the milk began to bubble. Problem solved. The little queue of customers gave me a small ripple of applause and I turned to take a modest bow.

Flo came back around the counter and took the jug out of my hands.

'Here, give us that. That bloody thing needs replacing. One of these days you're gonna take a swing at it and it'll go off like a rocket.'

'I can't afford a new machine, Flo, you know that. I'm barely making enough to cover costs as it is, let alone have any spare.'

'Maybe you'll have a bit extra once you've finished this catering job?' she asked, hopefully.

'Making desserts for some random corporate event isn't really going to help much,' I said. 'Besides, I really only did it as a favour to Liz.'

'I did tell you to charge her more, didn't I?'

'Yes, Flo, you did. Several times actually.'

'Well, she took the right piss, all that faffing about changing her mind, leaving it all to the last minute. I know she's your friend, but she was a pain in the arse. Uppity little madam.' I marvelled at how Flo managed to deliver this speech whilst simultaneously serving customers and wiping up spills on the counter. She was seventy years old, but she was still as feisty and energetic as ever; I couldn't manage without her, despite her occasional bouts of rudeness towards anyone with too much facial hair.

'Look, it's done now. I've just got to drop off the last batch of tarts and then it's over with. No more corporate catering for me.' I draped my arm around her tiny shoulders and dropped a kiss on her head. I'd known Flo all my life. She was one of my mother's oldest friends and although she might look tiny and fragile, she was formidable.

'Well, bugger off, then, go and get rid of those cakes.'

'I'll be back as quick as I can,' I said, pulling on my jacket. Now where did I leave the van keys? I rifled through the pockets, pulling out old tissues and other assorted bits of crap until Flo jingled the missing keys in front of my face.

'What would I do without you?' I said, taking them from her and heading into the kitchen.

'You'd manage. Look, there's no need for you to rush back. I can take care of everything here. We're not exactly rushed off our feet, are we?'

I looked back out to the café. It was true; business hadn't been brisk. I had been hoping that a glowing review in the local paper might drum up a bit more trade, but there was no chance of that now. The development of the nearby market had been great for anyone in its immediate vicinity, but not for us. We were just that little bit too far outside the 'development zone'. It wasn't just my café either – all the shops in this little forgotten corner of East London were struggling to stay afloat. I pushed those thoughts to the back of my mind. There'd be plenty of time to obsess about my failing business later, hopefully whilst relaxing in a hot bath with a glass or three of wine.

'Are you sure you'll be all right on your own?' I didn't want to take liberties; Flo might be mighty, but she was still seventy years old after all.

'Positive. You've worked hard on all this.' She gestured at the last batch of boxes I'd wrestled into my arms. 'You deserve a few hours off.'

'Okay. I might go and see if I can find a nice going-away present for Lucy.'

'Lovely. Off you go, then, and I'll see you in the morning. And tell Liz I said she got you cheap.'

I took the boxes and pushed my way through the back door. Flo was right of course; Liz had got me cheap, but she was my best friend. What was I supposed to do? She'd begged me to help her out after her other caterers had let her down; I wasn't going to say no, was I? Charging her more would have felt like taking advantage of her desperation. It would have come in handy though, there was no doubt about that. Between my daughter's imminent departure for university, the temperamental coffee maker and, now as I stood there looking at it, a delivery van that was on its last legs, my finances were stretched to the limit. The van, with its faded green paintwork and peeling pink cupcake on the side, sat in the yard looking old and knackered. Fifteen years of trips to the cash and carry and school runs in London traffic had taken their toll on the old girl. I knew how she felt. I secured the last of the boxes into the back of the van and shut the doors.

14

Chapter 2

By the time I arrived at the venue for the party, my mood had taken a further nosedive. Between the awful traffic and Liz's constant texting to check on my whereabouts, I was quietly seething. I brought the last pile of boxes into the office that was doubling as a makeshift kitchen and dumped them onto one of the countertops. No doubt I'd squashed whatever was in the bottom box but by that point I didn't really care. I turned back to the exit but was stopped by the sound of Liz's voice.

'My darling, thank Christ you're here at last!'

I turned to see her heading towards me, all jingling jewellery and perfectly coiffed hair, and before I could make good my escape she grabbed me by the shoulders and pulled me into a hug. Liz was a big hugger – me, not so much. I pulled out of her grip. Despite her outwardly polished appearance I could tell that she was in the middle of a full-on panic attack. She had that wide-eyed look of someone who'd bitten off more than they could reasonably be expected to chew.

'I'm here, Liz, stop stressing. Everything's fine.'

'Everything is not fine – it's a disaster! Bloody

caterers!' she hissed. 'I should have let you do all the food, not just the desserts. They're useless, Abby. I mean, just look at this.' She snatched a tray of canapés from a passing waiter and waved them under my nose. I wasn't sure what I was meant to be looking at but clearly something had her all riled up.

'I wanted dill on the smoked salmon, not parsley! Parsley is so common – I told them I wanted dill!' she exclaimed.

'All right, calm down. They look great, even with the parsley.' I tried to suppress a smile; it was only garnish, for God's sake, but Liz just looked as if she was about to cry. She'd put a lot of pressure on herself with this event and I knew she was desperate for it all to go well. She dropped the tray of canapés down onto the counter with a clatter and wiped her hands on a napkin.

'Liz, it's a tiny detail.' She tried to protest but I held up my hand. 'In about half an hour all the guests will be drunk on free booze from the bar, at which point you could be serving them anything for all they're likely to care. Just calm down.'

Flo was right, Liz could be an uppity little madam, but it didn't stop me from liking her. We'd been friends since meeting at catering college, more years ago than I cared to remember. We'd formed an instant bond over our mutual dislike of all the other students on our course. That, coupled with the fact that we were both mothers of young children, meant we got on like a house

16

on fire despite having little else in common. Liz was pretty, confident and the poshest person I'd ever met. I was dumpy and shy with an enormous working-class chip on my shoulder. She'd swept into the first day of classes in pristine kitchen whites, with a shiny new set of knives and a Mont Blanc pen to take notes with. I'd had second-hand whites and knives and a biro with a chewed lid.

We'd seen each other through a lot over the years, some good, some less so. No doubt this was the reason I agreed to help her with the party in the first place, despite my previous experiences of mass catering only extending as far as cooking bacon sandwiches and cupcakes in the café. That being said, when I saw the results of my hard work, all laid out on silver serving plates, I will admit to feeling more than a little proud of myself.

'Come and look at the decorating, Abby. I need your opinion.'

Before I could argue that in my flour-covered jeans and trainers, I was clearly not dressed for venturing out of the kitchen, she'd taken my arm and all but shoved me through a set of double doors. I was stunned; she was a miracle worker. The room had been transformed, with walls draped in a soft white fabric that also hung in swathes across the ceiling. It gave you the impression of standing inside a marquee rather than a boring conference room. Little candles in jars flickered on almost every surface and bunches of roses sat in vases and bowls on all the tables.

'Oh Liz, it's beautiful. Everything is perfect. I'm so proud of you.'

She grabbed my hand and squeezed it tight. 'I couldn't have done all this without your help, you know that, don't you?'

I started to deny that I had been any help at all, but she stopped me.

'I mean it, Abby. All those times I got in a flap about one situation or another, calling you a dozen times a day to bitch and moan about this and that, you were always happy to listen and help.'

'You weren't that bad.'

'Bollocks. I've been a total pain in the arse and you know it.'

'Well...'

'Exactly! You stopped me from becoming a total basket case, Abby, and I owe you one.'

'You owe me more than one.' I smirked.

'I'll expect your bill to reflect the additional stress and aggravation of having to deal with me and my lunacy.'

If only. 'Well, I think my work here is done so I'm going to head home and leave you to your success. Try and enjoy it, okay?' I turned to go back through the doors and into the kitchen.

'You can't leave me, Abby, not now. Please, I need you. I don't think I can do this on my own,' she pleaded.

I looked down at my jeans and then at Liz in all her designer glory.

'You never said I'd have to stay at the party! I'm not dressed for that – I'm a mess!'

She looked me up and down and dismissed my objections with a wave of her perfectly manicured hand.

'I knew you wouldn't come prepared, so I brought you something of mine to change into. I've thrown in a bit of make-up too. Here, you can change in the loo over there.' She pulled a small leather holdall out from under one of the tables and handed it to me. Sensing my reluctance, she gave me a not so gentle nudge towards the door.

'Get a wriggle on, then; I've got more important things to do than stand here with you all day.'

I took the bag and before I could protest again she'd gone, berating some poor waiter about dirty champagne glasses as she hurried away.

Thankfully the toilets were empty. I scurried along to the last cubicle and locked the door behind me. Closing the lid of the toilet, I sat and placed the holdall on my lap. Unzipping it tentatively, as if whatever was in there were about to jump out and bite me, I peered inside.

'Bloody Nora.' I pulled out a pair of nude leather high heels and dropped them on the floor, then I stuck my hand back into the bag. My fingers landed on something soft and velvety, and I already knew what the dress was going to look like even before I pulled it out.

I'd seen Liz in this dress before; it was made of butter-soft red velvet and it clung to every curve. She looked gorgeous in it because she was tall and confident and just curvy enough; I was none of those things. What was she thinking, picking out this dress for me? I was a thirty-seven-year-old woman whose body hadn't seen the light of day since ra-ra skirts and lace fingerless gloves were all the rage.

True to her word, I also found make-up in the bag and some of the most uncomfortable-looking underwear I'd ever seen. Seriously, how could you wear knickers that looked as if they could slice you up the middle if you so much as coughed? And as for the bra – there was no way I was going to be able to fit anything of mine into its tiny cups. I tried to recall what underwear I'd thrown on that morning under my baggy jeans and T-shirt and quickly realised that none of it was going to work under that skin-tight dress. Why was I even considering doing this? It was way beyond my duties as the supportive best friend. I was just going to have to go out there and tell her, 'No'. Better still, I could just sneak out and text her later – yes, that was a much better plan. She probably wouldn't even notice I'd gone, she'd be far too busy, I reasoned. I stuffed all the items back into the holdall and was about to unlock the door of the stall when I heard footsteps. Maybe Liz had come to find me?

'I'm not sure the décor out there really works, do you? I mean, it's a business launch not a country wedding. What do you think?'

It was a woman's voice and it sounded American. 'Don't get me wrong, it's very pretty but I'm just not sure it's what he was looking for.' I heard a zip and then the pop of a lipstick tube being opened. After a few seconds the voice carried on.

'I guess it's not really up to me, it's his company after all. And I guess it's too late to do anything about it now. I just wish he'd asked my opinion, that's all.'

Her voice faded away as the door closed behind her. Whoever she'd been talking to hadn't replied much beyond a murmur but the thought that there might be at least one person out there about to give Liz cause to doubt her work was enough. I unlocked the cubicle door and stepped out. I knew there was no way I could leave Liz on her own now, not with someone out there poised to spoil all her good work. I looked at my reflection in the mirror. 'Get that dress on and get out there, you idiot. Your best friend needs you!'

After ten minutes of heaving and tucking, I was finally in the dress and the underwear, praying that nothing was going to pop out when it shouldn't. Thankfully the mirror in the toilet wasn't full length otherwise I would have had a nervous breakdown. Although the dress wasn't as short on me, it was still short. I kept trying to tug the hem down a bit but every time I bent over I felt as if my cleavage was about to explode out of the bloody bra. I took a few deep breaths and headed out to the party. I saw Liz waving at me from across the room, so I tottered slowly across towards her, doing my best to walk in the heels and clutching the bag that held my 'real clothes' across my body like a security blanket.

'The holdall does nothing for that dress,' said Liz. She prised it from my grasp and despatched a passing waitress off to the kitchen with it.

'Where is she going with that?' I squeaked. 'All my stuff is in there. I need—'

'What you need is a drink, my darling. That dress always looks best when accompanied with a glass of champagne.' She grabbed two long-stemmed flutes from a nearby table and handed one to me.

'Cheers.'

'Liz, I can't drink this. I've got the van.'

'Bugger that – you can just get a cab later, don't worry about it.'

Later? I didn't want to be there at all, let alone later. I thought about explaining this to her but decided there was no point. Liz was never the first to leave a party and couldn't understand anyone who was.

'There are quite a few people here now, aren't there?' I said, as I discreetly put down the champagne and picked up an orange juice. Liz didn't notice, she was too busy scanning the room.

'I don't think everyone's here yet. Some of the guests are coming from the States. The owner of the company is from Boston,' she said. I remembered the American woman I'd heard in the toilet.

'A man or a woman?' I asked.

'What?'

'The new owner. Is it a man or woman?'

'Oh, a man. I've met him already. He was here last week. We had a meeting to finalise the plans for all this.'

'He was happy with all the plans, then?'

'Abso-bloody-lutely. He loved it. Mind you, if he'd hated it I would have been more than happy to change things for him.' Liz gave me a little grin and then a wink.

'Why?' I asked, already suspecting I knew the answer. Although happily married, Liz was a real flirt and it had been known to get her into trouble.

'Because he was knicker-droppingly gorgeous, that's why.'

'Oh, Liz, for heaven's sake.'

'What?' she replied, all wide-eyed innocence. 'It's true, he's beautiful. And a real sweetheart.'

I shook my head and took another sip of my orange juice.

'Don't give me that look. He'll be here later and you can see for yourself.'

I figured now was a good time to tell her that I had no intention of hanging around for that long.

'Liz, look, I really can't stay, I've got to get back, I'm —'

An enormous crash came from the direction of the

kitchen.

'Christ Almighty! What now?' exclaimed Liz. 'Here, hold this for me. I'll be back in a sec.' She thrust her glass into my hand and headed off towards the source of the commotion. I watched the waiting staff dart away as she approached the kitchen and I couldn't help smiling. That woman was a force to be reckoned with. Not for the first time, I thanked my lucky stars that she was my friend rather than my foe.

Liz had left me holding her half-empty glass of champagne, as well as my orange juice. I tipped one into the other and then got rid of the empty glass. I stood and sipped my drink, hoping that I didn't look quite as awkward as I felt. Social occasions like this were my worst nightmare, not that I'd been to many in the last few years or so. I'd been too busy; raising a daughter on my own for the past eighteen years hadn't left me much time for a social life. Well, that was my excuse anyway; I was very out of practice when it came to party small talk. Thankfully, my inept social skills weren't given the chance to be put to the test. Within a few minutes, I saw Liz walking back in my direction; she stopped briefly to talk to a man with his back to me. I couldn't see his face but whatever he leaned in to whisper to Liz made her nod and smile. I drained my glass and popped it down discreetly on the table behind me, next to the other empty glass. Liz came over and caught sight of my little collection of empties.

'Looks like I've got some catching up to do?' She beckoned to a passing waiter and handed him the empties, before taking two full glasses off his tray. He stood for a minute, unsure of his next move. Liz waved him away. 'Off you go then, don't dawdle. And do something about that tie whilst you're out there – you look like you've just rolled out of bed. Chop-chop.' The young man scuttled off to the kitchen.

'You have such a way with people, Liz. Has anyone ever told you that?'

'Don't be sarcastic, Abby. It doesn't suit you. Here, bottoms up!' We clinked glasses and sipped our champagne.

'What was all the commotion in the kitchen about?'

Liz rolled her eyes. 'Someone dropped a whole tray of champagne glasses. There goes my deposit with the hire company. Still, never mind, it'll be worth it if this all goes well. What do you think? Is it going well?' She scanned the room nervously.

'Everyone seems to be having a great time, don't worry.'

Liz nodded and went back to surveying the crowd. 'Ooh, don't make it obvious but have a look over by the main door. See that woman? The tall one wearing all the jewellery.' Liz tilted her chin slightly in the direction of a group of about half a dozen people, all of whom were laughing and chatting animatedly. I sneaked a discreet glance in their direction and it became immediately obvious who she was talking about. Although my view of her was partially blocked by a man with his back to me, I could see enough. The woman was thin, blonde and very glamorous, with that unmistakeably pristine look of entitlement that only very rich people who'd never done a day's work in their lives possessed. Her telltale red-soled heels and the obvious twinkle of diamonds on her wrist screamed 'designer chic'.

'Who is she?'

'That's Lexie Morgan. From what I can gather she's a good friend of the man in charge.' Liz leaned closer to me and whispered, 'Of course, when I say friend I mean fuck buddy obviously.'

'Liz! Don't say things like that – you don't know.'

'What I do know is that she's been at every meeting I've had with the guy in charge. She's in all the pictures I saw online before I met him. It would seem she's a bit of a minor celeb in America, on the Internet or something. She has a lifestyle blog, one of those things where they tell us poor mortals what our make-up should look like and what we should all be wearing or eating. Lucy would probably know her.'

'Yes, probably. She's always watching some person or other on the Internet. Personally, I don't get it.'

'You're just too old and uncool, Abby.'

'Cheers. And what does the bloke do?'

'He's one of those tech millionaire types. I think he sold some apps or something. This little do is for a new business he's launching in London. I want to say software development, but I'm not totally sure.'

I shook my head at Liz's ignorance of her own clientele.

'What? Look, I don't need to know the ins and outs of their business in order to be able to plan a party. This could all be an elaborate cover for some international drugs ring, I suppose.'

My mouth dropped open in shock and Liz burst out laughing.

'Look at your face! You need to get out more, Abby. It's fine – David checked everything out before he let me loose.' David – Liz's ever reliable accountant husband, the tonic to Liz's gin.

'Anyway, between her youth and glamour and his hot bod and massive...'

I raised my eyebrows.

'... fortune – I was going to say fortune – they're quite the little power couple. Everything the tabloids feed off. And in every picture, there she is, hanging off his arm and no doubt off his every word.'

'Well, good luck to her. I can't imagine anything worse than having to pander to some rich bloke's ego in order to feel worthy.' I took a large mouthful of champagne and Liz raised her glass to me in a toast.

'Well said. Bugger all those rich men who would dare to patronise you with the offer of jewels and cash.'

'You know what I mean, don't take the piss. I might

not have much but what I have got I've worked bloody hard for.'

'That you have, my darling. I'm only teasing. I'd still love it if you could find someone who wants to spoil you occasionally though. Even if it is just a night at the cinema and a jumbo popcorn.'

'I don't need anyone, Liz. I'm okay just as I am.' She didn't look convinced.

The room had filled up a bit now, and I saw an older gentleman making a beeline for Liz; surely this wasn't the man she'd been telling me about? He was kind of handsome but more Flo's age group than ours. And I definitely wouldn't have contemplated dropping my knickers for him, to coin Liz's phrase.

'Hector! My darling, you came! That is so sweet of you. Abby, this is Hector. He's the company's lawyer and an old friend of my family. Hector, this is my friend Abby. She made all the desserts you're eating tonight. Isn't she clever?'

The man held out his hand for me to shake and I saw him take in my cleavage; to be fair the bra was doing a very good job of thrusting my assets up and into the spotlight.

'It's very nice to meet you, my dear. I was just admiring your... er... tarts. They look delicious.'

'Now, don't be a pervert, Hector.' Liz rolled her eyes at me and linked arms with the old man. 'Come with me. There's some people I need you to introduce me to.

You have to talk me up, tell them how great I am at event management.' She dragged a bewildered-looking Hector away and left me alone again. It was the perfect time for me to quietly disappear. The party was in full swing and no one had run screaming for the exit when confronted with salmon canapés garnished with parsley and not dill. I drained my glass of champagne and made my way out to the kitchen area. I needed to find my things.

'Excuse me... sorry... have you seen a brown leather holdall out here anywhere?'

A waitress, a young girl with thick brown plaits, too much eyeliner and a nose ring, huffed at me as she tried to squeeze past.

'Sorry... don't mean to be a nuisance but I... oops!' I almost knocked a tray of salmon and parsley canapés – Parsley! So common! – flying in my haste to locate my things. No one was really listening to me; they were all far too busy. Probably terrified of incurring Liz's wrath, I thought. Bugger this, I'm just going to get a cab, Liz can find my stuff for me later. As long as Lucy had put the spare key back where it belonged – under the window box – I figured I'd be fine. It was a risk but one that I was more than happy to take if it meant I could get out of this party and out of this outfit. I weaved my way past waiters and trolleys laden with food and drink, over to the exit.

'And where do you think you're going, Mrs?' Liz's

unmistakeable voice stopped me before I even got a hand on the door knob.

'So close,' I muttered under my breath before turning and smiling in her direction.

'I'm going home, Liz. You don't need me here holding your hand. Everything's going great.'

'Oh, no, you don't,' she said, striding purposefully across the kitchen and grabbing my hand. 'I'm not going to let you scurry back into your mouse hole now I've got you out and all dressed up. What a waste of an outfit. Besides, that gorgeous man I told you about is here and he wants to meet you.'

'Really? Why the hell would he want to meet me?' I was in no mood to make small talk with boring business types. I wanted to go home.

'Because he just does, so let's go. And stop fiddling with the hem on that dress. You've got great legs and a very impressive cleavage – it's time to use it.'

Liz walked me across the kitchen and back out to the party. People were milling around in groups, drinking and laughing and enjoying themselves – lucky buggers. Liz pulled me along so fast I was struggling to keep up in the stupid shoes she'd lent me; I was so focussed on not falling arse over tit that I didn't even notice the man she was introducing me to until I finally re-established my centre of gravity and looked up. For a split second I didn't recognise him, my brain was just sending those 'Blimey he's gorgeous' messages but then I started to feel something else; a memory was tapping on my libido's shoulder, begging to be heard. I couldn't quite believe what I was seeing.

'It's you, isn't it? I mean, obviously, you're you... but... Jack?' I must have sounded like a burbling idiot but I couldn't help it; it was really him. After all these years, he was back.

'Hello, Abigail. How are you?'

His voice had changed a bit; I detected a slight trace of an American accent. I liked it, very sexy.

Stop that, Abby, he's just an old friend that's all.

Old friend my eye, he's your first love.

Get a grip girl, he just wanted to meet the woman behind the tarts, he didn't know it was you!

My brain and my 'missing presumed dead' libido were having a battle over who was steering the ship. I must have looked like a total idiot. Liz was eyeing me quizzically, waiting for more information, but I couldn't speak. Jack Chance, my childhood crush, was standing right there in front of me, for the first time in over twenty years.

'Abigail Turner lost for words, I don't believe it.' He reached out and took my hand in his.

Liz gave me a confused look. I hadn't gone by that surname for so many years that I sometimes forgot I ever did. A sudden flash of memory took me by surprise – Jack and me holding hands as we walked home from school. Although neither of us knew it at the time, it

31

would be the last contact between us for two decades. The touch of his hand and the memories it had triggered were so vivid they knocked me off balance. I think I mumbled something about needing to leave and I tried to make a move towards the door, but my feet wouldn't work.

'Abigail? Abigail, are you all right?' Jack's concerned face moved closer to mine and I tried to remember how to breathe.

Chapter 3

'Abigail?'

The sound of Jack's voice brought me back to the here and now.

'I'm fine, just went a bit dizzy for a minute. Too much champagne. I'm all right.'

I was acutely aware that he was holding my arms and his touch was doing weird things to my insides. He looked worried. I tried to move out of his grip but he wouldn't let me go. He probably thought I was about to keel over.

'Are you sure you're all right?'

I nodded and he lowered me down into a waiting chair. 'Here, drink this.'

I took the glass he handed me and sipped. He was kneeling in front of me and I had an almost irresistible urge to reach out and touch his face, just to make sure he was real. I didn't of course. It was hard to process the fact that he was there, in my present, rather than just a memory. I took another sip of water and then handed the glass back to him as I stood up.

'Whoa, where are you going?' He tried to push me back down into the chair but I refused to let him.

'I'm all right, really. I feel much better now.'

'You see, Jack,' said a voice behind him, 'she says she's fine. Give the woman some room.'

What was her name again? Trixie? Dixie? No – Lexie, that was it. She'd made her way through the little crowd that had gathered around us and was standing beside Jack, resting her hand on his shoulder. It's all right, I get the message, I thought. She might as well have branded him on the forehead with a big 'He's Mine!' sign. God, was I ever that young and desperate for a man's attention? I hoped not but I couldn't be sure. That thought made me shudder.

'Are you cold? You're shivering, Abigail. Here, take this.' Jack shrugged off his jacket and draped it around my shoulders.

'I'll look after her, Mr Chance, it's fine,' interrupted Liz, putting herself between me and Jack. 'Let's get you sat down somewhere quiet, now, shall we?' I let her guide me back towards the kitchen and as I passed I handed him back his jacket.

'I don't need this but thank you. Please go back to your party.'

Jack opened his mouth to speak but Lexie cut between us.

'Yes, Jack, you must come back to the party. There are some people that you really should meet.'

I turned away before he could speak and followed Liz across the room.

'What's that gloomy look for?' she asked as we sat down in the kitchen.

'Nothing.' I felt exhausted, drained of all my energy, and I knew why. I'd thought about Jack Chance plenty of times in the last twenty years, imagined meeting him again, but never in any of those daydreams had he reappeared in my life with a human Barbie doll fixed to his side, guiding his every move.

'Are you feeling better?' Liz asked.

'Yes, I'm fine. I didn't have any lunch, that's all. Too busy dealing with some irritating party planner who kept changing her mind about cake flavours right up until the last minute.' I threw her a pointed look. 'Two glasses of champagne on an empty stomach – I'm just a lightweight, I guess.'

'Yes, you are. Now—' she reached across and punched me on the arm '—you never told me you knew Jack Chance!'

'Ow! That hurt!'

'Serves you right for holding out on me. Spill the beans.'

'I promise you, Liz, it's a very small can of beans. We were just kids when his family moved away. I didn't know he was the man you were working for. You said he was from Boston. I had no reason to think it might be some boy I used to know from school.'

'It's like the beginning of a movie. I can see it all now.'

'Shut up, you daft cow. He won't even remember who I am.'

'You didn't see his face when you had your funny turn. He looked really worried about you.' Liz had a dreamy look in her eyes and a stupid smile.

'You've read too many books.'

I stood up, still a little unsteady on my feet. 'I really do need to get home. I think these knickers you lent me are trying to kill me. Maybe they're the reason I went a bit dizzy – they're cutting off my circulation!'

Liz laughed. 'Okay, now I know you're better – you're making jokes. You should think about keeping the dress though. It looks way better on you than it ever did on me.'

I was about to object when I heard Jack's voice coming from behind me.

'I agree. You look amazing.'

I turned and saw him leaning on the door jamb. His voice was low and his gaze was fixed on my body. I could feel it travelling up and down and I was suddenly very self-conscious.

'I don't think this is a very practical look for my kind of work, do you, Mr Chance?' I emphasised the 'Mr Chance' in a way that made him smirk a little.

'Surely you must socialise sometimes, Ms Turner. Or are you just locked in your little café all the time with no thoughts of fun and games?'

'My last name is Cowan, not Turner. Not anymore.'

I didn't elaborate on my response; I just wanted to get out of there. The kitchen had become very hot all of a sudden. When I didn't offer any more information, I could see him mentally putting two and two together and coming up with five.

'I'm sorry, *Mrs* Cowan, I didn't see a wedding ring. My apologies.'

I didn't correct his mistake and I could see Liz frowning at me. Oh, yes, it was definitely time to leave.

'No problem, it's fine. But I do need to be going so if you'll excuse me?' I tried to move past him but he grabbed my hand. I felt a jolt of something, like an electric shock, fizz through me at his touch.

'You almost passed out just now. I'm not letting you drive yourself home, Abigail, no way. Just wait and I'll take you.'

'Don't be silly, I'm fine. I'm not going to drive, I'm not that stupid. I can just grab a cab. This is your party. You can't leave now.'

He was still holding onto me; he looked down at my hand in his, but he didn't speak. Neither of us moved for a few seconds. I could feel the warmth of his touch so keenly and my mouth was suddenly dry. I swallowed and Jack lifted his gaze from our joined hands to my throat. My insides turned to liquid as he raised his eyes – those beautiful enormous eyes – to look at me. Then, without a word, he let my hand drop.

A strangled 'Thanks' was all I could manage as he

turned and walked away. I heard a man's voice call out to him and then he was gone, swallowed up by the crowd. I turned back to Liz, who was staring at me, open-mouthed.

'Good Lord, I thought he was going to rip that dress off and have you right there on the lino! What the hell was all that about?'

'You should go back to the party too, make sure everyone eats all those bloody tarts. I didn't do all that work for nothing, you know.' I ignored her shocked expression and tried to give her a gentle shove back out to the party, but she wasn't quite done with me.

'Why did you let him think you were married?'

'What? Oh, you mean the name thing. I don't know, just easier, I guess. I wasn't about to start giving him a potted history of my life. I barely know the man.'

'Bollocks.' Liz possessed a very finely tuned bullshit meter and, despite being one of the poshest people I knew, her language was sometimes more akin to a dockworker than a duchess.

'Oh, shut up. Just get back in there and do your thing. And see if you can find my proper clothes at some point. I'm going to try and get a cab outside and you better hope I don't get mistaken for a hooker in this outfit.'

She feigned mock horror. 'I'm appalled! You're more high-end call girl than hooker, if you please. That little lot cost a bloody fortune!' She smiled and gave me a hug, before turning on her heel and striding away.

I left the warmth of the building and stepped out into a damp, drizzly London evening. Bloody perfect – finding a cab in central London, in the rain, was almost impossible! Figuring I'd probably have more luck up by the station, I started to walk but it soon became obvious that Liz's nosebleed-inducing high heels were going to be the death of me; I was walking like Bambi on an icy pond. Holding onto a nearby lamppost for support, I took them off before I fell and broke my ankle.

'Abigail! Wait!'

I looked up to see Jack striding purposefully towards me clutching a long coat of some sort.

'I said I would take you home.' He moved to place the coat around my shoulders but I shrugged it off.

'I don't need that, thank you. I just need to find a cab.'

Clutching my shoes in my hand, I made a move to walk away but he blocked my path.

'I said I would take you.'

'It's really not a problem, Jack. I'm quite capable of taking care of myself.'

By now the drizzle had turned into a full-on shower and I was getting soaked, the red velvet dress was clinging to all my curves and I had to admit I was starting to shiver a bit. Jack looked at me as if he wanted to throw me over his shoulder and march me back inside – I could see the tension in his jaw, as if he was grinding his teeth.

'Fine. Have it your way.' He stepped away from me and over to the kerb. I was about to tell him that it was pointless trying to get a cab here when he stepped into the road and immediately managed to wave one down. Flash git. He held the door open for me as I tried to climb in without flashing too much leg. I don't think I managed it as I saw him smiling as he closed the door. Walking to the front window of the cab, he leaned in to the driver. I couldn't hear what he was saying but the driver was nodding. He stepped away from the cab and waved, before walking back inside. I gave the driver my address. I was hoping that Liz wouldn't be cajoled into telling him too much about me, but she'd always been a sucker for a pretty face. What if he turned on the charm? She wouldn't be able to resist. I needed to tell her to keep her trap shut but my heart sank as I remembered I didn't have my phone. I'd left it with my clothes and keys back at the party venue. *You could go back to the party,* said a voice in my head. No way, I knew trouble when I saw it and Jack had grown up into a very fine specimen of trouble.

I leaned back in my seat and closed my eyes, trying to focus on anything else besides what had just happened. It was impossible. Jack's face kept swimming into view. Admittedly he looked good but that just made me even more annoyed. How was it fair that he looked better now? After twenty years? Couldn't he at least have been overweight and balding? The injustice made me want to spit. Twenty years on and all I had to show for it were wrinkles, bags under the eyes, cellulite and a few grey hairs! Bastard! Don't get me wrong, I knew I wasn't quite ready for the knacker's yard. I was only thirty-seven and I generally scrubbed up all right when I put the effort in, it was just that there hadn't been much call for it lately. I spent most of my working days with my shoulder-length blonde hair scraped up in a ponytail and my less than perfect body hidden behind an apron. I had curves where all the magazines told me I shouldn't and I wouldn't have been able to squeeze myself into skinny jeans if my life depended on it. My mum liked to blame it all on the fact that I'd 'had a hard life'. She told people this by way of an explanation for my apparent lack of interest in my appearance. Always so tactful.

My life to this point hadn't exactly been the stuff of fairy tales, that was true. Pregnant at nineteen, then a single parent. I inherited my café from Ted and Rose. I'd started working for them as a Saturday girl when I was fourteen, and I was overwhelmed when they generously left me the premises and business when they retired. They told me that I was the daughter they never had, and I considered them as much my family as I did my mum and brother. When my dad disappeared and my mum lost the plot, Ted and Rose and their little café provided me with a reason to be out of that house; away from a mother who hid in her room all day with the curtains drawn and grandparents who'd been reluctantly roped in to look after all of us. They were my mother's parents and they never missed an opportunity to remind my brother and me that they were only there because our 'useless layabout father' had buggered off and left us.

The sudden appearance of Dad in my mind made me sit up. I hadn't thought about him for a long time; I was surprised by how long actually. There was a time when he was all I could think about: where had he gone and why? Would he ever come back? But time passed and thoughts of him gradually became less of a daily occurrence and more of an occasional nuisance. Thinking about him left me feeling confused and frustrated so it eventually became easier to just not think about him.

'Damn you, Jack,' I muttered.

'What's that, love? Did you say something?' The cab driver was looking at me through his rear-view mirror.

'No, nothing, sorry.' My stomach was churning; maybe I was coming down with something? That would have explained the dizziness. It had nothing to do with seeing Jack again – it was the start of the flu! Yes, that definitely made more sense than me getting all flustered at the sight of him. That would be too pathetic. But I could still feel his hand in mine and see the way his eyes had burned when he'd looked me up and down in Liz's dress. Oh blimey! No one had looked at me like that since, well, probably since I last saw him. Lucy's dad never gave me the impression he was burning with desire for me, but Jack had always been different. Even as a teenager, he'd had an intensity that most boys his age lacked.

*

'Direct hit!'

'Hey! Watch the jacket, it's new!'

I duck down behind the bench, laughing uncontrollably.

'Shh! He'll hear you,' says Jack.

I try to stop but the harder I try, the more I giggle. That last snowball I threw landed right between Kevin Warner's purple-nylon-clad shoulder blades. His new tracksuit is now sporting a very fetching damp patch on the back. I sneak a look over the top of the bench. I can see Kevin brushing down his jacket and trying to see where the attack came from.

'Serves him right,' I say. 'He shouldn't have taken the piss out of me in class this morning.'

Jack stops squishing snowballs together and looks at me.

'What did he say?'

'It was nothing. He just made some stupid comments about my blazer. He said it was a hand-me-down from my brother and that it suited me 'cos I look like a boy anyway.'

'He's a twat. That doesn't even make sense. You've got long curly hair. How do you look like a boy?'

I'm too embarrassed to answer so I just cast a quick glance downwards to where my boobs have obviously not materialised yet. I'm fifteen, I've got lank hair, mild acne and armpit fuzz but I remain resolutely flat-chested. Jack looks at my chest then quickly looks away again. He coughs and then mutters something under his breath.

'What was that?' I say.

He fidgets around, tossing a snowball from one hand to the other, before standing up and lobbing it at the back of Kevin's head. Satisfied that he's achieved his goal, Jack comes back to sit beside me on the ground.

'I said, you're gorgeous. Kevin Warner is an idiot.' Jack turns to face me, his expression intense. 'Ignore him. Ignore anyone who tries to tell you that you're anything other than perfect.'

*

Jack had been right; Kevin Warner was an idiot. And thankfully my boobs did eventually turn up – the devastatingly uncomfortable bra I was squeezed into at that moment was testament to that fact. But Jack had gone by then and I had been left at the mercy of those other stupid teenage boys. None of them had ever made me feel the way Jack had; a fact that had, apparently, not changed in the last twenty years. Fan-bloody-tastic.

I could see I was almost home and it dawned on me that I had no money to pay the cab fare. What the hell was I going to do?

'You can drop me here, just on the right.'

The driver indicated and pulled smoothly up to the kerb. I was about to confess to having no way to pay him when he said, 'That gentleman sorted out your fare, no need to worry, love. But if you want to give me a tip I won't say no'. He flashed me a big nicotine-stained toothy grin. What? How? Jack must have paid the driver when he leaned in to talk to him. Part of me was incredibly relieved but the other part was furious that Jack assumed I wouldn't be able to pay my own way.

'R-right,' I stuttered. 'Thanks'. I hopped out of the cab and walked towards the stairs that led up to my flat above the café.

'I'll take that as a no to the tip, shall I?' the cab driver shouted.

Ignoring him, I took the stained concrete stairs two at a time, clutching my shoes to my chest and trying not to think about what I might be stepping in. I made it to my front door and knocked, silently praying that Lucy was home to let me in. Please let the universe be on my side today – just this once. To my relief the door opened and I was greeted by my surprised-looking daughter.

'Bloody hell, Mum, what are you wearing? And where's the van?'

Chapter 4

'So, you just left the van and all your clothes there?' My daughter Lucy was stirring milk into my cup of tea and looking at me as if I were some sort of freak.

'Yes, I already told you. Your Auntie Liz forced me into this little get-up so I could meet people, I couldn't find my stuff, so it was just easier to get a taxi home.'

She brought my tea over to the kitchen table and plonked herself down in the chair opposite me. With her dark hair piled on top of her head in a messy topknot, Lucy's resemblance to my mother was striking. Tall and slim, she had graceful hands that fluttered about when she spoke and piercing blue almond-shaped eyes that could fix you with the same penetrating stare my mum had.

'Who did you meet, then?' she asked.

'What? No one, why? What do you mean?'

'You said Auntie Liz made you wear that to meet people. I was just asking who you met.' She gave me a quizzical look and I instantly became very interested in my cup of tea. Looking at the small bits of scum on the surface, I abruptly decided that this would be a good time to descale the kettle. I got up and went to the cupboard under the sink, pulling out a packet of limescale remover and some yellow rubber gloves. I could feel Lucy watching me fuss around in the kitchen.

'Mum, you can't clean in that dress. What's the rush to do that now anyway?'

'It needs doing. But you're right about the dress – it deserves better. I'll just go and change.'

As I headed to my room, I prayed that Lucy wouldn't follow me. I knew if she saw the underwear I had on under the dress, I'd never hear the end of it! No such luck. It had been just the two of us since she was a baby so it was normal to wander in and out of each other's rooms whenever we wanted. Sure enough, she followed me straight into my room and flopped down onto my bed.

'Nan called earlier. She wanted to know where you were and why you didn't go round yesterday.'

'I never told her I would see her yesterday.' Did I? Visits to my mum were usually only undertaken when I'd run out of excuses. Between work, Lucy, cleaning the toilet, defrosting the freezer, there really wasn't much time left to visit; at least that was what I told myself. I loved my mum, in my own way, but our relationship was difficult. To say the least. When my dad left she locked herself away in her room for two years and when she eventually emerged, I'd learned how to take care of myself. I found that I didn't need her, not in any practical sense at least. At the time, to my young mind anyway, what she did to us was almost as bad as what my dad had done. He'd left us to fend for ourselves and so had she and I'd never really forgiven her for that.

My brother, Matt, who was two years older than me, had always been much closer to her than I had. He'd always seemed more willing to forgive and tried to play peacemaker. He wasn't ever able to convince me though. As far as I was concerned, I'd managed just fine without her for two years, so when she'd tried to slip back into that maternal role I'd fought her at every turn. Our relationship had got better as the years had passed but that was because I tried not to let her get too involved in my life; there was always a part of me that was frightened to rely on her just in case she faded away again. She was a good grandmother to Lucy though, and I made sure that their relationship wasn't tainted by my feelings. It was hard at first – seeing how close they were used to make me feel sad and envious – but I got over it. There was nothing I could do about it now anyway – too much time had passed and I couldn't go back and change things. No matter how much I might have wanted to at times.

'You're being weird, Mum. What's going on?'

I was standing in the middle of my room, lost in thought. 'Nothing's going on. I just want to get out of this ridiculous dress and get back to normal.'

'It's not ridiculous, it's lovely. I was just surprised to see you in something other than jeans and an apron, that's all. You look gorgeous.'

I turned to look at myself in the mirror. All I saw were the bags under my eyes, the hair in need of a trip to the salon and a body that wasn't quite what it used to be. Sighing to myself, I pulled the dress off my shoulders and pushed it down to the floor. This should be interesting, I thought. I stood back up and saw Lucy's open-mouthed expression as she took in what I had on underneath. Liz's tiny thong underwear and half-cup bra, that barely covered anything it was supposed to, proved too much for my daughter. She curled up in a ball on the bed and began laughing uncontrollably at the sight of me in such skimpy items.

'Thanks, Lucy. What happened to "You look lovely, Mum?"'

She sat up and wiped her eyes with her sleeve.

'I'm sorry. It's just a bit of a shock, that's all. Normally you're a bit more conservative in your underwear choices.'

I assumed that 'conservative' was just another word for 'boring' but I couldn't argue with her. I picked up a pair of crumpled blue pyjama bottoms from the chair in the corner and shoved my legs into them, then pulled on an oversized grey sweatshirt with the word 'awesome' emblazoned on the front. I surveyed myself in the mirror and decided that this was much more me. I gave my daughter a little twirl.

'There you are, Mum's back to normal.' I hung the

lovely red dress on the outside of my wardrobe door and vowed to return it to its rightful owner, along with the shoes and underwear, as soon as I'd had it dry-cleaned. 'Now, where did I leave my rubber gloves?' The ping of Lucy's phone told her she had a text; I went back to the kitchen.

I busied myself putting the little sachet of nasty-smelling chemicals into the kettle and filling it with water. As they mixed together I watched the liquid begin to fizz and bubble, eating away at the scale in the bottom of the kettle. Would there be a market for a similar kind of product that you could use on your brain? Something to erase the scaly build-up of all those memories you'd rather forget. What a relief that could be. So many things in your past that you'd rather rub out, only keeping the good stuff. Unfortunately, the brain isn't a dirty kettle, and when memories start to get rubbed out it's indiscriminate, descaling the mind of the good as well as the bad. I had watched that happen to Ted and Rose, the couple who used to own the café. Rose went first, just little things to start with, mixing up names and faces, forgetting recipes she'd been making for years. Then came the panic and confusion when she would find herself out shopping but forget where she was or how to get home. Towards the end of her life she refused to leave the flat at all, preferring to stay inside where she felt safe.

Once she passed away, it was Ted's turn. Without her

there to focus on, to live for, he just slipped slowly away. I would sit with him in the retirement home and read to him from the newspaper or from one of his favourite books, but he rarely even acknowledged me. The only time I saw a spark of recognition from him was on the last day I visited before he died. We'd been sitting in our usual spot in the day room of the home. I hated that room. All those stiff, high-backed, wipe-clean chairs and the television always on, playing to no one. It was a cliché to talk about the smell in those places but it was true. It was a potent mix of disinfectant, boiling vegetables and urine. I'd gone to visit, doing the same things I always did with no real response from him; there was nothing to make me think that this would be the last time I saw him. When I leaned in to kiss him goodbye he suddenly grabbed both my hands and wouldn't let go.

'What is it, Ted? What's wrong?'

'You should have been told, Abby. They shouldn't have kept it from you; it wasn't right.' He was shaking his head and his eyes filled with tears as he spoke. 'Rose and me, we tried to make sure you were all right, we wanted to look after you and Matt but we didn't know what to do.'

'It's okay,' I said. 'Me and Matt have turned out fine. We're all fine.' I didn't understand what he meant – what should I have been told about? He held my face between his hands; his papery skin felt rough, and for a brief minute he looked at me as if he knew exactly who I was. He looked relieved to see me, as if he'd been waiting for me to come, even though I'd spent hours with him every week since Rose died.

'You can go now, Abby. Everything will be all right, you'll see.' I didn't know what to say to him, so I just nodded and put my hand on his.

'I'll be back tomorrow, Ted. I might be able to sneak some chocolate and a can of Guinness past Gestapo Nell on the front desk, eh? What do you reckon?' But it was too late; the fog had descended again and he was lost.

I got the call from the home later that same evening. He'd just passed away in his sleep. No fuss, no drama, just like Ted. I told Mum what he'd said to me but she dismissed it.

'He was old, Abby, confused. It probably didn't mean anything. Don't worry yourself about it. Ted was always a silly old sod anyway.' There wasn't any way of knowing for sure so I forgot about it and moved on. So why was I thinking about it now? In the middle of descaling a kitchen appliance, for God's sake – what was the matter with me?

'Who's Jack Chance?' Lucy's voice made me jump and I dropped the kettle into the sink, splashing myself with hot, scaly water.

'Oh shit! What? Who?' I grabbed a tea towel and tried to wipe the water off my sweatshirt.

'Jack Chance – Auntie Liz just text me to say she has

your phone and stuff. She asked if you'd told me about Jack Chance.'

Bloody Liz and her big mouth! I wasn't planning on telling Lucy anything about Jack – ever! She'd recently become quite obsessed with getting me out on a date. Any man that showed the slightest interest in me had become a potential target for her matchmaking. This had led to quite a few awkward situations; the most recent one had been when she'd 'accidentally' trapped me and the boiler repair man in the cellar for half an hour because she'd thought he was flirting with me. According to Lucy, I'd been a bit slow to pick up on his signals so she'd thought she'd give me a shove in his direction. So much for her intuition; whilst trapped in the basement the gas man had spent the time telling me how funny his husband would find this whole story. She had since been warned off any further attempts to matchmake, but the mention of Jack's name had obviously piqued her curiosity.

'He's just someone I used to know, from school. He used to live around here but he moved away.'

'And now he's back?'

'Yes. But please don't start getting carried away, all right?'

Lucy eyed me suspiciously. 'Auntie Liz said he was gorgeous so I looked him up. She's right – he is bloody gorgeous, Mum.' She turned her smartphone round so I could see and there he was: Jack Chance looking gorgeous in a dinner jacket at some charity event. I recognised the woman standing next to him as Lexie Morgan. They looked like the perfect couple. And Lucy was right, he did look good. He had just enough designer stubble to contrast the smart evening wear, making him look a little rebellious even in the formal picture. His dark hair was just messy enough without looking unkempt. No doubt some very expensive hair products had gone a long way towards helping with that look. He was tall and obviously worked out – a lot! The caption underneath the picture read, 'US entrepreneur Jack Chance and Internet star Lexie Morgan attend charity gala held at the US Embassy in London."

'She's that annoying woman on YouTube. Always banging on about lipstick and kale. I don't think much of her, do you?' said Lucy.

'I didn't really look, to be honest,' I lied. 'I think I'm just going to head downstairs for a bit. Get some stuff done before tomorrow.' I didn't have any reason to go downstairs to the café, but I wanted to be on my own for a while. As if sensing something was off, Lucy came over and gave me a massive hug. She was a little taller than me so she had to lean down a bit to give me a proper reassuring squeeze.

'Love you, Mum.'

I could feel the tears pricking my eyes and my throat was tight. I mumbled, 'You too,' into her shoulder before I pulled away and headed down the stairs that led from my kitchen into the café.

The staircase was dark as I went down; I could have switched a light on but I didn't want to. I liked the dark. It was calming and quiet. I unlocked the door at the bottom into the café and I stepped into my own little kingdom. The only light was coming from the street lamps outside, but I didn't need it; I knew this place like the back of my hand. It made me sad to think that one day, probably sooner than I'd like to think about, this place, and all the other shops in this little parade, would be gone.

The parade had been built before the age of the supermarket, back when people used a greengrocer, a butcher or a baker. The little row of eight shops had been the centre of day-to-day life. Customers had come for bread, or had gone to the boot menders, or the off-licence that sat at the very end of the row. They'd shopped, they'd lingered, they'd gossiped. But those days were long gone. The off-licence was still there but was now more of a convenience store, carrying everything from milk to mousetraps. There was a nail salon, a mobile phone shop, a betting shop and my café. The rest of the shops were empty, and according to Mrs Owen, who ran the nail salon, some local developers were just waiting for the rest of us to go under so they could swoop in and build luxury apartments. All in the name of progress, obviously.

Now I was down in the café, I didn't know what to

do with myself. I paced around a bit, straightening tablecloths that didn't need straightening and wiping the countertop unnecessarily. As I stood behind the counter I looked across the room to the table by the window – the best table in the house, Ted used to call it. Although I'd changed some things when I took over, I'd kept the layout of the café pretty much how it was when I'd started coming here with my school friends all those years ago. When I was a teenager none of my friends ever really wanted to go home. We always preferred hanging out in a crowd and keeping away from whatever dramas were going on indoors. Before my dad left, my parents argued a lot, usually about his lack of employment and his inability to provide for us, so I never wanted to go home. Then after my grandparents moved in to take care of us, I stayed out because I couldn't bear seeing the state my mum was in or listening to my grandparents go on about how much they'd had to sacrifice to come to our rescue.

There was usually a group of about twelve of us who would hang out in the café after school and between us we could count four absentee dads, one dead dad, two dead mums, assorted petty criminal relatives and a handful of alcoholics. In fact, before he disappeared from my life, Jack's family had been the only seemingly normal one. His parents were happily married and his dad had a responsible job in our local bank. Jack used to say he wished he had more drama in his life but I don't think he meant it. He'd sit with me in the café and listen to all the other kids make jokes about how crap their families were, laughing along when Jamie Bristow would tell us another story about his drunken mum and her escapades. He found all their stories funny but the minute I told one he would stop laughing. One day, I remember it was just the two of us sharing a plate of chips, sitting at that table by the window, and I asked him why he never laughed at my stories.

'Because I don't like it when bad things happen to you, Abigail. It makes me feel helpless and I hate it. Stupid, eh?' He grabbed a chip and dipped it in tomato sauce, shoving it all into his mouth in one go, before smiling nervously at me, and I remember my stomach doing somersaults. That was the first time he'd ever said anything like that to me and I think I fell in love with him right there and then.

Chapter 5

What are they saying? I can't make out the words. Why won't they help me? I can see Matt. Help me, Matt, get me out – I can't breathe. Please help me. Don't walk away – I can't hear what you're saying. I don't understand what's happening.

*

I woke early the next morning feeling exhausted and miserable. What little sleep I'd managed had been disturbed by the reappearance of a nightmare that I hadn't had for years. I'd almost forgotten about it, but last night it had returned. In the dream I'm trapped behind glass, watching friends and family come and go. They talk to me but I can't hear them. I try to make them understand but it makes no difference. They stare at me through the glass, their mouths forming unheard words, and then they leave.

I'd started having the dream after my dad disappeared. That sounds a bit dramatic, doesn't it? As if he were abducted by aliens or something. It wasn't like that. He left the house one day and just never came back. I was only fifteen so when I should have been obsessing about pop stars and lipstick I spent my days trying to get someone, anyone, to tell me where my dad had gone. Everyone else knew something, that much was obvious. I caught their raised eyebrows and meaningful glances to one another any time I brought the subject up.

I knew my questions affected Mum most of all; the more persistent I became in my quest for answers, the more she seemed to fade away. Every day that passed saw her grow more fragile. Eventually she retreated to her bedroom and would only come out once she knew everyone else was in bed for the night. I would hear her door open and the gentle creak of the stairs as she floated down them like a ghost. I never followed her. I came close once; I opened my bedroom door just enough to see her heading for the top stair. When she heard me, she froze and looked up like a startled deer. Her face was so full of sadness and I could only hold her gaze for a second before I retreated behind my door. I never did it again.

After a few months, my grandparents moved in to take care of me and my brother, since mum seemed incapable of functioning on any level. They arrived one afternoon; I came home from school and there they were, unloading suitcases out of the back of their old Rover.

*

'What you got in these bags? All your worldly possessions? How long we bleedin' staying for, Eileen? Three months?' Grandad shouts.

'Shut yer face and get those bags inside. Stop making a show of yourself.'

I have to squeeze past two suitcases already in the hallway to get to the kitchen. I find my brother sitting on the back doorstep, smoking a cigarette and muttering under his breath.

'I'm seventeen. I can look after us. They don't need to bloody move in.' He gestures behind him, sending orange sparks of cigarette ash floating down to the concrete.

'According to my teacher, we need proper adult supervision,' I say, sitting down next to him. 'The headmaster told my form tutor this morning.'

'And we'll get that from them, will we?' Matt says, jerking his head back in the direction of the front door. 'She hates kids – she told me as much when she got here.' He stubs out his cigarette. 'Fuck that. They're gonna drive me nuts. George's mum said I could go and stay with them for a bit if I wanted. I might take them up on it. Better than being here with those two old farts.' Matt stands up and brushes cigarette ash off his jeans.

'You can't!' I wail. 'You can't leave me here on my own. Please don't move out, please!' Matt looks at me for a minute and then obviously takes pity on me. He leans down and pulls my ponytail.

'Fair enough, Midget, I won't leave you. But you owe me for this, big time.' He sticks out his hand and I stand up and grab it eagerly.

'Let's go and help the old people unload their crap, then, shall we?'

I nod, happy that I've managed to convince him to stay. My brother and me, united against the world.

*

In the end, my grandparents stayed with us for almost two years; until one morning, when my mum suddenly appeared in the kitchen with her hair done and a full face of make-up on. She made us breakfast and a pot of tea and acted as if the previous two years hadn't happened. The house was suddenly spotlessly tidy all the time, and my mother became obsessed with my comings and goings. It was stifling but also unnerving; the slightest thing could set her off and she would rant and rave about what a worry I was to her. All of this made living with her a daily adventure. I never knew quite what mood she'd wake up in or what would be the thing that would set her off. Walking on eggshells didn't really do it justice, but it was the best description I could think of. Actually, if you replaced eggshells with landmines, you might be nearer the mark. Despite all outward appearances to the contrary, she never got over what happened.

I gave up asking questions about Dad; what was the point when no one ever gave you any answers? The noiseless voices of the people in my dreams represented all the unanswered questions I had about him and what had happened to him. I stopped talking to my mother, beyond the occasional yes, or no, or grunt. A horrible cloud of silence descended over us all and when an opportunity of escape presented itself, I took it. I stopped having nightmares, buried any feelings I had about my father and moved on. I figured that I'd learned a valuable lesson – sometimes people just left.

*

I lay in bed, trying to get my racing brain to calm down but I was restless; I decided to go downstairs to the café and start work. To try and make some extra cash, I'd started offering my services as a birthday-cake maker; I hadn't had that many customers but there were two cakes downstairs that I had to finish and deliver that day, so I needed to crack on. I brushed my teeth and pulled my hair back into a hasty ponytail, before grabbing my well-worn jeans and a T-shirt and jamming my feet into my favourite green Converse shoes. I caught sight of myself in my mirror as I passed; I looked tired and scruffy. The picture I'd seen of Jack and Lexie popped into my head. They'd looked so glamorous, so right for each other, and I felt a little bit sick suddenly. I told myself not to be so silly. I hadn't seen the man for years – what did I expect? That he'd lived like a monk after he left London? Stupid woman. But I couldn't help thinking about him. I was just trying to picture myself next to him in that photo when Lucy poked her head round my door.

'I heard you moving about in here. Are you going to fetch the van?' she mumbled sleepily.

The van! I needed it for my deliveries later and it was still parked in the car park at yesterday's party venue. What was I going to do? I didn't even have the keys – Liz did. I looked over at my bedside clock; it was six a.m.

'I hope Liz likes early morning calls,' said Lucy and she disappeared, presumably headed back to bed.

'Whoa! Not so fast, lady,' I called after her. 'If I've got to go and pick up the van, then I'm going to need you to open up for me and cover until Flo gets in.'

'Does this constitute overtime? Extra pay for unsociable hours?'

I shook my head at her barefaced cheek but I wasn't that surprised. Lucy was desperate to save up as much money as possible before she left for university in a few months, and she'd been working for me to earn some cash whenever she could. Truth be told, I hadn't been paying her wages out of the business; there wasn't enough in the till for that. It had been coming out of my savings and my brother had been chipping a bit in too.

'You drive a hard bargain. We'll discuss the specifics later, but right now I need you to get dressed and make a start downstairs for me, please.'

'All right, all right. How will you ever manage without me once I head off to Bristol?'

That unwelcome thought made me want to cry but I held it together. The thought of her leaving made me feel sick; I didn't want to face the idea that she would be gone soon and I'd be alone. It wasn't that I didn't want her to go to university. I wanted her to have the kinds of opportunities I never did, but I couldn't pretend it wasn't going to hurt like hell when she finally left.

'I'm sure I'll find someone willing to help me out – they might even be cheaper!' I shouted after her as she walked away.

Lucy stuck her tongue out at me by way of a reply and disappeared into the bathroom. I grabbed the phone in the hallway and dialled Liz's number; I knew she'd already be awake. Liz was a terrible sleeper. The phone only rang twice before she picked it up.

'Hello.'

'Morning, Motor Mouth, it's me.'

'Motor Mouth? What's that for?'

'Never mind, I'll tell you later. I need to get my van keys and phone from you. Is it okay to pop round now?'

Liz and her family had recently moved to a rather trendy part of East London, which was only about twenty minutes away from me on the Tube. It still made me laugh, every time I went to her lovely new house with its secure parking and well-manicured gardens, remembering how it had been when I was growing up. It had been a definite no-go area for me and my friends. But the decrepit old flats and run-down terraces had been revitalised in an effort to attract a 'better class of people'. The drug dens and betting shops had been replaced with studio apartments and chic eateries. Even the old bingo hall had been refurbished and now housed local artists and craftspeople selling their handmade wares. All very lovely but it meant that a whole generation of families had been forced out of the areas they grew up in because they could no longer afford to live there.

'How are you going to get to the office to pick up the van once you have the keys?' asked Liz. Bugger, I hadn't thought that far ahead. That would be another Tube ride. At this rate, I wasn't going to have enough time to finish the birthday cakes and deliver them. Luckily Liz had a plan.

'Tell you what, give me about half an hour and I'll come to you, then I can drive you over there.'

'You're an angel, thank you. I'll see you in a bit, then.'

I hung up and decided to fire up my laptop to check my emails whilst I waited for her. At least that was my intention when I first opened it up. After a cursory glance at messages from suppliers and assorted other junk, I found myself typing Jack's name into the computer. I hesitated for a second before I clicked on the search button, but only for a second. I couldn't help it; I just couldn't stop thinking about him. I felt like a teenager with a crush; it was totally ridiculous. I was a grown woman, I told myself, I didn't need a man to make me happy and I certainly didn't need a face from my past forcing its way back into my future.

Don't turn this into a three-act play, Abby. You saw him for a few minutes and he's probably forgotten about you already.

When his face appeared on my screen, I couldn't help smiling. He looked so handsome, much better than he did when we were younger. Money obviously suited him. I found a close-up of his face, some business magazine cover. He was staring down the camera lens, as if he were looking just at me. His hair was short except for the top, which was brushed back off his face, revealing sharp cheekbones and a well-defined jaw. I read a few news articles about him, about his company and what they did. Something very high-tech and obviously pretty lucrative – all to do with computers and apps; it might as well have been written in Mandarin for all I understood of it.

Interestingly, the articles made no mention of his being born in London, or the fact that he went to a normal crappy comprehensive. At some point, it seemed that Jack had decided to completely reinvent himself and remove all traces of the boy he was. But he couldn't fool me; I could still see him because I knew where to look. He was still there, in that slightly crooked smile, the one that used to make my insides fizz, and in those twinkling brown eyes, the same ones that used to watch me across the classroom. He always had a real knack for that – looking right through all the layers of emotional armour I wore to hide my many fears and insecurities. I tore my gaze away from those eyes and looked at his slightly crooked grin. Bad idea! I couldn't stop looking at his mouth now and imagining all sorts of things. Stop it, Abby! The sound of someone outside, leaning on their car horn, made me jump.

'Mum! I think Auntie Liz is here. You'd better get out there before she wakes up half the bloody street!' shouted Lucy, from the kitchen.

I grabbed my jacket and headed out onto the landing that ran along the front of the flats. I ran down the stairs as quickly as I could, trying to get to Liz before she let out another deafening round of her car horn, but I was too late. She leaned on the horn again, this time for a bit longer, and was treated to the sight of my neighbour hanging out of his window in his vest, shouting something at her in Greek. I jumped into the car just as Liz was about to stick her head out of her window to shout something back.

'Liz! No! Just drive the bloody car!'

'What a rude man. Makes me wish I could speak

67

Greek.'

'It's barely seven in the morning – you can't blame him for being a bit pissed off to be woken up like that.'

'Fine. I'll let him off just this once.'

I was struck by a sudden image of Liz boning up on her Greek in preparation for the possible next round. I wouldn't have put it past her.

'So why were *you* hurling abuse at me this morning, then?' For a second I didn't know what she meant, but then I remembered my 'motor mouth' reference from our earlier phone call.

'Why did you have to tell Lucy about Jack? You know what she's like about trying to get me involved with someone. She's become obsessed lately. I really don't know what's got into her.'

'You don't?' Liz eyed me, quizzically. 'You really haven't worked it out?'

I shook my head.

'My God, woman, when it comes to reading the signs you are totally shit! She hates the idea of leaving you all alone when she goes in a few weeks!'

'Really?'

'Really! Honestly, Abby, you can be so dim at times. Lucy wants to make sure you've got someone so you don't waste all your time missing her. She wants you to have a life – as do I, my darling.' She gave me a sympathetic smile.

'I have a life, thank you very much. Running the

business keeps me very busy. I don't need anything else.'

'Okay, I shall rephrase – you don't just need a life; you need a sex life.'

Before I could reply, Liz hurtled on.

'You haven't had sex for God knows how long! Not that I know of, anyway, and don't think you can lie to me about it because you can't. You are in danger of shrivelling up inside if you don't start living a life that involves more than just work and Lucy.'

'I have Mum and Matt too!' I protested, weakly.

'Judging by the way he looked at you yesterday, you could quite easily throw the lovely Mr Chance into the mix as well.' Liz turned and gave me a wink. 'He seemed very pleased to see you after so long.' I knew she was waiting for me to say something but I didn't, so she kept talking.

'He wanted to know how long you'd been married or if you had kids.' I turned in my seat to protest but she held up her hand. 'Don't worry, I didn't tell him anything. I pretended that we didn't know each other that well so I had no information for him. I don't think he really believed me, but he let it drop anyway.'

I let out the breath I was holding and I shook my head. I wanted to ask about the blonde on his arm, but I didn't dare. I knew if I showed the slightest interest Liz would be all over me. Instead I moved to safer ground and asked about the party.

'Did all those desserts get eaten?'

Liz smiled and nodded enthusiastically. 'Of course, they did! Well, except for the few that I took home. I couldn't resist – they were delicious.'

I was pleased. It was nice to know I was good at something at least. Liz started talking about how well the event went and about how she'd had lots of interest in her new company, but I wasn't really listening. The mention of Jack had sent my head spinning again and I couldn't concentrate; I kept seeing that picture of him in his dinner jacket. Conveniently in my mind he was minus the blonde and I couldn't stop picturing his eyes; those gorgeous eyes that used to look at me as if I were the only person in the room. Liz snapped her fingers in my face.

'Hello? Earth to Abby – anybody there?'

I sat up sharply and batted her hand away. 'God, I'm sorry, I was thinking about those two cakes I have to deliver this afternoon.'

'Yes, of course you were, my darling. Tell me, in your imaginings did Jack pop naked out of the top of one of them?' She had a huge grin on her face and I couldn't help but smile back.

'Don't be so ridiculous... that's not even... I mean, for God's sake... I don't even...'

Liz laughed at my stammering excuses.

'I knew it!' she cried, slapping her hand down onto the steering wheel. 'There is something more to this than you let on yesterday. You have to tell me everything,

70

right now.'

'Liz, it was such a long time ago, I don't know why it matters.'

'Because it's exciting! Humour me, please. I've been with the same man for all of my adult life and I need to live vicariously through you now!'

Now it was my turn to laugh; Liz and her husband, David, had been together since they were fifteen, but they still adored each other. She liked to complain that her life was dull and boring, but I knew she wouldn't have it any other way. Her marriage was something I envied. David would do anything for Liz and for their children; he was the ultimate family man. It didn't hurt that he was also quite cute, in a Hugh Bonneville/Colin Firth kind of way, and he worshipped Liz.

'You're not going to shut up about this, are you?' I asked.

Liz shook her head. 'No. Now spill those proverbial beans if you please.'

'Okay, okay, but there really isn't that much to tell. We lived in the same street, went to school together, he was my first kiss and then suddenly he was gone. His family just moved away and never came back. I never heard from him again.' That was it – our potted history.

'First kiss, eh? That's heady stuff. You never forget your first kiss, Abby.'

'Well, I did. No time to dwell on that when you've got a baby to take care of on your own.'

'Did he know Lucy's father?'

'Yes, he knew Martin. We were all in the same class at school.'

Liz wisely decided to leave that subject alone. The story of my relationship with Martin was a pretty ugly one; the only good thing to have come out of it was my daughter.

'What about when your dad... you know... buggered off?'

'Dad had been gone for a few weeks before Jack and his family left. So yes, he knows about it.'

'So why is this the first I'm hearing about this man? I know practically everything else there is to know about you, Abby, why not this?'

'I'd forgotten all about him,' I lied. 'A lot of things happened after he went and I just got on with my life.' I decided not to mention the weeks of waiting for the phone to ring, waiting to hear his voice on the other end telling me that he was coming back for me.

Liz reached over and took my hand. 'I know you had it tough at the beginning, Abby, but look at where you are now. All that's behind you. It's time to get out there and start really living.'

'I'm all right, Liz, really. I have everything I want. I don't need complications, especially when they come in the shape of a man.'

'Just promise me that you'll give it some thought, okay? Make some room for the possibility at least.' Liz pulled up at the kerbside outside the party venue and watched me as I unbuckled my seat belt, waiting for some reassurance that I'd heard her.

'I'll call you later.' I leaned across and pecked her on the cheek and then got out of the car. I made my way into the car park, grateful to be out of Liz's car and off the topic of Jack Bloody Chance.

Chapter 6

Oh, for Christ's sake! I couldn't quite believe what I was seeing. There was a bloody great black Mercedes parked right across in front of my van. How on earth was I supposed to get it out? No doubt some arrogant tosspot from one of the offices upstairs had just left it there. I started conjuring up a picture of a big, sweaty idiot in a badly fitting suit, up in his posh office, bossing around the little people.

Over by the entrance barriers there was a small office with a glass front window; the sign on the door said 'Security'. A man in a navy uniform was sitting inside, behind a bank of CCTV screens. As I approached he looked up and I gestured to him through the window.

'My van, over there, blocked in.' I waved in the general direction of my little green van and he nodded. Reaching across his desk, he picked up a phone and started talking to someone. After a brief conversation, he put the phone down and gave me the thumbs up; I assumed that meant the owner of the car was coming to move it, so I went back to my van to wait.

The poor old girl looked incredibly scruffy, parked in there alongside sleek Mercedes and BMWs. Maybe it was time to bite the bullet and get a new one? I could get a loan, I supposed. I thought about it for a split second then came to another conclusion. I didn't need a new van; what I needed was to just get the hell out of that car park full of overpriced penis replacements and get back to my life! Where was this inconsiderate idiot anyhow? I was rummaging around for my keys in the bag Liz had given me, when I heard footsteps coming across the car park. I was about to look up, ready to blast the inconsiderate git with a few well-chosen words, when I dropped my bag on the floor and my phone skittered across the ground to the man's feet. He bent to pick it up at the same time as I did and we bashed heads on the way down.

'Ow!' I cried out, putting my hand up to the crown of my head.

'Oh, God, Abigail, I'm so sorry! Are you all right?' It was Jack – of course it would have to be him, I thought, because the universe likes to mess with me. He placed his hand on mine and suddenly my brain was melting from the warmth of his touch. I pulled out of his reach.

'I'm fine, honestly. It's nothing.'

'Let me see. That was quite a crack.' Stepping towards me, he tilted my head down so he could get a better look and my face was suddenly buried in his chest. I fought the sudden urge to smell him and instead put both hands on his chest to push him away.

'No permanent damage done that I can see. Do you

75

need to sit down though?' he asked. His hands were now holding the tops of my arms and I was blocked in, unable to get out of his reach.

'What I need is for the idiot who owns this bloody car to get down here and get out of my way so I can leave! What kind of brainless git parks his car right across a parking space?' As soon as the words flew out of my mouth I knew the answer; that crooked smile appeared and I was looking at the Jack I remembered.

'It's your car, isn't it?'

He nodded. 'I'm afraid it is. And that's *Mr* Brainless Git, if you don't mind.'

I managed a smile and held out my hand. 'Nice to meet you, Mr Brainless, I'm Mrs Foot in Mouth.' He shook my outstretched hand and then gave me my phone, the screen of which was now sporting a very fetching crack right down the middle.

'Looks like you're gonna need a new cell phone.'

'Did you just say cell phone?'

He looked a little embarrassed. 'Sorry. Too many years in the States, forgot where I was for a minute. You're gonna need a new *mobile*.'

'Much better.'

'We aim to please, Mrs Cowan.'

Would now be a good time to correct his assumption that I'm married? I wondered. Yes, screamed my libido. No, bellowed my common sense. Leave it alone, if he thinks you're married then he won't bother you. Was that what I wanted? Yes, I told myself, I didn't need him. In order to confirm this, I reached into my bag and pulled out my purse.

'I think I owe you some money for that cab yesterday, if you'll just tell me how much?'

He put a hand out to stop me.

'Please, don't worry, it's fine. You don't owe me anything, really.'

Was he being patronising? I couldn't tell. Maybe I was letting that working-class chip on my shoulder get the better of me again, but I didn't like owing people. I especially didn't want to owe him anything. I managed to pull a ten-pound note out of my purse and thrust it into his grasp. He grabbed my hand and shoved the note straight back again.

'We could stand here like idiots doing this all day, but I promise you I will not take that money.'

I knew he was serious but I was determined not to owe him a penny; I decided to put it in the post and send it to him later. That would shut him up.

'Don't take it, then,' I said, stuffing the note back into my purse. 'I don't need your money, Jack. I'm doing fine.'

'I know. I can see that. I'm not trying to imply anything else – don't be so defensive. You always were a stubborn girl.'

He kept hold of my hand as he looked at me.

'I can't believe it's really you, after all this time. It's so good to see you, Abigail. You look great.'

'That's a lie but thank you anyway.'

I looked down at my tatty jeans and Converse trainers and felt very underdressed. By contrast, Jack looked immaculate in a grey three-piece suit and grey tie and I could see a very expensive-looking watch on the wrist of the hand that was still holding mine. We were so different now; as kids we'd been equals but not anymore.

He was still holding my hand, in no rush to let it go, it seemed, and although I knew I should move away I didn't. I was looking up into the face of a grown man but all I could see was the boy he was. The same sparkling eyes, the quirky smile and slightly unruly hair that, despite so many years gone by, could apparently still make my stomach do somersaults. He was the first one to break the silence.

'You look beautiful to me.'

I wasn't sure I'd heard him correctly; it was hard to make out the words above the sound of my heart thudding in my chest. I felt very hot and he was standing very close – too close. I should have got into my little van and driven away as fast and as far as I could, but I didn't. Why? Because you wanted him to kiss you, screamed my libido, which appeared to have recently woken up after a prolonged nap. No, I didn't want that – did I? He left me, he didn't even try and get in touch, he just left. He knew what my father's disappearance did to me, how it devastated me, and yet within weeks he'd done the same thing. I wasn't stupid, I knew it would have been his parents' decision, but he never even tried to contact me. I think that was what hurt the most. I hadn't gone anywhere, my phone number was still the same, so was my address. If he'd wanted to reach me then he could have done; now it was too late. The anger began rising, like a bubble inside my chest, and I couldn't control it. With my free hand, I slapped him – hard – across his cheek.

'What the fuck! What was that for?'

'Get away from me, Jack. What are you trying to do to me? What do you want from me?' I shouted. 'You may be the rich boy now, but you can't just come in here and call me beautiful like nothing ever happened!' That last remark sounded ridiculous – why was I complaining about being called beautiful? But I was so angry. I reached up to pound my fist on his chest, but he was too quick for me; he grabbed both my wrists and held them still.

'You only get away with that once, Abigail.' He was angry with me, but I didn't care.

'Could you move your car, please? I have work to do; I have to go.'

'No.'

'What? You can't keep me here, Jack. I have to go.'

'Then tell me how I can reach you.'

'No,' I said firmly.

He shook his head, exasperated. 'God, you're so frustrating, Abigail. You ran off yesterday – couldn't wait to get away from me, I seem to remember. And now you're looking at me like you want to do the same again. Why?'

Because looking at you, being so near to you, is making my heart hurt, I wanted to scream at him. When I didn't reply, he reached up and gently touched my cheek.

'You haven't changed, you know, not to me. As soon as I saw you yesterday, even from right across the room, I knew it was you.'

He stroked my cheek lightly with his thumb and looked at me as if I were the most amazing thing he'd ever seen.

'I was so stupidly happy to see you but you couldn't get away from me fast enough. Why?'

'I have to go, Jack. Please let me go.'

'You haven't answered my question. Why did you run? Why do you look like you're about to do it again? You look almost scared of me.'

I'm terrified of you, I wanted to scream, I'm terrified of how you can make me feel even after all this time. I straightened myself up to my full height, which admittedly wasn't much compared to him, and took his hand away from my face.

'I'm not scared of you, Jack,' I lied.

'Please don't run away from me, Abigail. There's so

much we have to talk about. It's been so long. Can we meet somewhere? Just to talk, to catch up?' His eyes were searching my face, pleading for a response; he reached out to hold my arms again. His touch seemed to burn through the fabric of my shirt. He looked so desperate that I almost gave in but I knew deep down that there would be no point in our meeting.

'I can't imagine what we'd have to say to each other after all this time. Can you let go of me, please?'

Reluctantly he released me from his grip and dragged his hand through his hair. He seemed as if he wanted to say more but we were interrupted by a female voice, coming from across the car park.

'Jack, there you are!'

We both turned to see Lexie Morgan coming towards us; I wondered how long she'd been watching. As she drew closer my heart sank to my scruffy shoes; she was even more glamorous than I remembered. She was dressed in an immaculate white trouser suit, her blonde hair pulled back into a neat ponytail, which emphasised her perfect skin and high cheekbones. Full lips, glossy hair and a perfect white smile – every normal woman's basic nightmare and the perfect companion for Jack Chance, high-flying tech millionaire and man about town. I was desperate to get as far away from the pair of them as I could – and fast.

'I've been looking everywhere for you. I thought we could head out to that place in St Katherine's Dock for breakfast.' She came to stand between us.

'It's become our absolute favourite place to eat since we've been here.' That last remark was directed at me and I smiled graciously.

'That sounds lovely. Mr Chance and I have concluded our business so I'll be on my way. If you'd be so kind as to move your car. It was lovely to meet you, Miss?' I pretended I didn't know her name. Very childish of me, I knew.

'Morgan. Lexie Morgan.' She shook my hand. 'Have we met somewhere before?'

'Yes. We met yesterday. I catered some of the food for the party.'

'You made the desserts!' she exclaimed, letting go of my hand. 'You are so talented. They were fabulous.'

I couldn't tell if she was being sincere or not. 'It was just a few cakes and pastries, nothing special.'

'Are you kidding me? They were amazing. Tell her, Jack.'

'They were delicious, Abigail. You did a great job,' said Jack.

I looked at him and he held my gaze for a few seconds. Something sparked between us, a moment of connection that scared the shit out of me. It was too much; I had to get out of there. Lexie coughed awkwardly and the moment evaporated. Jack turned to her, as if he'd only just realised she was there.

'Get in the car, Lexie. I'll be there in a minute. Mrs

Cowan and I still have a few things to talk about.' Jack guided her around to the passenger side and opened the door for her.

'Such a gentleman, isn't he? It was nice to see you again, Mrs Cowan.' Her head dipped inside the car and she was gone, hidden behind the tinted windows. I took that opportunity to get into my van, but Jack grabbed the door before I could shut it behind me.

'You never told me how I could get hold of you again if I needed you, Mrs Cowan.'

'You're right, I didn't. You won't need to get hold of me again, Jack. Our business is done.'

I grabbed the door handle and pulled it shut so fast that he had to jump out of the way. He looked momentarily stunned. I was half expecting – or was that hoping? – that he would rip it open again but he didn't. He stared at me for a second or two and then walked to his car and got in; Jack and Lexie, in their own little world of luxury upholstery and tinted glass, and me, back in my crappy green van. It's better this way, I told myself. I'm happy where I am and I'm sure they are too. Jack's car pulled away and I was finally able to manoeuvre out of my parking space. By the time I exited the car park he was long gone and I had to fight an unexpected urge to cry.

Chapter 7

'He did that on purpose! Just so you wouldn't be able to sneak in and leave! That's so romantic!'

After dropping off my afternoon deliveries, I'd called Liz and told her about my encounter with Jack. Unsurprisingly she'd rushed straight over and insisted on all the gory details.

'Don't be silly, Liz, he couldn't have known it was my van.'

'Of course he knew it was yours! I told you he was interested, didn't I? This is so exciting!' She bounced up and down in her chair, looking like a toddler who needed a wee.

'Keep your bloody voice down, will you? Flo's still cleaning up in the kitchen – I don't want her to hear. She'll feel compelled to tell Lucy and I definitely don't want her knowing anything about all this. It's bad enough you gave her his name yesterday.'

Liz placed one hand on her chest and raised the other. 'I promise I will not mention to your daughter that there's a very real possibility you will be having some hot sex in the near future. You have my word.' She was grinning from ear to ear and I looked shocked, which just made her laugh uncontrollably. As she wiped away a tear she said, 'Why do you find it so hard to believe that a man like that would want you? Have you not seen yourself? Have you been hiding behind that sodding apron for so long you've forgotten what you look like?' She stood up and gripped me firmly by the shoulders.

'I'm no Lexie Morgan. She looked stunning, Liz. I felt quite the dumpy troll stood next to her in her designer suit and killer heels.'

'Pah!' Liz gave a dismissive wave of her hand. 'That little girl doesn't stand a chance against you and the power of first love. You mark my words; this is not the last you will hear from him.'

'You're being ridiculous. You should have seen them together – the designer couple. And she's not as awful as I thought. She was very nice about my food.'

Liz didn't look convinced by my assessment. 'Well, she was bloody awful yesterday. Never stopped complaining.'

'Maybe she was nervous or having an off day. She really did seem quite...' I paused '... sweet.'

'Ugh.' Liz pretended to gag. 'The sweet ones are the worst. You should watch your back.'

'What for? We're not in competition. I don't want Jack – she can have him. They seem well suited. It's all good.' I moved across and started clearing away some empty cups from the next table.

'Why won't you let yourself be happy?'

I stopped wiping up some spilt sugar and looked at her. 'What do you mean?'

She came across to me. 'It doesn't always have to end badly, you know. You should take a risk now and again, let someone in.'

I shook my head, mainly because the lump that had formed in my throat was stopping me from speaking. A fat tear rolled traitorously down my cheek.

'Sweetie, I didn't mean to make you cry. I'm sorry.' She stepped back and held me at arm's length. 'I just get so frustrated with you and your total inability to see the good in yourself.'

'Take no notice of me. I can't seem to stop crying at the minute. You're very sweet, Liz, and I know you're just trying to help, but there's really no need. I'm all right.' I wiped away my tears with the sleeve of my shirt and plastered on a bright smile.

'Just think about it, Abby, that's all I ask.'

'I will,' I said. I think we both knew I was lying.

'All righty, then, I shall leave you to your cleaning and head home.'

'You could stay and help. I'm sure I've got a spare apron somewhere.'

Liz wrinkled her nose. 'I'm sorry, do we know each other? When have you ever known me to clean?'

I laughed. 'Fair enough. I'll call you tomorrow.'

'Make sure you do, my darling.' She gave me a peck

on the cheek and then shouted towards the kitchen. 'Goodnight, Florence!' When she didn't get a response, she leaned in to me and whispered, 'She really doesn't like me, does she?'

'I'm afraid you're just too posh and too rich for Flo.'

'Oh, well, can't please everyone, I suppose.' She threw me an air kiss and then she was gone. I breathed a sigh of relief and flopped down into the nearest chair, exhausted. Flo came out of the kitchen holding her coat and handbag and sat down next to me.

'She's gone, then, has she?'

'Yes, Flo, she's gone. You should give her a chance, you know. I think the two of you would hit it off. You're very similar in a lot of ways.'

'Ha!' she exclaims. 'I don't think so. What could we possibly have in common?'

'Me.'

Flo turned to look at me, her eyes full of concern. 'Are you all right, Abby? You look tired.'

'Just been a busy day, that's all.' I pushed myself up out of the chair and Flo stood too, shrugging on her coat.

'Have an early night, then, sweetheart. Go to bed with a cuppa and a good book – that's what I'm going to do. I'm reading a great one at the minute. It's got an Italian prince in it who falls in love with a common servant girl and they get up to all sorts. It's really naughty but it's good, very tastefully done,' she said with a wink. 'I'll lend it to you when I'm finished if you want.'

As much as I would have loved nothing more than to curl up with a good book, not necessarily one of Flo's soft-porn volumes, I had something else that I had to do that evening.

'I've promised to go and see Mum tonight, so no early bedtime for me, I'm afraid.'

Flo smiled. 'I spoke to your mum this morning and she did mention that she hadn't seen you for a while. I told her how busy you've been with all the extra work for Liz. Don't worry about it, Abby. I'm sure she understands.' Flo didn't sound convinced and neither was I. I was pretty sure I'd have to spend most of the evening justifying my lack of visits to my mother, just like always. It didn't matter though – nothing I did was good enough. I could have spent every day with her and it would still be wrong. Flo patted my hand reassuringly.

'Your mum is one of my oldest friends but sometimes even I want to strangle her. Don't let her upset you.'

I smiled at that. Flo was the only one of mum's friends who'd stuck around after her breakdown. She would turn up at our door, armed with cake and sweets for me and Matt, and then she would go up to Mum's room and sit with her for hours on end. She'd never told me what they'd talked about but, then again, I'd never asked. I was frightened that I'd scare her off with my questions and she'd stop coming to see us.

'I'll be fine, Flo. I promise not to strangle her, not tonight anyway.'

'Night-night, love.' She pecked me on the cheek and made her way to the door. 'Be sure and lock this behind me, now, won't you?'

'Yes, Flo. I always do.'

Shrugging her coat collar up around her ears, she walked out into the street. I watched her tiny form as she made her way up the road and when she got to the corner she turned and gave me a little wave, just as she'd done every night for the last ten years. But tonight, that little gesture made me want to weep. Enough with the tears, Abby! What is the matter with you? I swiped my hands across my cheeks and took a deep breath before leaning down to fasten the bolt at the bottom of the door. I turned and looked around at the empty café and my eye wandered over to the table by the window. Suddenly I was fifteen again, sitting there with Jack, holding hands and wondering how my life had been turned upside down.

*

'What do you mean he's just gone?' Jack asks me. 'He can't have just gone.'

'I'm telling you, Jack, he has. I haven't seen him for three days now. Mum won't talk to me about it – I've asked her but she just keeps saying it's better this way or

89

something.' I'm clutching Jack's hand and I can't stop the tears from falling. Immediately he moves from his place across the table and comes round to sit next to me. I bury my head in his shoulder and I sob. After a few minutes Ted comes across to us.

'What's the matter, Abby? What's happened?' Ted's brow is creased with concern. I can't seem to speak without sobbing so Jack tells him everything.

'It's Abby's dad. He's gone, just left them. Abby's mum won't tell her anything.'

I finally manage to find my voice as I wipe away snot and tears with my sleeve. 'She's just been sitting in her bedroom crying and I don't know what to do.' Ted is shaking his head sadly but he won't meet my eyes.

'Where's he gone, Ted? Why won't anyone tell me?' I'm pleading with him but he doesn't say anything, instead he just turns and walks back out to the kitchen. I see Rose putting her arm round his shoulders and then looking past him, out to me in the café. They are deep in conversation for a few minutes and then Rose pushes through the beaded curtain and comes over to me.

She's quite a formidable-looking woman. Her red hair is set in curls that are kept under a headscarf whilst she's at work. It's the same hairstyle she's had since she was a young woman, but she will admit to getting a bit of help with the colour now that she's developed a few grey hairs. She has it set once a week, in the salon next door, and trapped in the chair under the hairdryer is probably about the only time you will ever see Rose sitting still. She never stops; she's always doing something useful.

'Idle hands breed idle minds' she often says to me, as we mop the kitchen floor or wipe down tables for the umpteenth time in a day. She is short and stocky, with veiny forearms that tell the tale of many years of sheer hard graft. She worked with her father at Billingsgate Fish Market in London before she married Ted and they opened the café. She would tell me stories about how no one cared that she was a girl; she would be expected to lug the same boxes of fish and ice around that the men were. 'My dad wouldn't hear any excuses about my being weaker 'cos I was a girl. He'd tell me that it was me mother's fault for not giving him any sons to help out with the business.' I thought that sounded awful but Rose wouldn't have any of it.

'Taught me a valuable lesson, Abby: never let anyone tell you that you can't do something just 'cos you're a woman. We're strong, we can do whatever we set our minds to – you'd do well to remember that.'

As she sits across from me at the table now, I can see she's been crying too. She folds her arms across her formidable bosom and looks me straight in the eye. Jack is next to me, still holding my hand, and she gives him a strange look before leaning across the table. She speaks in a very low, no nonsense kind of way.

'You need to be strong for your mum now,

sweetheart, do you hear me? Your dad, well, let's just say he's made a bit of a mess of things.' As she speaks she's fiddling with the ring on her left hand, turning it round and round.

'What mess? What's he done? Has he run off with another woman? I heard some girls at school saying he'd gone to Spain to be with his girlfriend or something. Is that it?'

Rose shakes her head. 'The details aren't important. Your mum thinks it's best that you all just move on with your lives. You do as she says now, Abby. Don't you go making more trouble for her.'

I can't believe what I'm hearing! How can wanting to know where my dad is be classed as making trouble?

'She just wants to know what's going on. That's not making trouble – he's her dad. He can't just disappear, and no one tell her anything – that's not fucking fair!' exclaims Jack.

'Life isn't bloody fair and you mind your fucking language, young man – you're not too big for a clip round the ear, you know!' Jack sits back in his chair, stunned. Neither of us have ever heard Rose swear like that before. She takes a deep breath and straightens the front of her tabard; I'm bracing myself for another onslaught but instead she smiles at me kindly.

'I know none of this makes any sense to you now but one day maybe it will. Your dad doesn't want you and your family ruined by his stupidity. That's all I can tell you, Abby. He went because he didn't feel like he had any choice.'

I'm hit by the realisation that my dad's gone and he's not coming back and I don't think I'm ever going to know why.

'You're not alone in this, Abby. Ted and me are always going to be here for you, no matter what happens. You're surrounded by people that love you, my dear, remember that. You're going to hear lots of stories and idle gossip in the next few weeks. Just ignore it, all right? Focus on looking after Mum and your brother and you'll be fine.' She reaches across the table and gives my arm a reassuring squeeze before walking away.

'And I'm here too, Abby. I'll look after you. I promise,' says Jack.

*

'But you didn't look after me, did you, Jack?'

The memory of Jack's words brought me back to the here and now, standing in the middle of my café with tears streaming down my face. What must I look like to anyone walking by? The soppy middle-aged woman, clutching a tea towel and staring into space.

Don't be a fool, Abby. Why dwell on the past? You can't change it and you can't make it better. At some point, you have to decide to not let it rule your future. That was what I'd been doing for most of my life so what had changed? Why couldn't I hold back this sudden tide of memories that was threatening to drown me? It was Jack's fault – seeing him after all this time was dredging up the kind of crap I'd fought so long to bury. I needed to keep him out of my life; it was that simple. My sanity depended on it. I wiped my face with my hands and headed to the back to get my coat; the sooner I got to Mum's, the sooner I could get away.

*

It was only a five-minute walk to her house – it sat at the top end of the same road that the café was in – but it might as well have been a million miles considering how often I managed to drag myself there.

The walk was just long enough to give me time to develop the sweaty palms and upset stomach that always seemed to accompany my visits. I didn't think I was overstating it when I said that I hated that house. I never used to; before Dad went it was just a house. It was never exactly overflowing with warmth and love – Mum and Dad used to argue too often and too loudly for that ever to be the case – but I liked locking myself away in my room and listening to music or reading book after book. Sometimes Matt would hide away with me and we'd talk about what we were going to do with our lives when we grew up and left home. Matt was going to be a pilot and I was going to be a famous actress. I would imagine myself up on stage, listening to the thunderous applause as I stepped up to collect my most recent award. What a joke that turned out to be.

I pushed open the front gate and made my way up the cracked concrete path to the door; I'd never noticed before how run-down and old the house was looking. The frames in the front bay window were starting to rot a bit and the painted red brickwork around the small porch was peeling and worn. I reached up to knock but the door was yanked open before I got the chance.

'I thought I heard someone creeping around out here.'

'It's just me, Mum. No one's creeping around.'

My mother looked past me, as if expecting to see someone else. When she realised that I was on my own she stepped back to open the door wider and I walked inside.

'I thought maybe Matt or Lucy would be with you,' she asked, hopefully.

'Nope, sorry, just me. Lucy's out with friends and I don't know what Matt's doing. I haven't spoken to him today.'

'Oh well, never mind. I'm sure he'll pop in later if he can. He usually does. Tea?' She didn't bother to wait for a reply, she just bustled off down the hallway to the kitchen at the back of the house.

I took off my jacket and dropped it onto the stairs; from the kitchen I heard her call out, 'Put your coat in the under-stairs cupboard.' The woman was obsessed with tidiness. I contemplated pretending I hadn't heard her and just leaving my jacket where it was – did I dare? No, you don't, said the voice in my head. I picked up the jacket and pulled open the door to the under-stairs cupboard. It was so neat; just like everywhere else in the house, everything had its perfect place. Mum's shoes sat in a tidy row on the little shelf she'd made Matt put up for her and her coat hung on one of the hooks above. There was a spare hook for my jacket but in a childish act of rebellion I ignored it, chucking my jacket over the upright vacuum cleaner in the corner instead. How very mature, Abby. I couldn't help it; there was something about being in that house that always made me want to act like a naughty teenager rather than a mature adult.

Closing the door on the evidence of my childishness, I made my way down the hall and into the kitchen. I stood in the doorway for a minute, watching my mum potter about, fetching the teapot from the cupboard, laying out a mug for me and a cup and saucer for herself, and I wondered how many times I'd watched her do the exact same thing over the years. The kitchen was the same one that had been there since before I was born: high-gloss purple cupboards that she always seemed to be wiping fingerprints off and dark orange ceramic floor tiles. The unforgiving fluorescent strip light that ran down the centre of the ceiling filled the room with an unnatural yellow light that made everyone look jaundiced and it gave off a low-level buzzing noise that used to drive me bonkers.

'Well, are you going to just stand there or are you going to sit down? You look like you're not stopping.'

If only, I thought. 'No, I'm stopping. Sorry,' I mumbled as I parked myself in the nearest chair. She poured out the tea and brought it over to the table. We each took a sip and then sat in silence. I started picking at the skin around my fingernails; one particularly stubborn bit refused to budge so I raised my hand to my mouth, ready to pull it off with my teeth.

'Don't bite your nails, Abigail,' my mother snapped. 'It's a disgusting habit. I don't know how many times I have to tell you.'

I dropped my hand into my lap.

'That's better,' she said, taking another sip of tea. 'Flo tells me you've been busy working for that friend of yours. Lyn, isn't it?'

'It's Liz,' I corrected her, 'and yes, I was helping her cater a party. I made the desserts for her.'

'Couldn't she get a proper caterer for that?' Mum asked, eyeing me over the rim of her cup.

'She had a proper caterer but they let her down so she asked me to step in and help out.'

Mum nodded – her knowing look said that obviously Liz was desperate and now it all made more sense to her.

'Well, I'm sure you did your best, love. That's all that matters.'

I wanted to shout at her that actually my best was fucking brilliant and that everyone raved about my food, but I didn't; past experience had taught me that it wouldn't have made the slightest bit of difference, so I just went back to drinking my tea and changed the subject.

'I met someone at the party, actually. Someone I used to know, so did you – you used to be friends with his parents.'

'Oh, really? Who's that, then?' Mum got up and took her cup to the sink; her back was to me as she turned on the hot tap and started to fill the sink.

'Jack Chance. His family used to live a few doors down. Do you remember? Jack's dad worked at the bank on High Street.'

Mum turned off the tap and just stood looking out of the window above the sink. After a few seconds, she turned and started wiping her wet hands on a tea towel.

'No, the name doesn't ring any bells. Are you sure?' She folded the tea towel neatly and laid it on the worktop next to the sink.

'They lived four doors away, Mum. You and dad used to go out with them now and then. Oh, bloody hell, what were their names again?' I said, racking my brains to remember. I could see them quite clearly in my mind's eye; Jack's mum was always very glamorous for a housewife and his dad was such a sweet man. Suddenly it hit me. 'Brian and Sally!' I exclaimed. 'That's it! Brian and Sally Chance. Thank God for that – it would have really started to annoy me if I couldn't remember,' I said, bringing my mug over to the sink. Mum took it from me and I noticed her hands were shaking a little.

'Do you remember them, then?'

'No, Abigail, I don't!' she shouted. 'I've just told you I don't – why are you still going on about it?' She looked pale.

'Are you okay, Mum? Do you want to sit down?'

'No, I'm fine. Don't fuss.' She sloshed hot, soapy water into the mug and when she'd finished she started with the obsessive hand-drying again. Her hands looked sore and I took the tea towel from her.

'Mum, stop it. Look at your hands – you've made them all red.'

She looked down at them. 'Oh, yes, look at that. I should get my hand cream.'

I watched her scurry out of the room and all but run up the stairs, no mean feat for a woman of her age. I followed her out into the hallway and called up after her.

'Is everything all right? Do you want another cuppa? Shall I put the kettle on?'

'No.'

I stood at the foot of the stairs, unsure of what to do. Should I follow her and check she was all right? I took a step up and then stopped; I heard her slamming drawers up in her room. I'd just wait for her to come down.

Coward, said a voice in my head. I knew I was, but I couldn't deal with her when she was upset. She became too unpredictable and I didn't like it. It made me feel off balance. That was how she'd always made me feel. After she'd recovered from her breakdown she'd put on a good show for everyone. She'd managed to convince them all that after two years of shutting herself away and being barely able to function she was now better. My grandparents had been happy to believe her since that had meant they were free to move out and get away from us, and the few friends she'd had left had gone along with the pretence, because it was easier for them to think that they no longer had to worry about her doing something stupid. But I knew better; I lived with her. I heard her crying at night or, when she couldn't cry any more, obsessively cleaning and tidying the house. From the moment she 'recovered', until the day I finally moved out, I walked around our house in a permanent state of high alert, just waiting for her to fall apart again. And even after all this time, I knew I was still just waiting.

I went back into the kitchen and sat at the table, listening to her moving around upstairs. I heard her talking to someone. I couldn't make out what she was saying but I could hear the muffled sounds of crying interspersed with words. After about ten minutes she came back into the kitchen, a smile plastered firmly in place. She looked surprised to see me still sitting there.

'I thought you'd gone,' she said.

'No, what made you think that?'

She just shrugged, as if it didn't matter to her either way, and I realised that this little exchange perfectly epitomised our relationship. She ran from the room upset, I didn't feel any desire to follow her or offer comfort, and she really couldn't give a shit either way.

'Matt's coming round,' she said, filling up the kettle with water.

'Matt? What for?' I knew that was who she'd been talking to upstairs. She called and he came running, just like always.

'He enjoys coming to see me, Abigail. He doesn't need a reason.'

I loved my brother dearly and we were very close. He helped me raise Lucy and we would do anything for each other, but his blind devotion to my mother and her moods, and his willingness to overlook everything she put us through, really pissed me off.

'I'll leave you to it, then,' I said. I went to the cupboard and retrieved my jacket.

'You don't have to go, Abigail. Why don't you stay and we can all spend some time together? We haven't done that for ages. It would be nice to have both my children under the same roof for once.' Mum looked at me hopefully but I shook my head.

'I can't, Mum, got loads to do at the café. Tell Matt I'll catch up with him another time.' Shrugging on my jacket, I leaned in and gave her a quick peck on the cheek and then opened the front door.

'Abigail, I...'

I turned to face her and her eyes were filled with tears.

'What? Mum, what's wrong?' I reached out to touch her arm but she moved away. I saw a look of something flash across her face but she quickly tucked it away behind a fake smile.

'Nothing. It's fine. I'll see you soon. Bring that beautiful granddaughter of mine with you next time, all right?'

'Yes, Mum. See you later.' I walked out of the house and the door had closed behind me before I even made it off the front step. I was filled with a sense of sadness and unease that stayed with me as I slowly walked home.

Chapter 8

Why won't they talk to me? I know they can see me but they just stand and stare. Help me, I call out, help me, please. There's Dad! I can see him. I try and get his attention but he turns and walks away. The crowd behind him parts and he's swallowed up into a sea of faces I don't recognise.

*

I locked the door of the café and leant against it – it had been a very long day. It had started badly, with a reminder from the bank about my outstanding loan payments, and then it had just got progressively worse from there. I'd probably only served about a dozen customers all day; a fact that was starting to feel depressingly normal. I'd sent Flo home early – there was no point in both of us wasting our time – and I'd spent most of the day trying to come up with ways to make some money, but to no avail. What was I going to do? I didn't want to lose the business but, more importantly, I didn't want to lose my and Lucy's home. I knew she was leaving in a few weeks but I had to make sure that she would always have somewhere to come back to if she needed it, didn't I? The sensible part of me, the part that was usually in control, knew that moving on, letting the business go, was the practical solution. Matt had already told me I could move in with him for a bit if it helped, but that wasn't ever going to be a long-term fix; I needed a plan, and fast.

I couldn't believe, after working so hard for all these years, I was facing the prospect of being broke and homeless once again. All that was supposed to be behind me now – this was going to be the part of my life that wasn't going to be a struggle. No more worrying about whether or not I had enough cash to put credit on the gas meter key. No more hiding when people came to the door looking for debts to be paid. I'd done enough scrimping and saving to last me a lifetime and where had it got me? Still staring into a cavern of debt, that was where. The flat was rented from the council; all I owned was the café downstairs. That was the part that Ted and Rose had bequeathed to me. I could sell the café, but by the time I'd paid off my debts I wouldn't be left with very much; certainly nowhere near enough if I wanted to stay in this part of London. And this was my home. Ted and Rose's generosity had started out as a blessing, giving me and baby Lucy a roof over our heads and an income, but over the years, as the bills had risen faster than the profits, just staying afloat had become increasingly difficult.

I pushed myself wearily away from the door, weaving between the tables and chairs, towards the kitchen. I was fantasising about a nice hot bath and some peace and quiet when I heard knocking on the shop door. That was just typical. I didn't see a soul all afternoon and then when I was ready to go home some git came and banged on the door. I spun round and stomped back towards the front of the café.

'I'm sorry, we're closed for the day now,' I yelled. I couldn't make out who was there. They were tall, I could tell that much, and they obviously couldn't read the 'Closed' sign on the door because they were still banging.

'All right, I'm coming. Hold on.' I bent down to undo the bottom bolt, then the top, before finally yanking open the door.

'Hello, Abigail. Can I come in?'

Jack. On my doorstep. What the hell? I noticed he hadn't shaved; his designer stubble looked a bit untidy. He was wearing a tight grey T-shirt and jeans – very impressive chest, I noticed – and a black leather jacket; he looked annoyingly handsome. Bastard! He could at least have had the good grace to look like crap occasionally.

'What are you doing here?'

'I just wanted to see you. No hidden agenda, I swear.'

'How did you find me?'

'You're not exactly hard to find, Abigail. I had

105

someone on my staff trace your van. This is the registered address for it.'

He has staff – of course he does, he's a millionaire. Don't they all have staff?

'Tell your *staff* to stay out of my business. I already told you we have nothing more to say to each other.' I stepped out of the doorway, forcing him back a little, and then pulled the café door closed behind me. The last thing I wanted was for Lucy to hear him down here; she'd have him upstairs in the flat and drinking tea before I knew it. I threw him my best defiant glare, the one I usually reserved for stroppy customers, but it had little effect on him. He moved towards me ever so slightly and I took a step back. I was now trapped between the door and Jack's body. His dark eyes examined my face and I could feel my cheeks beginning to flush. He was so close, I allowed myself the luxury of a good old-fashioned ogle. No more fleshy, boyish cheeks; his face was more angular, the cheekbones more defined, the jawline more severe. All this new angularity was softened by the warm brown eyes I remembered so well; eyes that I would so often find focussed on me.

'I think we have plenty to talk about, Abigail.'

The scent of his aftershave filled the air between us and I could see a small pulse throbbing at the base of his neck. I'd quite like to just lean forward and bite it, I thought. Wait – what? Where did that spring from? I tried to regain my composure, taking several deep breaths before I could trust myself to speak.

'Don't be ridiculous. We haven't seen each other for twenty years, what could we possibly have to discuss?'

'Twenty years is a long time. A lot has happened to us both, *Mrs Cowan*.'

His voice was heavy with sarcasm and I realised that he'd uncovered my lie. No point denying it any more. I held up my left hand.

'No ring.'

'I can see that, but that isn't how I found out.'

'Your staff?'

He nodded.

'Bloody hell, Jack, stop snooping through my life! You have no right to do that!' I shoved both hands into his chest but it was like trying to move a boulder. I felt powerless and I didn't like it. He was unrepentant.

'You didn't leave me much choice. You keep running away from me, every chance you get. How was I supposed to see you?'

'You weren't. That's the whole point. Don't you get it?'

I was trying not to raise my voice – I didn't want to disturb the neighbours or Lucy – but he was being so aggravating. He was looking at me as if I were insane, as if he hadn't done anything wrong. After running out on me all those years before, he was standing there as if he had nothing to be sorry for.

'Why are you so angry with me?' he asked. 'You're

the one who broke my heart, remember? All those letters I wrote, begging for you to get in touch and nothing! No replies!'

'What the hell are you going on about? I never saw any letters!' He was lying, he must be.

'You were my first love, Abigail, my first kiss. Did you seriously think I would just leave you? Knowing how much it hurt you when your father left? Did you really think so little of me?'

His dark eyes searched my face, looking for some sort of response.

'What happened to all these letters, then, Jack? Where did they magically disappear to?'

He opened his mouth to speak but stopped himself; holding up his hands, he stepped away from me. I felt the cold air rush into the gap between us and for a moment I was tempted to draw him back towards me. He shoved his hands into his pockets and stood very still, looking me up and down for a few seconds.

'I didn't come here to fight with you, Abigail. Can't we just talk, like grown-ups? I just want to talk to you.'

I knew I should say no, but I suspected he would have an answer all ready for whatever objections I raised, and I didn't have the energy to argue. You also want to know what he has to say, said a little voice in the back of my mind.

'All right, fine,' I snapped, 'but you can't come inside.'

He looked mildly amused. 'Whatever you want, Abigail.' He walked away from the café, over to the railing opposite that enclosed a small patch of grass; the only patch of green left along the street.

'It's stupid, I guess, but I hadn't expected it to look so different.' He looked up and down the little row of shops that was home to my café. 'In my mind this all still looks like it did when we were kids.'

I stepped out from the doorway and went over to stand beside him, leaning against the same railing. He put his hand over mine and kept it there for a few seconds before he eventually pulled away. He walked over to peer into the window of the next shop along the row.

'What happened to the hair salon next door? That place was responsible for my first, and last, dodgy perm, I seem to remember.'

'Oh, God! I'd forgotten about the perm!' I started to laugh. 'That was truly awful. Mind you, it was the eighties – I think we all made some pretty poor hair choices, if I recall.'

'Wet-look gel and Lynx deodorant – those were the fragrances of my youth,' he said, walking up to the shop window and peering inside.

'So much hairspray, so little ozone layer,' I replied.

He turned back to me and grinned and then jerked his thumb towards the café.

'I promise to behave myself if you let me in.'

'I thought you just wanted to talk,' I replied.

'I do.'

'We can do that just as well out here.' I didn't feel as if I needed to say any more. If I didn't want him to come in, then that was up to me, wasn't it? No need for explanations; I was the one in control here. Jack might have been surprised but he kept it well hidden; he replied without missing a beat.

'Doesn't matter. We can just sit on the front step, like we used to, remember?'

I did remember, every detail, which was precisely the problem.

'I'm too old to sit on cold concrete steps anymore,' I said.

'I'd suggest you sit on my lap, but I don't suppose you'd go for that.'

I threw him a look that answered that question and he laughed.

'Thought not. Here, sit on this.' He took off his leather jacket and draped it over the step. I saw the designer label in the lining; there was no way I was about to park my arse on something that expensive. I picked up the jacket and threw it at him.

'Don't be so bloody ridiculous.' I plonked myself down on the hard step and he sat down next to me.

'You are a tricky one, Abigail.'

'Yes, so I've been told. What do you want to talk about, then? Anything specific or will the weather do?'

There wasn't much space on the step. I shifted my position so I was half facing him, trying to put a little distance between us, and absent-mindedly brushed something off my apron – anything other than look at his face. I could feel him staring at me.

'Don't be a smart-ass, Abigail. It's been so long. I want to know what's been going on with you, that's all.'

What should I say? I opted for brief and simple. 'Let's see, now. Got pregnant, got dumped, went to college, inherited a café. Ta da!' I held my arms out wide, to illustrate my vast empire.

'But not married?'

I laughed at the suggestion. 'No, not married. The surname change was Mum's idea. Something to do with all of us needing a fresh start after Dad buggered off.'

'And the baby?'

'Isn't a baby any more. She's just about to leave her poor old mother all alone and start university.' That thought brought a lump to my throat but I swallowed it down and quickly changed the subject.

'And what about you, Mr Moneybags? I don't suppose I need to ask you how your life's been, do I?' I think the mention of his money made him uncomfortable, as he squirmed a little. I wasn't about to be put off; he wasn't the only one who had questions. 'What exactly is it that you do?' I said. 'You never told me.'

'You never asked.' He looked at me so intently, I

couldn't hold his gaze. I was asking the questions and yet I still felt like the one being examined. I needed to take charge of the conversation – and fast.

'Your girlfriend, Lexie, seems very sweet,' I said.

He raised his eyebrows in surprise. 'What on earth makes you think she's my girlfriend? That's ridiculous.'

'Oh. I thought you two were an item. You seemed very close.' I couldn't tell him about all the pictures I'd seen whilst I was looking him up on the Internet. I'd look like a stalker.

'She's a friend of the family. I've known Lexie since she was a teenager.'

'Well, she's all grown up now. And she's in love with you, obviously.'

Jack acted surprised by my statement. 'What? That's crazy. She's more like my little sister. She's not in love with me.'

I raised an eyebrow at his emphatic denials; I wasn't entirely convinced they were genuine. Or maybe I was being unfair; I wasn't sure. It reminded me again of how little I knew about the man in front of me.

'Men are so dense,' I said. 'I've only met the girl twice and even I can see it.'

Jack shook his head. 'I'm telling you, she's just a friend.'

I held my hands up in mock defeat. 'All right, if you say so. But I know I'm right.'

Jack puffed out an exasperated breath. After a few

minutes' silence, he said, 'It is really strange to be back but, sitting here with you, I can't explain it, it just feels right to me. I—' He stopped abruptly, as if he wasn't sure what to say next. He didn't need to say it; I knew what he meant. There was something comfortingly familiar about the two of us together. It felt safe and reassuring. And temporary, my logical brain piped up. In a few days he would be gone again, back home to his life in America. There was no point sitting there romanticising about it, I told myself. This was just two old friends catching up. I needed to get the conversation back onto safer ground.

'Are you a spy or something, then?'

'What?' Jack laughed. 'Why would you say that?'

'I ask you about your work, you change the subject, or you're very vague. I just figured it must be top secret if you won't talk about it.'

'I don't talk about it because it's very dull and there are plenty more interesting topics we could be discussing.' He nudged my shoulder and gave me a flirty smile. I didn't reply. He sighed.

'It's just computers. Very boring. My company designed a few programs that various government agencies found useful.'

'Government agencies? Ooh, so you are a spy!' I punched him on the arm, not surprised when my fist landed on a very firm bicep. My brain took a little detour and I had a brief vision of what his body might look like under his clothes. Bloody Nora. I felt a little hot suddenly, the two of us squeezed onto the doorstep, so close our bodies were touching. I had to swallow down the involuntary murmur that almost escaped my lips, but I could feel the flush that was heating my cheeks.

'Are you all right? Abigail?'

Pull yourself together, woman, I chastised. 'Yes, I'm fine. Sorry. You were saying?'

Jack smiled and I had to resist the urge to punch him again.

'I wasn't saying anything. Computer programming and developing software. That's it. We've just started working with some companies over here, hence the reason we opened the new office and why we had the party you catered for.'

The party. That seemed like a lifetime ago but it had only been a few days.

'So, if there's no romance between you and Lexie – which I'm still not convinced about, by the way – is there anyone else in your life?' Even as I asked the question I realised that I wasn't totally prepared for the answer. If he suddenly announced he had a wife and three kids tucked away somewhere, I wasn't sure what I would do.

'No. There's no one. I haven't exactly been blessed in that department. I work long hours and most of the women I've dated haven't been keen on playing second fiddle to my business.'

'No children?'

'None that I know of and I've been pretty careful about that.'

'A workaholic, then? Sounds lonely.'

He shrugged. 'It is what it is. I've had to make sacrifices to be successful. It isn't a big deal.' His expression contradicted his words; he looked sad and I found myself feeling sorry for him. I'd be lost without Lucy, without family and friends. No amount of success could compare to the love and support of family. That wasn't a sacrifice I could ever see myself making. Which probably explained why my business was in the toilet and Jack was flying first class around the world. The comparison made me smile.

'What's funny?'

'Nothing. Everything. I was just wondering where my life might have taken me if things had been different. Being left on your own to bring up a baby when you're barely an adult yourself isn't exactly a recipe for career success.'

'Lots of women do it.'

'They do, you're right. Perhaps they're lucky enough to have the help of a loving partner.'

'Maybe, but I still think you're selling yourself short. Your daughter's off to college, the world is your oyster now. What do you want to do with your life?'

There were lots of things I wanted to do – it was just

that, at this moment, I couldn't think of any.

'I can't just up and leave... go wherever I want... Lucy's still going to need me... I'm the only proper parent she has... I need to be here... for her...' It sounded so pathetic, I knew that, but I wasn't ready to look beyond the next few weeks. The thought of the future terrified me, but I was buggered if I was about to let him know that. I think he sensed my discomfort so he changed the subject.

'Lucy's father isn't in the picture at all, then?' Jack looked a little nervous as he waited for my answer.

'No. Martin sends her a birthday card with a ten-pound note in every year but that's about it. He left just after Lucy was born.'

'What about his family? Didn't they want to help?'

'Good God, no!' I exclaimed. 'The Church family couldn't really be considered upstanding members of the community, despite their surname. Besides his mother always hated me, thought I'd trapped her little boy on purpose by getting pregnant.' That thought made me chuckle, as if Martin were some prize catch that I'd snagged with my wily ways. When it came to her son she was always very good at conveniently overlooking his many flaws.

I think I saw the exact moment that the penny dropped for Jack, as he processed the information I'd just given him. He knew Martin Church – we were all in the same class at school – and he hated him.

'Hold on a second. Lucy's father is Martin Church? You slept with Martin Church?' He stood up and walked away from me, raking his hands through his hair. 'That useless asshole is the father of your kid? Abigail, seriously, how could you do that?'

I attempted a laugh in the hope of masking my embarrassment. 'I was young, stupid, I guess...'

'Stupid is a fucking understatement,' he exclaimed. 'He was a useless little shit even when we were kids. I can only imagine the kind of man he grew up to be.'

I jumped to my feet and strode over to him, my feelings of embarrassment now replaced with anger. How dare he stand there and judge me?

'He grew up to be the kind of man who would gamble away what little money we had, shove me about a bit and then piss off and leave me with a baby to look after. That kind of man. Happy now?'

I noticed the flash of anger that crossed his face at my reference to Martin's violent temper.

'God, Abigail, why would your pain make me happy?'

I just shrugged and then crossed my arms defensively. I couldn't look at him. I couldn't bear to see the disappointment in his eyes.

'Abigail. Look at me. Please.' His voice was soft and when I looked up there was no trace of anger or disappointment in his gaze, only warmth and tenderness. 'Talk to me.'

'First Dad left and then you. Mum had gone from creeping around the house like a ghost to then acting like my own personal prison warden. Always watching me, always criticising – I couldn't breathe.' The memory of that time still made me shudder. 'Martin was nice to me.'

'Yeah, I'll bet he was,' said Jack.

'It wasn't like that – we were friends. We hung around together. To be honest I don't think his home life was any better than mine. I'm pretty sure his dad used to knock him and his mum about.'

'Explains a lot,' said Jack, sarcastically.

'You know what, just forget it. It's very easy for you to sit there in judgement of the rest of us. The ones you left behind.' I stood up and turned round, ready to go back into the café and slam the door in his face.

'Wait, look, I'm sorry. I'm not judging. I'm just trying to understand.'

'Understand what?'

'How someone as amazing as you could have ended up with him.'

'We all make mistakes, Jack. Martin was one of mine. We just sort of fell into a relationship. Then Lucy happened.' I smiled at the mention of my beautiful daughter. 'We decided we could do it – we could be better grown-ups than the ones we knew. So, we got a shitty bedsit and gave it a try. But something changed. We had responsibilities. We weren't playing at being grown-ups any more. This was real. I guess Martin never fully managed to rise to the occasion. He was always unemployed. I worked in the café, but it didn't pay that well. Martin couldn't ever seem to hold onto a job. He'd started drinking and gambling a bit as well.'

'You said he shoved you around…'

I nodded.

'Spineless little fucker.'

'He'd always been a bit handsy – he would push me or shout in my face – but he'd never actually hit me. Until that last night.'

I could remember it as if it were yesterday. Even now, so many years later, the sound of a door slamming still made the hairs on the back of my neck prickle.

'I remember the door being flung open so hard that it rebounded off the wall and cracked the plaster. He was so angry and so drunk. He'd lost some money, he'd been gambling on God knows what. I never asked.' I hadn't spoken about this with anyone for so long and I was amazed at how vividly I could still recall it.

'He smelt like beer and sweat. I told him to stop shouting because I'd just got Lucy off to sleep. He didn't like that. Took great exception to being told what to do.'

'Abigail.'

I heard Jack's voice, but I couldn't stop talking – it was as if now I was back there, I had to get to the end. To make him understand.

'He said he was going to teach me a lesson, to show me who was boss. He grabbed me and tried to kiss me, but I shoved him away and then he hit me. Back of his hand right across my cheekbone.' Instinctively I raised my hand to my face. 'It was like a thousand light bulbs all went on at once. I knew he'd do it again and I knew that I couldn't allow it. He tried to apologise but that was it. I shoved his drunk, lazy arse out of the flat. I locked the door, put the chain on and told him to fuck off.' My heart was thumping in my chest by the end of my story, the memory still enough to send adrenaline coursing around my body.

'I wasn't going to be a victim. I was sick of things just happening to me. I felt like I had no control over my own life. I decided enough was enough; I had a child to think about. She was my responsibility and I knew that the only person I was ever really going to be able to depend on was me. Other people just let you down. I didn't need anyone else.' I took a deep breath and cast my eyes to the sky. I felt strangely uplifted. Remembering what I'd done, how I'd taken charge, made me feel powerful, not sad or regretful. Jack reached out and gently touched my arm.

'I'm just sorry I wasn't here to keep you from all that pain. I'm so sorry, Abigail, I didn't...'

I stepped away from him, out of his reach, and he looked hurt.

'My life is nothing to do with you. And I refuse to let

you make me feel guilty or ashamed about my relationship with Martin because it gave me the best thing I have in my life. My daughter is bright, beautiful and kind and I would willingly go through everything I have all over again if it meant I was rewarded with her at the end of it.' My voice was catching in my throat as I finished my little speech, but I meant every word. 'You weren't here to save me then and I sure as shit don't need you here to save me now, Jack. I needed you twenty years ago, but you left and I got over it. Your concern for me is too little, too late. You should go.' I turned and started to walk away but his voice stopped me.

'I did try to get in touch with you, Abigail. I wasn't lying about that. I wrote to you but you didn't reply.'

I turned to face him. I'd had enough. I didn't want to hear any more of his pathetic explanations. 'And it's taken you twenty years to remember where I live, has it, Jack?'

He opened his mouth to speak but then closed it again.

'That's what I thought,' I said.

He took another step towards me. 'Abigail, please...'

I held up my hand to stop him from coming any closer but that was as far as I got. The door to the café was flung open and a distraught-looking Lucy came flying out and into my arms.

'Mum! I didn't know where you were! I was shouting

for you.'

'What is it, Lucy? What's the matter?'

'It's Nan, she's in hospital. She's had a stroke!'

'What are you talking about? I saw her yesterday – she was fine.'

'Uncle Matt just rang... he said that he'd... he'd been trying to reach her all afternoon and when he couldn't he... he... went to the house. He found her on the front-room floor.' Lucy was frantic, her explanation punctuated with tears and sobs.

'He called an ambulance and they took her. He's at the hospital with her now... we have to go, Mum!' Lucy took my arm and pulled me into the café, with Jack close behind. I fell into the nearest chair and leant forward with my head in my hands. None of it made any sense. She was fine; I saw her yesterday. Jack knelt in front of me but turned to face Lucy when he spoke.

'Which hospital?'

Lucy looked at him and then at me. She must have recognised him from all the photos she'd trawled online but I introduced them anyway.

'Jack, this is my daughter, Lucy. Jack is...' I stopped; what was Jack? He extended a hand to Lucy, who shook it politely.

'Your mum and I were good friends back in school. I'm happy to meet you, Lucy, although I wish it were under better circumstances.'

Lucy was still staring at him. She had her head tilted

slightly to one side while she assessed him – she'd done the same thing ever since she was little – mentally weighing up the pros and cons of whether to speak to him or not. Finally, she said, 'She's at St Mary's. I need to fetch my coat,' and ran up the stairs in the corner, back to the flat. Jack turned to me and took my hands in his.

'I have my car here. Let me drive you to the hospital.'

'There's no need. I can drive us in the van. It's fine.'

'Abigail, you look as white as a sheet. I'm not letting you drive anywhere. I'll take you, it's no problem.' I nodded and then stood up so suddenly I almost knocked Jack back off his feet.

'I need my bag... I need my jacket... I...'

I stood, frozen to the spot. I couldn't seem to connect my brain to my legs. Jack placed his hand at the small of my back and gently guided me over to the stairs.

'I'll be here. Get what you need. I'm not going anywhere. Okay?'

All I could do was nod my reply. As I reached the top and walked towards my room, I felt as if I were in a dream. The one where you knew you were walking, taking steps, but you weren't getting anywhere fast. I felt as if I were knee-deep in quicksand and every step took almost Herculean effort until suddenly, almost without realising how I got there, I was in my room. I stood in the middle of the chaos trying to take it all in: Mum's in hospital; she's had a stroke. I needed to get to her. I was galvanised into action by the sight of myself in the mirror, still wearing my apron. *Get on with it, you have to move. Now.* I grabbed my jacket and handbag from the back of the door and raced back out into the hallway and over to the stairs. As I made my way down the steps and into the café, I could hear that Jack was on his phone.

'She's a friend, she needs me, that's all. I know that... but it can't be helped. Go without me if it's so important to you, Lexie.' He turned and saw me just as he finished speaking. I felt as if I'd intruded on his conversation and should be apologising for earwigging, until I remembered that this was my home and I could go wherever the hell I liked. He finished the call and put his phone back into his jacket pocket.

'Are you supposed to be somewhere else?' I asked. 'Please, don't feel obliged to help. I told you I can manage on my own.'

'I want to help, Abigail. Can you please just let me do that?'

I didn't reply; his need to be a knight in shining armour was his issue. I shrugged on my jacket and shouted up the stairs to Lucy.

'Lucy, are you ready? We need to go.'

When she appeared, coat in hand, I could see she'd been crying. Wrapping my arms around her, I murmured into her hair that everything was going to be fine, as I used to do when she was small. The truth was that I wasn't sure everything would be fine. All I knew was that I needed to get to the hospital.

Out on the street Jack pointed us in the direction of his car but I knew which one it was. I recognised it from the car park the day before. It was sleek and black and expensive-looking. He opened the back door to let Lucy in and I was about to follow when she stopped me.

'Sit in the front with Jack, Mum. I'll be fine.' She gave me a little smile and a wink. 'Don't want him to look like a glorified cabbie, do we?'

I was ready to refuse but he was already holding the front passenger door open for me, so I got in. Lucy's head appeared between the seats.

'Are you all right, Mum?'

'I'll be better once we get to the hospital. Did Uncle Matt say anything else about what happened? How long had she been lying there for?' A horrible image of her lying on her front-room carpet for hours, not being able to get up or call for help, swam into my mind. And what had I been doing all the time she'd been lying there? Reminiscing with some bloke from my past and acting like a stupid teenager with a crush. See, this was what happened when you let yourself get caught up in the romance of what might have been. It was time to get a grip and focus on reality. Having Jack hanging around wasn't going to help with that. Why was he here anyway? What did he want from me? I couldn't say. All I knew was that he didn't belong in my life. If I wanted to make sure I kept my sanity intact I had to keep well away from him.

The drive to the hospital was interminable, the silence only punctuated by the sound of Lucy tapping out messages on her phone one after the other. A thought suddenly occurred to me.

'Does Flo know about what's happened?' I turned in my seat to look at my daughter.

'No. Matt said not to worry her until we know more.'

'Yes... he's right... makes sense.'

Who else would need to know? Mum didn't have a huge circle of friends and as far as family went, Matt and I were pretty much it. I decided to text Liz, more for something to do than any other reason. I pulled out my phone and began typing.

> Had to go to hospital – mum had a stroke – no news yet – will call tomorrow xx

Out of the corner of my eye I could see Jack watching me as I typed; he seemed to be struggling with what to say so I decided to help him out.

'I'm assuming this is not how you saw the evening ending up when you were lurking outside my café?' I asked.

'Not exactly, no.'

'Then what were you expecting?'

'Nothing. I told you I just wanted to see you again,

126

that's all.'

'Well, now you've seen me again, you can get on with your life, can't you? Curiosity satisfied.' I knew he wanted to say more but he couldn't with my daughter sitting in the back. He decided to change tack.

'How is your mum? I mean, you know, before this. God, that sounds awful, I'm sorry, I didn't mean...'

'It's okay.' I stopped him before the conversational hole he was digging for himself got any deeper. 'She was, is, fine. Never really been the same since he left but you knew that already.' He nodded; he didn't have to answer. In the weeks after Dad went and before Jack's family did their disappearing act, there were plenty of days when I would just bunk off school so I could stay at home and keep an eye on Mum. I was terrified she was going to do something silly to herself, or, worse than that, just disappear too, like Dad. On those days, Jack would come to my house after school and help me catch up on the work I'd missed, so I didn't fall too far behind. It was on one of those visits that we had our first kiss.

*

'So, Mr Marshall gave us these to do today. They're pretty simple – you shouldn't have any problem with them.' Jack is sitting on the end of my bed with a maths textbook open on his lap. I'm peering across, trying to make sense of what I'm looking at, but it's all just a mess of numbers to me. I can't concentrate on anything.

'Thanks. Just leave them there. I'll get to them later.'

I'm sitting at the top end of my bed, clutching my pillow in front of me.

'How is your mum today? Have you seen her?'

I shake my head. Despite being in the house all day to keep an eye on her, I haven't seen her since I poked my head round her bedroom door this morning. I crept into the darkened room to see if she wanted a cuppa but she just waved me away and buried her head into her pillow.

'I think she comes out of her room at night when everyone else has gone to bed. She doesn't want to talk to any of us.' I'm fighting to hold back the tears; I'm so fed up with crying.

'She's being unfair, Abby! He left you too – doesn't she see that?'

I shrug. 'It's not her fault. Nan told me that the tablets she's taking make her just want to sleep all the time, then she doesn't have to think about what's happening. I get that, sort of.' I don't really, I just said I did so my Nan would stop talking to me.

'I still think it's wrong of her to shut you and Matt out like this. If it wasn't for your nan and grandad who would you have to look after you?' he asks.

'You,' I say.

'I'll always look after you, Abigail, always.' His sincerity is the final straw; I can't fight the tears any longer. As I sob he moves to put his arms around me. He murmurs gentle words and holds me tightly and for the first time in ages I feel safe and happy. Jack moves so he can gently hold my face in his hands. As he looks at me I see something in his eyes change, a sudden realisation that this is it, this is going to be our first kiss. I tilt my face slightly up towards his, I close my eyes and I wait. But nothing happens. I open my eyes and Jack is staring at me, still holding my face ever so gently.

'What's wrong?' I ask. 'Don't you want to?'

'It's not that... I want to kiss you, so much, but I don't want to mess it up.'

'You won't, you couldn't. Please just kiss me.'

For a second I think he's going to refuse, but then he slowly leans in to me, his eyes searching my face, and I nod and put my arms around his neck. Our lips meet and his mouth feels so warm and soft.

*

'Mum, we're here.' Lucy's voice from the back of the car dragged me back to the present. As we approached the hospital, Jack was scanning the car park for a space. This is it, I told myself, do it now, tell him to leave you alone and then everything will get back to normal.

'You don't need to park. You can just drop us at the front, no need to come in.' I undid my seat belt and gestured to the hospital entrance. 'You can just drop us here, it's fine.'

'I can come inside with you. It's no problem.'

'No, really, you should get back to Lexie. She's obviously waiting for you. Thank you for the lift though. It was very kind.'

'Yeah, thanks, Jack, it was great to meet you,' said Lucy as she hopped out of the car and walked towards the hospital doors.

'When can I see you again, Abigail?'

That was the question I'd been waiting for. I wanted to say, whenever you like, Jack, come into the hospital with me now and never leave my side again, but I didn't. Instead I summoned up all my courage and told him the one lie that I knew would drive him away for good.

'Look, it's been nice catching up and all that, but I don't think we have anything else to say to each other.' I looked down at my hands in my lap. 'I did get your letters, Jack, and you're right, I didn't reply. I'd moved on by then... we were only kids, after all, it... It didn't mean very much really, did it?' I tripped over the words, getting them out as quickly as I could as I fumbled with the door handle. I was out of the car before he could reply. Head down, I all but ran over to the hospital entrance, hoping that he wouldn't follow me. I needn't have worried; as I reached the hospital doors I heard his car screech away from the kerb behind me.

Chapter 9

Lucy was waiting for me just inside the door of the hospital. 'They've taken her up to a ward. We have to go this way,' she said.

I nodded and followed her lead. We turned down a corridor and stopped to wait by a bank of lifts. I could see my reflection in the metal doors; I looked old and tired. What a shocker. Maybe I should watch one of Lexie Morgan's online make-up tutorials. Or maybe not. Why was this lift taking so long? I pressed the call button again; maybe the stairs would be quicker? I was about to suggest this when the lift doors slid open. My reflection was replaced by unfamiliar faces. No one made eye contact, everyone just bustled out, heads down. I stepped to one side to let people pass, then got into the lift. Lucy took my hand. Whether it was to reassure me or herself I couldn't tell, but I was grateful for it nonetheless. I squeezed her hand and gave her a smile.

'She's going to be fine, Lucy. I'm sure it will all be fine.' She nodded but we both knew that I was making that up. I didn't know any more than she did. I watched the neon numbers on the display go up until the doors eventually opened on the fifth floor. I didn't want to get out. I let go of Lucy's hand and grabbed the rail behind me. Lucy turned to look at her insane mother, holding onto the rail like a child who didn't want to go into school.

'Mum, we're here. We have to get out of the lift now.'

'Yes, I know, sorry, I'm coming.' I forced myself to let go and stepped out. I could hear beeping and alarms going off somewhere along the corridor. A nurse at a desk over by the wall looked up as we approached.

'Can I help you?'

'We're here to see my nan, I mean, Mrs Cowan. Where is she?'

The nurse looked down at a clipboard on the desk and then clicked something on the computer screen in front of her.

'Mrs Cowan has only just come up to us from A & E. We're just getting her settled. I'll show you to the relatives' room and you can wait in there.' She came round from behind the desk and placed her hand gently on my arm, guiding me towards a door across the corridor.

'There's a machine for tea and coffee in the corner if you want one. Take a seat and I'll come back for you as soon as Mrs Cowan is settled.' She gave me a reassuring squeeze on the arm and then left.

The room was small and blandly decorated; nothing

to intrude on your consciousness while you worried about whoever you were there to visit. It had little boxes of tissues placed at strategic points around the room; by the side of chairs, on a low table by the window, on a shelf underneath a little mirror fixed to the wall. I couldn't think why you would need a mirror in a room like that. Just so you could see how shitty you looked when they came in and told you that someone you loved was dead? My brother, Matt, was sitting in a high-backed chair over on the other side of the room, checking his phone; he hadn't noticed us but Lucy ran across and threw herself into his lap.

'Hey there, Lucy, are you all right?' he said, putting his arms around her. She sank into his embrace easily; Matt was more like a father to her than an uncle. After her dad left us, Matt had moved in to help me take care of her. He'd only been twenty-two at the time. He should have been out partying with his mates and getting off with girls but instead he'd been at home with me, helping with night feeds and changing nappies.

I'd had many conversations with him over the years about why he did it and he'd always said that having to be there for us had saved him. Matt had gone off the rails a bit after Dad left; he'd been getting into fights or staying out all night and not telling anyone where he'd been. Our grandparents had just been there to stop social services from putting us into care; they didn't really give a crap about what Matt was getting up to as long as he didn't get himself arrested. But he'd seemed intent on screwing up his life.

That had all changed the night that I threw Martin out. After I'd locked the door on the drunken bastard, I'd sat down on the floor and congratulated myself on my strength and courage and tried to ignore the throbbing pain in my face. I could do this on my own, I'd told myself, I didn't need a man. But after about half an hour Lucy had started to cry and she wouldn't stop. To begin with, it had just been a gentle mewing sound, like a kitten – aww, how cute – but within minutes it had turned into a full-on screaming wail, complete with tiny clenched fists, purple scrunched-up face and flailing legs. I'd picked her up and tried to calm her down, checked her nappy, made her a bottle, but nothing had worked.

As her cries had continued, I'd started to panic. What had I been thinking? I couldn't do this all by myself. What the fuck? Why wouldn't she stop? All those nagging doubts about my skills as a mother had suddenly transformed themselves into a mountain of doubt that I hadn't been able to see the top of, let alone get over. Lucy had carried on crying and by then I was too. My baby had every right to be upset, I'd told myself, because even she knew how shit I was at this. I'd convinced myself that my tiny daughter was distraught at the prospect of being raised by me, a totally inept single mother. In the midst of this full-on anxiety attack, my brother had turned up. He'd taken one look at me and my crying baby and, without a word, he'd taken Lucy from my arms and rocked her until she'd fallen asleep. He moved in with us the next morning. He stopped going out and getting into trouble; instead he got himself a job at the local boxing gym, cleaning toilets and wiping sweat off the mats. Over time he'd worked his way up to Manager and then eventually he'd become part owner of the place with Keith, the man who'd given him his first job all those years ago. I was fiercely protective of him, even though he was six feet four and built like a brick shithouse. I went to sit in the chair next to him and rested my head on his shoulder.

'What happened, Matt?'

'I don't know. I'd been calling her all morning, but she didn't answer. I left messages but she never rang me back. It got to about six o'clock and I just thought I should go and check on her.' Matt closed his eyes as he remembered. 'I let myself in. There were no lights on, no telly on. I almost tripped over her, just lying on the front-room floor, not moving. I thought she was dead at first.'

Lucy got up from his lap and went to stand by the door, looking out into the hall.

'How long does it take to get someone into a bed?' she demanded.

'They'll come and get us as soon as they can, don't worry,' said Matt. He got up and started to pace the room; he looked like a bear trapped in a cage. His phone buzzed in his pocket and he pulled it out to read the message. Shaking his head, he typed a quick reply and put it back.

'Who was that?' I asked.

'Just Karen, nothing important. She wanted to come but I told her not to bother.'

I was glad; Karen was my brother's current girlfriend. She was barely older than Lucy, with one of those high-pitched baby voices that she thought was sexy but that just made me want to rip off her head and beat her with it. After his slow start with the girls my brother had more than made up for it in recent years, but his choices hadn't always been that great. There'd been a long line of bubbly bimbos all convinced that they could be the one to get him to finally settle down; Karen was just the most recent.

We sat and waited patiently for about twenty minutes or so, until the nurse we met earlier came to find us.

'Your mum's doing fine. She's all settled in. You can see her now,' she said. 'The doctor will be here to speak to you in a little while, to explain more about what's happened. Just sit with her for now, let her know you're here.'

Matt took my hand and we walked together with Lucy following behind. The nurse guided us into another side room that had two beds. My mum was in one and the other was empty; an orderly was stripping the sheets from it. I wondered if the patient in that bed had got better or died.

Matt stood at the foot of Mum's bed, looking awkward and unsure of what to do next. Lucy, however, had no such qualms. She positioned herself at the top end of the bed and sat down in a chair so her head was level with Mum's. She gently placed her hand on top of Mum's where it lay on the blanket. It was hard to see her face behind the oxygen mask she was wearing but I could see there was a cut on her forehead, just above her left eye.

'What's that?' I asked the nurse as she busied herself looking at Mum's chart. After a quick scan of the clipboard she said, 'She banged her head, we assume when she collapsed at home. It looks worse than it is, don't worry.' How could I not worry? All I knew was what Matt had told me and that wasn't much.

'It's all right, Nan, we're here. You're all right now.' Lucy was whispering words of comfort to her and I felt as if I should go and sit closer, but I didn't move. We'd grown so far apart after my dad left and we'd never been able to find our way back to each other. I'd built a life for myself that meant I wasn't reliant on her for anything. I'd spent years cultivating my survival strategy, so much so that when she'd eventually resurfaced, after so many years of pushing me away, I'd had no room left in my life for her.

My brother moved to sit opposite Lucy. 'We're all

here, Mum, don't worry, everything will be all right,' he murmured. I thought I saw her eyes open slightly but the moment passed so quickly I wasn't sure if I'd just imagined it. A very young, very tired-looking doctor came into the room, picking up the chart at the end of Mum's bed and studying it for a bit before looking up at us.

'Your mother has had a stroke. I'm sure they will have told you that down in A & E.'

'Yes. They sent her for a scan. They said it was a bleed on her brain or something like that,' said Matt.

'Yes, that's right. We're giving her some IV fluids and she's getting oxygen from the mask she has on, but until she regains full consciousness it's impossible to predict what her recovery will look like. If indeed there will be any.' He looked at his watch and then made a note on the chart.

'What do you mean? People recover from strokes all the time, don't they?' asked Matt.

'The next twenty-four to forty-eight hours are critical. We'll keep an eye on her, monitor her pulse, respiratory rate, things like that. The bleed was relatively small, but she may still need surgery to relieve any pressure. We'll keep a close eye on that. Her situation probably hasn't been helped by the amount of time that elapsed between the stroke and her getting treatment.'

'She lives by herself. She's a very active lady – she didn't need looking after,' Matt said to the doctor. 'I called the ambulance as soon as I found her.' He looked pleadingly at me, like a little boy who'd done something wrong but didn't really understand what. I felt a sudden flash of anger. How dared this doctor make us feel responsible for this?

'This stroke has come completely out of the blue. No one could have seen this coming,' I said. 'If you're trying to imply that this is in some way our responsibility...' I left the question hanging in the air and watched as the young doctor began to stutter out an apology.

'No, no, of course not, I'm sorry, I didn't mean to imply that at all, forgive me if it seemed that way. But it is a fact that the sooner a stroke patient receives treatment, the more chance they have of regaining whatever functions the stroke has damaged. As I said, we won't really know anything for sure until she regains full consciousness. We have to wait. If you will excuse me, I have other patients to see.' He replaced Mum's chart and left the room. Matt slumped back in his chair; he looked exhausted.

'Why don't you go home, Uncle Matt? We can stay with her,' said Lucy.

Matt shook his head. 'No. I'm not leaving her now.'

'It's not our fault, Matt. You don't have to feel guilty. It just happened.' Even as I said the words I knew they'd fall on deaf ears. Matt was always the one who'd been there for Mum. He reached across the bed and took her hands in his. She was so tiny that she barely made an impression under the sheets. Looking at her lying there, unconscious and helpless, with Matt and Lucy sitting attentively on either side of her, I felt like an intruder. I wasn't capable of feeling any of the same things that they were; I didn't belong there.

'I need to borrow your car, Matt,' I said, suddenly. 'I'm going to fetch Mum a few things from home. She'll need them when she wakes up.'

'Where's your van?'

Before I could reply, Lucy chimed in. 'Mum's old friend brought us here in his swanky Mercedes.'

'What old friend? Who's she talking about, Abs?'

'Jack Chance. You won't remember him. He moved away years ago. I haven't seen him in ages. Are you giving me your keys or not?' I snapped. I really didn't want to talk about all that now.

'All right, all right, touchy old cow.' He fished around in his jacket pockets, searching for the keys. I reached out to take them, but he pulled his hand away at the last minute. 'I think I do remember Jack, as it goes. Was he the one you spent months being miserable over? He just upped sticks and left, didn't he?'

'Yes, he did. And I never spent months being miserable, more like five minutes, now give me the bloody keys.' I snatched them out of his hand before he could pull them away.

'Why has he showed up again, then? What's he after?'

'What do you mean? He's not after anything. It was just a coincidence, us bumping into one another.'

Matt seemed to have more to say on the subject, but I wasn't in the mood to listen; I had to get out of that bloody hospital.

'Call me if anything changes. I won't be long.' I hesitated for a second before I moved to the top of the bed. Leaning down to give her a kiss on the forehead, careful to avoid the cut above her eye, I waited to see if there was any movement from her, but there wasn't.

Chapter 10

The street was dark and quiet as I pulled up outside the house. There were no lights on inside and I felt oddly nervous about going in by myself. I couldn't remember ever having been in the house when my mum wasn't there; even when she was nothing more than a shadow, hiding away in her room, I always sensed her presence. Now I felt like a trespasser, to be honest.

I switched off the ignition and the silence squeezed in around me; it wrapped me like a blanket and held me safe. I didn't want to get out of the car; I wanted to stay right there, suspended in time and protected from whatever lay ahead. I couldn't shake the feeling of foreboding that was growing in the darkest parts of my heart, a shifting feeling of unease that signalled bad times on the horizon. You're just being silly, I told myself, sitting here in the dark and imagining things. Now get off your bum and get on with what you came here for.

Reluctantly I stepped out of the car, immediately getting hit by a gust of wind that was so cold it made my teeth hurt. It whipped my scarf across my face and momentarily blinded me. I yanked it back down but was knocked off balance and caught my foot on a loose paving slab. I sprawled across the pavement in a very unladylike heap, spewing curse words and handbag contents in all directions. There's your sense of foreboding, said my pragmatic self. You were worrying about the impending end of the world when you should have just been looking more closely at where you were stepping. Silly girl. I scrabbled around on all fours, collecting the contents of my handbag, and then I stood, grimacing slightly at the soreness in my right knee and the hole I'd ripped in my jeans. 'For fuck's sake,' I hissed. I limped a bit pathetically up to the house and let myself in.

Standing in the hallway, I could hear next door's TV but that was all. Mum had already told me that her new neighbour was as deaf as a post and had his telly blaring away at all hours. She'd tried to talk to him about it, but he just made out he couldn't hear her. Mum was convinced that this was a ploy. 'He's only bloody deaf when it suits him,' she'd said.

I switched on the small lamp on the hall table and saw her coat hanging over the banister at the bottom of the stairs. Odd that it wasn't in the cupboard. Should I take it with me when I went back? Would she need it when she came home? Or would that be 'if' she came home? I couldn't think about that now.

The light from the hallway was spilling into the living room and I could see that the armchair and coffee table had been moved, shoved to one side by the paramedics, I assumed. The disruption would have driven my mum bonkers if she were there to see it. She liked everything to be 'just so'. I caught myself thinking of her in the past tense already; I gave myself a mental rap on the knuckles as a reminder that this wasn't yet the case. Tidying the living room was going to have to wait though; first I needed to collect her things from upstairs.

I made my way up slowly, creeping up the stairs as I had done so many times when I was a teenager. I could still remember which were the treads to avoid in order to prevent telltale creaks, and exactly how far up I could go before I'd have to drop to my hands and knees to avoid detection. No need for any of that though; there was no one there to catch me unawares. I reached the half-landing at the top, before the stairs turned to the right, and saw the little brown wooden plant stand that had been there for as long as I could remember. It sat, tucked against the wall, with a vase of faded silk roses sitting daintily on top.

A flash of memory stopped me dead. I see a different vase, a cut-glass one, filled with fresh roses, not silk ones, soaring high in the air, glinting in the sunlight, as my mum lobs it at my dad out of an upstairs window. In my mind's eye, I watch it rise and fall in slow motion, until it hits the concrete path and shatters into diamond shards at my feet. I know they're my feet because I'm wearing my favourite pink jelly shoes, which means the water from the vase has splashed onto my socks and my feet are wet and squeaking inside my shoes. I hear a voice screaming, 'You stupid bastard! How could you do this to us?' I think it sounds like Mum's voice; I can't be sure.

When did I see this happen? Or maybe I didn't see it. Perhaps I heard about it later, or maybe I'd made the whole thing up? I couldn't be sure. Slightly shaken, I finished climbing the stairs and opened the door to her bedroom. Not for the first time I marvelled at just how tidy the room was. The rest of the house was by no means messy, but Mum's bedroom took tidiness to a whole new level. The bed was made up with sheets and blankets, pulled tight and neatly tucked under the edges of the mattress, not a wrinkle in sight. Mum had been appalled at the duvet and its rise in popularity; the casual way it could be flung across a mattress and the bed considered 'made' was a source of real irritation to her.

Her slippers were tucked neatly under her side of the bed. I picked them up but I didn't know what to do with them next, so I just stood there like an idiot, holding them for a few seconds. A bag! That was what I needed – something to put everything in. I pulled open her wardrobe with my free hand. On the shelf at the top I saw what looked like two brown leather handles; figuring they must belong to a bag of some sort, I pulled. Sure enough, I managed to drag out a small brown leather holdall but in my haphazard rush I also succeeded in pulling half the contents of the shelf out with it. A beautifully folded pile of jumpers, all arranged by colour, I noticed, upended themselves onto the floor and all I could do was watch it happen. I had the slippers in one hand and the bag in the other; I couldn't even manage a half-arsed attempt to catch them. Mum would have been bloody furious. I dropped the holdall onto the bed and threw the slippers in, before returning to the sorry pile of clothes on the floor. Picking them up, without bothering to sort or refold them, I shoved them back onto the shelf. When Mum sees it she'll go barmy, I thought. Or maybe she won't be here to see it? There was that niggling voice of negativity again.

Pushing those thoughts away, I moved over to the chest of drawers by the window and pulled open the top one: Mum's underwear drawer. It all felt so wrong to me; it was too intimate, standing there looking at her knicker drawer and wondering which ones to take. Without thinking I grabbed a few pairs, and a bra, and stuffed them into the bag. Opening the next drawer, I found nighties and socks, much easier, I thought. But no, it wasn't. Which nightdress should I take? Did she have a favourite? I should know which one that was, shouldn't I? What kind of a daughter was I? Matthew or Lucy should be here. They'd know which one she'd like. Why hadn't I let one of them do this instead of me? I grabbed the top one on the pile and as I did I saw something stuffed into the corner of the drawer; it was the socks I'd bought Mum for Christmas last year, still with the price tags on. Yes, I'd bought my Mum socks for Christmas, don't judge me. She was awful to buy gifts for; she'd always ask for the receipt 'just in case'. I took these unworn socks as further proof, if any were needed, that I was the wrong person to be here. I didn't know her; I couldn't even be trusted to buy a pair of socks that she liked.

With the back of my hand I roughly scrubbed away the tears that I hadn't even realised were falling and went back to filling the holdall on the bed. I found toiletries in the bathroom and just grabbed everything I thought might be useful. Half of it was probably unnecessary but I took it anyway, unwilling to spend any more time dwelling on how little I really knew my own mother.

Back in the bedroom, I zipped up the holdall and surveyed the room. The bed cover was wrinkled and a couple of the drawers were slightly open where I'd left random bits of clothing poking out of the top or side. I didn't tidy them up, the belligerent child in me wanted to provoke her, I think, wanted her to tell me off because at least that would have been communication of a sort. How sick and twisted was that?

I stomped heavily down the stairs and flung the holdall into the corner by the front door. I went over to the living room and hit the light switch. My eye was immediately drawn to the bloodstain on the rug in front of the fireplace. It wasn't huge but its presence on the cream carpet still made me uncomfortable, reminding me of the fact that my mother had been lying there bleeding before anyone found her. Should I just roll up the rug and get rid of it? No, better to try and clean the stain, I thought, ignoring the little accusatory voice in my head that was telling me I should be going back to the hospital rather than scrubbing a carpet.

There was carpet-cleaner foam under the sink in the kitchen and I found a cloth; I was about to start filling the plastic washing-up bowl with warm water when I saw there were three cups in the sink. A cup and saucer and two mugs, to be exact. I knew the cup and saucer belonged to Mum – she never drank her tea out of anything else – but who'd used the mugs? The paramedics that Matt called wouldn't have had tea whilst in the middle of treating an elderly stroke victim, would they? No. So, who were the mugs for? I walked back down the hall still wondering and went into the living room to begin my task.

Kneeling on the rug, I sprayed cleaning solution onto the stain. The white foam sat there for a few seconds and then it started to turn slightly pink. I left it to work and set about sorting the pile of magazines that was strewn across the coffee table. On top of the pile there was a business card. It had an official-looking police emblem in the corner and a name – Joanne Clow, Family

Liaison Officer. Did the mugs in the sink belong to the police? Matt hadn't said anything about calling the police to the house. Or maybe he had and I just hadn't been listening?

I started scrubbing at the now baby-pink foam on the carpet; some of the blood came out but there was still an ugly-looking mark left behind. It was obviously ruined, so I rolled it up and carried it out to the wheelie bin at the end of the front garden path. I turned to walk back into the house and I spotted a large black car, a Range Rover, parked across the street. The windows were tinted so I couldn't see in, but I got the feeling that whoever was inside was watching me. I crossed my arms defensively across my chest and headed quickly back into the house. Turning off the overhead light in the living room, I stood by the window, watching the car. After a few minutes, it drove away. I felt slightly freaked out. It was just a car, Abby. Stop jumping at shadows.

I sat in Mum's armchair in the now dark living room and took out my mobile phone. I had four missed calls and half a dozen text messages – all from Liz.

> R u ok? Anything I can do? Please let me know if
> there is, sending love xx

The next message was much the same but by the third one she was getting irate; I needed to reply, if only to stop her from jumping in her car and racing to the hospital. I loved her but the last thing I wanted was her striding onto the ward and bossing the nurses around. I typed in a quick reply.

> Mum still in hospital. Will call when I know more xxx.

Almost instantly another message pinged into life on the screen; the number was unknown.

> I hope everything is okay with your mum. Am heading back home in a few days, thought I would let you know. Jack.

Heading home? Back to America? That thought made me feel sick. Isn't this what you wanted? You wanted him to leave you alone and now he is – he's buggering off back to America with his beautifully young girlfriend, end of story. Happy now? I felt a flutter of panic; did I want that? I didn't know.

The deaf old man next door must have gone to bed because I couldn't hear his TV anymore; all I could hear was my own rapid breathing and the tick of the clock on the mantel. Jack's reference to 'home' had brought me back to earth with a bang; London wasn't his home any longer. He belonged somewhere else, somewhere I had no business being. If I was being totally honest, I'd always known that our futures would take us in different directions. Even as a teenager he'd been adamant that he wanted to get away. We'd spoken about it a few times; in fact, one of our last conversations had been about just that.

We were sitting on the top field at school. It was summer – that was the only time we were allowed on the field; the slightest chance of rain and we were all sent to play on the playground to make sure we weren't traipsing mud into school. On this day it was warm, and Jack and I were propped up against one of the old oak trees. There were two of them and their massive, sprawling canopies used to cause havoc with all games of rounders or cricket. Balls always ended up stuck in their branches, but they were such beautiful old trees that no one ever thought about removing them. The ground underneath was bone dry and grassless, there was just a fine dirty dust that managed to get into your shoes and make your socks dirty. Jack was staring up at the sky, watching a plane leave jet trails in its wake.

'That's gonna be me one day,' he said.

I looked up. 'Really? Where do you want to go?'

'Anywhere. Anywhere that's not here. Somewhere exciting and far away. There's nothing to keep me here,' he said.

I swallowed the lump that had suddenly formed in my throat; I couldn't believe he would say there was nothing for him here. When I didn't reply straight away, Jack sat up and looked at me.

'What's up?'

'Nothing. Just got a bit of dirt in my eye, that's all. I'm fine.'

'Here, let me have a look.'

He took hold of my face and pulled my eyelid down to check for this phantom piece of dirt.

'Looks all right,' he said. I nodded, and he sat back down next to me.

'You'd better start saving, then, if you want to get away so badly. Y'know, if it's so awful to be here with all of us boring ordinary people.'

'I didn't mean you.' Jack reached across and took my hand, interlinking our fingers and making butterflies take off in my tummy.

'We're going to go together. Wherever it is, we'll be together. I promise.'

It had all sounded so simple back then; we were two stupid kids, what did we know? And now he was leaving again and this time there was no question that he was leaving me behind. It was better this way, I told myself, much easier to let him go now before something happened that we'd both likely regret. There was no version of this story that ended with us together.

As I threw my phone onto the coffee table, I noticed the card again. I was confident that Matt would know what that was all about; I knew Mum would have undoubtedly shared it with her favourite child. I picked up the card and stuffed it in the back pocket of my jeans and then, with enormous effort and a large dose of reluctance, I hauled myself out of the armchair and into the hallway, picking up the bag of Mum's things as I passed.

*

I'd only taken a few steps into the hospital foyer before I realised that I couldn't remember which way I needed to go. I looked around, trying to find something, anything, that would jog my memory, but every corridor looked depressingly similar. The information desk was empty, so I wandered across to a map of the hospital. No, still no fucking clue. She was in a critical care ward, that much I knew, but the map might as well have been written in hieroglyphics. Someone had scratched off the helpful 'You are here' arrow, as well as the names of some of the wards. Great. I was about to pull out my phone and dial my brother until I heard his voice bellowing at me from the hospital café.

'Oi, Midget! Over here!'

I weaved my way between empty tables and chairs, over to where he was sitting, his large body wedged into a tiny plastic chair in the corner of the café.

'I couldn't bloody remember which way to go. Good job you were here. I could have been wandering these corridors for hours.' I dropped the bag and slid into the chair opposite him.

'Do you want a cup of coffee or tea? The counter's not open but there's a machine in the corner.' He was holding a flimsy plastic cup, full of something that resembled dirty dishwater. I wrinkled my nose in disgust.

'No, it's fine, I'll get something later. How's Mum doing?'

'She's still unconscious. Lucy's up there with her. I couldn't sit there looking at her any longer. I needed to get out of that room... She just looks so small... I can't...'

I reached over and put my hand on his arm. 'It's okay, Matt. Lucy's with her. When she wakes up she won't be on her own.' I said 'when' not 'if', but I couldn't shake the feeling that I was being unduly optimistic. He nodded and took a mouthful of his coffee.

'Fucking Nora, this stuff is awful!' he exclaimed, pushing the cup away from him. The coffee sloshed up the sides of the cup and formed a puddle around the base.

'She's going to hate the tea in here when she wakes up,' I said. 'I might have to bring her a decent cuppa, in a flask or something.'

'Yeah, she'd like that.'

I nodded and Matt went back to looking at his phone.

'How come you went to the house?' I asked. He looked up and gave me a non-committal 'Hmmm?'

'I said, how come you went to the house? What made you think something was up?'

He continued scrolling through messages on his

154

phone for a few seconds and then placed it on the table.

'I told you, I'd called her a couple of times but she wasn't answering, which I thought was a bit odd, so after I finished work I went round.'

'Oh.'

'Why do you ask?'

'No reason, just curious.'

'Balls. What are you getting at, Abby?'

I shrugged. 'I dunno. I feel bad, I guess. That's all.'

'What for?'

I picked at the skin around my thumbnail for a bit and didn't look at him as I answered. 'When you don't hear from her you're concerned enough to make the effort to go and check on her but when I don't hear from her I feel… well, relieved I suppose is the best way to describe it. I'm relieved I haven't had to struggle through another conversation with her and that makes me feel terrible.'

I stared down at the puddle of cold brown coffee sitting around the bottom of his cup and felt a sudden urge to wipe it up. I stood up quickly, my chair made a loud scraping sound that echoed round the empty canteen, and I scurried over to the napkin dispenser by the counter. I yanked on a napkin and managed to pull another twenty or so out along with it. Armed with my wad of paper I went back to the table and made a half-arsed attempt to mop up the coffee, before slinging the whole dripping mess of paper into a nearby bin. I sat back in my chair.

'Are you done?'

'Yes... sorry... stupid bloody napkins... had to wipe it up, it was annoying me.'

'Mum understands, you know. She always has done, about the way you two are together. She gets it.'

He looked so sincere and I got a very unkind urge to giggle. I seriously doubted my mum 'got it', or got me, any more than I got her.

'She doesn't understand, Matt, because she doesn't want to. That would involve her having to take some responsibility and she won't do that. And I feel awful for thinking that way, but I can't help it. I can't just bury how I feel in the way that you seem to have managed to.'

He shook his head at me and gave me a pitying look.

'Don't do that. You always give me that look whenever I try and talk to you about how she makes me feel. You shake your head and treat me like I'm a pathetic little girl who doesn't know any better. It's so bloody patronising!'

'I wish I could have made you understand, Abby. Mum loved us both so much, protecting us was all she ever wanted to do.'

Not this old chestnut again. 'Protect us from what? How did she think she was protecting us when she stuffed herself full of Valium and hid behind her bedroom door?'

I started to feel the beginnings of the headache that always accompanied this conversation. I pinched the bridge of my nose and closed my eyes.

'Why can't you let it go, Abs? She did her best, you don't know all of it... you don't understand.'

My eyes flew back open. 'Of course, I don't,' I hissed, 'because no one would ever tell me anything, would they? I was just supposed to take your word for it, wasn't I? Just go along with the idea that everyone had decided what was best for me, no questions asked.'

Matt slumped back in his chair, looking exhausted. 'I don't want to fight with you, Abs, not right now. Please?'

I wanted to argue, to tell him that I was sick of always being kept in the dark and lied to, but I didn't. Instead I went with a petulant, 'Fine.' The loud metallic rattling of the shutter going up over the counter stopped any further comment from either of us.

'I'm going to get a drink. Do you want something?' I asked, standing up from the table.

'No, thanks, I'm fine.' Matt returned to looking at his phone, another indication that any more discussions were off limits for the time being.

There was a young man behind the counter, just putting the cash drawer into the till. He looked up as I approached and smiled.

'What can I get you?'

'Just a cup of tea, please,' I asked, 'milk, no sugar.'

'Coming right up.' He turned to the tea urn behind him and I started rummaging around in my pockets for some change. From the back one I retrieved the business card I'd found at Mum's. I thought about just stuffing it back into my pocket and forgetting it. After the conversation we'd just had, perhaps it would be better not to stir things up. That thought lasted for about two seconds – I knew that whatever the story was that went along with the card, I wanted to hear it. I paid for my tea and walked back to Matt. I sat down and slid the card across to him. He picked it up and glanced at it, trying to appear casual, but I saw a brief flash of shock skitter across his face. He regained his composure quickly, but I knew what I'd seen. I waited for him to start talking; the silence was awkward and I was determined to stay quiet until he decided to talk.

'What's that?' he said, eventually.

'You're going to claim ignorance, then?'

'What do you mean?'

'Pretending you don't know anything about this card.'

'I don't.'

I knew he was lying to me. I'd known him for too long and I'd seen him lie very convincingly to the many girlfriends he'd had in tow over the past few years.

'Don't lie to me, Matt, just tell me what this is all about. For once, please, just tell me the truth.'

A loud crash came from behind the counter and I

jumped in my seat. Matt didn't move at all; it was as if he hadn't even heard it. The man who'd served me my tea appeared behind the counter, clutching a mop.

'Sorry, sorry, everyone. My fault – I dropped a pot!' He scurried back out to the kitchen. After a long few minutes Matt sat up straight in his chair and reached across the table to take my hand.

'I'm sorry, Abby, but I can't. It's not my story to tell.'

'Then whose is it?' I wanted to force him to tell me, I was angry that he couldn't see how badly I needed to know, but before I could go on the silent cafeteria was disrupted by my daughter, screaming my name.

'Mum! You need to come! Something's happened to Nan!'

Chapter 11

Lucy dragged us both out of the café and over to the stairs. 'We can't wait for the lift. We have to go now!'

She led the way, taking the stairs two at a time. Matt took the bag I was carrying and gestured for me to go in front of him. The urgency in Lucy's voice was fuelling our ascent and we burst through the double doors at the top so loudly that several disapproving heads turned in our direction. I didn't care; all I wanted to do was get to Mum.

We raced back into the side room and stood at the bottom of the bed. There were two nurses and a doctor working on her tiny body.

'What's happening?' I could see panic in Matt's eyes; Lucy pulled me close and sobbed into my shoulder.

'Oh, Mum! It all happened so fast! She opened her eyes, we thought she was coming round, but then her breathing went funny... She was making this horrible noise.'

'It's okay, love, the doctor will help her...' Even as I said the words I knew that they weren't true. The nurses had stopped what they were doing, and I heard the doctor declare the time of Mum's death.

'I'm so sorry,' he said, turning to face us. 'It appears your mother suffered another stroke. We did everything we could but she never regained consciousness.'

I nodded and held Lucy even tighter as she cried. Matt sat down heavily into the chair next to the bed and put his head in his hands. He was crying silently, tears sliding between his fingers. I was the only one that wasn't crying; what was wrong with me? My mother was lying on the bed in front of me and I couldn't cry. 'What happens now?' I asked.

One of the nurses was disconnecting a bag of fluid. 'We'll need to do a few things for Mum, to get her ready, but there's no rush. You can just sit with her for a bit if you'd like.'

I nodded. 'I'll stay with her.'

Matt got up from the chair. 'I don't want to stay, Abs. I don't want to see her like this, with all this stuff —' He stopped abruptly.

'It's okay. Take Lucy outside for me. I'll come and fetch you in a bit.'

They both left the room, followed by the nurses. I pulled a chair nearer to the bed and sat down. I could hear pieces of conversations going on in the hallway outside, orders being given, discussions about lunch breaks and rotas; all the trivial stuff that showed how life went on. After a while I managed to zone out all the noise and a strange peace fell over the room; it was like being inside a bubble, just me and her. I'd felt the same on the night that Lucy was born. After all the noise and trauma of a twenty-one-hour labour – she was stubborn even then – I was taken up to the maternity ward with my new baby. It was the middle of the night, the ward was dark and quiet and, once the nurse had settled me in, I was left alone with Lucy for the first time. The overwhelming feeling that it was just me and her now hit me like a tidal wave and I had to fight hard to suppress a feeling of panic that was almost choking me. How could I be responsible for this tiny little thing? What the hell was I supposed to do? I had that feeling again, right then, looking at my mum's small, lifeless form. What was I supposed to do now?

I moved my chair closer to the head of the bed and took hold of one of her hands. It was still warm and soft. I gently rubbed my thumb back and forth across the top of it. Her papery skin wrinkled as I stroked it; she was still wearing her wedding ring. She'd never taken it off, even after Dad left. I'd never understood why but I didn't dare ask her about it. Now I'd never get the chance to ask her, about that or the million other things I wish we'd talked about. The reality of never being able to speak to her, to hear her voice again, hit me like a punch in the stomach; I was winded, knocked off balance by how strongly I already felt her absence. I'd thought I'd grieved the loss of my mother already; she'd removed herself from my life so completely all those years ago, it had all but felt as if she'd died to me then. That feeling would be nothing compared to the pain I knew I was about to experience. I released her hand and leaned closer to her face.

'I love you, Mum.'

*

After we left the hospital, clutching information leaflets on bereavement and an appointment time to register Mum's death, it seemed only natural that we would go back to her house. Lucy went straight into the kitchen to make tea, the universal cure for everything. I didn't want tea, but I didn't have the heart to tell her. I could hear her opening cupboards and rattling cups.

Matt was standing in the middle of the living room, staring at the spot where the rug had been. 'Couldn't save the carpet, then?'

'No, I couldn't get the stain out, so I threw it away.'

Matt just nodded and walked across to the fireplace. 'It's weird, isn't it? One minute she's here, the next she's not.' He looked over at me, but I didn't know what to say to him.

I was holding a plastic bag full of Mum's things; they'd given it to us at the hospital and I'd been clutching it all the way home but now I couldn't wait to get rid of it. It felt slightly disrespectful to be carrying all her possessions in what was essentially a bin bag and I dropped it onto the sofa.

Lucy came into the room, carrying a tray laden with a teapot and mugs. She hesitated for a minute, unsure as to where she could put it, so I cleared a spot on the coffee table. She knelt beside the table and began pouring milk then putting sugar in one cup for Matt. She looked like a little girl playing with her favourite tea set.

'What?' she asked, as she looked up and caught me watching her.

'Nothing, it's nothing,' I said.

She shook her head but she was smiling. 'Shall I be mother?' she asked, picking up the teapot. I nodded and she poured three mugs of steaming tea. Matt picked up his and took it over to the window. Something across the street appeared to catch his eye and he leaned closer, slightly pulling the curtains back to get a better view of whatever it was.

'Whose car is that, Abs? I don't recognise it, do you?'

Lucy got up and went to stand by him at the window. 'Blimey, that's one expensive-looking car. Come and have a look, Mum.'

I only knew one person who had that sort of money, excluding Liz and David. And since I figured that they wouldn't be sitting outside keeping an eye on me, that only left one possibility.

'Don't worry about it, it's probably nothing.' I wandered over to the window and wrenched the curtains back so whoever was out there could see that I'd spotted them.

'Bloody hell, Abby!' exclaimed Matt, ducking back away from the window 'What are you doing? You'd make a really crappy spy!'

The car didn't move. I'd expected it to drive away once I'd made it clear I knew they were watching. Maybe I'd been wrong? Maybe it wasn't anything to do with Jack? After all, why would he care what I was doing? He was going back to America; he'd told me so himself. I went back to sipping my tea and tried to ignore the churning in my gut. My phone pinged to alert me to a new message – it was Liz.

Just checking in – how's Mum? Anything I can do?

'It's Liz, I'm going to call and tell her what's happened,' I said. Lucy and Matt were still peeking through the curtains, trying to guess who the car belonged to, so I took my phone out into the hallway and dialled Liz's number. She answered it after barely two rings.

'Darling girl, I've been so worried! How are you? What's happening?'

'Hi, Liz, I'm fine but... um... Mum, she didn't make it. She passed away a few hours ago.'

'Oh, Abby, I'm so sorry. What happened?'

'The doctor seemed to think that she had another stroke. It was just too much for her. She never woke up. I didn't get a chance to say goodbye or anything. She just went... I don't know what to feel, Liz. It's all so confusing.'

'I know, my darling. Don't try and make sense of it now. It's too soon for that. Give it some time; you'll find a way through it, I know you will.'

'Thanks. But I think you're giving me too much emotional credit. I already feel like the world's worst daughter. I haven't even been able to cry. What the fuck is that about?'

'It's the shock, that's all. Don't read too much into it. And don't sit there wallowing in self-pity either. Your relationship with your mother was as much her responsibility as it was yours, so don't go putting all that guilt on yourself, okay?'

When I didn't reply, she followed up with another stern, 'Okay?'

'Okay.' I wasn't okay. At that moment, I was about as far away from okay as it was possible to get but with Liz it was sometimes easier to just agree. I needed to divert her attention away from my emotional well-being and onto more practical ground.

'I need your help with something.'

'Anything. Just tell me what I can do.'

I smiled at her reply; she didn't even wait to find out what I needed before she agreed to do it. Not for the first time, I thanked the universe for giving me such a loyal friend.

'Matt and I will need to organise the funeral and there'll have to be a wake. I can have it at the café but I could use some help with the arrangements… Could you —?'

She cut me off before I could finish. 'Consider it done. I'll sort it all, don't you worry. Just let me know how many and when. You are not to give it another thought, my darling. Where are you now? Do you want me to come over?'

'I'm at Mum's house with Matt and Lucy. I'm all right. We're here together.' I was pacing up and down the hallway as I spoke; I couldn't seem to stand still. I felt wired, on edge.

'You should get some sleep, Abby. Go and have a lie-down, even if it's only for an hour or so.' She was trying to help but I didn't think I could have slept, even if I'd wanted to.

'I'll try, I promise. I'll call you later.'

'Make sure you do. Give Lucy a squeeze from me, tell her I'm thinking of her, all right?'

'I will. Bye, Liz, thank you.'

I went back into the living room. Lucy was stretched out on the sofa sleeping and Matt was propped up in the armchair, resting his head in his hand and snoring quietly. They must have been exhausted; I'd been out of the room for barely five minutes.

I walked quietly across to the window; the sleek black Range Rover was still parked across the street. Before I'd realised what I was doing, I'd flung open the front door and was marching towards it. I was powered by grief and lack of sleep; it was the only explanation I could offer for what happened next. I grabbed the rolled-up rug that was sticking out of the top of Mum's wheelie bin and I lobbed it at the car's windscreen. As soon as the bloody thing left my hands I regretted it – I had visions of it shattering the glass and then me having to pay for it. But that didn't happen. The rug just landed on the car bonnet with a very underwhelming thud. There was a large, bald man in a dark suit sitting in the driver's seat, reading a newspaper. No going back now, I thought, go big or go home. I headed to the driver's side window.

'Can I help you with something?' I shouted. He ignored me and turned his head to talk to someone in the back of the car.

'I said, can I help you?' I banged on the window. He turned around and opened his door. Shit. He didn't look happy about my bashing on his window. He stepped out of the car; the man was almost as wide as he was tall, and in a swift move he opened the back door.

'Get in the car, Abigail, before you wake up the whole goddamn street!'

Jack's voice came from inside the car, and I peered in to see him sitting in the back, laptop resting on his knee and a mobile phone in his hand. He looked ridiculously handsome, ensconced in the luxury interior of the car. He was dressed in a dark T-shirt and jeans; his hair was slightly mussed and he was wearing glasses with heavy black rims that would make anyone else look like a nerd but on him they had the opposite effect. I had to stand on the car's side step to get in and I sat down, tucking myself into the furthest corner of the car's back seat. Jack looked amused.

'I won't bite, Abigail,' he said. 'Not unless you want me to.' He flashed me a smile that I'm sure had separated countless other women from their knickers, but I was too angry with him to care.

'What are you doing here, Jack? I thought you were going back to America?'

'I am in a few days, but I was worried about you. You made me leave you at the hospital, Abigail; I needed to feel like I was doing something to help.'

'By having people spy on me? Parking outside my house in sinister-looking cars? That's you helping?'

He looked defiant. 'I didn't mean to frighten you, Abigail. The guys were under orders to stay close in case you needed anything.'

'And report back to you, I suppose.'

'They kept me in the loop, yes.'

'And when I came back here in Matt's car to get some things for my mum?'

'They followed and waited outside.'

He'd had me followed since we parted ways at the hospital?

'If it makes you feel any better, I've only just got here,' he said. 'I'm not some weirdo who usually does business out of his car so he can spy on girls.'

'No, I'm sure most of the women you know would love the idea of being stalked by a handsome millionaire.'

'But not you?' He sounded almost disappointed.

'Not me.' My body sagged back into the soft upholstery and I felt a wave of tiredness wash over me. Resting my head against the seat, I closed my eyes. Jack didn't speak or move but I could feel him watching me.

'You're doing it again,' I murmured, without opening my eyes.

'What?' he asked, softly.

'You're watching me.'

'I can't seem to help it. Whenever you're around I can't look at anything else, Abigail.'

I opened one eye to look at him. 'That's very funny, Jack, but I'm not in the mood to be mocked.'

'I'm not mocking you, Abigail. Why would I do that?'

'Fun, sport, mental illness. Take your pick.' I closed my eyes again; I was so comfortable, I thought maybe I could just go to sleep for a bit. No one knew where I was. I could hide in this little protective cocoon of leather upholstery and plush carpeting and never face the world again.

'She's gone, Jack. She died,' I said, my voice cracking as I finally allowed the realisation of that fact to sink in. My throat tightened and suddenly I was crying; fat, salty tears were running down my face and splashing into my lap. In an instant he was beside me, his arms around me, holding me tight. He whispered his condolences into my hair as I sobbed quietly into his shirt. I felt safe here, in his arms; it all felt so familiar, so right. The feeling was welcoming and forbidding all at the same time; I knew I could get used to being in his arms but what would be the point? He would soon be leaving again, going back to a life I had no place in. Why put myself through yet more rejection? I knew I was right to push him away at the hospital; there was no reason to rethink that decision now. I was just feeling vulnerable, I told myself. That was all it was. I pushed myself away until he was holding me at arm's length, studying me with those gorgeous eyes.

'Please tell me what I can do, Abigail. Let me help you.'

'There's nothing you can do, Jack. I told you that at the hospital. Whatever was between us is ancient history. We're different people now. I moved on years ago.' I looked him straight in the eye, hoping he was convinced. He wasn't.

'You're lying to me, Abigail. What I can't figure out is why. Why do you keep running away from me? What are you afraid of?'

'Are you joking? You're seriously asking me that question?'

'Yes! If you're so over what we once had, then why are you trying to push me away when all I want to do is help you?' He didn't release his grip on my arms and my skin burned under his touch.

'You appear back in my life after all these years, you poke your nose into my business, you… you… turn up at my flat and then have me followed. You make it impossible for me not to think about you. Which is something I really don't want to do since it's taken me twenty years to get over you leaving without a word!' I was shouting but I didn't care. I needed him to finally hear me.

'Without a word?' he said. 'Hang on a second. You told me at the hospital that you'd read my letters. You said they didn't mean anything to you.'

I paused for a minute – what could I say?

'You didn't get my letters, did you? You lied to me at the hospital.' It was a statement, not a question.

'No,' I said, my voice practically a whisper. 'I didn't get them. I don't know where they went but they never reached me.' I kept my eyes firmly fixed on my hands in my lap; I couldn't look at him. I knew that if I looked into his eyes, I'd be lost. I moved to grab the door handle behind me.

'Stop.' His voice was strong and calm. 'Look at me.'

I shook my head; I couldn't do it. I couldn't let him in. *Yes, you can, just do it, Abby.* Jack reached out and gently tilted my chin so I had no choice but to meet his eyes. I fought to get my breathing under control, surprised to find that he seemed to be struggling too. His gaze was penetrating. I couldn't hold it for more than a few seconds, the intensity was too much and I had to look away. He tenderly placed both hands on either side of my face.

'Look at me,' he repeated. I did as he asked and I was treated to a smile that melted my heart.

'Kiss me, Abigail.'

'Why?'

'Because you want to. It's just me and you, so kiss me.'

I think he was waiting for me to push him away, but I didn't. He was right; despite all my good sense telling me that it was crazy, all I wanted was to kiss him. I moved my face closer to his and he needed no more invitation than that. His mouth closed gently over mine, his lips lingering for a few seconds, and then he pulled away, as if he was afraid to go too far. I lifted my hands and rested them lightly on his chest. I could feel his heart beating fast beneath my palms.

'Kiss me, please, Jack, I need you to kiss me, right now.' Another heart-stopping smile, and then he kissed me, hard. His mouth was crushing mine, parting my lips with his tongue; I moved my hands up to his hair, grabbing fistfuls of it, trying to pull him closer to me. His hands moved around my waist and he pulled me onto his lap. As he took his lips away from my mouth, I moaned in protest, until he started trailing kisses down the side of my neck. Oh, God, it felt so good but what was I doing? Was I crazy? All my doubts disappeared as he ran his hand down the front of my shirt and stopped when he reached my breast. He lifted his head to look at me.

'I want to see you, Abigail. You are so fucking gorgeous. Let me see you, baby.'

I nodded and he grabbed the hem of my shirt as I raised my arms; he pulled it off over my head and threw it to the floor. I said a silent prayer to the laundry fairy for washing my one good bra.

'Do you have any idea how many times I've imagined seeing you like this since you walked past me in that dress at the party?' His eyes roamed my body hungrily. 'I knew it was you; I made your friend go and fetch you. I had to see you again, Abigail.'

'I don't usually dress like that – that outfit was all Liz's idea.'

'Then remind me to send your friend Liz a big fucking thank-you present,' he said, lowering his head to kiss between my breasts. I moaned loudly and Jack raised his head, grinning like a fool.

'I'm glad I raised the privacy panel.'

I looked across to the front of the car, feeling my cheeks flush with embarrassment.

'Oh, God! I forgot about him,' I said. 'What must he be thinking of me?'

'I don't pay him to think about you; that's my job.' He grinned lasciviously as his mouth returned to its onslaught. He moved his hand between my legs, the seam of my jeans causing just enough friction for it to feel so, so good. His mouth was on mine, his tongue probing deeper and harder. I could feel his arousal; I needed to get closer. I moved out of his lap and turned to face him, sitting astride him. My insides turned to liquid as he pulled me down into a deep kiss that left us both gasping for breath.

'Oh, baby, you are amazing, so beautiful,' he murmured into my mouth, between kisses. 'Tell me what you want, Abigail. I want to hear you say it to me.'

He looked so beautiful, sitting beneath me with his sexily messed-up hair and eyes heavy with lust, and for a minute I almost believed that it might be all right. Then the little self- sabotaging voice in my head piped up. He's far too good-looking for you, it said. Why would he want you, a middle-aged mum with your stretch marks and M&S undies, when he could have the likes of Sexy Lexie? That thought was like a bucket of freezing water flung over my libido and my confidence; suddenly the wanton woman who'd placed herself in Jack's lap just a few moments ago was gone and all that was left was me.

'I can't do this... I'm sorry... I can't...'

Scrambling off his lap, I snatched my shirt up from the floor of the car and retreated to the very end of the seat.

'What happened? What did I do?' Jack asked,

watching me pull my top back on. He made a move to reach for me but I flinched away from his touch. What could I tell him? Everything was fine until I realised that you were way too good-looking for me? That in a few days you're going to leave me again and I don't think I can cope with the hurt that would cause? However real they were, all those excuses sounded pathetic, so I gave him the only answer I hoped would make sense to him.

'I'm sorry, it's not you… it's just… this is wrong.'

'It didn't feel wrong.'

'No… I mean… yes. It's just bad timing. My mum just died and I'm cavorting around in the back of a car with you, like some cheap slut!'

'Don't! Don't say that kind of shit about yourself, Abigail. I won't let you do that.' He tried to reach for me but I moved closer to the door and grabbed the handle, ready to open it and leave him behind.

'You're running away again, then?'

'I'm not running anywhere, Jack. I have to get back to my family.' I opened the car door and stepped out. 'Goodbye, Jack, have a safe trip home.'

He opened his mouth to speak but I'd already closed the door. As I walked back to the house part of me was hoping that he'd jump out of the car and follow me, take me in his arms and refuse to let me go, but he didn't. I heard the engine start and I turned to see his car pulling away from the kerb.

Chapter 12

'So, who's in the car?' My brother was waiting for me in the hallway as I came back into the house.

'No one important, Matt. Let it go.' He looked at me for a few seconds and then nodded.

'Okay, no problem. I'm sure you'll tell me when you're ready.'

I turned away and began walking down the hallway that led to the kitchen. My brother gave a little cough and I turned, letting out an exasperated, 'What?'

'You've got your T-shirt on inside out.' He gave me a wink and then went back into the living room.

'Oh, shit!' I headed into the kitchen to try and straighten myself up. As I passed the hallway mirror I looked at my tired reflection. Red eyes from crying, and rosy lips from the kissing, quite a combination. What must I look like? I adjusted my clothes and reminded myself that snogging in the back seats of cars was a young person's pastime. A woman of my age ought to know better. I touched my fingers to my swollen lips and remembered how good it felt to be kissed like that; by him.

'Are you okay, Mum?' Lucy walked sleepily down

the hallway towards me. 'Where were you?' Rubbing her eyes, still groggy from sleep, she followed me into the kitchen.

'Hmm? Oh, nowhere, love, just talking to someone outside, that's all,' I replied, vaguely.

'Jack has great taste in cars, Mum. I'll say that for him at least.'

I toyed briefly with the idea of denying it, but it was pointless.

'It's nothing, Lucy. He just wanted to see how everything was with Mum, that's all. I told him she passed away.' The words still sounded strange to my ears.

'Why didn't he come to the door and knock, or call you?'

'He didn't want to intrude.'

She gave me a sideways glance. 'He obviously wanted to get you on your own but what for, I wonder – hmm?'

'It was nothing, really. Anyway, he told me he's going back to America in a few days so that's that. Whatever *that* is,' I replied, trying to sound casual about the whole thing.

'And you're going to let him go, are you? Just like that?'

'I've got too much going on to worry about him and what he's doing. I need to arrange Nan's funeral. We'll have to sort out this place. God only knows what she's got stashed in the loft. There could be tons of stuff up there to sort through.' I was rambling on, trying to fill the void with a conversation that would take us away from the subject of Jack Chance and his impending departure. She put her arms around me.

'It's going to be fine, Mum. We can all help out, you know that. I just think it's a shame not to even allow for the possibility of there being a place in your life for Jack. He seems nice and he's obviously very keen on you.'

'When did you become so grown up? Shouldn't it be me giving you advice on your love life, not the other way around?'

'No offence, but what you know about having a love life could be written on the back of a postage stamp!'

'Hey!' I feigned disgust but she was right; my love life in recent years added up to a few really bad dates and one drunken fumble in an alleyway – not one of my proudest moments. Lucy's dad was the only man I'd ever slept with. Perhaps it was good that things hadn't gone any further with Jack, I thought. I probably wouldn't have remembered what to do. Or maybe I would? I'd been quite happy sitting astride him in the back of his car; I was pretty sure it would have all come flooding back to me. An image of him, all sexy hair and glasses, appeared in my mind, sending an involuntary shiver down my back. I remembered how his lips had felt as they'd placed hot kisses down my neck and onto my chest. My little flashback was interrupted by Lucy.

'If you expect me to believe that nothing just

happened in the back of that car then you must take me for an idiot. Look at you! The mere mention of him has made you light up like a candle! I don't understand why you would want to pass that feeling up.'

'He has a life in America, he's not going to give that all up for me and I certainly don't want to be anywhere else but here, so where would that leave us?'

'I'll bet you haven't even given him the chance to stay around for you, have you? Have you even asked him what he wants out of all this?'

'Lucy, stop, please, just stop.' I couldn't talk about this with her anymore; it was too exhausting. 'I need to focus on all this now anyway,' I said, waving a hand around the kitchen. She was desperate to say more, I could sense it, but thankfully she was interrupted by the doorbell.

'I'll bet that's him, come to carry you off in his arms!' she said as she headed down the hallway. For a second my heart leapt at the idea that maybe it was him, come to take me away from all this, to take me back to his hotel and make love to me for hours and hours. But it wasn't, and I was surprised by how much that disappointed me. He'd only been back in my life for five minutes; how had he become so important again, so quickly? I walked down the hall to the front door and I was surprised by the sight of a policewoman standing there holding a cardboard box.

'What's going on?' I asked.

'It's about Nan, I think,' said Lucy. 'This lady says she came to see her yesterday and she's here to follow up, or something.'

'I'm sorry for the confusion. I'm P.C. Joanne Clow, I'm a Family Liaison Officer with the Metropolitan Police. I came here yesterday with Father Michael, to see Mrs Turner. Is she around? I'm sure we can clear all this up.' The officer looked past me, down the hallway, as if she was expecting to see my mum.

'She died in the early hours of this morning, Officer. She had a stroke.'

The young woman suddenly looked very pale.

'I'm sorry, this is all very confusing,' said Lucy. 'Why were you here yesterday?'

'Perhaps I could come in for a few moments. This is a box of personal effects for your mum; I told her I would bring it to her.'

'Whose personal effects?' I asked. 'The hospital already gave us all of my mother's things.'

'These are your dad's things, from his cell. The prison sent them over this morning and I said I'd deliver them to her and see how she was coping with the news,' said PC Clow.

'I think you'd better come in,' I said, leading the confused-looking officer into the living room.

<u>Chapter 13</u>

The officer placed the box on the sofa and took a seat beside it. Lucy and I sat in the armchairs by the window and Matt stood by the fireplace; none of us spoke for a long time.

'You'll have to forgive us, Officer,' I said. 'It's just that we haven't heard from our father in twenty years. This must be some sort of mistake, a mix-up with paperwork or something?'

The officer shook her head. 'You are Mrs Turner's children, is that right?'

'Yes, we are, but she changed our surname to Cowan after our father left.'

'Right, I see. It's just that when Father Michael and I were here yesterday Mrs Turner, sorry, Mrs Cowan, told us that she had no one she could contact to come and be with her. We don't like to leave people, especially older people, alone when they've just had a shock.' PC Clow reached into the box and pulled out a slim brown folder. 'She said she was fine and we could leave her – she was pretty insistent about it actually. I left her my card and told her I would be back today with this.' She gestured to the box. I looked across to my brother but he wouldn't meet my gaze.

'Yes, I found your card. And you came here to tell my mum what exactly?'

'That her husband had passed away. He had a heart attack whilst he was working in the prison garden. Wormwood Scrubs – your father had been there for about twenty years. Didn't any of you know this?' she asked, amazed by our obvious ignorance. I looked to my brother for some sort of sign that this was all a big mistake; he just shoved his hands into his pockets and turned his back. My next comment was spoken as much to him as it was the harried-looking policewoman.

'Our dad disappeared, no one knew where he was for sure. But I don't think we ever thought he was in prison. I heard some gossip about him buggering off to Spain with another woman but not prison.'

'I'm so sorry, I don't know what to say. Father Michael offered to stay with her for a while – he's the prison chaplain; he was with me when I broke the news. But she said she was fine, even made us tea. I would never have left her alone if I thought she was ill.' The police officer looked as if she was on the verge of tears.

'She wasn't ill, she was fine. I'm guessing this must have just been too much of a shock for her, to find out where he'd been all these years. Don't you think, Matt?'

He just nodded. Lucy had been sitting silently in her chair the whole time we'd been speaking but suddenly she got up and left the room. The officer stared down at the brown folder on her lap, unable to make eye contact; my brother wouldn't even look at me.

Fragments of stories I'd heard growing up tumbled across my consciousness like pieces of a jigsaw falling out of a box. Yes, Spain, I was sure that was what I'd heard. Something about Spain, about my dad doing something stupid and running away. The memory I'd had earlier – the smashed vase and my mum's voice screaming recriminations – that must have been to do with that. He'd run off with another woman, not been locked in prison. I was convinced the officer must have got it wrong; some sort of bureaucratic mix-up. There'd been plenty of gossip about my dad after he left, but everyone had told me to ignore it. Ted and Rose, my grandparents, Flo – they'd told me that people just liked to talk – but I wasn't a baby, I was fifteen when he left. Old enough to know that something wasn't right but still young enough to want to believe that my family – the people who were supposed to love me – wouldn't lie to me about something so important. But had I ever really been convinced? Hadn't there always been a part of me that had suspicions and questions?

Lucy returned to the living room, clutching a picture in her hands.

'I found this in the bin when we got back and I was making tea in the kitchen. I didn't say anything; I didn't want to upset either of you by asking questions.' She held the picture out for us both to see; it was a photograph of me and Matt, standing with our parents, outside this house. I hadn't seen any pictures of my dad for years. I'd always assumed that my mum, or my grandparents, had got rid of them all. The photo was faded and had been repaired at some stage; yellowing sticky tape was holding its torn pieces together. I took it from Lucy and walked across to look at the brown box on the sofa.

'These are things from his cell?' I asked.

The officer nodded. I slowly lifted the lid. My hands were shaking, and Matt came across to stand beside me. Inside the box there were books and papers and a bundle of photographs. I lifted them out and took off the rubber band that was holding them all together. There must have been at least thirty or maybe forty of them. Some were old school pictures of me and Matt, and then there were other, more informal pictures. One of Matt with his first car, me in my old waitress apron, working in the café, one of me and Lucy on the day she got her A Level results – photos of all the milestones in our lives. I flipped through the stack and it was the final photo in the pile that really shocked me; it was a picture of me in the hospital, just after I'd given birth to Lucy. I looked exhausted and Lucy had hair matted with blood and tiny screwed-up eyes. I remembered Mum taking it; Lucy could only have been minutes old. She must have sent him all these pictures of us. I handed Matt the bundle of photos and then went across to sit back in the armchair by the window. I felt sick and weak; my legs didn't seem to want to hold my weight.

'She knew where he was,' said Lucy, echoing the realisation that had just dawned on me. 'All these years she said she hadn't heard from him, but she knew exactly where he was.'

Going to the box, Lucy lifted out another bundle, of what looked like letters. She took them across to the coffee table and began sorting through them; they'd all been opened and read, some of them many times considering the state of the paper, all of them except one.

'This one was only sent a few days ago, it's not even been opened yet.' Lucy lifted it up to show me and I recognised the handwriting on the front immediately.

'It's from Nan,' I said.

PC Clow stood up, looking eager to escape. 'I'm very sorry about all this,' she said. 'If there's anything I can do to help you sort this all out, please just let me know. Your mum seemed like a lovely lady. You already have my card so please stay in touch.' As she spoke she made her way over to the door.

'What's going to happen with Dad's body?' It was the first time Matt had spoken.

'It's in the mortuary at the moment. There'll have to be a post-mortem since it's technically classed as a death in custody, but that's just a formality really. You'll need to arrange for the funeral home to collect him after that.

All the paperwork you need is in the box.' She continued making her way out into the hallway and I followed her. I had so many questions but she wouldn't have any answers for me; she'd just been doing her job yesterday, delivering a piece of bad news to family.

'I am very sorry about your mum; I wouldn't have left her if I thought the news had affected her so much. She seemed okay, she really did.' Opening the front door, I gently steered her towards it. I needed her gone so I could begin to make sense of all this; she wasn't going to be able to help me navigate the unfolding soap opera that was my life.

'It's fine, you couldn't have known what would happen. Please don't worry about it. Thank you for bringing his... I mean... my dad's things, we appreciate it. We'll be in touch if we need anything.' I closed the door on her just as she was turning to speak to me; I had no more platitudes for her. Standing by the door for a few minutes, I tried to steady my breathing.

When I went back into the living room, Lucy had moved the coffee table and upended the contents of the box onto the floor. She'd already put the books in a small pile next to her and she'd started sorting through the letters. The unopened one sat alone on the mantelpiece, its contents unseen by anyone since Mum sealed up the envelope. I didn't want to read it, not yet, not until I understood more about this whole situation.

'Mum, this is proper big family secret type stuff. Did

either of you know anything about all this?' asked Lucy.

'That's an excellent question, Lucy.' I turned my attention to my brother. 'Matt?'

His head snapped up and he stared at me.

'Perhaps you can answer that one for her. Did either of us know anything about all this?'

He didn't reply, he just shook his head sadly and walked across to the window, anything to avoid making eye contact with me, it seemed.

'I need a fucking cigarette,' he announced, sharply.

'You don't smoke any more, remember?' He'd given up when he moved in with me and baby Lucy; an unwelcome thought popped into my head.

'Did you move in with us so you could keep an eye on me? To make sure I never found out about all this?'

He didn't answer. All these years I'd painted my big brother as the hero of my story, stepping in to save me when my life went to shit; when the reality was that he was there to protect himself, to keep me from finding out about the lies I'd been told. 'Well?'

'No, Abs, that wasn't why,' he said finally. 'I moved in because you needed me. It was nothing to do with all this other stuff, I swear.'

I wanted to believe him; I wanted to know that I could still put my faith in him, but how could I do that now? 'You need to tell me everything, Matt, all of it. I want to know.'

'I need a cigarette,' he repeated and made a move to

leave the room. I had to stop him; quickly I moved between him and the door to try and block his escape but it was no use. He ducked around me and then he was gone, the glass in the front door rattling as he slammed it behind him. Lucy looked up at me from her position on the floor; she was sitting cross-legged surrounded by piles of books, papers and photographs.

'What's he doing? He can't just walk out.'

'It appears he can,' I said as I paced across to the window; his car was already gone.

'How much of all this do you think he knew?' she asked, picking up a handful of letters.

'I don't know.' That was the truth; I might have had my suspicions but I didn't know anything for sure. I looked at the piles of letters and photos on the carpet. 'There must be replies to all those letters here somewhere, in the house.'

'Where do you think Nan would have put them?'

'I'm going to have a look upstairs in her room, see if I can find anything that helps to explain all this.' I gestured towards the piles on the carpet.

'Want a hand?'

'No, it's fine. You stay there. I can manage.' I left her sitting on the carpet, surrounded by the evidence of a family history that felt as if it belonged to someone else entirely.

*

It was hard to believe that I'd been in this room only a few hours ago, packing the things that I thought Mum might have needed in the hospital. That bag was sitting in the hallway downstairs, its contents no longer necessary. The room felt very different now, as if it was hiding things. Every drawer, every cupboard could be laden with secrets. I felt like a trespasser, as if my mum were going to poke her head round the door at any moment and demand to know what I was doing in here.

I sat down on the edge of the bed and looked around the room, wondering where I should begin my search. What was I looking for? Was I expecting to find a big box marked 'Family Secrets'? Her wardrobe seemed like as good a place as any to start so I pulled open the heavy dark wood doors. The inside smelt like a unique combination of her, beeswax and mothballs. Her clothes were hanging neatly in groups: trousers, skirts and dresses, followed by blouses, jumpers and cardigans. The untidiest part of the wardrobe was the pile of jumpers that I'd shoved back on the top shelf earlier. At the bottom were her shoes, all sitting tidily together in pairs. I hadn't followed in her footsteps when it came to neatness. My complete lack of interest in tidiness and order had been just one of the many things we'd fought about. She'd stand at my bedroom door and just shake her head in utter dismay at the state of my room.

'How ever do you find anything in this disgusting excuse for a room, Abigail?' she would say to me. I remembered thinking, in the way that moody teenagers did, that what I chose to do with the contents of my wardrobe and my room was my business; especially since she'd only just started taking an interest in me after two years of previously not giving a shit.

'It's been like this for ages, Mum. Why do you give a toss suddenly? Have you run out of pills to take? Just woken up?'

I cringed now at the memory of those horrible words and how often I'd used her absences from my life against her. I'd known she was unhappy; I'd known she'd had a nervous breakdown, although I hadn't really known what that was at the time. I'd known because that had been all anyone had talked about when it came to Mum. Neighbours would question my nan about how she was doing and she'd tap her temple with a nicotine-stained finger and say, 'She's still not right in the head. She's had a nervous breakdown, you know?' All the old crones would nod their heads sagely and talk about what an awful business it was. Had they known about Dad? *Of course they had, you stupid woman. Turns out it was only you who didn't know the truth.* I felt like such a fool. I'd managed to convince myself that the stories they told weren't about my dad. Not him, not the man who'd taught me how to ride a bike and watched *Grandstand* every Saturday, sitting in his pants, chain-smoking Benson & Hedges and swearing at West Ham's football scores. That man surely wasn't capable of doing the kind of things that would send him to prison for twenty years.

I was just sitting on the end of the bed, staring into the wardrobe, when Lucy appeared at the door. 'Didn't find anything, then?'

'What? Oh, no, not really, well, I haven't had a chance to look.'

She came and sat next to me on the bed. 'I don't think the answers are just going to leap out of the wardrobe, do you?'

I shook my head. 'Maybe there isn't anything to find. Maybe she burned all the replies to make sure I didn't catch sight of them.'

'I can't see Nan setting light to letters in her kitchen, can you? She wasn't some sort of secret agent and, besides, it would have made far too much mess.'

I smiled; she was right, of course, it was a ridiculous image.

'I think you should read this one, though.' Lucy held out a letter to me. 'I haven't gone through all the others, but this is the last one she sent, the one he never saw.'

I could see that it had already been torn open. She gave me a sheepish smile.

'Sorry, Mum, I couldn't resist. It's the last one she wrote; it's like the last piece of her.' She wiped away tears and I took her hand.

'It's all right, I understand. I just don't know if I have the strength to read it now, that's all.' I turned the envelope over in my hands and traced the outline of her writing with my finger.

'I think you need to read it,' she insisted.

Taking a deep breath, I slid out the single sheet of pale blue paper covered in my mum's shaky scrawl.

> Dear John,
>
> I hope this letter finds you well. It's been almost a month since I wrote last. I'm sorry it's taken me so long. I've been keeping busy though, there's always plenty to do. I hope you are keeping busy too. Everyone here is all right. Matt is still working hard, managing the gym and his complicated love life. He thinks I don't know about all the girls he's got on the go but I hear things. I'm not that fond of the new one, I think her name's Karen or Sharon or something. She's a bit of a trollop I think. Far too much make-up and she has the most annoying bloody voice.

That brought a smile to my face. We did have something in common after all; I didn't think Karen was good enough for my brother either. Lucy looked at me quizzically, but I didn't stop to explain.

Lucy is getting ready to leave for university. She's going to Bristol. I think I've probably already told you that, haven't I? I wish you could meet her, John, her photos don't do her justice, she's beautiful and so clever. She reminds me so much of Abigail at that age.

That remark stunned me; it was the nearest thing to a compliment I'd ever had from my mother.

Abigail is still doing well with her café business but I do worry about the rest of her life. I'm very worried that she's going to be so lonely after Lucy leaves. Not that she would ever tell me anything like that. We don't really talk anymore. She seems to get angrier with me as time goes on. I'd hoped that eventually she might come to forgive me for not being there for her but, if anything, it's got worse. I see her struggling with the guilt of how she feels about me and I want to tell her that it's all right, that I understand. But I can't seem to say it right, anything I say just seems to make her even angrier with me and pushes her further away. I wish I could make her understand but I think it's too late for that now.

There was more but I couldn't carry on reading; I couldn't see the page through my tears. I let the letter drop from my hands. Lucy didn't speak, she just sat beside me, resting her hand over mine. I looked down at our two hands together; my stubby fingers interlaced with Lucy's longer, slender ones, and I marvelled at how I could be holding the hand of a grown woman, when only yesterday she'd been a little girl. Why did everything feel as if it was moving so fast? Why there never enough time?

'Why didn't she just tell me the truth?' I sobbed. 'If she'd told me… I wouldn't have… everything could have been so different.'

'I know, Mum, it's all right.' She stroked my hair gently. After a few minutes I sat up, roughly swiping tears away from my cheeks, and I took a deep breath.

'Well, that's enough of that,' I said sternly. 'I'm meant to be taking care of you, not the other way around.'

'Don't be daft, Mum, it's all right to let me look after you for once.'

'I'm fine, sweetheart, honestly. This has all been a bit of a shock, that's all. Hard to take it all in.' I plastered on my brightest smile and stood up. 'I think we need to start sorting some of Nan's things out, don't you?' Wrenching open one of her drawers, I grabbed a handful of jumpers and dropped them onto the bed, trying to ignore the overpowering scent of her. In that moment, all I wanted to do was lie on her bed and bury my face in them. I wanted to close the curtains and lock the door and just hide there, surrounded by her things; just the way she did after my dad left. That thought shocked me into stillness; maybe I wasn't so different from her after all? Deep down I think I'd always suspected that I had more in common with my mother than I wanted to admit.

There was a time, Lucy was almost three, and I was working as many shifts as I could in the café whilst trying to get through my course at catering college. I was chasing round, never a free moment to stop, just trying to do everything at once. I'd thought I was managing all right, but the brain can be tricky. I woke up one morning and I couldn't get out of bed. It wasn't a physical thing – I still had four functioning limbs – I just couldn't muster the mental energy I needed to make them work. It was my 'Stop the world, I want to get off' moment and it frightened the shit out of me. No amount of tea or cajoling from Matt could persuade me otherwise. The guilt I felt about not being able to take care of my daughter was like an immense weight that sat on my chest and made it hard to breathe, but still I couldn't drag myself up and out of the depths; there didn't seem any point.

That must make me sound like a terrible mother and

I still sometimes cringed at the memory, but gradually I'd come to realise that I didn't have to be ashamed about those lost weeks because I couldn't have done anything about it, even if I'd wanted to. My brain had just decided it had had enough; enough of the broken sleep, the worries about money, the worries about being a good enough parent to Lucy. My brain had needed a rest just as much as my body. For two weeks all I did was sleep or lie there staring at the ceiling. I didn't wash – not my hair, not my body, not my teeth – I didn't eat and I hardly spoke. Matt and Liz, who at that point had known me for barely a year at college, took over Lucy's care. They gave me the time I needed to get back to a point where I could at least get up and get dressed in the morning.

In all that time, throughout those two weeks where I'd basically given up, my mother never came to see me. Not once. I'd never forgiven her; it had just been another nail in the coffin of our relationship as far as I was concerned. But now, after everything that had happened, I thought I understood why. It would have been too much of a reminder to her of the way she'd been after Dad left. She'd pulled herself out of that dark place and hadn't been keen to go back. She hadn't abandoned me after Dad went away; she hadn't been able to help her breakdown any more than I had mine. It was so obvious to me in that moment, but it was all too little, too late for us.

'Mum, you don't have to do that now.' Lucy gently took the pale blue cardigan I was holding, out of my hands. She put it down on the bed and then pulled me into a hug. We stood together like that for a few minutes, until we were interrupted by my brother's voice.

'Room for one more in there?' He was standing by the bedroom door; he looked awful. I opened out one arm and he came across to us, burying his face in my shoulder. I heard him sniffing back tears and trying to mask the fact that he was crying with an awkward little cough every now and then. That was enough to start Lucy off again and then we were all crying.

'I don't mind the tears, Abs, but you can keep the snot to yourself, thanks,' he said, reaching into his pocket for a tissue. I took it and blew my nose loudly.

'Bloody hell, you sound like Nelly the Elephant!'

I slapped him across the shoulder, which probably hurt me more than him since he was all muscle. He laughed and rubbed his arm. I offered the tissue back to him; he refused it with a disgusted look.

'No, thanks, you can keep it.'

I stuffed it in my pocket and started to pick up some clothes from the bed to fold; I needed something to do. 'I'm going to fold while you talk.'

'And I think I'm going to make myself scarce,' said Lucy, sidling out of the room before either of us could stop her.

'Keeping your hands busy so you don't punch me, is that it?' said Matt.

'Something like that. I want to know everything, Matt. I mean it. You don't get to stop talking until you've told me all of it.'

'I can only tell you what I know, which is by no means all of it.'

I raised an eyebrow at this, unsure of whether to believe him or not.

'It's true, Abs, I swear. Mum only told me the bits she thought I needed to know in order to make sure you were protected.'

'But you knew that Dad was in prison?'

'Yes. She told me that Dad had been a "very silly man" and that he'd got himself mixed up with the wrong sort of people. In Mum's version of the story, the one she fed me at least, Dad was just in the wrong place at the wrong time and didn't deserve to be where he ended up.'

'And you believed her?'

'At first, yeah. But then you hear things and I did a bit of digging of my own.' Matt was pacing back and forth across the bedroom floor. 'No one was really that keen to share what they knew, it's like the whole subject made them nervous, but I eventually found out which prison Dad was in and what for.' He stopped pacing and turned to look at me but didn't speak.

'And?' I prompted him.

'It was an armed robbery. Him and six other blokes. They robbed a security van.'

'Armed robbery? What the fuck did Dad know about guns?'

Matt shrugged. 'Mum didn't want you to know about any of this, Abby.'

'And what about Dad? What did he want?'

Matt gave a wry laugh. 'No one knew what he wanted.'

'But all those letters downstairs? Mum wrote to him all the time.'

'She wrote to him but he never wrote back. She kept sending him letters and photos, even though she never heard from him again after he got sent down.'

'Then why did she keep writing to him? I don't understand.'

'I told you, as far as she was concerned he was just unlucky. He got lumbered with the blame, that was all. She still loved him, Abby. She never stopped loving him. And it was important to her that you still loved him too. That's why she didn't want you to know; she didn't want it to change how you felt about him.'

'How I felt about *him*? What about the effect it had on the way I felt about her? Didn't she care about that?'

'Yes, of course she did, but I think she thought that you'd eventually get over that and maybe forgive her, in time.'

'This is such a fucking mess, Matt.' I plonked myself

heavily down on the bed and he came to sit by me.

'I know. I wanted to tell you, Abby. There were so many times I almost did, but Mum would get so upset if I mentioned it. She'd disappear to her room, refuse to eat, refuse to come out. It frightened me, Abs – she'd revert back to how she was… when… y'know…'

'How she was when he left, you mean?'

Matt nodded. 'It freaked me out, Abs. I couldn't cope with it so I just left it. I'm so sorry. I should have been stronger. I should have stood up to her and told you everything. Now it's too late, isn't it?'

I shrugged. 'I guess it is.'

'What about me and you, though? Are we all right? Please say we are. I don't know what I'd do without you and Lucy.' A panicked look flickered across his face at the thought of the damage this might have done to our relationship. The thought of losing what little family I had left was enough to push me towards my answer.

'It's going to be fine, Matt. I've lost a mum and dad in the same day; I'm not about to lose a brother too.'

Matt let out the breath he'd been holding and pulled me into his arms. I wanted to return the gesture with the same gusto but I didn't feel able to – not yet. He sensed my reluctance and let me go.

'Not quite ready to forgive me yet, are you?'

I shook my head and he nodded. 'I understand. Just promise me that you'll try, tell me that you'll let me have a good go at making it up to you. Please?'

'I promise, but you have to promise me something too.'

'Anything. What?'

'Promise me that you won't lie to me any more about any of this. If there's anything else I need to know, you have to tell me now; because if I find out later that you're still keeping things from me I won't be able to forgive you.'

Matt didn't reply straight away; he just sat there staring at the floor for a few moments. I took this to mean that he had something else he needed to get off his chest.

'What is it?' The silence was killing me; what the hell was he gearing up to tell me now?

'Martin,' he said, eventually.

'What? Who?' I snapped.

'Lucy's dad, Martin Church.'

'What about him?'

'I might have something to do with why he left you and Lucy that night.'

That didn't make any sense; Lucy's dad had been a drunk and a bully and, despite the fact that Matt had offered to sort him out for me many times, in the end it had been me that had thrown him out.

'What did you do?'

'Don't panic, I didn't break his legs or anything, although I would have loved to. I just warned him off. Reminded him that there were certain things that you didn't know about and I told him I'd like it to stay that way. That's all.'

'You were worried he was going to tell me about Dad?'

'I was in the pub that night you threw him out. I heard him mouthing off to people about how you were a snotty cow who needed to be taken down a peg or two. That maybe you wouldn't be so full of yourself if you knew you were the daughter of a criminal.'

Suddenly some of the things that Martin used to say to me started to make sense. He would accuse me of acting as if I was better than him and his family, telling me what a joke that was and if only I knew the truth. I'd put it down to the drink talking and the fact that he'd seemed to enjoy insulting me.

'He was a useless twat, Abs. You were better off without him.'

'I know that. It still wasn't your place to warn him off! He's Lucy's Dad! She deserved the chance to have some sort of a relationship with him!' I yelled.

'Bollocks!' Matt shouted. 'If he'd wanted to be in his daughter's life then no amount of threats from me should have made any difference. If I had a daughter no one would be able to keep me from her.' I looked at my brother's earnest expression and knew he was right; Matt had just given Martin an excuse to do what he'd always been going to do anyway.

'What did you say to him?'

'Not much. I just gave him a gentle reminder of how important it was to me that you shouldn't find out too much about Dad and what had happened.'

Thankfully he didn't elaborate on the form that this 'gentle reminder' would have taken. He gave me his best innocent choirboy look and I couldn't help but smile. I should have felt angrier with him, but to be honest the idea of Martin getting a taste of his own medicine didn't upset me that much. Did that make me a bad person? Maybe, but I'd get over it. I had one more question for him before I let him off the hook.

'Tell me how it's possible that I've never heard of any of this before?'

'Dad had a lot of friends, Abby. I think word got around that it didn't pay to gossip about the Turner family, and then when Mum lost the plot most people stopped coming round anyway, and that was that.' He said it so matter-of-factly that I wanted to slap him.

'But what about people at school, my friends? If Martin knew then so did everyone else in my class.'

Matt rubbed the knuckles on his right hand and my eyes were drawn to the scars there; I had a feeling I knew the answer to that one.

'How many of my friends did you beat up, then?'

'It wasn't like that, Abs. Eventually people moved on, they all had their own shit to deal with, Dad's story got lost, forgotten about. Occasionally it would rear its ugly head again, but I dealt with it. Life went on.'

I couldn't help feeling sorry for Matt, feeling as if he'd had no choice but to stick around and be my protector. What kind of life had that been for him?

'Mum should never have put that kind of burden on you. That wasn't fair. You could have gone anywhere, travelled the world, except you didn't because she'd made you into some sort of secret keeper for me.'

'Don't be daft, Abby, where the fuck was I gonna go? I like my life. I've got my own business. I'm my own boss. Besides, what would all the girls round here do for entertainment if I just upped and left and took all this gorgeousness with me?' He flexed his pecs and winked at me.

'That's disgusting, Matt. I don't even want to go there.'

'It made you smile, though, didn't it?'

'I'm not smiling; I'm trying to suppress my gag reflex.'

'Ha ha!' Matt clapped me on the shoulder and laughed loudly.

'Well, that all sounds a lot more positive,' said Lucy, as she came back into the room. 'What are you laughing about?'

'Trust me, Lucy, you don't want to know. I wouldn't want to scar you for life,' I said. Matt stuck two fingers up at me in a vulgar salute.

'Fair enough. Do you need help with anything?'

'We need to think about making some arrangements,

I suppose,' said Matt. 'I need to go and see the funeral directors, talk to them about what she wanted and all that. Be nice if I had some company.'

Lucy nodded. I didn't have a clue what Mum wanted when it came to her funeral; I was kind of surprised that Matt did either.

'Did she talk to you about it, then?' I asked.

'Yeah. It just came out in conversation one day, wasn't like I asked her about it or anything. She was watching something on the telly about wicker coffins, I think some singer she liked had one when he died. She said that's what she wanted, said it would burn better than a proper coffin when she was cremated.'

'She wanted to be cremated? I thought she'd want to be buried next to her parents.'

'No, she said she wanted to be cremated and then she wanted her ashes scattered over the Thames, off the side of the Woolwich Ferry.'

The Woolwich Ferry! That ugly metal boat that carried traffic from one side of London to the other!

'You are joking, aren't you?' I tried hard to hide my amusement at the image of the two of us, weaving our way between lorries and cars on board the ferry, then scattering Mum's ashes over the side. Unfortunately, the ridiculousness of it was too much for me; within seconds I was bent double, holding my sides and laughing uncontrollably. Matt was watching me. He looked horrified at my laughter and his serious face just made it worse. I was laughing so hard that I couldn't catch my breath. Lucy looked at me and then back at him, and for a split second I thought she was going to tell me off, but then her face cracked into an enormous grin.

'The Woolwich bloody Ferry?' she exclaimed. 'That's hilarious. I never knew Nan had such a sick sense of humour!'

Matt just looked despairingly at both of us. 'You're bloody mental, the pair of you. I'm going to see the funeral directors. Hopefully they'll be a bit more respectful,' he said, and left us clutching each other for support as our laughter subsided.

'He's right, of course,' I said, wiping away tears. 'That probably wasn't very nice, was it?'

'Probably not, but, after everything that's happened today, if you can't laugh about it then what's the point?' She leaned in and gave me a quick peck on the cheek. 'I'll go after him; we can't have him organising the funeral on his own, can we? Uncle Matt, wait for me, I'm coming.' She ran out of the room and I heard her thumping down the stairs. Picking up all the stuff that I'd emptied out of drawers, I began folding it into neat piles on the bed.

Chapter 14

'You know you should have just shagged his brains out when you had the chance, don't you?' said Liz, as she lay on my mum's sofa. She'd come to see me after Lucy and Matt had left a couple of hours ago. I'd told them that I wanted to stay behind to start sorting some of mum's stuff but the truth was I just didn't want to go home. Being in this house made me feel closer to her and after everything I'd learnt about my mum today, I needed to feel that closeness.

Liz had insisted she come over to join me, to stop me from 'getting maudlin'. She'd brought two bottles of wine, which we'd made short work of, and once we'd polished those off I'd dragged out some musty port from the back of one of mum's cupboards and we'd had a couple of glasses of that. I was drunk and, if I'm being totally honest, a little bit sick. I'm not sure how old the port was; the bottle had been very dusty.

'He has a girlfriend and he lives on the other side of the world, Liz. Why does everyone keep overlooking those very important facts?' I was lying on my back on the floor in the living room, with my forearms across my face. Every time I opened my eyes the light in the middle of the ceiling above me seemed to spin very fast. I'd tried to sit up just now but quickly realised that was a bad idea.

'I thought you said, that he said, that girl was just a friend?' Liz hiccupped.

'He did.'

'Then what's the problem?'

'The problem is I don't believe him. She looks at him so adoringly and she's in so many photos with him. There has to be something going on.' I lifted my glass and realised it was empty – probably just as well.

'Even if there is something between them, he didn't seem bothered about it so why should you be? His perky little girlfriend was the furthest thing from his mind when he got you topless in the back of his car a few hours ago!'

'Urrggh! Stop, Liz, please don't remind me. I'm so embarrassed. I don't know what the fuck I was thinking.' I shook my head, and instantly regretted it; my brain swirled about inside my skull, which didn't do much to curb the nausea.

'I don't know how you managed to drag yourself off his lap – he's bloody gorgeous, darling. I mean, look at him.' Liz thrust her smartphone in my face, showing me the pictures of him she'd found online. He was good-looking, no point denying that fact, but that didn't change anything.

'That face, those eyes,' Liz swiped through the

pictures, 'Bloody hell – I've found one of him naked!'

'What?' I tried to grab the phone but she snatched it out of my reach.

'Gotcha! There aren't any naked pictures of him, you wally. But admit it, you were curious, weren't you?' She gave me a knowing wink and I stuck two fingers up in reply.

'Well, that's charming, that is. Here I am trying to show my support for you and that's the thanks I get.' She let out a huge yawn and I looked across to the clock on the mantel; it was almost midnight.

'I'm sorry, I didn't mean to keep you so late. You should have said something.' I crawled across to where she was sitting on the sofa. 'Do you want me to ring for a cab?'

'I think that would probably be a good idea, my lovely. I'm in no fit state to be driving anywhere.'

I dragged myself up off the floor and staggered to the phone in the hallway. Miraculously I remembered the number of the taxi firm, and after a rather confusing initial exchange, during which I thought I might have ordered six cabs rather than one, I managed to organise Liz's ride home.

'He'll be here in about ten minutes. Liz?' She'd wriggled down the sofa into a completely prone position and was snoring lightly. How on earth was I going to get her into a cab? I nudged her shoulder gently but got no response. I nudged her again, this time slightly harder, but that made her turn over. All this effort had made the room start spinning unpleasantly – I needed a glass of water. In all honesty, I was way beyond the point where a glass of water would be of any use. I also needed to find some painkillers. I made my way down the hallway, wobbling from side to side as if I were trapped inside a pinball machine. I couldn't remember the last time I'd been this drunk; definitely not since I'd had Lucy, probably not since I was about seventeen and I'd taken a sudden liking to White Lightning cider. It had been cheap and had got you shitfaced really quickly; something that I'd found came in very handy when I'd been trying to cope with my crappy existence. God, I'd had a boring life. I flicked the overhead light on in the kitchen and immediately regretted it.

'For fuck's sake.' I winced at the fluorescent glow and banged the switch again. Feeling my way over to the sink, I switched on the little lamp that sat on the window ledge – much better. I rifled through the drawers by the sink, looking for headache pills, only finding cutlery and tea towels in the first two. The next one held scraps of paper, old bills and dried up biros, and an old ice-cream tub full of spare keys, random screws and rubber bands. As I moved the tub, my eye landed on a blue envelope tucked underneath. It had grease stains on the front and what looked like the ring from a coffee mug but the most unusual thing about this envelope, tucked away in the bottom of my mum's 'crap' drawer, was the fact that it had my name on the front. 'For Abigail' was written quite clearly in my mother's distinctive hand. I pulled the envelope out and placed it on the kitchen table, propped up against the salt cellar. I stared at it for a few minutes, as if I were expecting it to self-destruct now it had been pulled from its hiding place. It was probably just an old birthday card, I thought, nothing more than that. I reached out tentatively towards the envelope but snatched my hand back when a car horn sounded loudly outside – the cab! I left the envelope propped against the salt cellar and went to open the front door. I waved at the cab driver and turned to go and fetch Liz. I almost knocked her flying, as she was already standing behind me, looking weary and a bit green.

'Are you going to be okay? Do you need the loo before you go?'

She shook her head, almost as if she was too afraid to open her mouth.

'Mmm... K... Just need... home, bed,' she mumbled.

I walked her to the car and saw the driver eyeing her cautiously.

'She ain't gonna chuck up in my cab, is she?'

'No, no, of course not. She'll be fine, she's just a little tired that's all, long day, you know how it is.' I gave him my best cheery smile and slammed the door. He was shaking his head as he pulled away and I prayed that Liz was going to be able to hold it together for the twenty-minute cab ride home.

The house was quiet when I went back inside. I collected the empty wine bottles and glasses from the living room and took them out to the kitchen. A sudden whiff of wine from the bottles gave me a brief urge to throw up but I managed to keep it down. After rinsing glasses and emptying the bin under the sink, I sat at the kitchen table, contemplating that bloody envelope. I picked it up and turned it over before putting it back down on the table. There was every chance that the envelope held nothing more than some old receipts or a forgotten birthday card. On any other day, I would have assumed exactly that but after everything that had happened, what I'd learned about my family and its talent for keeping massive secrets, I wasn't so sure. I didn't want to deal with any more crap; not by myself anyway. You should call Jack, the treacherous little voice at the back of my mind piped up; no doubt fuelled by all the lady petrol I'd drunk. Call Jack and tell him you need him, that you want him, said the voice.

I went to the living room in search of my phone and found it buried under a pile of photos on the coffee table. On top of the pile was the photograph that Lucy had rescued from the bin earlier; the one of all of us standing outside this house. I held it up close to my face to get a better look at my dad. He didn't look like some gun-toting master criminal. Stonewash jeans, a Fred Perry polo shirt and white trainers; he was your typical

1980s Dad. I could see him now; standing in the front room in nothing but that polo shirt and his pants, ironing his jeans with a cigarette hanging out of the corner of his mouth. I could hear Mum's voice coming from the kitchen. 'Don't you drop bloody fag ash on my carpet, John!' The memory was so vivid, so full of detail, I swear I could almost smell the cigarette smoke. I wished Liz hadn't gone home, I didn't want to be on my own.

On impulse I opened my phone and Jack's last message appeared on the screen.

> Am heading back home in a few days, thought I would let you know.

My sense of recklessness stirred a little, blame it on the wine. If he was going home, then why shouldn't I take advantage of our obvious mutual attraction, just once? Then he'd leave and my life would return to normal. Why couldn't I allow myself to have some fun? Where was the harm? Lexie's face suddenly popped into view – there was the harm. Despite his claim that they were just friends, I wasn't the type to be cast as the other woman. Okay, so I wouldn't sleep with him then; maybe we could just talk? My subconscious raised a sardonic eyebrow in disbelief but I was undeterred. We were adults after all. I dialled his number before I could change my mind. It was only when it started to ring that I remembered what time it was. Shit – what had I done?

My finger hovered over the end call button but I didn't press it. It was too late; the phone was ringing. After a few seconds, I heard Jack's sleepy voice on the other end of the line.

'Hello? Abigail, is that you?'

Bugger it – what should I do? Should I answer? Put on my best fake voice and pretend I'd got the wrong number? I was rubbish at lying under pressure so I owned up. 'Yes, it's me. Sorry, I didn't realise it was so late.'

'It's fine, what's wrong? Did you need me?' I heard the rustle of sheets in the background, as if he was getting out of bed, and my sex-starved brain immediately began conjuring up images of him in bed wearing nothing but a smile. Stop it!

'Just hang on a minute,' he said, whispering into the phone, and it dawned on me that he must be sneaking out of bed to talk to me. No doubt sneaking away from a sleeping Lexie, who was obviously there with him. God, what an idiot, what was I doing? I'd just dragged him out of the bed he shared with her; for all I knew I'd interrupted them in the middle of shagging each other's brains out. He wouldn't have stopped halfway through to answer his phone, would he? It had been a while since I was in that position myself, but I was pretty sure that the etiquette on not answering phone calls during sex couldn't have changed that much.

'Are you still there, Abigail?' I heard what sounded

215

like a door closing.

'I'm here.' There was a long silence. I didn't know what to say. Think, Abby, you need a reason for calling him in the middle of the night otherwise he's going to think you're a lunatic; my mind went blank.

'What is it? What's wrong?' he asked.

'Nothing's wrong, I'm fine. Oh, God, I'm so sorry, Jack, I shouldn't have called you... don't know why I did really... Let's blame it on the wine and leave it at that, shall we?' Please say we can leave it at that.

'Are you drunk-dialling me, Abigail? That doesn't sound like the responsible woman I know. How much have you had to drink? Are you at home? Are you alone?'

'Hold your horses, that's too many questions all at once. I'm still at my mum's and, yes, I'm alone.' Although what that had to do with anything I didn't know. 'I am undoubtedly a little drunk. I apologise for my childish behaviour; I will let you get back to your grown-up life now, Mr Chance.'

'Wait, hang on. Don't go. I think we should talk, don't you?'

'I can't, Jack, it's too... difficult.'

'We used to be able to talk about anything, Abigail. No one knew me better than you did.'

'We're not kids anymore.'

'No, we're certainly not kids anymore.' The heat in his voice made my cheeks burn. 'I think we proved that

216

a few hours ago.'

'That was a mistake, Jack. I was upset, that's all.' A flashback of the moment I slid onto Jack's lap and he relieved me of my shirt popped into my mind.

'It was more than that and you know it, but I'm not going to force you to say it out loud,' he said softly. For a few seconds neither of us spoke; all I could hear was my own breathing.

It was Jack who broke the silence. 'What's happening with your Mum's funeral? Do you need any help with the arrangements?' Although a bit taken aback by the sudden change of subject, I was relieved to be able to talk about something else.

'Liz is helping me, it's fine.' I paused. 'We have to bury my dad as well.'

'What are you talking about? Your dad? You found him?' He sounded as confused as I was.

'He died in prison, a few days ago. That's where he's been all this time. The police came to tell us today, it's complicated, too much to explain really…' I didn't get to finish the sentence.

'Stay where you are. I'm coming to you,' he said.

'What? No, Jack, don't be silly. I don't need you to…'

'Jack, what are you doing out here? Who are you talking to?' I heard Lexie's voice in the background. I wanted to cry. I'd been right: she'd been there with him the whole time. I felt so stupid.

'I shouldn't have called you, Jack. This was a mistake. I have to go now. Have a safe trip home.'

'Abigail, wait, please, don't—'

I disconnected the call before he could finish.

Chapter 15

Please stop! I'm still in here, don't do this to me!' I'm trapped inside my glass box again. I'm being watched by a crowd of people who are all dressed in black. I'm at a funeral; my funeral. The people come to the glass and point and laugh, they're talking but I can't hear what they're saying. I pound my fists on the inside of the glass but they just walk away. Now the box is being lowered back into a hole and I watch as the box slides down deeper and deeper until it reaches the bottom with a thump. Panic fills my throat, like bile; I can taste it. The mourners are peering over the edge of the pit.

Help me, please.' I scream but no one comes to help me. Then the handfuls of dirt begin falling on the lid of the box. Bang, bang, I pound my hands on the top, on the sides. I kick my legs out but I'm trapped and they just keep piling on the dirt. Why can't they hear me? Bang, bang.

*

The sound of hammering on the front door woke me up. It took me a few minutes to work out where I was. I

219

wasn't trapped in a box being buried alive. I was lying on the sofa in my mum's living room. The clock on the mantel told me it was almost two in the morning. I'd only been asleep for an hour or so but I felt as if I were waking up from a coma. My head was groggy, my mouth was bone dry and when I stood up my legs felt like jelly. I limped tentatively to the door, conscious that the banging was now making my head hurt. Why did they have to bang so loud?

I opened the door, readying myself to give whoever was there a few choice words about courtesy, but I was stopped short by the sight of Jack standing on the doorstep, all wild-eyed and angry-looking.

The only response I could muster was, 'Oh, for fuck's sake.'

'Why the hell haven't you been answering your phone?'

I turned away from the door and started to walk down the hallway to the kitchen.

'I need a drink,' I muttered.

'I think you've probably had enough to drink, don't you?'

I wheeled round to face him. 'What the fuck has it got to do with you? I meant I need a coffee, not more alcohol.' I considered cracking open another bottle of wine just to spite him. Unfortunately, my stomach had other ideas, as the very thought of more wine made me feel as if I was about to throw up.

'Would you like a cup of coffee?' I asked, sweetly. Jack looked as if he wanted to throttle me; I could see a small muscle ticking in his cheek. He turned to close the front door and by the time he turned back he seemed to have composed himself enough to answer me.

'No coffee, thanks, can't stand the stuff. Can I have a cup of tea?'

'That's not very American of you. I thought all you Yanks loved coffee.' I walked down the hallway and into the kitchen. I filled the kettle and put it on to boil before pulling two mugs out of the cupboard. I threw a teabag into one of them and a spoonful of instant coffee into the other.

'It's the latent Englishman in me. Can't beat a cup of builder's tea and a digestive biscuit,' said Jack as he came into the kitchen behind me.

'You're going to love me, then. Look what I just happen to have here.' I pulled out a packet of digestives from the cupboard and put them on the kitchen table.

'I love these things. There's nothing better than a digestive for dunking into your tea.' He'd lost all trace of his American accent as he uttered that last sentence; he was back to being the London boy I remembered.

The kettle clicked off and I poured scalding water into the two mugs. I poured milk into my coffee and then started to take the teabag out of Jack's mug.

'Wait, wait. It's only been in there for a few seconds, leave it alone for a bit.' He came over and took the

221

teaspoon out of my hand. 'Your mum would be appalled at your tea-making efforts.'

'I know. I can hear her now, telling me off for making it in the cup and not in a proper teapot. "That's not how it's done, Abigail, you've got to put the tea in and leave it to draw."' I never understood that use of the word 'draw' but all my family said it. I used to picture a plume of steam emanating from the spout of the teapot and making pictures on the kitchen tiles.

'There, that's more like it.' Jack squeezed the teabag against the side of the mug and then dropped it into the bin. As he added milk I watched the tea turn from almost black to something resembling weather-worn terracotta.

'Perfect. You can't get proper tea like this in America. You can get the teabags but there's something about the water, or the milk, I guess, makes it taste different.' He blew across the top of the mug and then took a sip. An enormous grin slowly crawled across his face.

'I'm gonna miss this when I go back, and these.' He opened the biscuits and pulled out two. He dunked one into his mug and then took a bite. 'Lexie hates it when I dunk.'

The mention of her name reminded me of her voice on the other end of the phone. I didn't want to talk about her.

'Well, Lexie isn't here, so your secret's safe with me.'

We both sipped our drinks in silence for a few

minutes, the only sound Jack munching on his biscuits. I watched him as he carefully lowered each one into his tea and then whipped it into his mouth before it crumbled. His mouth was beautifully distracting. As he finished his last one he leant back in the chair and licked crumbs from his fingers. I felt my face heat as I watched those long fingers dip in and out of his mouth; that gorgeous mouth. Holy shit, what was I doing? I was so obsessed with staring at him that I didn't realise he was staring at me. Quick, Abby, say something to distract him.

'Careful with those, Mr Chance, we can't have you developing middle-aged spread. I suspect Lexie wouldn't approve,' I said, trying to hide my embarrassment at having been caught perving at him.

'Are you saying I'm getting fat?' He stretched his shirt across his stomach and I got a preview of the muscular body underneath. God help me.

'Yeah, fat and bald,' I hurried on, 'so make sure you marry Lexie before things get much worse. Nab her while you're still at least reasonably attractive.' I got up from the table and took my mug over to the sink. I tried to focus on washing up but then I felt him standing behind me, pressing his body against mine and placing his hands either side of me on the counter. I could feel his breath in my ear as he spoke, sending shivers down my neck and making my insides clench.

'Why do you keep saying things like that? I told you,

we're just friends.'

'Let's just say I'm sceptical.'

'She's never been to London. When I said I was coming here for business she asked if she could come with me, and I agreed. It was easier than having her pester me until I gave in. She can be quite persistent when she wants something.'

'Yes, well, it all sounded very cosy at your end when we spoke on the phone earlier. How did she take you climbing off her and coming here to me?'

'Is that what you think? That I'd sleep with her and then leave her in my bed to take a phone call from you? Is that the kind of man you think I am, Abigail?'

I looked up at our reflection in the kitchen window in front of me. The handsome millionaire businessman and me.

'I don't know what kind of man you are, Jack. I don't know you.' I needed to get out of his arms, but I was hemmed in. I could feel his body pressed against mine.

'Bullshit,' he said, his voice low in my ear. He leaned closer and I felt as if I was sinking into him. For a moment, I was tempted to just stay there, to lean my head back against his shoulder and see what could happen next. But what would have been the point of that? I saw him watching my reflection in the window.

'Thinking about how you can get away from me again?'

I turned around to face him, hoping that would make

him take a step back but it didn't; he stood firm but released his grip on the countertop and placed his hands on my waist. We were practically nose to nose. His gaze was locked on mine. He was waiting for something from me, my permission to go further, but I didn't give it; I couldn't.

'Let me go please, Jack.'

He didn't speak, just let his arms drop from my sides, and returned to his seat at the kitchen table. He took a sip of his tea before he eventually spoke.

'Why do you keep insisting on pushing me away? You and I have a connection, you know it as well as I do, but you keep denying it and I can't figure out why. Explain it to me, would you?' He eyed me closely over the rim of his mug and waited for my response; I didn't know what to tell him. How could I explain it to him when I didn't really understand it myself?

'Would you like another cup of tea?'

I saw the telltale muscle in his jaw tighten as he clenched his teeth.

'Goddamn it, Abigail, no, I don't want any more fucking tea.'

'Then I think it's time for you to go, don't you?'

'No,' he said simply. 'Tell me about your father.'

'You're not going to leave until I do, are you?'

'Nope.' He leaned back in his chair and folded his arms across his chest. Get it over with, Abby, tell him everything and then he can leave. I moved to sit across from him at the table.

'I don't know where to start. A police officer came here today. She had a box of Dad's things, from his cell, she said. She was here yesterday too, with the prison chaplain. They told Mum about Dad dying and then they left.'

'They couldn't have known what would happen to her, Abigail – no one could.'

'I know. I assumed it was the shock of getting the news that caused her collapse, but I was so wrong.'

Jack looked puzzled.

'She knew all along where he was. The box that the officer brought had letters in it she'd written, photos of all of us that she'd sent to him over the years. Baby pictures of Lucy, pictures of me and Matt.'

'Jesus! This is… I mean… I don't know what to say. I can't believe it. Surely someone must have said something to you, or Matt?'

'Matt already knew,' I said. 'Mum told him years ago.' I started pushing biscuit crumbs around the table top. I'd managed to scoop up quite a pile before Jack's hands closed over mine and held them tight. His touch was warm and reassuring.

'They shouldn't have kept that from you. That wasn't fair.'

'I don't think fair ever really came into it. Mum was trying to protect me from the truth about Dad and what he'd done. She wanted me to carry on loving him. She didn't want to destroy what few memories I still had. In a weird way, I think I understand. I've done the same thing with Lucy. I've always tried to keep the worst of Martin's behaviour away from her, to protect her.'

The mention of Martin's name made Jack's eyes darken.

'The other night, outside the café, you told me that Martin had hit you.'

'Do we have to go over all that again?' I rubbed between my eyebrows, trying to ease the thumping in my head. 'I really don't want to talk about my disastrous romantic past.'

'It's just hard for me to hear shit like that,' said Jack.

'It was even harder for me when he gave me a black eye and a suspected broken cheekbone. But I can see how difficult just hearing about it could be for you,' I replied, my voice dripping with sarcasm.

Jack looked embarrassed. 'You know I didn't mean it like that... I'm sorry... I didn't mean to sound patronising. Forgive me.'

'Forget it. I'm just tired. I didn't mean to be a bitch.'

'You weren't. I had no right to say that.' We stood in awkward silence for a moment until Jack finally spoke. 'I just can't reconcile the girl I knew with the girl that ended up with the likes of him.'

I shook my head, sadly. 'Yeah, well, what can I say? The girl you knew disappeared a long time ago.'

'Not to me. I still see her, every time I look at you.

She's still there.'

'That's a nice idea but it's not true. It's like what you said the other night, about how you were expecting all the shops to look the same as when you left. In your mind, nothing's changed here. But in reality, everything is different. You, me, everything. It's just the way things are now.'

'It doesn't have to be.'

'But it is. Face it, Jack. You left, and as far as I can see you got yourself a pretty fantastic life. But I stayed and ended up with a different life. It's not exactly the stuff of fairy tales but I've done all right. Martin Church notwithstanding. And don't give me that look.'

'What look?'

'Like I'm some pathetic little girl that you need to feel sorry for. It's irritating.'

He held up his hands. 'I didn't mean to irritate you.'

'Well, you did,' I snapped. 'It's ancient history, over and done with, and I don't want to talk about it anymore. All right?'

Jack nodded but he wasn't quite finished with this topic. 'Just so you know, though, if I ever see Martin again, I will kill him.'

I started to laugh but stopped when I realised he was serious.

'Don't say stuff like that, Jack. I don't like it. It would make you no better than him and we both know that's not who you are.'

'So now you're saying you do know me after all? You are a mass of contradictions, Abigail.'

'All part of the wonder that is me,' I said, smiling, attempting to lighten the mood. Thankfully he took my cue to move the conversation on to a new topic.

'What's going to happen now? With your dad, I mean?'

'Matt and I have two funerals to organise, I suppose. What else can we do?'

'I'm really sorry about your mum.'

His comment brought me up short – for a moment I'd forgotten all about it. That sounded awful but it was true. Thoughts of Dad, Martin and my train-wreck of a life had momentarily pushed Mum out of my head. But Jack's words of sympathy brought her loss to the front of my mind and a wave of grief rushed in to fill the void, like sea water flooding a rock pool. My eyes filled with tears and I couldn't stop them from falling. In an instant Jack was out of his chair and standing in front of me.

'Please don't cry, my beautiful girl. I'm here.'

His gorgeous face was so full of concern and affection. Reaching out, I touched his cheek. He pressed his face into my hand and then kissed my palm ever so gently.

'Please just let me in, Abigail. I want to be here for you.'

His heartfelt plea tipped me over the edge and I couldn't fight it any more. Slowly I leaned forward and kissed him gently on the lips; this was all the encouragement he needed. He took my face in his hands, his thumbs gently brushing away the tears on my cheeks, and he lowered his mouth to mine. He returned my kiss gently at first but gradually the kiss deepened. His mouth devoured mine, as if he couldn't get enough of me, and I returned his fervour. I wanted more, so I slid my hands under his shirt to feel his hard body. I was rewarded with a low growl from him as he tore his mouth away from mine. We were both breathing heavily; Jack's eyes were dark and full of intent. Swiftly he lifted me up, encouraging me to wrap my legs around his waist, as he walked us backwards and we slammed into the kitchen wall. I could feel the full force of his body pressed against mine and he trailed kisses down my neck as I grabbed fistfuls of his shirt and held him tightly. It felt so good, so right, as if I'd just been waiting for him to come back to me.

'God, you are amazing. You're so beautiful, Abigail. Look at me. Look at what you do to me. I'm a mess when it comes to you. I can't stay away.' His mouth claimed mine in a powerful kiss and I could feel just how much he meant what he said. But what about Lexie? Did he tell her the same things? My logical mind snapped back into action – what the hell was I thinking? This couldn't happen.

'Jack, stop, please, we can't do this.' At first, I thought he hadn't heard me as he didn't release me from his grip, but when he pulled back to look at me I could see the hurt and confusion in his eyes. He lowered me to the floor and stalked across to the sink, his knuckles white as he gripped the edge of the counter.

'I'm sorry, Jack, I just can't...'

'Can't what? What can't you do?' He whirled round to face me. 'Can't bring yourself to be near me? Can't get over the fact that I left and somehow you think that makes this—' he gestured back and forth between us '—impossible to even consider. What is it?'

'You should go. Go back to Lexie, go back to your life.'

'Is that it? Is this about Lexie? I told you, Abigail, that's nothing. Why won't you believe me? What do I have to do to convince you?'

'It's not nothing. She loves you. I heard her calling your name when we were speaking on the phone earlier. She was there with you.'

'Goddamn it, Abigail! I have a suite of rooms at the hotel. She has one of those rooms. I wasn't sharing a bed with her.'

He walked towards me and I instinctively backed away. I didn't get far; I hit the kitchen table and I was stuck. He stood in front of me, effectively preventing my escape, looking as weary as I felt.

'I can't control how Lexie feels about me. As far as I'm concerned, we're just good friends. She's a sweet kid but that's all. There could never be anything between us, especially not now. I knew that the minute I saw you at that party the other night. I don't want anyone else, Abigail. I only want you.'

'That's how you feel now but you're getting caught up in memories, that's all. It's not real, it's in the past and you need to forget about it.'

'That's bullshit and you know it. The way I feel about you isn't just fucking nostalgia. It's more than that.'

I shook my head. 'I can't take the chance that you'll wake up tomorrow and realise I was right. I'm not willing to risk it, Jack. I'm not strong enough.'

He stepped away from me with a pained look on his face.

'I want you, Abigail, more than I've ever wanted anyone, I think. But I can see that you're not going to believe me. I'll go if you really want me to but be careful – if I leave now, then I won't be back. I'm not a masochist and I don't enjoy being tormented.'

'And I don't enjoy being bullied,' I replied. 'I'm not trying to torment you, Jack. I'm trying to be realistic about our situation. It would never work and I'm getting too old to mess around like a teenager. If that means that we can't at least be friends then so be it, but that's your decision not mine.' My voice was full of a strength that I didn't really feel but I was grateful I could at least muster the appearance of a backbone for the moment. Fuck him and his ultimatums. He shook his head and then leaned in to kiss me on the cheek.

'Goodbye, Abigail. Take care of yourself.'

And with that he walked away, down the hallway and out of the door without looking back. I sank to the kitchen floor in an ungainly heap and started to cry.

Chapter 16

It was amazing how time flew when you were organising the funeral of your mother and long-lost father. It had been almost two weeks since Jack had left me in that pathetic heap on the kitchen floor and he'd kept his promise; I'd heard nothing from him. I'd like to say that I hadn't given him a minute's thought but that would be a lie. There had been plenty of nights in the last couple of weeks where I'd replayed that last scene between us and imagined it ending very differently. In my fantasy, I didn't stop him from kissing me and we ended up making love right there on the kitchen floor. I didn't have stretch marks or saggy bits and he adored every inch of me. But that was only in my head, of course. I was sure the reality would have been somewhat different. He'd probably have taken one look and run a mile, right back to sexy Lexie. But I'd never know now, would I? Whatever the fantasy, I knew I couldn't waste any more time on what might have been. I needed to deal with my life the way it really was, rather than the way I wished it could be.

I shook away thoughts of Jack and tried to focus on the situation in hand. I was late – I should already have been at Mum's house. There was a bit of good old East End tradition to get out of the way before the funeral tomorrow – my parents were coming home to spend their last night in our old house. I'd been against the whole idea at first; I wanted to remember Mum as she was and I certainly didn't want the first time I saw my Dad in twenty years to be when he was laid out in a coffin looking like a waxwork version of himself, but Matt had insisted.

'It's tradition, Abs, and that's how she wanted it done,' he'd said. I didn't feel as if I could argue; he knew so much more about Mum's wishes than I did.

Our family had always followed the same ritual when it came to funerals: the body was brought home, in an open casket, so friends and relatives could come and pay their respects. The one exception to this that I could remember had been Great-uncle Freddie – he'd blown his head off with a shotgun so an open casket would not have been the best choice.

When my grandad had died, my nan had insisted he be laid out at home for almost a week before the funeral. The house had been freezing because all the windows had been wide open to keep it cool. I'd overheard the funeral director telling one of his colleagues that if his body had lain there much longer we wouldn't have been able to get the smell of death out of the house. It might well have been a family tradition, but it didn't mean I had to like it. I'd made it very clear to my brother that I had no intention of sitting by their coffins all night. I was going to stay in the kitchen, making tea and washing up cups, and nodding politely when people expressed their condolences.

We'd already had a few strange phone calls from people claiming to have been 'business associates' of Dad's – I assumed that was just a handy euphemism for criminal – and they all seemed very interested in coming to view his corpse. What fun.

I took a last look in the mirror. I couldn't put it off any longer; it was time to go. I left the flat and walked along the landing, feeling as if I were wading through water. I was walking into the sea, fighting against the tide to make any kind of progress. I made my way down the concrete stairs at the end of the landing and out onto the street.

As I walked past familiar front doors and shops, I looked down at my feet stepping over the same kerbs and cracks as they had done when I was fifteen. I'd get off the bus at the top of the road and walk the last bit home, usually with Jack. He'd been such an important part of my life then and when he'd left I'd been lost for a long time. I'd got over it though, eventually. I'd managed to forget how important he'd been to me. His recent reappearance in my life had disturbed my carefully cultivated peace, made me remember feelings that I'd rather forget, and his most recent absence had almost turned me into that sad and lonely fifteen-year old all over again. I felt raw and vulnerable and I hated him for coming back and doing this to me, but I hated myself even more for letting it happen.

But this is what you wanted, Abby. You said you weren't strong enough to face the inevitable end and you sent him away. You said it would be better that way. Does it feel better?

I pulled my coat tighter around my body to ward off the sudden chill I felt.

*

There was a black van parked outside the house when I arrived; two very sombre-looking men were fiddling around with some flowers in the back. I walked past them and into the house.

The coffins were already in the front room. I could see them out of the corner of my eye as I passed the door. I didn't linger; I went down the hallway and into the kitchen. Matt was there, filling the kettle, and I saw four mugs on the side.

'It's started already, has it?' I asked, placing my coat and bag onto a kitchen chair. Matt turned when he heard my voice.

'Hey, I didn't know you were here. Yeah, just making a cuppa for the gents in the living room. It's the least I can do.' He flicked the kettle on to boil and came over to give me a hug. We stood there for a few minutes, neither of us keen to break the contact.

'I know you're not totally comfortable with all this, Abs. I just felt like I had to do it, for her,' he mumbled into my shoulder.

'I know, I get it. I'm just not ready to go in there.'

He nods and swipes away a tear. 'What about Lucy? Is she coming?'

I shook my head. 'She doesn't want to see them, not like this. She's keeping an eye on the café for me.' I knew I had no right to try and force her. 'She said she didn't want her last memory of her Nan to be the image of her in a coffin.'

'Fair enough,' Matt sighed. 'Better get this tea done for them,' he says, pulling away from me. He started putting teabags into the mugs.

'Don't do it like that. It'll be better if you make a pot.' I opened the cupboard next to the fridge and pulled out the old brown teapot. I put the teabags in and then poured on the hot water.

'Can't give them weak tea, can we?' I said.

Matt laughed. 'Ha! That's one of the things I do remember about Dad – he hated weak tea. Piss-water, he called it. He had his so strong you could stand your spoon up in it.'

'And he always used the same cup. Never washed it, just rinsed it out under the hot tap between drinks,' I said, surprised to find that memory so readily available. 'The inside of that cup was so brown no one else would go near it.'

Mum had lobbed that mug at the kitchen wall a few days after he'd left; that was where that fond recollection ended, in pieces on the kitchen floor. Oblivious as to where my treacherous memory had just taken me, Matt poured the tea and took the mugs to the men in the living room. Shoving unhappy thoughts to one side, I busied myself wiping down the worktop where he'd spilt milk and sugar.

'Sorry to disturb you. I just wanted to come and see how you are.'

I turned to see one of the funeral directors standing in the doorway.

'Your brother tells me you're not keen on the idea of having your parents here.' He looked at me quizzically, as if there was something wrong with not wanting to share a house with two dead bodies. He looked young. I'd always assumed that funerals were an old man's job. Wearing a black three-piece suit and a black tie, he looked very smart and respectful. His comment annoyed me; surely how I felt about all this was up to me, wasn't it?

'I don't mean to imply anything by that – please forgive me if that's how it came across.' He had a very nice voice; deep and soothing. I imagined it would come in handy for calming grieving relatives in situations like this. He wasn't that bad-looking either but perhaps it was the suit; I've always been a sucker for a nice suit.

And good shoes – good shoes were very important. I glanced down at his feet: black, nicely polished but not too shiny. What was I doing? The man was organising a funeral, for God's sake. Was I so sex-starved that this was what I'd been reduced to? Perving over the funeral director?

'No, you didn't... I mean... it's fine...' I babbled like an idiot and he smiled kindly at me.

'It's a difficult time for all of you. And it's quite a unique situation, as I understand it.' He was trying to be tactful but I couldn't let it go.

'You mean because sitting with my father's corpse in the living room will be the most contact I've had with him in the last twenty years,' I snapped. 'Yes, I suppose that counts as a unique situation.'

He looked down at his feet, unsure of what to say next.

'I'm sorry,' I mumbled. 'That was very rude of me.'

'No, it's fine. I'm the one that should be apologising. There was no need for me to mention it.' He drained his mug and put it into the sink. 'Thank you for the tea,' he said and walked out of the kitchen. What a bitch I was. The poor man was only trying to be sympathetic. The people-pleaser in me wanted to go and apologise but that would have meant going into the other room and I wasn't ready for that. Matt came back into the kitchen with empty mugs.

'Thirsty work huh?'

He just nodded, as he filled the sink with water.

'Everything all right?

He was concentrating intently on scrubbing out a mug. I thought he hadn't heard me but then he mumbled, 'Yeah, just a bit weird to see them both in there, laid out like that.'

My new friend appeared at the kitchen door before I could reply.

'We're all done now, Mr Cowan. We'll be back tomorrow for the last part of Mum and Dad's journey.' He gave a respectful little nod and then walked away. I heard the front door go and then there was silence; we were alone with our parents and neither one of us knew what to do. Matt went back to scrubbing mugs in the sink and wiped down the worktop even though it was spotless. A knock at the front door saved us from having to talk about the elephants, or should I say bodies, in the room.

'Fuck me,' Matt exclaimed, 'were they just hanging about outside waiting for the van to go or what?'

'Probably. You'd better let them in before they start forming a queue down the street.'

Matt took a deep breath and plastered on a smile, before walking to the front door. I heard him greet my mum's deaf neighbour warmly, and loudly.

*

The flow of well-wishers, and those just morbidly curious, kept up for most of the day. They ranged from close friends to casual acquaintances that I either didn't know or just didn't remember. I stayed in the kitchen, much to the bewilderment of a few guests who tried to persuade me to go with them into the living room. People kept making it their mission to get me to see my parents; it became like a challenge to see which one of them would finally succeed. But I stayed put, content to make tea, slice cake and deal with the washing-up.

'Everything all right out here, darlin'?' Flo came into the kitchen carrying some dirty plates and cups. She dropped them into the sink, rolled up her sleeves and then plunged her hands into the soapy water.

'You don't need to do that, Flo. I can manage.'

She shook her head. 'I don't mind. I'd rather be in here, with you. It's a bit odd in the other room, to be honest. People standing around chatting and drinking tea with your mum and dad all laid out.' She gave a slight shudder. 'I know it's what she wanted but it still gives me the willies. Always did.'

I didn't have to explain how I felt about all this to her; she knew already. She'd found me hiding in the kitchen when she'd arrived. Flo finished washing up and dried her hands before coming over to me. She smoothed a stray hair away from my face and smiled.

'You look so much like her sometimes it's frightening.'

'Really? I've never thought that.'

'She was only a few years older than you are now when your dad went away.'

'I know.'

'She was still young. She thought she had a lifetime to spend with the man she loved and then he was gone.'

'I think we had more in common than I wanted to believe. I know what being a single parent feels like but I don't know how I would have handled what happened to her. I had some say in what happened to me, I threw Martin out, but she had that decision made for her. There was nothing she could do about it.'

It made me feel so desperately sad for her; left to deal with two teenagers, gossip and the disapproving stares of friends and relatives.

'I wish I could take back all the shitty things I said to her over the years. If she'd just told me the truth we could have sorted it out, made things right between us.'

'I know, dear, and so did she. You don't have to feel guilty – she wouldn't want you to.'

I sniffed back a few tears. 'Despite everything, I think I'm a little envious of her, envious that she had someone in her life that she loved so much, a man she cared so deeply for that she stayed loyal to him for twenty years. That kind of love is a rare thing.'

'It certainly is but I don't know that it really did her any good in the end. She sacrificed so much for your dad, the rest of her life, her relationship with you, they all suffered because of her devotion to him. To a man who wouldn't even return her letters. Still, she made her choices and she had to live with them. Same as we all do in the end.'

She gave me a weak little smile and then ambled down the hallway. I watched her as she stopped briefly at the living room doorway before gathering herself and going in.

*

I was waiting for the kettle to boil for at least the hundredth time that day, when I was joined in the kitchen by an older gentleman in a dark overcoat and trilby hat. He looked as if he'd just stepped out of a gangster movie. I guessed he was about the same age as my parents and I thought I vaguely recognised him. He had broad shoulders and his face was tanned but wrinkled, as if he'd spent too much time in the sun. He didn't speak to me at first; he went and sat in one of the chairs by the kitchen table, just watching me as I moved round the room. After a few minutes, I couldn't stand it any longer; the silence was too uncomfortable.

'Did you know them well?'

He didn't reply, he just removed his hat, stroked away a piece of fluff from its brim and placed it on the table before raising his eyes to me.

'Don't you remember me, then, Abby?'

'Er, no, I'm sorry, I'm afraid I don't.' The way he was looking at me made me feel a bit uneasy but I was curious about him. He certainly looked familiar, but it was his voice that I recognised more than anything else. I'd heard it somewhere before but I couldn't place it.

'It's been a long time. I'm not surprised you can't remember me. I was a good friend of your dad's, and your mum. I haven't been around much these last few years – got myself a nice little place in Spain, you see. Had to get away from the crappy British winters.'

That explained why he looked like a bit of wrinkled shoe leather: too much sun and sangria, obviously. 'How did you hear about the funeral? If you live abroad, I mean.'

'A mutual friend read the notice in the local paper and got in touch with me. I flew straight back as soon as I heard.' The man stood, unbuttoning his coat and taking it off, before laying it neatly over the back of a chair. Underneath the coat he was wearing a white shirt and I could clearly see the tattoos that covered his arms and chest showing through the fabric. Diamond studded cufflinks twinkled at his wrists and a large gold sovereign decorated the middle finger of his left hand.

'I'm sorry, I didn't catch your name?'

'Don't be sorry, Abby,' he said, with a smile that reminded me of a snake about to swallow its prey. 'The name's Terry, Terry Egan.'

Egan? I remembered that name from when I was

growing up. The Egans had been a bit notorious. They'd always passed themselves off as innocent scrap-metal dealers, but everyone had known they were no such thing. Two of the Egan boys, Joe and Michael, had gone to my school although they were older than me, so I hadn't really had much to do with them. I'd had no idea that our families were friends. But that voice; I couldn't explain it but there was something about that voice that made me feel anxious.

I could hear my brother saying goodbye to some people at the front door; everyone else had gone. I was relieved to see him walking down the hallway towards the kitchen. 'Finally,' he exclaimed. 'I thought we'd be at this all night.' He stopped abruptly as he entered the kitchen and saw we still had company.

'Matt, this is a friend of Dad's, Terry—'

'Terry Egan. I know who you are.' My brother's voice was hard and cold.

'Well, well, Little Matthew Turner. You've grown into quite a strapping young man, ain't ya?'

My brother's hands balled into fists at his sides, as if he was about to take a swing at the mystery man in our kitchen. What the hell was going on?

'Mr Egan has come all the way from Spain to pay his respects, Matt. He says he was a good friend of Dad's but I'm afraid I must seem rude because I don't remember him.' Matt hadn't taken his eyes off Egan.

'Not at all, darlin', not rude at all. It's been a long

time. You were a lot younger when I was hanging around with your dad. No reason you should remember all that. Is there, Matthew?' Egan walked across to my brother; the pair of them were practically toe to toe.

'You should leave, Mr Egan,' said Matt. 'I suspect you've got what you came for now, haven't you?'

A lazy smile spread across Egan's face as he looked my brother up and down one more time before turning to pick up his coat. He took his time putting it on, adjusting the cuffs of his shirt so the glint of diamonds in his cufflinks was obvious, and then he picked up his hat. Matt was watching him intently, coiled like a cat ready to pounce. The tension in the room was palpable.

'I certainly did, Matthew, thank you.'

'What's he talking about, Matt? What did he come here for?'

'I came here to make sure your dad was really dead, my dear. And luckily for him, he is.' Egan put on his hat and turned to walk out of the room. 'I'll let myself out for now, but I'll be in touch.'

'For what reason?' asked Matt.

'Oh, I've got a million reasons, actually.'

He looked me up and down and then, with a last oily smile, he walked away.

After I heard the front door slam, I was frozen to the spot. My brother relaxed his fists and leant up against the kitchen counter.

'What the fuck was all that about?' I demanded.

'Nothing, Abby, just leave it. It's done now.'

'What's done? What are you going on about?'

'For Christ's sake – just let it go!' he shouted, stalking out of the room. I followed behind him, clipping at his heels like an annoying puppy. I'd followed him into the living room before I could stop myself and I was confronted by the sight of my parents, laid out in their wicker boxes, looking like two life-size dolls. Their faces had that artificial bloom in the cheeks and lips. Mortician's make up, and whatever other chemicals had been pumped through their systems, had smoothed out the lines around their mouths and foreheads. It was ironic that my mum should have fewer wrinkles now than when she was alive, I thought to myself.

My brother was sitting in one of the fold-up chairs that the funeral company had left by the side of Mum's coffin. Between the caskets, at the top end, there was a substantial wooden crucifix and two large fresh flower arrangements on either side of the fireplace. The living-room windows were open, and I could hear sounds from the street outside. Although it was starting to get dark, there were still kids playing on the patch of grass across the road. I walked over to the window and looked out at them enjoying the last bit of daylight. A couple of boys were playing football and a small group of girls were sitting on the grass watching them. One of the boys was skilfully manoeuvring his way to the far end of the field and the makeshift goal they'd set up there. He kicked the ball and it curved high into the air and over the poor goalie's head. The goalkeeper held his head in his hands and shouted something to his teammates that I couldn't hear. The lucky scorer jogged over to one of the girls and was rewarded with a kiss. I didn't know them, didn't know anything about their lives or their circumstances, but, in that moment at least, they appeared to be carefree and happy. I think I could remember feeling that way once, as if anything was possible if you just wanted it enough. In my head it didn't feel like that long ago; in reality it might as well have been another lifetime.

'What else is there you're not telling me, Matt?' I stayed facing the window; I didn't want to look at him if he was about to tell me another lie.

'It's nothing, Abby, it's not important. Nothing for you to worry about.'

'And yet strangely I find myself worried anyway.' A black 4X4 drove past the window and for a minute my heart leapt to think that it might be Jack, but the car didn't even slow down.

'I asked you not to keep anything else from me, didn't I? And yet here we are with more shit to deal with.' I turned to face my brother. He nodded. 'So, I'm asking you again. What are you not telling me?'

There was a long silence before my brother finally spoke.

'Terry Egan is my dad, Abby.'

Chapter 17

I grabbed blindly at the window ledge behind me as the room started to spin.

'That man is your dad. I don't understand... How is that...? I mean... Oh, God.' I slapped my hand across my mouth. I was going to throw up. I ran down the hallway to the toilet and made it just in time. I retched again and again until there was nothing left for me to bring up. Matt came and knelt beside me, stroking my hair, and I slid into his lap and sobbed into his chest.

'Every shirt I've had on for the last few days has ended up with your tears wiped on it,' he said.

'Think yourself lucky I don't wear as much make-up as most of the girls in your life – things could be a lot messier.' I crawled across the floor and pulled the roll of toilet paper off the holder. Unravelling way too much, I blew my nose on it. The horribly acidic taste of vomit lingered in my mouth, sticking to my teeth. I shuffled over to the sink and turned on the tap, cupping handfuls of water into my mouth. The reflection in the mirror above was one of a tired-looking middle-aged woman; it was a face I was quickly becoming all too familiar with.

'I need a drink,' I said. 'Wanna join me?'

'Fuck yeah.'

I pulled him up off the floor and we went to the kitchen. I took a bottle of wine from the fridge and grabbed a beer for Matt. Once we were settled at the table, we raised our drinks to each other.

'Cheers,' he said, taking a long mouthful of his beer.

'Up yours,' I replied. I took a large gulp of my wine and then waited for Matt to start talking. He didn't; he just picked at the label around the top of his bottle and avoided making eye contact with me.

'Come on, Matt!' I exclaimed. 'How long have you known?' I wasn't sure what answer I wanted. I looked across at him – my brother – the only man I thought had never let me down. He took another swig of his beer before he spoke.

'Since I was eighteen. Almost a year after Dad… erm… went away.'

'How did you find out?'

'Mum told me. I'd been out late and drinking a bit too much. We were arguing and I said something about how she couldn't stop me doing what I wanted 'cos I was a grown-up. Typical arrogant teenage-boy crap.' He cringed at the memory. 'That's when she screamed at me that maybe she should call my real dad and he could come and give me the arse-kicking I deserved.'

'How come you never said anything to me?'

'She regretted telling me the instant the words left her mouth. She was so upset, she made me swear never to tell you. She knew how close we were; she didn't want anything to change that.'

'And she thought more lies would be better? Jesus, this is unbelievable!'

Matt reached across the table and tried to take my hand. I shrugged him off and he went back to nursing his beer.

'She only ever wanted to protect you, Abby. She thought she was doing the right thing. It was in the past. Nothing any of us could do about it.'

'Have you ever met him before? Egan, I mean.'

'I'd seen him around – his sons were about my age – but I knew what everyone used to say about the Egans and what they got up to. I didn't want to broadcast the fact that he was my real dad. I remember him coming to the house a few times when Dad was still around.'

That was it! That was why I recognised his voice. It was a few months before Dad left; I remembered hearing shouting coming from the kitchen. Two voices, one was Dad and the other belonged to Terry Egan. I couldn't remember what was said – from my place at the top of the stairs I couldn't hear everything – but I could remember the tone of his voice; it was so full of anger and violence.

'What was all that stuff about making sure Dad was really dead? What did he do to piss him off so badly that he'd want him dead?'

'Terry Egan was part of the crew that robbed the

security truck. Dad worked for him but if anyone had reason to be pissed off it should have been Dad.'

'How do you mean?'

'Once the police started sniffing around after the robbery, Egan just disappeared. Went to Spain and left everyone else to take the blame.'

'What happened to all the others? You said there were six of them.'

Matt drained his beer. 'They're all gone, Abs. Only Dad went to prison. He turned himself in for some reason. Dunno why. Never got to the bottom of that one. He could have buggered off to the Costa Del Crime like Egan did and lived a long life off the money they nicked. But he didn't.'

'How long have you known about what Dad did? About where he was?'

I could tell that my brother was weighing up the pro and cons of what he was about to tell me.

'Don't baby me, not now. The truth, please,' I said.

'It was about a year or so after he left.'

I was shocked. 'Mum could barely string a sentence together at that point, she was so depressed. How the hell did you manage to get her to talk to you about all that?'

'Mum wasn't the one who told me, Abby. It was Keith.'

'Keith from the gym?' Matt's former employer, now his business partner, had been almost like a substitute father to him over the years. I credited his influence for keeping Matt in line and ensuring that he hadn't gone the way of some of his former school friends.

'I was always hanging around the gym, even before I got my job there, and I was young but I wasn't stupid. I saw how blokes would come and go, some of them would work out but lots of them wouldn't. They'd come, disappear into the locker room and then leave again. I knew they were obviously dealing drugs out of the gym and so did Keith, but he didn't seem to be able to stop it.' Matt got up from the table and started pacing the room as he spoke.

'One night a fight broke out in the locker room. I think one of the Egan boys was involved – he stabbed another bloke. I wanted to call the police but Keith stopped me, said that it would be taken care of, and then he made a comment about how none of this would have happened if John Turner had still been around to run things.'

'Dad never had anything to do with the gym.'

'He didn't mean running the gym, he meant running "things".' Matt gestured to the whole room. It took me a minute to figure out what he was getting at.

'Wait, you mean Dad was some sort of local gangster or something? Like… I dunno… The Krays?' It was crazy.

'No, not as bad as all that, but I think he was involved in plenty of dodgy stuff over the years.'

Matt took another beer from the fridge and came to sit back down at the table with me. My head was spinning and it wasn't from the wine. It was surreal. My whole world had been turned on its head and my immediate reaction was to giggle like an idiot. I laughed so hard, I couldn't seem to stop. It was like something out of a film, a very bad film with cops and robbers and shady deals in dark alleyways. This was not my life. I could tell Matt wasn't quite seeing the funny side, so I took another mouthful of wine and swallowed down my hysterics.

'Keith panicked, realised he'd said more than he should and he tried to backtrack. But I knew what I'd heard and I made him tell me everything.'

'Even then I wasn't sure whether to believe him or not. It was only when I confronted Mum about it that I knew. She didn't have to say too much; I could tell from her expression that it was the truth. That's when she begged me to help her protect you from finding out.'

I didn't need to go over all that again; if I had to hear any more about how my mother thought that lying to me was a good idea I was going to lose my marbles. I changed the subject back to Egan.

'Mum had an affair with that... that... man.' This amazed me; I couldn't believe she would have had anything to do with a man like that.

'She told me it wasn't an affair; it was just one drunken night. She'd had a bad fight with Dad and—'

I interrupted him. 'And so she went and slept with someone else?'

My brother just shrugged. 'There's no point getting all judgemental about it now, Abs. It's done with. Can't change it.'

He was being so calm about it all, but then he'd had a bit more time to get used to it – about twenty years more.

'Did Dad know?'

Matt didn't speak, he just nodded. I needed more wine. I got up from the table and poured myself another glass; I'd drunk more in the last three weeks than I had in the last three years.

'This doesn't change who we are to each other, you know that, don't you?' I said.

'I've known about all this for years and it's never made a difference to me.'

I smiled at his answer and went to put my arms around him. 'I love you, you know that, don't you?' I squeezed him tight.

'Blimey, Abs, give me some room to breathe, you daft cow. You're strangling me.'

I laughed and released him a little but not totally. I could feel the tears starting to come and my throat was so tight I could barely breathe.

'Hey, what's all this?' Matt turned round in his chair and pulled me onto his lap. I buried my face in his neck and carried on crying. After a few minutes of listening to me sob he leant back and I was forced to look at him. He had such an earnest look on his face that I almost started to cry again.

'It's just too much. Mum, Dad, all this.' I gestured towards the living room. 'I can't take it all in.'

'And Jack? Are you upset about him too?'

'What? No, of course not.' I shook my head. 'He's the last thing on my mind.'

Matt raised an eyebrow at my reply. 'Really? Are you sure about that?'

'Of course I am. I've got too much other stuff to be dealing with to worry about him and whatever he's doing. I don't expect I'll be hearing from him again.' A horribly leaden feeling settled in the pit of my stomach as I said those words. Wiping my face, I stood up and busied myself putting away cups and plates. Any hopes I had that Matt would take that as a hint to drop the subject were dashed by his next announcement.

'He came to see me, you know – Jack, I mean. He came to the gym.' Matt gave me a sheepish smile and held up his hands. 'I know, I know. I should have told you.'

I shrugged as if I didn't care, as if I weren't desperate to find out what he'd said. I carried on clearing away and when I was done I turned to face him.

'What did he want to see you for?' I asked, in my best attempt at nonchalance.

'I'm not really sure, to be honest. He didn't say much.

He was only there for a few minutes. Long enough to say he was leaving and to say he was worried about you, about how you were dealing with everything that was going on.'

Worried about me? His concern would probably have been more plausible if he'd been in touch at all since he'd left. Not so much as a text message in the last two weeks and yet I was supposed to believe that he was so concerned about my welfare that he had to go and see my brother.

'Well, how nice,' I snapped, 'and what else did the two of you chat about during this visit?'

'Nothing. He didn't want to talk about anything except you, really. Made it clear that I needed to make sure you were looked after and then he left,' Matt said, with a shrug.

'How dare he?'

'I don't think he meant anything by it. He was obviously worried about you. He did mention something about you and your drinking habits, which I thought was funny, but...' Matt gestured towards my empty wine glass on the side.

'Don't be bloody ridiculous, Matt. I don't drink that much. He's got some bloody nerve.' I was so angry I felt like pouring myself another glass of wine just to prove a point, but I didn't.

'All right, all right, just saying.'

'Well, don't!' I picked up the half-empty wine bottle

off the side and tipped its contents into the sink.

'You don't need to worry about my drinking habits just because Jack told you to. That man has no right to any opinions on me or what I do with my life.'

'Fine, sorry I mentioned it.'

'I should bloody well think so. You know me better than anyone.'

'I do, but I also know that a lot has changed for you, for both of us, in the last few weeks. It's been hard trying to deal with all this shit.'

'I'm not planning on turning into an alcoholic any time soon, so don't worry.'

Matt came over and planted a kiss on my forehead before walking to the kitchen door.

'I can't stop being your big brother, Abby. I just want to make sure you're all right.'

'I'm fine.'

'Yes, so you keep saying. I'm not sure I believe you, though, that's the problem.'

'Go to bed and stop fussing.' I waved him away.

'All right, then. Need my beauty sleep before tomorrow. Goodnight, Midget.'

'It'll take more than a few hours' sleep to improve your face, you ugly bugger!' I yelled. He carried on walking away down the hall, treating me to a two-fingered salute as he went.

'Idiot,' I muttered under my breath.

Chapter 18

After Matt went to bed I sat in the kitchen. The only light was coming from under the cooker hood on the wall opposite me. Almost an hour passed with me just sitting there. I had, albeit briefly, contemplated making myself a cup of tea but I couldn't seem to find the energy or the will to get up from the table. I sat and listened to the sounds of my brother moving around upstairs, getting ready for bed. I heard him in the bathroom, the sound of water running, and teeth being brushed. I heard him turn off the light and climb into the single bed in the spare bedroom. Listening to the creaking of the bedframe, complaining under my brother's weight, and his intermittent swearing as he tried to get comfortable, I didn't feel alone. But the house had gone quiet now and I felt like the only person in the world.

People say that silence is just the absence of noise and most of the time I suppose it is. When you turned down the loud music or switched off the television at the end of the day, the noise disappeared and you were left with a kind of silence; a version of it that still included the distant whoosh of traffic or the occasional faint sound of people outside or sirens in the distance. It wasn't often that you experienced real silence, that dense cloud of nothing that filled your ears as completely as the loudest music could. That was what surrounded me then, sitting in my dead mother's kitchen in the middle of East London, and it was suffocating.

It reminded me of how quiet the house was after Dad left. The only sounds I could remember were my grandad shouting, either at my nan – 'Bring us me fags/Guinness/newspaper, Eileen!' – or at the football on the telly – 'Bloody West Ham! What a shower of shit!' And then my nan shouting back – 'Get 'em yerself, ya fat-nosed bastard! I ain't yer bleedin' skivvy!' And that was it. No memories of music filling the house, or cosy evenings spent watching the telly together. Everyone retreated to their own spaces and stayed there. I came out for food and to go to school and that was it. No one questioned it, no one asked how my day was when I got home. I would drop my bag in the hall, grab a bag of crisps and a drink from the kitchen and then go up to my bedroom. If Matt wasn't off doing God knew what with his mates, he might poke his head round my door; although a cursory 'All right, Midget?' was all I'd get.

Before he left, Jack would come home with me and we'd sit in my room. That was the other amazing thing – I was fifteen and I had a boy in my room and no one cared! All my friends' parents refused to let their boyfriends further than the front room, but not mine. All our classmates were convinced that we must be 'doing it' on a regular basis. We weren't. We did our fair share of snogging and I think Jack might have touched my boobs, such as they were, once or twice. But it was strictly 'over the shirt' action, nothing more. We weren't in any rush; we thought we had all the time in the world. As it turned out we were wrong. Fate was lurking around the corner, just waiting to wreak havoc on our plans for the future.

Everything that had happened in the last few weeks began to play on fast forward in my mind: Jack, Mum and Dad, Terry Egan. My racing brain couldn't seem to stop the sudden inrush and I felt as if my head were about to explode. When my phone buzzed over on the worktop, I leapt out of my chair and grabbed it, grateful for the distraction. The message was from Lucy.

Go to bed Mum.

She knew me too well. I messaged her back.

Am in bed already – don't stress x x.

Almost instantly my phone buzzed with her reply.

Liar! Get to sleep xx.

She was right: sleep was the best thing, but I felt fidgety and restless. My hands were shaking slightly as I turned the kitchen light off and walked to the stairs.

When I reached the bottom step I turned towards the closed living-room door. The faint whirr of an electric fan was the only sound I could hear. The funeral director had told us we should leave it on to keep the room cool. My parents were in there, lying in their wicker caskets, closer together in death than they had been for the last twenty years in life. I heard a car pass by outside and I remembered standing at the living-room window earlier, watching a car I thought might contain Jack drive by the house. The window had been open then – had Matt closed it? I couldn't go to bed and leave it open – what if someone broke in? They'd get a bloody shock, that was for sure, but still.

Terry Egan and his oily smile came into my head; he'd said he'd be back – what if he got into the house? I knew I wouldn't be able to settle upstairs until I was sure that window was locked. I went to the door and slowly pushed it open. Inside, the room was dark, apart from the orange glow cast by the streetlight outside and a battery-operated candle that flickered artificially on the mantelpiece. The window was closed but unless I tested the handle I wouldn't know for certain that it was locked; I had to go into the room.

I tiptoed over to the window – why was I tiptoeing? I wasn't going to wake anyone up, was I? Taking bolder steps, I reached the window and tested the handle – locked. The street outside was quiet and it had been raining. When had that happened? I saw a flash of movement out of the corner of my eye; it was a fat ginger cat. It came to sit on the front garden wall and stared at me: the funny lady peeking out of the curtains in the middle of the night. It tilted its head and eyed me for a few seconds, before it turned, dropped down off the wall and sloped away down the street. I watched it until it turned the corner at the end of the road and was gone. I was envious of that cat; it got to walk away, to go wherever the mood took it, whenever it wanted. I couldn't do that. I was stuck there with two dead parents and no life to speak of, dreading what the next day would bring. That thought was enough to drain away what little energy I had, reminding me that I needed to get some sleep.

I turned away from the window and faced the room; the candle was flickering and I could smell the freesias that were somewhere in the flower arrangements. Freesias had been Mum's favourite; she would always have a little bunch of them in a glass on the kitchen windowsill, because she said they were the only cut flowers that smelled of anything. I looked over at her lying there, looking for all the world as if she were sleeping. I went and kissed her on the forehead. Her skin was cold and hard against my lips and I immediately wished I hadn't done it. It was like kissing a doll. The fan in the corner moved strands of her hair as it sent sweeping draughts across the room. The hair briefly rested on her cheek before being lifted away again. I found myself expecting her to reach up and tuck the wayward bits behind her ear as normal.

I looked across to my dad, reminding myself that nothing about any of this was normal. He was wearing a dark suit and shirt and tie. Matt had dealt with all that; I'd refused to go to the funeral home. I'd felt no urge to see him, which had surprised me. After spending so many years wondering, I'd thought I'd at least be a little curious but I wasn't. It didn't seem real. I'm sure someone far cleverer than me would be able to explain why, but I was choosing not to overthink it. I didn't have the space in my brain for that kind of self-analysis; it was too exhausting. Maybe afterwards, maybe that's when I'll have time to process it all, I thought. Just get through tomorrow and everything will be fine.

Looking at him lying there, I was surprised by how little he'd changed. His hair was peppered with grey, more at the temples, his face was a bit fuller, but it was still the same face I remembered. Looking inside the coffin, I noticed that there was something tucked into my dad's left hand. I reached in and removed it carefully. It was a strip of photographs, taken in a photo-booth; four pictures, all in faded colour, of me and Matt and Mum and Dad. I couldn't remember them being taken – in the pictures I looked about six or seven – but we must have been at the seaside somewhere as Matt was clutching the biggest stick of pink rock I'd ever seen and Dad was holding a cloud of candy floss on a stick. He'd only managed to get half of his face into shot for the first two pictures, but in the last two it was just him and Mum. They were biting opposite sides of the candy floss and laughing. By the next one, the last picture on the strip, they'd eaten the candy floss, or dropped it, and their lips were pressed together. They were trying to keep straight faces and my mum had turned her head slightly towards the camera. The happiness in her eyes was so obvious. It made me yearn to be able to remember them like that. I wanted to be back there, in that little family, before everything got completely messed up. Before the shouting and the smashed plates holding ruined dinners. Before the anger and before the eerie stillness, with Dad gone and Mum hiding in her room.

I was almost tempted to keep the photos as a reminder of better times, but I knew I couldn't. Someone had put them there, probably Matt, and it wouldn't have felt right to sneak them away for my own selfish reasons. Reluctantly, I slipped them back into Dad's hand and walked to the door, sending a whispered 'Goodnight' to my mum and dad.

*

I woke the next day with a terrible headache and an even worse mood; I'd had a crappy night's sleep. I'd been tormented by that dream where you felt as if you were falling and then you wake up suddenly. I was sure I'd read somewhere that it happened when your heart skipped a beat, which sent a signal to your brain for you to wake up – presumably so you didn't die in your sleep. That was probably a load of old rubbish, although I was too exhausted to question it.

The morning brought the kind of grey, murky light that made you want to dive back under the covers; I knew I didn't have that option. Lucy and Matt would not have been very impressed if I'd just refused to get out of bed and sent them off to deal with everything without me.

I'd slept in Mum's old room. Matt had declared that her mattress was too soft and he would be more comfortable in the spare room. Sleeping in her bed hadn't been either of our first choices but there weren't many other options. I'd put different sheets on the bed; the other ones just smelt too much like her. The room still looked as if she were about to walk in; in fact, the whole house was like that. I'd made a few half-arsed attempts at sorting stuff out over the last few weeks, but I'd barely scratched the surface of what needed to be done. I knew I was just putting off the inevitable. After today, I told myself, after they were both gone, I would make a start. Tomorrow, or maybe next week. Or maybe never.

The clock by the bed said it was almost nine; I needed to get dressed. I wearily pulled back the covers and stood up just as my phone started to ring; it was Liz.

'Good morning, my darling, how are you? All ready to face the world?'

'No, not really, I was just wondering if I could get away with staying in bed all day. I'm sure no one would miss me.'

'Nonsense, darling, I would miss you and so would Lucy. She needs you today as much as you need her.'

'More so probably,' I said. It was true; Lucy had been close to my mum, closer than I'd ever managed to be.

'Everything's ready at the café, you know, for afterwards.' Liz faltered a little as she spoke.

'Thank you, for everything.'

'Don't be silly. I'm just glad to have been of some use, that's all,' she said. 'Right, well, I'm going to get dressed and I will see you at the service in a bit.'

'I'll see you soon.' I pressed the end call button and sat with my phone in my hand. I wanted to call Jack but I knew I couldn't. What time was it in America anyway? Middle of the night probably, but what difference did that make? I couldn't call him, not after I'd let him go like that. No matter how desperate I was to have him there with me, to hold me close and tell me everything was going to be all right.

God, that's pathetic, I mentally shook myself. You don't need a man to tell you everything's going to be okay, you are enough, you've got this. You've been doing things on your own for most of your adult life.

Don't turn into some weepy weakling who can't function now.

After giving myself a good old-fashioned bollocking, I took a deep calming breath, threw my phone onto the bed, and started getting ready to face the day.

*

I was just finishing my make-up when I heard a gentle tap on the door; it was Lucy.

'Hey, Mum, you look nice,' she said. 'Is that all right to say to someone at a funeral? Sorry, I'm just... I don't know what...' With that she began to cry.

'Everything's going to be okay. Don't cry,' I said. I made her sit down next to me on the bed; I put my arms around her and rocked her gently back and forth, as much as it was possible to gently rock an eighteen-year-old back and forth anyway. It was nice to be sitting there like that with her; I couldn't begin to imagine what my life was going to be like after she left. I'd be alone in the flat. Who would I have to talk to or just laugh with? The thought of it brought a lump to my throat and I blinked back the tears that were threatening to ruin my eye make-up. What kind of idiot wore mascara at a funeral?

'Look at the pair of you, sat there blubbing. Mum would not have approved.' Matt was leaning against the door frame, watching the two of us. His remark made

Lucy smile and she sat up.

'That's true, she would be shaking her head in disapproval at all this emotion,' Lucy said, scrubbing away tears with the backs of her hands. 'She was always a bit, well, shall we say reserved, when it came to her feelings.'

'That's a fucking understatement, but we don't have enough booze here to talk about it now,' said Matt. 'It's almost time. The cars will be here in a minute.'

I took a deep breath and stood up, holding out my hand for Lucy.

'Ready?'

She nodded and took my hand and we made our way downstairs.

Chapter 19

I'd decided I was a horrible person. I had to be; only a horrible person could get the giggles at their parents' funeral. It all started as they were brought out and placed in their respective hearses. Mum came out first, in her lovely wicker casket, the handles decorated with little posies of ribbon and flowers. All I could think about was how the squeaking of the wicker coffin sounded like my nan's old laundry basket. She would heft it down the stairs, full of dirty socks or Grandad's sweaty vests, effing and blinding about how heavy it was, and the basket would creak and squeak as if it too were complaining about being filled with such foul cargo. I tried to maintain an air of dignified calm but it got very difficult. The more they creaked and squeaked, the more I wanted to laugh out loud.

'What's the matter with you?' muttered Matt.

'Nothing, I'm fine, really, I...' I held my hand over my mouth to cover my smile – he wouldn't have been impressed if I'd shared my train of thought. He shook his head and walked to the waiting car.

'Ready, Mum?' Lucy appeared beside me and slipped her arm through mine.

'As I'll ever be, I suppose.'

*

The drive to the crematorium was a quiet but blissfully short one. I watched people on the street as we passed: some didn't even acknowledge us; a few older gentlemen removed their caps out of respect as we drove by and a toddler in a pushchair waved at me. I noticed a couple of people suddenly register the fact that there were two cars with two coffins; I would have loved to hear their theories about that.

'At least the weather's brightened up,' said Matt.

'Yes, it has,' replied Lucy.

'It's not going to make much difference. We aren't standing by a graveside – we're indoors watching them slide behind a curtain,' I said, matter-of-factly.

'That's true,' said Matt. We descended back into awkward silence.

'We're almost there now.' The driver's voice was a welcome intrusion. The funeral director had got out of the first car and was leading our procession up to the chapel. He walked slowly, with his head bowed, and the rest of us followed. Our car pulled up to the chapel and as we passed I was shocked by how many people were waiting for us at the crematorium. I had a quick flash of panic; how were we going to get them all into the little chapel?

'Bloody hell, Matt, where did all these people come from? I don't even recognise half of them.'

'There are a few I know but not all of them.'

The funeral director I'd been so rude to yesterday approached us as we got out of the car. I smiled, and he gave me a small nod in response. I saw Liz and her husband, David, standing with Flo just by the entrance to the chapel, but I couldn't seem to move. I didn't know what to do. From behind me I heard the warm voice of the funeral man.

'It's okay, Mum and Dad are going to be taken in first and you and your family can follow us when you're ready,' he said. When I turned to thank him he'd already moved away and was quietly giving guidance to the pall-bearers. He was very efficient and businesslike, whispering quiet instructions so that everything happened in the correct order and with the minimum of fuss.

Liz and her husband, David, made their way over to me, with Flo following along behind. As she reached me, Liz opened her arms and pulled me to her.

'You look tired, my darling. Did you get any sleep at all last night?'

'Yes, a bit. Not enough, obviously, if I look that bad.'

She stood back and held me at arm's length. 'I'm just worried about you. I don't think you're taking care of yourself. You should come and stay with me for a few days so I can feed you up and make sure you get some rest.'

'Stop fussing, Liz. I'm sure Abigail knows what she's doing. Ignore her, my dear, you look fine,' said David, leaning in to give me a peck on the cheek.

'I'm just worried about her, that's all.'

'You should listen to your husband,' said Flo, forcing her way between me and Liz and taking my arm. 'She knows she's always got me if she needs anything. Don't you, dear?'

This battle between the two of them for my attention was something I was used to and normally I could find the positives in it, but not today; today I found it bloody irritating.

'I'm all right,' I snapped. 'I just want to get this day over with as soon as bloody possible.'

Flo and Liz exchanged angry stares and Flo let my arm drop.

'Then let's get inside and do just that, then, shall we?' she said. I nodded and we walked over to Matt and Lucy; they were talking to a lady I thought I vaguely recognised. She turned and gave me a polite smile before walking away.

'Are you ready to go in?' asked Matt.

'Who was that?'

'Mrs Vaughan, old friend of Mum and Dad's, she said.'

'I don't remember her, do you?'

'Not really, but she's come to pay her respects. I

didn't want to be rude.'

I looked across the pathway. Mrs Vaughan was standing with a group of men and women, all of them around my parents' age; more faces I didn't recognise. Then my gaze came to rest on one of them – Terry Egan. My insides felt as if they'd dropped to my feet and I felt a shiver run through me. Egan turned around. Had he sensed me watching him? He tipped his hat to me and smiled.

'Matt.'

My brother turned and followed my gaze across to the crowd. I saw his shoulders tense.

'What the bloody hell is he doing here?' muttered Flo. 'I thought he'd pegged it years ago. Vicious bastard, he was.' She shivered and Matt put his arm round her tiny shoulders.

'Let's all just go inside, shall we?'

*

The chapel was packed with people. Matt, Lucy and I made our way to the front pew with Flo, Liz and David. Mum's casket was already on the plinth that would carry her away at the end of the service; Dad was on wooden trestle legs that had been draped with a rich purple and gold cloth. There was music playing quietly: Louis Armstrong singing 'A Kiss to Build a Dream On' – one of Mum's favourites. Was it a song that Dad would have chosen too? I felt a pang of guilt; I didn't know the answer to that. I couldn't recall ever hearing him play music or sing along to anything. I remembered that he spent a lot of time in the pub, he chain-smoked Benson & Hedges and he loved a strong cup of tea. That was all I could recall about a father who'd been there for the first fifteen years of my life and it made me feel bloody awful. Why couldn't I remember more? Had I buried it all so deeply that it was as if I'd never had him in my life? The fact that no one spoke about him – ever – meant that there had been no stories to keep him alive in my memory. And now he was gone for good.

Lucy whispered, 'Nan loved this song, didn't she?' I nodded my reply, afraid that if I tried to speak I wouldn't be able to stop the tears. I sat quietly, chewing the inside of my cheek, and waited for the choking feeling to pass.

People were still filing into the pews behind us; there were lots of murmured greetings and people muttering, 'Excuse me,' as they tried to find a place to sit. I turned to look and the first face I saw belonged to Terry Egan; he was sitting at the end of the back row. He'd taken off his hat and I was struck by how much my brother looked like him; it was unnerving. Or perhaps I was just seeing things because now I knew the truth. Matt turned to see who I was staring at.

'Ignore him, Abs. He wants to cause trouble. Don't let him get to you.'

He was right, of course, I knew that, but it irked me to see his smug face at the back of the chapel. I was so focussed on him that I wasn't paying much attention to anyone else until my eye landed on another familiar face – Jack. He was standing at the back of the chapel, wearing a dark suit and black shirt. He looked very sombre but he gave me a tiny smile that instantly took my breath away.

'You might have to stop holding your breath, my darling. It's really not good for you,' Liz leaned in to whisper to me.

'He's here. He came.'

'What? Who? Oh!' she exclaimed as she clocked who I was looking at. 'Did you know he was coming?'

'Know who was coming?' Lucy chimed in, looking round to see who we were talking about.

'Stop looking at him, the pair of you, turn around,' I said.

'Who's he with?' asked Liz. 'He hasn't brought the Barbie doll, has he?'

I hoped not but I couldn't tell without turning around again. I risked another look and this time he raised his hand and gave me a discreet wave. He wasn't with the Barbie doll.

'He's on his own, I think.' I couldn't believe he was there. My stomach was in knots. Liz and Lucy both made a move to turn round again but they were stopped by my brother.

'You three look like bloody meerkats bobbing up and down! Turn round and sit still, for God's sake!'

*

The service seemed to pass by in a flash and for most of it I felt as if I were having an out-of-body experience. I listened to the priest talk about my parents as if he knew them, even though he didn't, and I listened to my brother give a moving speech about how our parents were finally reunited after so many years apart. It was a good speech; he skilfully managed to avoid mentioning the reason for that separation and instead he chose to focus on memories of happier times before Dad left us – none of which I could remember. Everything was going as planned. I even managed to hold it together as each of their coffins disappeared discreetly behind the curtains. I was willing the proceedings along, mentally ticking off the order of service, praying for it to be over. We sang the last hymn, 'The Lord is My Shepherd', all very traditional, and then I heard a voice from the back of the chapel that made my blood run cold.

'I'd like to say a few words, Vicar, if no one minds, of course.' Terry Egan was making his way down the aisle.

'What the fuck is he doing?' asked Matt.

'I have no idea,' I replied, 'but I'm buggered if I'm about to let him ruin our parents' funeral.' Without a second thought, I stood up and stepped out in front of him and Matt got up to stand behind me.

'Whatever you're thinking about doing, Mr Egan, I'm asking you very politely to reconsider,' I said, with as much attitude as I could muster. He smirked at me and leaned closer.

'I suggest you sit down, young lady, before I lose my temper and do something I might regret.' The threat in his words was obvious, no nuance or subtlety about it, and I knew that if things turned ugly then my brother wouldn't back down from a fight. The look on Matt's face was the same one I'd seen the night before, when Egan had been standing in Mum's kitchen; I knew I couldn't let him get hurt protecting me.

'Just say what you need to and then leave.' I turned and forced Matt back into his seat. As I sat down I saw that Jack had moved towards the front of the chapel too and he was wearing the same murderous look as my brother. I shook my head at him and he took a few steps back.

Mr Egan was a man who liked an audience; that much was obvious from the first. He walked slowly to the podium and placed his hat down in front of him. Looking up at the expectant faces of the crowd, he smiled, safe in the knowledge that he could take his time since we all seemed powerless to stop him.

He took a long look at the photo of my father that stood on an easel at the front of the chapel.

'When I first met John Turner he was a nobody. He

had no job, no money and hardly any friends, but what he did have was a gift for making people do whatever he asked them to. He was a very persuasive man. It was a unique talent that he employed on my behalf many, many times.' Egan was on a roll and he was enjoying himself.

'I think most people here will know how our friendship ended. It was… an unfortunate turn of events, shall we say?' This remark seemed to cause a few murmurs from somewhere at the back of the room and Egan held up his hands to demand order be restored. 'Now, now, let's not dwell on the past. John had a right to protect his family and I'm just here today to let them know that there are no hard feelings.' Egan looked over to my brother and me before he continued.

'Matt and Abby – looking at you both today – I know that your parents would be very proud. Very proud indeed. You've both done so well. Abby, with your little café, and Matt with the gym. You've achieved so much with so little, it would seem. Congratulations to you both.'

What the fuck? I'd never heard anyone make a compliment sound so sinister. Where was he going with this? I looked across to my brother, who just shrugged.

'We all have to live with the choices we make, and the consequences of those choices can last a lifetime. But time has passed, we've all moved on and that's the end of it.' With those last words, Egan looked towards a small group of men at the back of the room and a few of them nodded. 'Let's just say that all is forgiven and leave it at that.' With a final glance at me, he picked up his hat and strolled down the aisle. The heavy oak door of the chapel banged shut behind him and an awkward silence settled over the room. The vicar stepped cautiously up to the podium, looking around to see if anyone else had anything they'd like to share.

'Yes... well... um... forgiveness is certainly something we advocate here.' He let out a nervous little laugh. 'If you would all bow your heads, we will end with a final prayer.'

*

The sun was shining brightly as we left the chapel. I said a few words to people offering their condolences, although I wasn't paying much attention to them. I'm a little ashamed to admit that I was looking for Jack.

'Bloody hell, I felt like an extra in one of the *Godfather* movies at the end there. Who on earth was that man with the hat?' said Liz, shrugging on her coat.

'An old friend of the family's apparently. He came to the house last night and introduced himself,' I said.

'Are you ready to head over to the café?' asked Liz. My heart sank at the thought that this ordeal wasn't quite over yet. I had a bloody wake to get through.

'I need to find Lucy and Matt.'

'I think they're already in the car waiting for you, see, over there.' Liz pointed towards the big black car I'd come in and I saw my new funeral buddy holding the door open, waiting for me. I kissed Liz on the cheek and walked over to the car. I stepped in and sagged back heavily on the seat, relieved to be out of sight.

'Well, that was interesting,' said Lucy. 'Who was the gangster at the end?'

'Just someone who knew your nan and grandad a long time ago,' replied Matt. 'He's no one important.'

'He certainly thought he was important. Stood up there looking all menacing, talking about Grandad and what he did for him. Urgh.' Lucy shuddered. I reached over and took her hand.

'It's nothing. Just an old man trying to make himself look interesting. Isn't that right, Matt?' He just grunted in reply and then turned to face the window.

Matt and I didn't speak for the rest of the journey; he wouldn't even turn around to look at me. Lucy tried to fill the uncomfortable silence with chatter but gave up when she realised that no one was in the mood to talk.

When our car eventually pulled up to the kerb outside the café, Matt was the first one out; he didn't even wait for the funeral director to open the door. As I got out I could see that Liz had put signs in the café windows – 'Closed for Private Function' – and guests were already milling around inside.

'I hope everything went the way you wanted it to,'

asked the funeral director.

'What? Oh, yes, it was lovely. Thank you for everything you did,' I said, as I held out my hand for him to shake.

'No trouble at all, really.' He took my outstretched hand and held it for a few seconds; was he flirting with me? At my parents' funeral? No, he couldn't be. We stood there looking at each other for a moment; I wasn't sure what to do next.

'Would you like to come and have a cup of tea? Before you have to go, I mean?'

'Thank you, but no, I'm afraid I have to get back.'

'Hot date?' I blurted out. He looked at me with a mixture of shock and confusion.

'God, that's awful, sorry, why did I say that?' I was utterly mortified. 'You mean you have another... um...'

'Funeral, yes,' he interrupted, saving me from further embarrassment.

'Okay, then, well, goodbye.' I turned and walked away as fast as I could without breaking into a run.

The café was crowded. Liz was over by the counter, taking cling film off trays of sandwiches, and Lucy was pouring tea from a huge stainless-steel pot; there was no sign of my brother. Flo was talking to a group of ladies all about her age, their grey heads close together as they whispered about something. As I got nearer, Flo looked up and said something to the little group that made them all stop talking.

'Have you seen Matt?' I asked. 'I can't seem to find him anywhere.'

'I think he went upstairs to the flat,' Flo said. 'Is everything all right, Abby? You look ever so tired. Don't she look tired, Iris?' Half a dozen grey-haired heads all nodded in unison, then they started talking about interrupted sleep and stress levels and all the many other reasons for my current haggard state. None of it was doing much for my already shredded self-esteem, so I left them to it, and went in search of my brother.

I didn't have to look far. He was upstairs in my flat, sitting at the kitchen table, picking the label off the neck of a bottle of beer.

'This was supposed to be my hiding place today. Go and find your own spot to skulk in.' I nudged him on the shoulder as I passed; when he looked up I could see the worry etched across his face. Going to sit opposite him, I reached across the table to take his hand, but he shrugged me off. He leaned back in his chair and downed his beer, then got up and went to the fridge. He took out two more bottles, popped the cap off each and handed one to me.

'Cheers,' he said mournfully, tapping his bottle against my mine. He leant on the counter by the sink and took a long swallow from his beer.

'Go on, then,' I said, 'get it off your chest. Whatever it is.'

'It's nothing, Abs. I can sort it. Don't worry.'

'Why do people say that? Don't worry. As soon as you tell someone not to worry it's the first thing they do. It's fucking pointless.'

Matt came and sat back down and then reached for my hand, but this time it was my turn to shrink back.

'Is this something to do with Egan and his little performance at the funeral?' I asked. My brother kept his head down, but I wasn't about to be put off. 'Matt?' Finally, he took a deep breath and looked at me.

'Egan thinks we've got some money stashed away somewhere and he said he's coming to collect.'

'Money? What bloody money?'

'The police never recovered all the cash that Dad and his cronies robbed from the security van. Egan has this theory that Dad left it with us before he turned himself in.'

'How much?'

'Just under a million quid.'

'Is that what all that bollocks at the funeral was about? All those snide remarks about the café and the gym and how well we've done for ourselves?'

Matt nodded. I couldn't help myself – the laugh, and a large amount of beer, were out of my mouth before I could stop them.

'Shit, Abs! Careful!' Matt leapt out of the way just in time, my beer spray just catching his sleeve. He grabbed a cloth from the side and wiped his arm.

'He thinks we have a million pounds stashed away

somewhere?'

'Yep.'

'He's insane. Or just plain stupid. If I had that sort of money I certainly wouldn't still be here, scrabbling around to make a living with a café that's barely breaking even!'

'I know, it's ridiculous. He's been telling people that he doesn't believe you inherited this place and he's convinced that I must have had money from somewhere to be able to go into partnership with Keith at the gym.'

'Who told you all this? Did you speak to him?' I asked, trying to ignore the vision of Egan jumping my brother in a dark alley somewhere to threaten him. Matt shook his head. 'No. I thought that's why he came to the house yesterday, but he never said anything. No, all of this came from Jimmy, one of the old faces at the gym. You remember Jimmy?'

I shook my head.

'Yeah, you do,' Matt continued, 'ginger fella, big beard. Everyone calls him Scotch Jimmy.'

'Is he Scottish, then?'

Matt laughed. 'No! They call him Scotch Jimmy 'cos he's always four parts pissed. I was surprised when he rocked up at the gym last week – I thought he was dead. Anyway, he said he'd heard some rumours about Egan coming back for Dad's funeral. He reckoned it was all a load of crap but thought he ought to mention it. Forewarned is forearmed and all that.'

'So, Egan hasn't actually said anything to you himself, then?'

'Nope.'

I was relieved – it was obviously just the rumour mill at work. Egan couldn't be so stupid as to think that we had a million pounds stashed away.

'If he was after money then he would have said something when he was here – he had the perfect opportunity the other night, but he didn't say anything.'

'No, he didn't,' said Matt, 'that's why I said don't worry about it, Abs. It's just people gossiping and hoping to stir up some trouble, that's all.'

We both went back to sipping our beers in silence for a while.

'I'm still finding the whole thing pretty hard to comprehend, though,' I said eventually.

'Which bit?'

'You know, Dad as gun-toting bank robber and all that. Doing Egan's dirty work. It's just not the way I remember him.'

'I thought you said that you didn't remember him.'

'I don't, not really. It's so confusing, I can't really explain it. I don't think I'm basing this on actual memories... it's more like... I don't know... more like just a feeling, I suppose.'

'You can't be that surprised, Abs. You remember what it was like growing up around here. Everyone was up to something a bit dodgy – that's how most of 'em made ends meet.'

It was true, we hadn't grown up in some suburban idyll. I knew about people like Aunty Pat, the lady who lived across the road and always had a kitchen full of stuff she would flog to people. You couldn't move in there for boxes of knock-off tracksuits, dodgy designer perfume or cheap cigarettes. Whatever you wanted she had it, or knew someone who could get it for you, at a price. But to me that all seemed like harmless stuff, not even close to the kind of crimes that could put you away for twenty years. I took a mouthful of my beer, but it just made me feel sick. I slid the bottle across the table to my brother. He raised an eyebrow at me.

'Is this 'cos I implied you had a drinking problem yesterday?' he said with a smirk.

'Oh, piss off! I need to keep a clear head, for the rest of today at least, just in case any more ghosts from the past appear downstairs.'

'Speaking of which – was that Jack I saw at the service?'

'Yes, it was. Did you know he was coming?'

'Nothing to do with me, sis, I swear.' Matt had started on my beer; that was three down in the space of about twenty minutes.

'Did you see where he went after the service?' I tried not to sound too interested in Jack and his whereabouts. I obviously failed as my brother gave me a knowing wink.

'Nope, sorry, Midget,' he said, standing up and ruffling my hair.

'Hey, leave off! We need to get downstairs – people will think we've abandoned them.'

Matt nodded. 'It's all ancient history now, you know, Abs, all this business with Dad and whatever he did. It's all over.'

I gave him my best reassuring smile but deep down I couldn't shake the feeling that it was far from over.

Chapter 20

Matt and I came back down into the café and he headed straight out to the kitchen, no doubt in search of more beer, I figured. The room was packed with people, most of whom looked about my parents' age. I recognised a few of them – I even spotted good old 'Scotch Jimmy' over in the corner by the makeshift bar, a giant man with a ginger beard and rosy cheeks. He saw me watching him and he raised his glass. I nodded and smiled and then turned my attention back to the room. I knew who I was looking for – Jack – but he wasn't there. In my heart of hearts, I knew he wouldn't be, but I had to admit – even if it was only to myself – that I had hoped he would come. I guess my rejection had done the trick; he'd obviously come to the funeral just to be polite. Move on now, Abigail, it's done with, I told myself. I felt a hand at my elbow and it made me jump.

'Steady up, girl, it's only me,' Flo's voice reassured me. I turned, feeling the familiar comforting warmth that her presence always gave me, and gave her a weak smile.

'You're a bit jumpy. What's the matter?'

'Nothing, nothing. You surprised me. What are you

doing lurking about behind me?'

'Just keeping me eyes out.' She gestured to the room full of mourners. 'Look at 'em all. Bloody rubberneckers. None of 'em came near or by when your mum was alive. Wouldn't have given her the time of day but here they all are – scoffing bloody sausage rolls and guzzling the free booze!' Her little body was shaking with barely contained fury by the time she'd finished speaking.

'It doesn't matter now, Flo,' I said, gently. 'She's at peace. They can't hurt her anymore.'

Flo reached up and gently touched my face. 'You're right, I know. Doesn't make me any less angry. Here, come with me.' She took me by the arm, across the café and over to the counter at the back. Once there, she dragged a chair over and, using the counter to steady herself, she climbed onto it.

'I have something to say,' she shouted. All heads turned in her direction and I realised that sweet old Florence was a little bit drunk. Lucy came to stand beside me.

'What's she doing?' she whispered.

'I have absolutely no idea.'

Flo took a minute to gather herself, took a swig from her wine and then started to speak.

'I just wanted to say, on behalf of my dear departed friend Esther, that you lot...' Flo stabbed a finger in the general direction of the crowd '... are a bunch of two-faced arseholes!'

There were some general murmurs coming from around the room, but most people were doing their best to try and ignore her. Flo was undeterred.

'You come in here, all of you, taking advantage of the catering, when you know as well as I do that you abandoned my friend and her children when they needed you the most. None of you were there for her, none of you!' Flo gesticulated wildly, sloshing her wine about all over the place.

'Flo, stop. Come down before you hurt yourself.' I reached up and tried to take her arm but she shrugged me off.

'No! This needs sayin'…'

'I'm sure, but maybe not right now,' I hissed. People were turning their backs, trying to ignore the crazy old bat on the chair.

'I wouldn't cross the road to piss on any of you, even if you was on fire!' she yelled and then drained her glass. Jesus! How much had she had?

'All right, that's enough now, Flo.' My brother appeared and gently lifted Flo down from her perch. 'What would Mum say if she could see you making such a show of yourself, eh?'

'Like I said, it needed saying. They need to know what they did. None of 'em are innocent. Look at 'em – all looking down their noses!' She made another move to try and get back on her soapbox, but she was thwarted by Matt, who held her around the waist until she stopped trying to jump back onto the chair.

'Just calm down,' he said gently. 'It's all over and done with.'

Flo sagged against my brother, drained from the effort of her little outburst. Matt guided her to another chair and lowered her down. He put his arm around her shoulders and sat beside her.

'Mum knew who her friends were, Flo. She always knew. Nothing else matters now, does it? She's at peace. With Dad.'

She smiled weakly at him. I sat on the other side of her and took her hand.

'You don't have to fight Mum's battles for her anymore. Or ours. We're big enough to take care of ourselves.'

She patted my hand and looked at me, tears filling her eyes.

'I know. It's just hard for me to stop after all this time,' she said, quietly. I realised then that she must have been exhausted from all those years of hiding things, protecting me from the truth. I also knew that she was waiting for me to tell her that I understood and that I forgave her for her part in the deception that had surrounded me for so long.

'It's all right, Flo. I know it all now. Everything. I think I'm even starting to understand why Mum did it.' Even as I said the words I knew that I didn't believe them – not quite yet. But my need to believe was outweighed by Flo's need to hear me say them.

'I'm so sorry, Abigail,' she said, earnestly. 'I wanted to tell you so many times but your mum... well, you know how she could get. She was always so fragile. I had to be so careful with her.'

'It's done now, over with. I just want us all to move on.' I looked across to my brother. He nodded and I gave Flo's hand one last reassuring squeeze before I stood up.

'Now then, let's get you a cup of tea and maybe a couple of sausage rolls to soak up some of that booze.'

*

Two hours after Flo's little outburst, there were only a few diehard mourners left in the café. People had started to drift away once they were sure there wasn't going to be any more entertainment. I'd shaken hands, been hugged and kissed by random people and accepted everyone's condolences, with a gracious smile. I'd done a fine job of keeping it together when all I'd wanted to do was tell everyone to fuck off. Flo had left about an hour ago; Scotch Jimmy had offered to walk her home. He was quite the gentleman, as it turned out, despite the drink problem.

Liz and David had started clearing up, rather obviously removing cups and plates from around the stragglers, trying to get them to take the hint and go. I should have been helping but I didn't have the energy.

I went through the kitchen and out of the back door, into the little yard behind the café. I leaned against the wall, grateful to feel the solid brick behind me; it made me feel grounded and safe. I tried to focus on my breath, in and out, slow and steady. I'd been fighting the tears all day, wanting to appear strong and capable, but I'd had enough.

Lucy appeared at the back door looking concerned. I plastered on my best smile and tucked my impending breakdown away for later.

'You should just go up to the flat. We can finish clearing up down here,' she said.

'I'm all right, love. Just a bit tired, that's all.'

'I know what you mean. I didn't know half the people in there today. I couldn't help feeling that they all knew lots about us.'

'It would seem there are plenty of people who've always known more than they ever let on.' I sat on the back doorstep and patted the space next to me. Lucy sat down.

'You mean Flo and Uncle Matt, don't you? He's been moping around for the last hour. He's had quite a bit to drink too.'

'He'll be fine. We all just need to get through this horrible day and then we can move on.'

'Can we?'

'What do you mean?'

'All that business with that bloke at the funeral. Egan. What does he want?'

'Nothing,' I lied. 'There's nothing here for him now that Dad's gone.'

'I can't believe Grandad worked for him. Who knew our family was so interesting?'

'Oh, Lucy.'

'What? It's not like he's around to get offended. I just think it's amazing that you seem to have grown up totally oblivious to it all.'

'I don't think I was totally oblivious. I was fifteen. I wasn't a baby. I knew he'd gone away and I knew enough to know it was bad. I thought he'd run off with another woman, or something. That was the story I told myself. I filled in the blanks with something that my childish brain could understand.'

'Wow. And you never thought about him?'

'I was a teenager – teenagers have short memories. Life moved on and other things became more important. Like you.' I nudged her shoulder. Looking back, I could see that all of my memories were coloured with the stain of what my relationship with Mum became. So many fights about curfews and coming straight home from school and now I knew why. If she kept me at home she could control who I saw and what I heard. Every decision she'd made had been based on her need to hide the truth, and it had been those decisions that had made me hate her. I'd hated my mother. The guilt of admitting that settled like acid in my belly and made me feel sick. I felt as if I was losing my grip. As if I'd fallen down the rabbit hole and I was stuck in a weird alternate reality; a life made up of completely different versions of everyone I thought I knew, including myself.

I could feel a sense of foreboding twisting itself around my insides and making its home in the pit of my stomach. I knew there was more to come; I could sense it. I wasn't ready for it. I wanted a rest, a break from the nagging questions that were spinning around inside my skull. I only knew one way to do that without the need for major surgery. 'I need wine,' I declared.

'Okay, I can sort that. Are you coming back inside?'

'Not yet. Can you just bring it out here for me?'

'Okay. But I'm sending Auntie Liz out here to sit with you. I'm not letting you get pissed and depressed all by yourself.'

'Fine, if that will make you happy, then go get Liz.' She nodded, pleased with herself, and gave me a swift peck on the cheek before dashing inside. I didn't want any company, not even Liz, but she hadn't given me much choice.

I leant forward and rested my head in my hands. My eyes were starting to hurt. Maybe wine wasn't such a good idea after all, I thought. Then I heard glasses clinking and someone sat beside me on the step.

'Thank fuck for that, I need a...'

Jack was sitting beside me, brandishing two glasses and a bottle of wine. A strange mix of feelings rushed through me: joy and surprise, tempered with a healthy dose of annoyance.

'Mind if I join you?' he asked.

All I could manage in response was an exhausted-sounding, 'Why?'

'Why what?' he asked, opening the wine and starting to pour.

'Why are you here? Why do you want to join me? You can answer whichever one you want. I don't care.'

He handed me a glass of wine and I downed it in one, then held it out again for a refill. He raised an eyebrow. Idiot.

'I know you think I have a drinking problem. Matt told me all about your little visit before you left.' He started to speak but I cut him off. 'I don't have a drinking problem and even if I did what the fuck does it have to do with you?' I jabbed my finger into his chest and slopped a bit of wine down myself. 'You don't get to come back here and pretend that you care after what you did.'

'After what I did? What the hell did I do?' he exclaimed. 'You told me to go so I did. That was your choice, Abigail, not mine!'

'I don't like ultimatums, Jack. You made it very clear that unless I was willing to have sex with you then you didn't see a future for us, not even as friends. You made that decision, not me!'

'Everything all right out here?' Liz appeared behind us at the door. 'I thought I could hear shouting.'

'It's fine, Liz, everything's okay. Jack and I were just catching up, that's all.'

Jack twisted his body round to face a flustered-looking Liz. 'It's nice to see you again, Elizabeth. Although I must say I'm surprised. The last time we met you insisted that you didn't know Abigail that well at all.'

To her credit, Liz didn't miss a beat. 'Yes... well... just looking out for my friend, that's all. I'm sure you understand. Abby is very special to me. I would do anything for her.' Her defiant declaration of loyalty made Jack smile. He raised his glass.

'Very admirable, Elizabeth. And I completely agree. Abigail is very special.' He turned back to face me and I felt myself blush. Bloody hell, how old are you, woman? Stop it.

'I'm glad we understand each other, Jack. I'll just leave you two to "catch up", then, shall I?' She mouthed the words 'Oh my God' behind Jack's back, giving me a thumbs-up sign before she ducked back inside. It made me smile and I went back to sipping my wine.

'A smile? Wow, haven't seen you give one of those in a while.'

'It wasn't for you.'

I could feel the warmth from Jack's body radiating

through mine as we sat so close together on the back step. All I would have to do was lean my head on his shoulder, I thought to myself, and I knew that would be enough for him to start our little dance all over again. I didn't do it. Jack poured himself a large glass of wine.

'Are you driving?' I asked.

'No. I got my driver to bring me back here. He can pick me up later, when I'm done.'

'When you're done? Done with what? 'Cos you're certainly not "doing" me if that's what you're thinking.' God, what an arrogant bastard! Arrogant he may be but at least he's honest about it, I thought. Don't pretend you haven't been sitting here imagining what would happen if you let him take you upstairs; don't be a hypocrite Abigail.

He held up his hands in mock surrender. 'I didn't mean anything by that. I just didn't know how this—' he gestured between us '—would pan out, that's all.'

I eyed him warily.

'Scout's honour,' he says.

I wasn't convinced. 'I thought you were back in America?'

'I was. And now I'm not.'

'Are you here for work, then?'

Jack looked at me. 'I'm here for you.'

'Me?'

'I thought you might need a friend, so I came.'

He made it all sound so simple. If only it were. I

didn't know what he wanted me to say, so I changed the subject. 'Must be nice to be able to fly off around the world at a moment's notice.'

'Where do you want to go, Abigail? Tell me and I'll take you there. Right now.'

He was serious. Bloody hell. 'Don't be silly, Jack. I can't just leave... I...'

'Why not? What's stopping you?'

'I... I have responsibilities... a business. There's also Lucy to think about.' I rambled on, trying to come up with a convincing list of reasons. Jack was having none of it.

'That's just you, getting in your own way. What are you so afraid of?'

'I am not afraid.' Liar! 'I just don't believe in letting people down. Don't you have people who rely on you back home?'

He shrugged. 'My company could run itself at this point, so, no, I don't.'

'What about friends? Or family? What about your parents?'

'I don't think my mum really cares what I do. After she remarried she kinda lost interest in me. Much more fun to be had spending my stepdad's money. Poor guy.'

'I didn't realise your parents weren't together any more. I'm sorry, Jack. When did they get divorced?'

Jack looked surprised. 'He died, Abigail. About a year after we moved away. I thought you knew.'

'I didn't even know where you were. How could I have known about your dad?'

'That's right, you didn't get my letters, did you?' he said, sarcastically.

'I didn't get your bloody letters! I already told you. Are you saying you don't believe me?'

'No, I'm not, it's just… I don't know… I can't believe no one told you anything about my trying to get in touch.'

'It would appear there were lots of things I wasn't told. You can just add that to the ever-growing pile.'

'We moved up to Glasgow to live with some distant cousin of Mum's. Dad got a new job, everything was going okay for about year and then he had a heart attack. Just dropped dead at work.' Jack drained his glass and poured himself another; he gestured to my glass and I nodded. What the hell? I could worry about the hangover later.

'I'm so sorry, Jack. I liked your dad. He was a nice man. Very responsible, like a proper dad. And he always came straight home after work without stopping for a pint or three on the way.'

'He dragged your dad out of the pub and got him home lots of times. Do you remember?' asked Jack.

'Not really. But that sounds about right. I can recall them being friends although I can't conjure up many details. I do have one vague memory. Both sets of parents sitting on patio chairs in our front garden, probably watching us while we played out on the street.'

'Making sure we weren't getting up to mischief.'

'Probably. I think your mum was convinced that I was going to lead you astray.'

'I wish,' he said, giving me a flash of his near perfect smile and suddenly looking like your typical all-American hero. Good teeth, nice hair and broad shoulders could really do things to a woman's libido. Before my traitorous brain started down that particular road, I changed the subject.

'I do remember asking Mum about it when you all left. I thought she might know something. She just told me it was adult business and that I should keep my nose out.'

'I got pretty much the same response from my parents. They always avoided talking about it. I guess when you're a kid nobody really gives a crap about what you think. You're just supposed to accept it and move on without asking too many questions.'

'Amen to that,' I said, raising my glass in salute. He clinked his glass to mine. An unfamiliar sense of peace settled over me. There was no denying that, sitting there with Jack, I felt more content than I had in weeks. But all the reasons I'd sent him away were still there, still squeezed in between us, no matter how closely we sat together on that back step. Nothing had really changed, had it? So, what was the point in letting myself get too comfortable?

'Stop overthinking it,' said Jack, as if he'd read my mind.

'I wasn't. I was thinking I should probably go inside and help with the clearing up. I can't leave it all to Liz and David.' I made a move to stand but he took my hand.

'Don't. Just stay here with me for a minute.'

'What for?'

'I like sitting here with you. Please?'

'Why?'

'Being around you makes me happy.'

I sat back down. 'You didn't look very happy the last time I saw you.'

He looked down at his drink; the silence stretched between us until eventually he looked up at me.

'I'm sorry, Abigail. I shouldn't have left like that. It was wrong of me to storm off like a bad-tempered teenager.'

I remembered the hurt in his eyes when I'd stopped him from kissing me in the kitchen that night and told him that nothing could happen between us. That memory was closely followed by another one – of how it felt to be kissed and wanted by him. I took another mouthful of wine to avoid having to speak.

'The minute I left I wanted to come back, to apologise. I let you down, Abigail, and I'm so sorry for that. But I'm here now and I need you to know how I feel.'

'Jack, please don't... I can't...'

'Let me finish. I should have come back and told you all this weeks ago, but I didn't know how to say it. Now I do.'

My heart was beating so fast I was sure he must be able to hear it. What the hell?

'I have to have you in my life, Abigail, for me it's that simple. I need it like I need to breathe. And if being your friend is the only way that can happen, then I'll take it. I'll take whatever you're willing to offer, just please don't send me away again. These past two weeks have been some of the worst of my life. To have you back and then have to face the prospect of losing you again was too much.'

I wanted to believe him but the man sitting next to me was a million miles away from the boy I once knew; I didn't know this Jack, not really.

'Who are you?'

He looked surprised. 'What do you mean?'

'I don't think I can claim to know you anymore, not really. You're a grown man, a man who's obviously had a very interesting life that's taken you a world away from here. So, I'm asking you – who are you now?' If my comments upset him, he didn't show it. Without missing a beat, he sat up straight, shook my hand and looked me right in the eye.

'Hi, my name is Jack, millionaire businessman and sex god, at your service. And you are?'

'Very funny, but I think you know what I mean. So much has happened, tons of which I wasn't even aware of, apparently, so I don't think we can claim to be friends, not really.'

'Then let's try. What do we have to lose?'

'Nothing, I suppose. I just don't want to give you any ideas, about this becoming something else. I'm not ready… I can't…' I stuttered nervously.

'You don't have to be frightened of me, Abigail. I would never do anything to hurt you.'

'I know that.'

'You have all the power here. We do this your way, whatever you need.'

I felt as if I should be the one to confront the designer-clad elephant in the room.

'How does Lexie feel about this burgeoning friendship of ours?'

'Lexie and I are no longer an issue. I told her it would be best if we stopped spending time together.'

'And how did that go down?'

He shrugged. 'It was fine.'

'But she was in love with you.' That was a statement, not a question.

'I told you before, it isn't like that with us. No matter what you seem to have convinced yourself.'

'You're still friends with her, though? I would hate to think I'd ruined that in some way.'

Jack smiled. 'I'm sure we'll stay in touch. Our parents

306

will probably be more upset. I think they were hoping we'd get together.' Jack laughed to himself. 'Not out of any real desire to see us happy, mind you – for them it was more like a business deal. The young Internet sensation and the tech millionaire. A true romance story,' he said, sarcastically.

'I'm sorry,' I said, and I genuinely was – sorry for Lexie and for him.

'That's what makes you so unbelievable, Abigail. You care about everyone. Your kindness is limitless. You're an amazing woman and I want that in my life. As a friend.' He smiled that bright, slightly crooked smile, the one that still had the power to make my heart soar. As a friend.

'All right,' I said, 'friends it is.'

'Great. And my first duty, as your friend, is to ask who the hell was the goon in the hat at the service today?'

Egan. I'd forgotten him for a minute.

'Terry Egan. A face from the past I'd rather forget, to be honest. He came to the house last night as well, making his presence felt.'

'What does he want?'

'I don't know what he wants,' I lied. 'He's the man that Dad was working for when he went to prison. A gang of them robbed an armoured security van. Dad went to prison and Egan buggered off to Marbella.' I swallowed the last of my wine. 'Still want to be friends?'

Jack reached for my hand.

'You're going to have to do better than that if you want to frighten me away.'

I relished the warmth that came from our closeness.

'What are you two up to now?' Liz reappeared at the door behind us and we both stood up. Jack was still holding my hand and I saw Liz glance at that and then take in Jack's beaming smile. I rolled my eyes and groaned; if I knew Liz she was going to assume that something had happened, probably that we'd had sex amongst the cardboard boxes.

'How are you both? Are you fine? You look fine.'

'Yes, Liz, we're fine,' I said.

'Um… well, then… that's just fine, isn't it? So… I'll just be going back inside, then. I mean since we're all fine.' She turned quickly and nearly tripped over in her rush to get away. No doubt she'd be searching for Lucy so she could share the news that Jack and I had been up to no good in the yard. I shook my head ruefully.

'What's up?' Jack asked.

'Nothing. I need to go in and help clear a few things up.'

'I'll come with you. I'm a dab hand at doing dishes.'

I didn't bother to explain that wasn't really what I meant.

'It's fine. You don't have to—'

'Friends help, Abigail. Okay?'

'Okay.'

Maybe this whole 'friends' thing could work for us, I thought.

Yes, of course it would; it was all going to be fine.

Chapter 21

The morning rush at the café, such as it was, was finally coming to an end; the queue of takeaway coffee drinkers had shrunk to two and, so far, the cappuccino machine had behaved itself. I had my back to the customers, wiping up spilt coffee grounds, when I heard a familiar voice.

'Do you have any wheatgrass? Or maybe a ginger shot?'

I turned to see Lexie Morgan quizzing a bemused-looking Flo about our menu.

'Grass?' exclaimed Flo.

'Wheatgrass. It's very good for you.'

'Grass is for cows, love, although there's a patch of weeds out the back I could shove in a sarnie for you, if you'd like.'

Lexie wrinkled her perfect nose in disgust. 'No, thank you.'

I took a deep breath and approached the counter.

'Hello, Ms Morgan. It's nice to see you again.' Lexie looked me up and down, then gave me a sweet, if slightly condescending, smile.

'I think your people could do with a few lessons in

customer service.' She looked pointedly at Flo, who ignored her and carried on serving the next person in line.

'I'm sure Flo didn't mean to be rude. Perhaps I can help you?'

Lexie stood for a long minute, examining the menu board on the wall behind me. Seeing her up close like this, I was struck by how young she was. She was dressed quite casually, a rich woman's version of casually anyway. Designer jeans, a fine-knit jumper that hugged every curve perfectly and just screamed money, all perfectly accessorised with the requisite oversized tote bag. Her long blonde hair was loose around her shoulders and every now and then she ran a pristinely manicured hand through it. She was beautiful, there was no doubt about that, but now I could see her close up I realised that everything about her seemed so contrived. The clothes were just the right side of casual, the hair just tousled enough to appear as if she'd just thrown this look together, when the reality was that she'd worked very hard to look this laid-back.

Finally, she spoke. 'I'll just have a green tea.'

My heart sank – we didn't have any green tea. She'd come to the wrong place if that was what she wanted. Despite being surrounded by an array of trendy coffee shops and eateries; Rosie Lee's had remained resolutely ordinary. People came here for a strong brew, a slightly average cup of coffee or one of Flo's famous egg and bacon sandwiches. I had no idea why they tasted so good; Flo would never divulge her secret. She'd told me that she would leave me full instructions for making them in her will.

I'd thought about updating the menu to fit in with the other places opening up around us, but every time I did I would hear Ted and Rose in my head. When they'd signed the business over to me almost fifteen years ago, this area had just been another run-down borough in East London. 'People like to stick with what they know, love,' Ted had said. 'It's a tried and tested recipe for success – stick with that and your loyal customers will thank you for it.' And they had at the beginning. But I don't think Ted or Rose could ever have envisioned the transformation that this whole area had experienced. Who knew – maybe if they'd still been around they might have been tempted by the lure of artisanal sourdough bread and small batch coffee roasting? I very much doubted it though.

Before I could apologise to Lexie for my café's shortcomings, Flo piped up.

'Right away, madam. I just need to fetch it – we keep it out the back. Only for special customers, you see.' She scurried off, leaving me looking confused.

'Anything to go with that? Cake? Or perhaps a croissant?' I asked.

'No, I'm good, thanks. Just the tea will be fine.'

She turned and weaved her way through the empty

tables, taking a seat at one by the window. Where was Flo? After her comments about feeding Lexie weeds in a sandwich, I was filled with dread at the thought of what she might try and pass off as green tea! I went to the kitchen and found her rifling through her shopping bag.

'Don't tell me you've got a box of green teabags in there, because I won't believe you.'

'Don't be daft. There was a sample one stuck inside the magazine I was reading this morning. Here it is!' Flo held up the page and ripped the sample bag off.

'You're a genius.'

'I'll stick it in a cup, you can slice a bit of lemon to go on the side. That ought to keep her happy. Who is she anyway?'

I opened the fridge and pulled out a rather shrivelled-looking old lemon. 'She's a friend of Jack's. I'm not sure what she's doing here.' I dropped the lemon slices onto the saucer that Flo handed me. 'Oh, bugger, what if she asks for a second cup?'

'We'll just reuse this one. This stuff tastes like cat's piss at the best of times – she'll never notice. Do you want me to take it to her?'

'No, it's fine, I can manage. What would I do without you?' I dropped a kiss on the top of her silvery head.

'I'm indispensable, what can I say? It's a curse.' She grinned widely, and I made my way out to Lexie. She was engrossed in something on her phone, so I just put the cup and saucer down and started to walk away.

'Would you sit down for a minute? I have some things I'd like to talk to you about.'

I turned back to her as she switched off her phone and put it into her bag. 'It won't take long.'

'Sure, why not?' I pulled out the chair opposite and sat down. Lexie leaned back in her seat and looked around. 'It's cute, your café, very… um… authentic.'

'Thanks, I think.'

'Jack told me you've lived here all your life?'

'Pretty much. I grew up in a house just down the road.'

'Wow. That's amazing. And you never felt the need to move away? Y'know, see the world and all that?'

'Bit tricky. What with this place and my daughter to think about.'

'Oh, yeah, that's right. Jack told me you had a kid. That's cool.'

I had to smile – Lexie was only a few years older than Lucy. I wasn't sure of what to say next. I fidgeted a bit; why did I feel so uncomfortable?

'I've always wanted to come to London. It's so exciting. That's why Jack brought me. I nagged him about it for so long. He gave in so I'd shut up about it.' At the mention of Jack's name, a warm smile spread across Lexie's face. My heart sank to my knees; she was in love with him. I could see it in her eyes.

'Have you and Jack been friends for a long time?' I asked.

'Since I was about thirteen. Jack's stepfather was in business with my father. Our families would get together quite a bit. You know the kind of thing. Barbecues, Thanksgiving, Christmas. The usual.'

I nodded and silence fell again. I could see Flo wiping out a mug and sneaking surreptitious glances across at me.

'I really should get back to work. The dishes won't wash themselves,' I said, making a move to stand up.

'No, please, just wait a minute. I really do need to talk to you.'

I sat back down and decided to broach the obvious subject myself.

'Look, Lexie, I'm sorry if my friendship with Jack has upset you. There's no reason it should – it's two old mates catching up, that's all.'

She considered this for a minute then said, 'I think we both know it's more than that, Abby. At least it is for Jack. I know him. The way he lights up when he talks about you. It's pretty obvious how he feels.'

She had this totally wrong. 'We're friends, good friends. I've known him for a long time. We have a shared history. He's obviously feeling a bit nostalgic about being back here. That's all it is.'

Lexie shook her head. 'It's not just that. That's why I wanted to see you. To tell you to be careful with him.'

'What do you mean?' I was confused.

'To be careful with his heart. He's trying so hard to

just be your friend, like you asked. But he wants so much more, Abby, and I'm worried that you're going to hurt him. Being in love with someone who just wants to be friends is a horrible thing to have to go through.' Lexie looked down at her cup and I saw her shoulders sag a little.

'You're in love with him, aren't you?' I asked.

Lexie didn't answer – for a minute I thought she hadn't heard me. She picked up her cup and took a sip of her green tea. Placing it back down, she said, 'Yes, I'm in love with him.'

Part of me wanted to leap up and punch the air – I'd been right all along! I wasn't imagining it! But that urge was dampened by the sight of the unhappy young girl sitting across the table.

'Does he know?'

Lexie shook her head. 'God, no. He sees me like a little sister, I think. In his eyes I'm still the same awkward thirteen-year-old he met at a Labour Day picnic ten years ago. Any hopes I might have had about that changing someday were shot to pieces the day he saw you again,' she said, smiling sadly.

I felt awful; what had I done to this poor girl?

'I don't know what to say. I'm sorry if you've been hurt... I never meant...' I mumbled out an apology until Lexie reached across the table and grabbed my hand.

'That's why I'm here. To tell you that there's no hard feelings. To tell you not to use me as a reason not to be with him. He had no idea how I felt about him. I'd got very good at hiding it. And let's face it, men can be a bit slow to pick up on the signals sometimes.'

I laughed. 'That's true, but I can't believe he didn't see it at all.'

'He's a good man, Abby, a kind man. He's not the type of man who would hurt someone intentionally. You can trust him.'

'I know.'

'And if he has to be with someone else, I'd rather it be someone like you. Someone he can love and share his life with. Better that than some of the gold-digging floozies that have cosied up to him in the past.'

'Really?'

Lexie rolled her eyes at me dramatically. 'Hell yeah. Some of them were awful. Luckily, they never stuck around that long – once they realised that he was in a strictly monogamous relationship with his work, they all gave up.'

'He works a lot, doesn't he?'

'Yes, of course, that's why he's so successful. But hey —' she squeezed my hand '—that's not something you need to worry about. I can't see Jack letting you play second fiddle to anything. He really cares about you.'

I didn't know what to say; Jack and I were just friends, nothing more. Sensing my discomfort, Lexie sat back in her seat and assessed me for a few seconds. After a while she said, 'You can't use me as an excuse to keep him away any more, Abby. I will always be Jack's friend, and I'd like to be a friend of yours too, but you're the one he loves. I think you need to ask yourself why you aren't willing to love him back.'

Was that true? Had I exaggerated their relationship in my own mind, as a way of keeping him at arm's length? *Of course you bloody well have!* screamed my common sense. I was more than a little ashamed of the fact that I'd just been so accurately second-guessed by a girl twenty years younger than me. Lexie took another sip of her tea, before pushing the cup away and standing up.

'If you don't want to be with him, that's up to you. Only you can answer that. Just do me one favour?'

'What's that?'

'Don't mess him around. Be honest. In these situations I've found it's always better to be up front.' She hoisted her bag onto her shoulder. 'How much do I owe you for the tea?'

'It's on the house,' I replied.

She nodded and walked over to the door. As she reached the handle she stopped and turned to face me.

'Who knows? Maybe if I'd taken my own advice and been honest with Jack about how I felt, things might have been different. For all of us.'

A cold feeling washed over me as I contemplated the implications of that. What would have happened if Jack had been with Lexie when I met him again? I knew enough about myself to know that I would never get involved with someone who wasn't single. Didn't I? As if she'd read my mind Lexie said, 'Or perhaps not. I can't help feeling that there's a kind of inevitability about your relationship with Jack.' She looked around at my café. 'Like coming home.' She pulled open the door and left.

'She gone, then, has she?' Flo appeared beside me and took the cup from my hands. 'She hardly touched her tea. I tore me bleedin' favourite magazine to get that teabag out. And for what?' Flo walked away grumbling to herself and I followed her back out to the kitchen, where I plonked myself down onto a stool.

'Everything all right, love? You look a bit peaky. Can I get you anything? I hear wheatgrass is very good for you,' she said, in the worst American accent I'd ever heard. We both burst out laughing. I could hardly breathe, I was laughing so hard. It felt good. I couldn't remember the last time something had made me laugh so much.

'Er, hello? Could I get a cup of tea, please?' The voice of a customer at the counter interrupted our fit of giggles.

'All right, hold yer horses. I'm coming.' Flo rolled her eyes at me and went out to serve him. I wiped away my tears with the hem of my T-shirt and just sat there. I felt weird. The conversation with Lexie had unsettled me. Despite her telling me about Jack's feelings, there was a

319

part of me that still doubted her story. Young girls liked to romanticise; I'd seen it plenty of times with Lucy. They hadn't been round the block enough times yet to realise that happy endings like that belonged in the movies, not real life. Although I was sure now that there wasn't any kind of romantic relationship between Lexie and Jack, I still wasn't convinced that it meant Jack and I had a future together.

I tried to focus on wiping down the workbench in front of me, scooping crumbs into a pile before walking over to the sink to drop them in. As I rinsed out my cloth and watched the water drain away, I reached what I felt was an important decision: just being friends with Jack was still the better plan. Did I mean better or safer? Was I still hiding? I shook away my doubts; I knew I was right. Being friends was just going to have to be enough. For now. Maybe. Definitely. God! Why couldn't I make up my bloody mind? Oblivious to my inner turmoil, my brother chose that moment to walk into my kitchen and put two containers, very gingerly, down on the workbench in front of us.

'Well, there they are.'

I looked at him quizzically. 'Who?'

'It's Mum and Dad. Their ashes are in there.'

'What's all this?' Flo stepped back into the kitchen, wiping her hands on her apron.

'It's Mum and Dad,' said Matt.

Flo picked up one of the jars. 'Bloody hell!' she

exclaimed. 'Are you sure they gave you the right ones? Esther didn't weigh this much when she was alive, let alone now she's just ashes!' She plonked the jar back down on the table. 'I think they've squeezed someone else in there with her!'

I started to laugh again; I couldn't help it. It felt so liberating and I didn't want to stop. My brother's serious face brought an end to my nonsense.

'Are you all right?' he asked.

'Yes, I'm fine. Sorry. Just being childish. I'll try to stop,' I said, stifling another giggle with my hand. Matt shook his head at me, like a disapproving parent.

'Are you still up for doing this today?'

'Doing what?' I coughed to cover up the last of my giggles.

'Scattering the ashes on the river. Off the Woolwich Ferry. Remember? We said we'd do it today.'

'Yes, I can do it, it's fine.' I didn't want to put it off. It had to be today. I didn't feel as if I could move on until it was done.

'Have you had breakfast yet, Matt?' Flo asked.

'Nope. Are you gonna make me one of your egg and bacon butties before I go, you gorgeous woman?' He gave Flo a little nudge on the shoulder and she whacked him with the nearest tea towel.

'Behave yourself. Go and sit your fat arse out there and I'll bring it over to you.'

Matt leaned down and gave her a peck on the cheek

before he left. Grabbing a newspaper off the counter, he took a seat by the door and started to read.

I was left in the kitchen looking at the two plastic jars of ashes. They were the same shape and size as the sweet jars that used to sit on the shelf in the local newsagent's, but these containers were made of burgundy plastic and thankfully you couldn't see what was inside. And we'd got to drop them off the back of the Woolwich Ferry; the whole thing was bloody ridiculous but it was what Mum wanted. God only knew what my Dad wanted but he wasn't really in any position to argue about it; he was getting flung over the side with her and if there was such a thing as heaven then they could scream at each other about it for the rest of eternity. For my part, I just wanted to get it over with, so I wasn't about to question the plan.

'Knock, knock. Can I come in?' Jack's voice dragged my attention back to the kitchen. He was leaning against the doorway and looking gorgeous, as usual. He was wearing a blue suit and white shirt but no tie; leaning nonchalantly against the door frame, he looked like something out of a menswear catalogue.

'The lovely Florence said I could come straight through, but you looked deep in thought. I didn't want to startle you.'

'Hey, Jack. It's okay, you can come in. Say hi to the parents.' I gestured to the jars on the table. Without a word, Jack came across and pulled me into his arms; I felt like a fraud. I should have been more upset, but I didn't feel anything. What was in those jars wasn't my parents – it was just dust. I had about as much emotional attachment to it as I did to the contents of my vacuum cleaner.

'I'm fine. There's no need to fuss, Jack.' I pushed myself away from him, a tricky thing, since being in his arms was a nice place to be. Just friends, Abby, I reminded myself, you're just going to be friends.

'Are you sure?'

'Of course. What brings you here anyway? Shouldn't you be working? Adding more zeros to your bank balance?' I hopped off the stool and busied myself stacking plates in the dishwasher. I knew he was watching me; I could feel it.

'Being your own boss means you're free to take off whenever you like. Fancy coming to lunch with me?'

'Can't. Sorry. I've got to go with Matt and scatter... those.' I gestured towards the urns. 'We're taking a little trip across the Thames on the ferry. Mum's final wish.' I slammed the dishwasher door closed a little too fiercely and heard the plates rattle inside.

'Take it easy, Abigail, you'll break something. We can do lunch another time, okay?'

'Sure.' We stood there awkwardly for a minute and then the silence was broken by my brother's voice. He was talking loudly to someone on his phone as he walked into the kitchen.

'What the fuck? How did that happen? Well, who left it on all fucking night? Jesus!'

Jack looked over to me. I just shrugged.

'Fine, I'll sort it. Yes… I said I'd sort it, all right?' He jabbed his finger on the end call button and let out a frustrated howl.

'What's the matter?' I asked.

'Bloody cleaner left the tap running in the utility room at the gym. It's been on all night! The water's pouring through the ceiling. I've got to go and sort it. We'll have to scatter ashes another time, I suppose.'

I hated that idea. 'No. Can't someone else sort the ceiling out?'

Matt gave me a sheepish look. 'To be honest, Abs, I wasn't really looking forward to doing it.'

'What do you mean? You've been banging on about how it's so important because it's what Mum wanted. Now you're telling me that you never wanted to do it?'

He shook his head. 'The idea of shaking their ashes out of those jars gives me the creeps a bit. I mean, what happens if the wind changes and they blow in the wrong direction? I don't want to end up with a face full of our parents.'

I couldn't believe what I was hearing. 'For a big bloke, you really are a pathetic bloody wimp, do you know that? I'm not going to do it on my own. I'll look like a loony, leaning over the side of the ferry. They might think I'm a terrorist scattering some sort of biological weapon over London.' Even as I said it I knew it sounded ridiculous, but I was desperate. My brother was smirking slightly, which just enraged me even more. I slapped him across the shoulder. 'I'll bet you planned this. I wouldn't put it past you to flood your own gym, just so you can get out of it.'

'Don't be daft, Abs. This is going to cost me a fortune to fix. Why would I do that?'

He came over to me and rested his hands on my shoulders. 'Do it for Mum and Dad, Abby. Please? Just do this one last thing for them.'

That was a low blow; I pouted for a bit then nodded and he kissed me on the forehead.

'Thanks, Abs. Maybe Lucy could go with you?'

'She can't. She's out with friends.'

'I'll come with you – I mean, if you want,' said Jack.

'There you go, Abs, problem solved. Jack can go with you, just to make sure you don't get dragged away by the police or whatever.'

'But...'

'Look, I've got to go. I'll call you later. Sorry.' He was gone before I could argue anymore. Bloody idiot.

'Where's he off to in such a hurry?' Flo appeared at the kitchen door, clutching a plate. 'I made him a sandwich.'

'Emergency at the gym, apparently.'

'That's the second time this morning that someone's buggered off before they've finished what I've made for 'em. Here, you have it.' Flo shoved the plate at Jack. 'You look like you could do with some proper food.'

He took the plate eagerly. 'Yes, ma'am.'

'What's with all these bloody Americans in 'ere this morning?' Flo muttered, walking back out to the counter. Jack had pulled up a stool and was devouring Flo's special egg and bacon sandwich.

'This is awesome,' he cried, biting into the thick white bread, leaning over the plate as the egg yolk broke and oozed out of the sandwich. He was getting in quite a mess. I should probably fetch him a napkin, I thought, but I couldn't seem to stop watching him eat. The look of pure pleasure on his face was very distracting, and when combined with the murmurs of satisfaction that kept spilling from his mouth, well, it was a weirdly compelling sight. I'd never thought I could get turned on watching a man eat a sandwich but, apparently, I was wrong. Stop it, Abigail, just friends you said, remember? I grabbed a cloth, in an attempt to distract myself from his amazing mouth and handed it to him.

'Thanks.' As he took it from me our fingers touched very briefly. He held my gaze for a few seconds, until I pulled my hand away and moved over to the other side of the workbench. I suddenly felt very warm and I was breathing very fast. Jack wiped his mouth and hands with the cloth without taking his eyes from mine. A sudden image, of the two of us writhing around on my kitchen workbench, popped into my mind and I gasped.

I had to slap my hand across my mouth to prevent any more telltale noises escaping, and Jack smiled.

'Everything all right, Abigail? You look a little... flustered.'

I was very grateful that Jack couldn't read minds. Oh, Christ – the whole 'just friends' thing was never going to work unless I could train my brain and my body to stop betraying me.

'Just waiting for you to finish your breakfast so we can go. I'm going to get my coat. You can wait there, or outside, whatever. I'll be right back.' I opened the door that led up to my flat and took the stairs two at a time. Grabbing my coat from the hook by the door, I caught a glimpse of myself in the hall mirror. My cheeks were flushed and my eyes were shining. Pull yourself together, woman, you are not a horny teenager, you are a grown-up. A grown-up who is perfectly capable of being just friends with a man. Admittedly he was an incredibly sexy, charming, sweet, kind and funny man, but he was just a man nonetheless. I gave myself a thorough talking-to in the mirror and returned to the kitchen, confident that I had my traitorous psyche well under control.

That feeling lasted for all of two seconds; I walked back into the café to find Jack helping Flo bring in a tray of bread that had just been delivered. He'd taken off his jacket and I could see the outlines of some very well-defined muscles in his arms and back. His shirt was stretched tightly across his very fine form and, as for his arse, god help me.

'Ain't he lovely, Abby?' Flo declared. 'Such a gent.'

'What? Yes... er... very helpful. Thank you. Um... right... well... shall we go?' I threw my coat on, grabbed the urns and then headed through the café and out of the door; Jack had to run to catch up with me.

'Hey, wait up.' He dropped into step beside me, not even slightly out of breath, I noted, and gently steered me towards his car. 'I don't think Florence really needed my help, but she was kind enough to let me feel wanted.'

'That's very nice of her. She's very sweet.'

Jack laughed – I loved that sound. 'I don't think sweet is quite the word I would use but she's definitely a character. And she adores you.'

I smiled. 'The feeling is entirely mutual. I don't know what I'd do without her, to be honest.' I didn't want to think about that – I'd lost enough in the past few weeks. I knew it would happen one day, I wasn't stupid, but the thought that I might be standing there holding her ashes in an urn at some point made me feel anxious and scared. I shivered slightly and Jack put his arm around my shoulders.

'Are you cold? Here, get in.' He held open the car door and I got in, placing my parents in the foot well.

'Will they be okay there?'

'They're not going anywhere. They'll be fine.'

He closed the door and I took the opportunity to snatch another look at him as he walked around the car.

No harm in looking, so long as he didn't catch me, I reasoned. I watched him pull out his phone and he tapped in a number. By the time he got into the car, he was talking to someone.

'I don't know how long I'm going to be. You should probably just go ahead and cancel everything.'

I felt guilty for pulling him away from work like this. Flapping my hands in front of his face, I tried to get his attention, but he swatted me away like an annoying fly.

'No, no. If he complains about rescheduling the meeting just tell him the deal's off. I can't work with people who aren't willing to be flexible. Okay, sure, that's great.' He ended the call and put his phone back in his pocket.

'You don't have to cancel things for me. I don't want you to miss anything important on my account.'

He took my hand. 'This is important. Being here for you is important. Now stop complaining and tell me where we're going.'

*

As usual the approach road to the ferry was heaving with cars and lorries and we hadn't moved for at least twenty minutes. I was sick of staring at the anatomically detailed drawing of some male genitalia on the back of the large van in front and I was running out of safe conversation topics. We'd covered the weather – 'grey and wet'. We'd covered the scenery – 'grey and uninspiring'. I had very little left in my 'just friends' conversational arsenal. When the traffic in front of us began to move I almost cried out with relief.

The staff on the ferry were very efficient and quickly loaded us on board. The line of vehicles we were parked in was close to the edge of the ferry, which meant it would be easy to just get out, fling the ashes overboard and then jump straight back in the car. I didn't want to attract the attention of the ferry staff just in case they tried to stop me.

'Okay. Let's get this over with.' I unscrewed the lids of the jars and pushed open my door. Jack got out of his side and came around to help me. I scurried over to the edge, ready to dump the contents of the jars over the rail, but Jack grabbed my arm.

'Wait, wait. What's the hurry? Don't you want to take some time, say goodbye? Say something?'

Did I? Should I? 'I don't know what to do, Jack. I've never done this before,' I hissed. A few people nearby turned to look at us, the strange woman with the sweetie jars and the handsome man trying to stop her from flinging them over the side.

'Look, I'm not sure if we're even allowed to be doing this. I told Matt that I thought we'd need to get proper permission or something, but he'd said not to bother. Which is all fine and dandy since he's managed to wheedle his way out of coming. Jammy bugger.' I cursed my brother and his ancient plumbing.

'Just hold on a sec, okay?' Jack opened the car door and leant inside. After a few seconds I heard music playing; it was beautiful, something instrumental. Then he went round to the boot of the car and produced a bouquet of white roses, pulling two from the arrangement and bringing them to me.

'Here you go. One for each of them.'

'Where did you get them? That bouquet...'

'Was for you. I was going to give it to you if you'd accepted my invitation to lunch.' He looked nervously down at his feet.

'Oh, Jack, I don't know what to say. Thank you.'

'What are friends for?'

At that moment, it took all of my self-control not to throw my arms around this kind, amazing man. But I couldn't – for many reasons, not the least of which was the fact that I was currently clutching two jars of ashes with no lids on. Instead I went to the rail; Jack took one of the urns from me as I took a deep breath and slowly turned the other urn over. The contents were immediately caught by the wind; they rose away from me, and all I could think to say was goodbye. Jack handed me a rose and I dropped it over the side, watching it get caught in the waves created by the ferry. It bobbed along in the muddy water by the side of the boat and then disappeared towards the back. I let out the breath that I hadn't even been aware I was holding and reached for the second jar; the plaque on the front told me it was Mum's. A piano began playing, the sound coming from somewhere inside the car; the music was so serene, it seemed out of place on this dirty, fume-filled ferry.

'Maybe I shouldn't do this?' I said, suddenly. 'Maybe she deserves more from me?'

'More?'

'Yes, more. More consideration, more care, more love. I didn't give her enough of that, of any of it, when she was alive. Maybe I can do that now, try and make up for everything. Shit, I don't know. Why the fuck is this so hard?' I shouted, but my voice was lost to the wind. Jack put his hand on my shoulder.

'Take your time, Abigail. There's no rush. What do you want to do?'

I knew the answer to that question without having to think. 'I want to go back,' I said. 'I want to go back to before everything turned to crap and I want to somehow be able to make it all better.' I choked the words out between sobs; people were looking but I didn't care. 'I want to have her back so I can tell her how sorry I am for everything I said, everything I did. I want to tell her that I understand and that it's all right.'

Jack pulled me closer to him. 'She knows, Abigail, she always knew. She was your mum and whatever she did, she did it because she loved you.'

He held me tight while I sobbed into his shoulder,

whispering words of comfort into my ear. When I had no more tears left and my sobs had turned into the occasional hiccup, he held me at arm's length and looked at me.

'What did she want, Abigail?'

'This,' I said and I shook my mother's ashes out over the river. The wind whipped them into a whirling mass and then they were gone. I threw the rose out, further away from the side of the ferry, and watched it ride the current as we moved past. I felt cold and I wrapped my arms around myself to try and counter the chill.

'Let's get back in the car,' said Jack.

I nodded. It was over; I'd done what she wanted. So why did I still feel like the worst person in the world? We got back into the car. I was shivering and my teeth were chattering hard enough to crack the enamel. Jack turned the heater on and then reached across to turn off the music.

'Don't turn it off. I like it.'

He sat back in his seat. Neither of us spoke for a long time; I was glad. I didn't want to fill the space with pointless chit-chat.

'Who is this?' I asked, as the music ended.

'Ludovico Einaudi. Do you like it?'

'It's beautiful.'

We went back to listening to the music. The sky outside had gone very dark, as if someone had thrown a blanket over the sun, and within minutes the slight drizzle that had been falling was transformed into fat raindrops. They landed heavily on the roof and the windscreen, practically drowning out the music. Jack had to shout to be heard above the noise.

'Where the hell did this come from?'

The downpour was so heavy it was almost biblical; I could barely make out the shapes of the other cars and lorries around us. It was like being in a car wash – that feeling of being trapped by the water, you couldn't open the doors or windows, you were in your own little universe. I loved that feeling; just for a few minutes nothing could get to you. I saw a film once, where a woman drove into a car wash but never came out. The car came out but somewhere in the middle of the rinse cycle she had just disappeared. The police were baffled, and the general feeling was that something horribly gruesome had happened to her, but I always liked to imagine a different scenario. In my version of the story, the woman in the car wash was somehow magically transported away from her ordinary life to a faraway tropical paradise. Someplace where the drinks had umbrellas in and hammocks always swung gently in the breeze. I pictured that woman on a long, white sandy beach, sipping her drinks and wearing bougainvillea flowers in her hair. Lucky girl.

By the time the rain slowed down, we'd reached the other side of the river and the ferry staff were offloading us. The rain had left everything looking brighter and cleaner; even the genitalia graffiti on the van in front had been almost washed away. Jack had hardly spoken a word in the last ten minutes, taking his lead from me, I suppose, but the silence was starting to get to me a bit.

'Thank you for today,' I said.

'It's no problem. Glad to have you back – you were lost in thought there for a while. Where did you go?' He turned slightly in his seat to face me, but I kept staring straight ahead. I couldn't look at him.

'Hammock. On a white sandy beach, wearing flowers in my hair and not much else.'

Out of the corner of my eye I saw him swallow and fidget a bit in his seat. What on earth had possessed me to add that last bit? Stop playing around, Abigail.

'I think it's our turn, Jack.'

His face lit up with a smile, and then he realised what I meant – the ferry master was directing us off the boat. He cleared his throat and started the car.

'Sure, yes, of course.'

I watched his strong hands put the car into gear and manoeuvre us smoothly onto the pier.

'I need to get back to the café. Flo will be wondering where I've got to and she'll need help with the lunch rush.' Who was I kidding? We hadn't had a lunch rush for ages.

'Of course. I'm assuming you don't want to make the return trip back on the ferry?'

I shook my head; I never wanted to get back on that

bloody thing ever again. Jack nodded his agreement and we drove away from the pier.

Chapter 22

As we pulled up outside the café I started to feel nervous, as if I were at the end of a first date. And what an awful first date it would have been. Hey there, good-looking man from my past, wanna go and scatter the remains of my parents? Then maybe catch a movie? What a showstopper. But we weren't on a first date, I reminded myself, we were just friends. I looked across at Jack and I was slightly cheered by the fact that he looked nervous too. He'd switched the engine off but had returned his hands to the steering wheel, as if he didn't know what to do with them. Was he waiting for me to invite him in? It seemed only polite after everything he'd done for me.

'Would you like to come in, for a coffee or something?'

'Don't you need to get back to help Florence?'

'Well, yes, but you can keep me company in the kitchen, if you like?' Perhaps he doesn't want to come and have a coffee, perhaps he's just trying to be polite? I thought. Maybe he has better things to do? Of course he has better bloody things to do, Abby, don't be ridiculous. 'Don't feel like you have to. I-I mean, I'm sure you've got more important stuff to be doing,' I stammered.

'There's nowhere I'd rather be than here right now.'

A feeling of relief took me by surprise; I hadn't wanted him to drive away and leave me, but I was damned if I was about to admit it.

Unsurprisingly the café was practically empty when we came in, just a few people sitting at tables nursing their mugs of tea or eating sandwiches. Lucy was at the counter serving a customer and she gave me a cheery wave when she saw me.

'That'll be three pounds fifty, please,' she said to the lady in front of her. It was Pam, the owner of the nail salon next door.

'Cheers, darlin',' she said, handing over the money then turning to me. 'Hello, sweetheart, how's it going? Everything all right?'

'I'm good, thanks. How's business?'

'Not great, to be honest. If it wasn't for my regulars I'd be up shit creek. It's getting a bit hard to drum up trade round here.'

'I know what you mean. Apart from the morning coffee rush, such as it is, and the customers we see at lunchtime, it's dead. I've been having to try and find other ways to prop this place up.'

'And what about him?' She tipped her head in Jack's direction; I noticed he'd taken a seat at our old table by the window. 'Is he helping to "prop you up"?' She put air quotes around the last bit. 'He's lovely. Where did you find him? Not from round 'ere, is he? Look at the suit – I can tell good quality tailoring when I see it.' She was staring and making no attempt to hide it.

'Actually, he is from round here. Or used to be, at least. He's an old friend from way back.' Her perving was starting to annoy me, but she seemed quite happy to hang around and ogle.

'He's gay,' said Lucy, leaning over the counter. Pam looked disappointed.

'Typical. All the good-looking well-dressed ones usually are.' She let out a sigh, giving Jack one last look before she grabbed her sandwich and left.

'Lucy! Whatever did you say that for?'

'She was ogling your man, Mum. She needed to be warned off.' She gave me a cheeky wink.

'He's not my man, don't be daft. We're just friends, that's all.'

'Yeah, yeah. Whatever you say.' She smiled knowingly and then grabbed a cloth to wipe down some tables. Pushing through the doors that led to the kitchen, I found Flo sitting on a stool, reading a magazine.

'How did it go?' she asked. I shrugged off my coat and hung it by the back door.

'It was all right. I'm glad I didn't go on my own.'

Flo put down her magazine and watched me as I retrieved my apron from the workbench and started putting it on. She didn't say anything; she didn't have to.

I knew how her mind worked.

'This wasn't a romantic date or anything, Flo. Just a mate helping me out.'

'I didn't say anything, did I?' She tried her best to look innocent, but it wasn't working.

'What's left to do, then?' I said. Flo narrowed her eyes at me but said nothing. I started loading some dirty plates and cups into the dishwasher and then went to the sink for a cloth to wipe the workbench; it wasn't even dirty.

'There's nothing to do. Lucy gave me a hand after you left, and we managed. We weren't exactly rushed off our feet.'

'I was going to make Jack a coffee. Do you want one?'

'No, thanks, sweetheart. I've just had a cuppa and at my age if I drink too many I'll be running to the loo every five minutes. Why don't you take Jack upstairs for that coffee? It's much nicer up there. Your flat doesn't smell like bacon fat and old Lenny.'

Lenny was a regular. He lived in the care home down the road, but he came in every day and sat in the corner for a few hours, nursing a single cup of tea.

'We can stay down here,' I said, 'what happens if you get busy?'

Flo raised one eyebrow at that remark. 'Yes, well, if coachloads of hungry people suddenly descend on us, I'll give you a shout.'

Looking back out to the café, I saw that Lucy had stopped clearing tables and was now sitting down opposite Jack. He was laughing at something she'd just said; what could she be saying to him? I hurried over to their table and interrupted them, hoping to stop Lucy before she could embarrass me.

'What are you two talking about?' I asked, in an overly chirpy voice.

'Nothing. I was just filling Jack in on what goes on around here. Which isn't much,' she said, more to him than to me.

'That's not true. You're always out with your friends.'

'I am, you're not.'

'Don't be silly. I go out, I do things, I'm just busy with this place, that's all.' I waved a hand around the empty café. Lucy and Jack smirked at each other. 'Oh, shut up, the pair of you. Do you want that coffee or not?'

'I definitely do.' Jack stood up and took Lucy's hand. 'It was nice to talk to you, Lucy. I hope I'll see you again sometime.'

Lucy shook his hand enthusiastically, grinning like an idiot. 'Me too. I'm sure we will.'

'Let's go upstairs to the flat.'

'Lead the way, Abigail.' He placed his hand in the small of my back as we walked and I felt a jolt of electricity flicker up my spine. Stay down here, Abby,

341

you idiotic woman, don't go upstairs. My rational mind was engaged in an epic struggle with my heart, as I tried to suppress all thoughts of what might happen if we were completely alone upstairs. I told myself I was an adult and I'd made the decision for us to just be friends. I knew Jack respected that decision, but I couldn't deny that there was still something between us.

'Everything okay?' Jack asked.

'Yes, of course. Everything's fine.' We walked across the café to the stairs that led up to my flat.

'Have fun, you two. And don't feel like you have to rush back. Me and Lucy can look after everything down 'ere. Can't we, love?' Flo called out. Lucy popped her head around the kitchen door and gave me a thumbs-up.

''Course we can. You two kids go and enjoy your coffee. I'll help Flo clear up and when we're done I'm going to Flo's for tea.'

'Are ya?' said Flo.

Lucy gave her a knowing look. 'Yes, remember?' She came out of the kitchen and put an arm over Flo's shoulders, leaning down to whisper something in her ear. Flo replied and whatever she said made Lucy giggle.

'Yes, that's right, she is,' said Flo. 'I thought it would be nice for us to have a bit of time together before she leaves.'

'And then after that I'm going to see Heather. Won't be back for ages,' Lucy said, emphasising the 'ages'. I chose to ignore their silliness and left the pair of them cackling away like Macbeth's witches.

'What was all that about?' asked Jack as we made our way up the stairs.

'I think that was a not so subtle attempt at a swift exit.'

'I see.'

I could hear the smirk in his voice and I stopped abruptly and turned to face him. He was two steps below me so we were practically nose to nose.

'Behave, Jack. Or else you can stay downstairs in the kitchen with Flo.'

He held up his hands in mock surrender. Satisfied that I'd made my point, I carried on up the stairs.

Once we were inside the flat, I started to feel a bit nervous but Jack made himself very comfortable at my kitchen table, just watching me flap about.

'Coffee or tea?'

'Tea would be great.'

'I just need to find the teapot. Why don't you go through into the living room and I'll be with you in a second?' Please go into the other room and stop looking at me like that, I thought.

'Do you need me to do anything for you?'

I didn't dare answer that one honestly; I was shocked by how easily I could come up with a very satisfying list of things he could do for me. I bit my lip to stop myself from saying them out loud and just shook my head. He nodded and wandered out of the kitchen and into the tiny living room across the hall. I let out the breath I was holding and leaned against the worktop for a minute. Christ on a bike! Behave yourself, Abigail. You just told him off for not behaving and now look at you.

I had to try and gather my scattered thoughts. I was so confused I could scream. Being friends was what I'd wanted, it had all seemed so much neater and easier to keep him at arm's length, but now he was here, sitting in my shabby-looking front room, being all handsome and considerate – that wasn't playing fair.

'Where have you gone for that tea? Ceylon?' His voice made me jump.

'I'm coming,' I shouted back, grabbing the tray holding the cups from the side.

When I walked into the living room he was standing by the window.

'Admiring the view?' I asked.

He turned and grinned at me. 'It's a lovely view. I like looking at it.'

Ignore it, Abigail, just give him his bloody tea. I passed him his drink and he took it and sat down on the sofa. Leaning back, he looked very comfortable and as if he wasn't going to be rushed. He patted the cushion next to him.

'Come and sit, let's talk.'

Oh, no, Mr Chance, no way. I'm not putting myself within touching distance. I perched on the arm of the sofa, out of reach. Jack raised an eyebrow but said nothing. He sipped his tea and looked round the room; I was embarrassed by how shabby it looked. It was clean and tidy, but I'd never really had any spare cash to waste on interior decorating. Maybe I should bring Terry Egan up here and show him around? I thought. That ought to be enough to convince him that I didn't have a million pounds squirrelled away somewhere. The thought of that man made me shudder and I wrapped my hands around my mug of hot tea to try and ward off the chill I felt. Jack sipped his drink, watching me over the rim of his cup. Eventually he spoke.

'What did Flo mean earlier, about "bloody Americans" in the café this morning?'

I was hoping he hadn't heard that.

'Lexie came to see me this morning. You only just missed her, actually.' A look of something I couldn't quite place flashed briefly across his face. He put his cup down and leaned forward, forearms resting on his thighs.

'What did she want?'

'A green tea. I tried to tempt her with a sticky bun, but she wasn't interested.'

'Ha, ha. Very funny. I meant what was she doing here?'

'I know what you meant. I'm just not sure whether I should be discussing this with you.'

'Why the hell not? What did she say? She didn't upset you, did she?'

'No. She was really sweet and surprisingly mature for a girl her age.' I recalled Lexie's laser-sharp insights into my motivations and it made me smile.

'What's funny? I'm not sure I like the idea of the two of you having secrets.'

'Why not? Got something to hide, Jack?' I asked, playfully.

'No. I'm an open book.'

I sipped my tea, trying to buy myself some time. What should I tell him? 'Be honest' – Lexie's words echoed in my mind. 'She felt like she needed to see me, to reassure me that there wasn't anything between the two of you.'

'Go on.'

'Well, like I said to her, it doesn't make any difference either way. You and I are just friends, right?'

'Right. Friends.' Jack took a large gulp of his tea and sat back in his chair.

'She also told me that she loves you.'

He didn't react. Instead he stared at the floor and sighed heavily.

'You knew that already, didn't you?'

He nodded.

'When did she tell you?'

'She didn't. Not in so many words anyway. The day after your parents' funeral, after you and I had talked and decided to be friends again, I told her about it. I told her that you were important enough for me to want to give that a try. She said that sounded great but there was something in her eyes, something sad that I hadn't ever seen before. I kinda guessed then.' He put his head in his hands and when he eventually looked up at me, I could see the guilt in his eyes.

'I felt bloody awful when I realised. I couldn't believe I hadn't seen it. I'm such an idiot. I've hurt her, someone I care about. I never meant to do that. I thought I'd always been very clear about my feelings. I'd always treated her like—'

'A little sister?' I interrupted.

'Yes. Exactly.'

I shook my head. 'And people tell me I'm shit at picking up signals. I hate it when I'm right.'

'You must think I'm a selfish arsehole.'

'You're not selfish, Jack. Ignorant, emotionally retarded, blind as a fucking bat, but not selfish.'

'Thanks, that's very good of you.'

'You're welcome.'

'I don't know what to do now. I want to make it right. I do care about Lexie, just not in the way she wants me to.'

'Don't do anything. Give her some time to get over you. It is possible to get over you. Take it from someone who knows.' Liar!

'So, you're over me, are you?'

'Totally. Your charms don't work on me. I don't care how big your bank balance is.'

'That makes a nice change. I've met plenty of women who were *only* interested in my bank balance.'

I tried to lighten the mood. 'Wow! Exactly how well off are you, then?'

'Don't joke, Abigail. Having money can cause as many problems as it solves,' he said, sadly.

'Funny how it's always the people with money who say that. I'd like to be a fiver behind you.'

'I know it must sound pathetic to you, after everything you've had to go through, bringing up a kid on your own, running your business. But at least you've had people you can rely on to be there for you, people who will watch your back, friends and family that care about you and what happens to you.'

'Don't you have that, then? You must have friends? And what about your mother? She loves you enough to want to see you married and settled.'

'Aah, yes, my mum. The woman who tried to convince me that I was better off settling for what Lexie had to offer rather than waste my time looking for real love. That's how much she cares about me.'

'I'm sure that's not true. I know a thing or two about emotionally distant mothers and I've come to realise that, however misguided their actions may seem, they usually come from a good place. And, of course, I also have the added bonus of speaking as a mother myself. No one tells you how to do this parent thing. They hand you a baby and then you just wing it and hope you don't do them any permanent damage.'

'You've done an amazing job. She's a great girl.'

'Yes, she is. But I didn't know that was going to happen when I had her. I could have done all the wrong things just as easily as I did the right ones and messed it up entirely. I'm sure your mum just wants you to be happy, that's all. That's all any parent wants for their kids really.' I reached out and placed my hand on his arm.

'Lucy's very lucky to have you.'

'I'm the lucky one. I've been able to watch her turn into this amazing young woman, ready to take on the world.' I could feel the tears coming. 'What am I going to do without her, Jack?' I said, quietly. Jack moved closer to me and pulled me into his arms. Once again, I found myself reluctantly pushing him away, but he didn't let me go completely. Taking my chin in his hands, he tilted my face up so I was looking into his beautiful brown eyes. I thought he was going to kiss me but then he let his hand drop and he picked up his cup of tea. Disappointment filled me.

'What do you want to do now, Abigail? With your life, I mean?' He sipped his tea and watched me closely over the rim of his cup. Was he playing games with me? My disappointment turned to anger – I wasn't about to be toyed with. I moved to the other side of the room.

'I'll keep running the café for as long as possible, take care of Matt and Flo, I guess. Nothing very exciting.'

'Well, Matt's big enough to take care of himself and I doubt Flo needs much help from you in that department either. Stop putting obstacles in your way – what do *you* want?'

'I don't know… I haven't really thought about it.'

'Then start thinking. You must have some ideas about what you want to do with the rest of your life?'

'Ideas are all well and good but they cost money. Money that I don't have.'

'If money is your only problem then I can—'

I cut him off. 'I don't want your money, Jack. I'm not a charity case or one of your gold-digging girlfriends.'

'Believe me, I know that. This isn't charity, it's business. You can pay me back.'

'Thanks, but no. Money and friendship don't mix.'

'Just think about it.'

'I don't have to think about it. It's not a good idea.' The last thing I wanted was to complicate our friendship even more.

'What about your parents? Did they leave you anything?'

I laughed. 'That depends on who you talk to.'

Jack looked confused and I realised I'd have to tell him everything now.

'I wasn't going to say anything – it's so stupid it's not even worth repeating, really.'

'What is it?'

'Terry Egan – the man from the funeral.'

'The gangster wannabe in the hat?'

'That's him.'

'What about him?'

'Apparently he's convinced that me and Matt have got a million pounds hidden somewhere and he claims it belongs to him.'

'What?'

'The missing proceeds of the last job that he did with my dad.'

'Jesus, Abigail!'

'I know, it's ridiculous. I mean, look at this place. If I had a million pounds I wouldn't be living in a flat with dodgy plumbing and a boiler that only works when it wants to.' I smiled but Jack looked serious.

'Has he threatened you? Or Matt?'

'Not as such. He's just a silly old man spreading stories, that's all.'

'I can get you some protection. Let me make some calls.' He reached into his pocket for his phone, but I went across and took hold of his arm.

'Don't be daft. I don't need protection, it's fine.'

He looked down at my hand on his arm. 'Abigail.'

He only said my name, but it was enough; I felt him tense underneath my touch and fireworks went off inside my brain. I moved my hand away and went back to sit on the sofa. Say something, Abby, you big dumb idiot, say anything.

'More tea?' I sat forward and reached for the pot.

Jack cleared his throat and then came and sat beside me. 'Sure, why not?'

I concentrated on getting the tea into the cup rather than all over the table, conscious of the feeling of his leg pressed against mine.

'What were your ideas, then?'

'Hmmm?'

'You said just now that you had ideas, but they cost money. What ideas?'

My mind went blank.

'To be honest, I think I've spent so long being Lucy's mum that Abby has almost disappeared. Everything's always been about Lucy. My one focus in life has always been to protect and care for her and send her out into the world as well prepared as she can be. I don't think I remember how to do anything else.'

'You're selling yourself short. You run your own business; that takes some doing. Believe me, I know.'

'But even that's been about Lucy, in a way.'

'How do you mean?'

'You've seen it – the café isn't a hugely successful endeavour. We're barely breaking even most months. I should have called it quits a long time ago, but I hung on here because this is Lucy's home. The little money I made was enough to keep us afloat so I just carried on.'

'What would you have done, then? If you only had yourself to think about.'

'I don't know. Closed the café maybe, concentrated

more on the cake-making side of things. Weddings, birthdays, corporate stuff. I think that's the reason I jumped at the chance to help Liz cater your party. It gave me a safe way to fulfil one of my own dreams for a change.'

'And you did brilliantly. Your food was amazing.'

'Thanks.'

'So, what now?'

I shrugged. 'Don't know. What if I don't know how to be anything other than Lucy's mum?' I said. 'Now who sounds pathetic?'

'You're not pathetic. You're strong and beautiful and you can do whatever you set your mind to. I have no doubt about that, Abigail, no doubt at all.' He smiled at me, a dazzling smile that made my insides fizz and the blood rush in my ears.

'Why didn't you kiss me just now?' I asked.

'Because I made a promise. That we would be friends until you decided that you were ready for something more. I'm a patient man, Abigail – when it's something I really want, I'll wait as long as it takes.'

I knew then what was going to happen next; if I'm being honest I think I'd always known. I was too tired to fight it any more. Why couldn't I have something for me? The idea that I might be about to do something that I'd promised myself I wouldn't sent a shiver through my body.

'Lexie told me that she thinks you're in love with me.'

'Is that a question?'

'No. Yes. Maybe.'

'Ask me the question, Abigail. If you really want to know, you just have to ask.'

My heart was racing and my skin felt as if it were on fire.

'Are you in love with me, Jack?' My voice came out in a strangled whisper – very sexy – and Jack smiled. I dropped my gaze; the intensity in his eyes was too much.

'Look at me, Abigail. Please.' His rich voice was gruff and full of emotion. I raised my head and looked into his eyes.

'I am very much in love with you.'

I couldn't control it; my breathing quickened and I could feel the first flush of something like desire start to heat me from inside. Jack's eyes ignited the fire in my own. He moved closer to me and took my face in his hands; his gaze roamed over me hungrily, just waiting. His beautiful mouth was so close, just one small move would have brought us together, but neither of us budged. We stayed like that, examining each other as if it were the first time we'd met, our breath coming in short, heavy bursts, until finally I couldn't wait any longer. I leaned in and brushed my lips ever so gently across his. He closed his eyes, his hands not leaving my face, and he rested his forehead on mine. Moving one hand to gently hold the back of my neck, he closed his mouth over mine with a ferocity that took my breath away. His kiss was hard and desperate and so full of passion that I couldn't help but return it with equal force. He pushed me gently back onto the sofa and pulled me underneath his body. I'd never been kissed like that. My whole body was covered by his lean and muscular frame. I ran my hands across his back, his arms, his chest; I wanted to feel every inch of him. He tore his mouth away from mine and looked at me lying beneath him.

'What now, Abigail? I told you before that you have all the power here and I meant it. Nothing is going to happen between us unless you want it to.' He kissed me softly on the lips.

There it was, there was my way out, I thought to myself, my way of making sure that this didn't happen. I could tell him no, right now, and then he'd never have to see me in my M&S undies. I wouldn't have to see the look of disappointment on his face as he compared my childbearing body, cellulite and all, to the Barbie dolls he was used to dating. He wouldn't have to pretend to be turned on by my less than perky boobs and saggy tummy. Just tell him to go now, it's easier in the long run, I told myself. Before I could speak, almost as if he could read my mind, he pulled me closer and I could feel his need for me.

'I won't pretend that I'm not desperate to drag you to your bedroom and spend hours making you come. You are so sexy, no matter what you've convinced yourself about the way you look, and I will spend all night trying to convince you of that if I have to.' His eyes burned into mine and I could see that he meant every word.

'What about Lucy and Flo? They're only downstairs.'

'I think we probably have their blessing after the performance they put on for us just now.'

I cringed a little at the thought that my daughter and a grey-haired pensioner probably knew I was about to have sex, even before I'd realised it myself. Jack laughed at my embarrassed expression. 'We're not doing anything wrong, Abigail. We've got nothing to be ashamed of.'

'I know.' I had no more excuses, no more reasons why it shouldn't happen. 'Yes,' I said, my voice barely a whisper.

'Are you sure?'

'Don't give me a chance to talk myself out of it; I want this to happen. I won't pretend I'm not bloody terrified, but I think I'm done with feeling scared.'

Jack's face was lit by an enormous smile and he pulled me close for a breath-taking kiss. He rested his forehead on mine and closed his eyes.

'I've missed you so much,' he says, 'and now you're here. I'm never leaving you again, you know that, don't you?'

'Don't make promises you can't keep,' I whispered. His eyes flew open at my response and he pulled his face away from mine.

'What do you mean?'

'We don't know what's going to happen, no one does. You have a life in America. You can't give all that up for me. I don't want you to do that. Let's just enjoy this for now. For as long as it lasts. I'm okay with that.'

'I'm not okay with that! If you think I'm just going to walk away from this...'

'And exactly what is this?'

'It's us, Abigail, you and me and the future.' He looked at me, his eyes pleading with me to agree. I had no answers, I didn't dare think that far ahead, so I leaned in and kissed him hard on the mouth. He returned my kiss with so much passion that within seconds everything we'd been talking about was forgotten. In that moment, we had only this, this fire, this passion that could be ignited by even the smallest touch. He lifted me into his arms and carried me over to the door.

'Bedroom...' I murmured into his mouth' ... that way.' I gestured towards the end of the hallway and he carried me towards my room. He kicked open the door and went inside, lowering me to the floor so we were standing face to face. I didn't know what to do next; he looked so out of place in my tatty bedroom, with his sharp suit and expensive watch making it obvious that he didn't belong there. What was I thinking? I felt awkward and shy. I wasn't totally inexperienced but I wondered if there were new things I should have learned? Perhaps I should have done some research – looked up 'New sex moves for the perpetually frigid' online – that might have helped. Or not. I decided to just power through and pray that I didn't do anything embarrassing. I pushed his jacket off his shoulders but then I didn't know what to do with it. I couldn't throw it on the floor; it was bloody Armani, I noticed. I lobbed it over onto the chair in the corner of my room and Jack laughed. God, I loved that sound!

'I don't care about the suit, Abigail. Tear it off me with your teeth if you want.'

I shook my head.

'I mean it. Now turn around.' I did as I was told; he lifted my shirt up and over my head and then began to drop kisses down my back until he was kneeling on the floor behind me. He grasped my hips and turned me back to face him. This was it, I told myself; this was the moment he would be confronted with my stretch marks and suddenly realise that this was all a dreadful mistake. He undid the buttons on my jeans and pulled them slowly down my legs. My knees were shaking as I stood there in my underwear, in front of a man who was so gorgeous it made my brain hurt. He was kneeling in front of me as if I were a goddess to be worshipped and, most startlingly, he hadn't fled from the room at the sight of my body! He began to nip and kiss my skin as he stood back up, his hands travelling slowly over my hips, until they came to rest on my breasts. I swallowed nervously as he reached around to unclasp my bra. In one swift move, he took it off and dropped it to the floor before cupping both my breasts greedily in his hands and kissing them gently.

'This isn't fair,' I moaned as he began to suck gently on one of my nipples. Oh, God, it felt so amazing. 'I'm practically naked and you're still almost completely dressed.' He raised his head from my breasts and just shrugged.

'What should we do about that, then?' he asked, coyly. I knew exactly what to do about that. Slowly, with my fingers slightly trembling, I unbuttoned his shirt and let it fall to the floor. Christ on a bike! I was confronted with the most beautiful chest I'd ever seen and a set of abs most blokes could only dream of. A faint line of dark hair disappeared down into his waistband; he was like something out of a magazine and I couldn't stop smiling.

'Are you laughing at me?' he asked.

'Good God, no,' I cried, 'but, I mean, look at you. And then look at me. It's ridiculous. You can't really want to—'

'Stop!' he exclaimed, grabbing both my hands. 'Just stop, okay?'

'What? I'm just being honest.'

He held my palms against his chest and I could feel his heart was thudding as much as mine. 'You are maddening, Abigail. How many times do I have to tell you how beautiful and sexy and strong you are before you believe it?'

I leant my forehead on his chest and tried to remember how to breathe.

'You are wonderful. You raised a child practically single-handed, a child who has grown into a beautiful and smart young woman. You did that, no one else. You don't know how strong you are. I am in awe of you, Abigail.'

I could feel tears pricking the backs of my eyes and my throat was choked with emotion. Wordlessly I pushed him back towards my bed and he sat down; I made short work of removing the rest of his clothes.

'Impressive,' he smirked. 'Your turn.'

I hooked my thumbs inside my underwear and slid them slowly down my legs.

'Gorgeous,' he said, his eyes raking over every inch of my naked body. I didn't feel self-conscious, I felt strong and desirable. I wanted this, I'd chosen to make this happen and, for once, I wasn't going to hold back. He pulled me onto the bed and we lay there, face to face. And yes, I was aware that this was not the best 'breast angle' for a woman of my age but I didn't care.

'Are you okay?' he asked. I'm sure he was just waiting for me to freak out and change my mind. To be fair, I had done that plenty of times to him recently, but he needn't have worried.

'I'm good, great, actually. I haven't felt this way for a

long time. It's a nice feeling.' I leaned closer and kissed him, gently at first but then it grew. The kiss deepened into something more passionate. My hands were in his hair, grabbing fistfuls and pulling him closer, as he slid his hand between my thighs and I gasped.

'I want you, Jack. Now. I don't want to wait any more.' My voice was thick with desire.

'You are my beautiful girl, Abigail. It's always been you.'

<u>Chapter 23</u>

I woke with a start and my heart sank as I realised I was alone; no sign of Jack. Perhaps I really had been that bad in bed and rather than face me he'd done a runner while I slept? I looked at my clock; it was 8.30 a.m. What the hell? Jack and I had spent most of yesterday in bed. He hadn't been joking when he'd said he wanted to spend hours making me come. I thought I'd managed to hold my own, as it were, but maybe not. I needed to get up. I couldn't lie there all day, obsessing over my obvious lack of skills in the boudoir.

I pulled on my pyjamas, but I couldn't find my dressing gown; I figured Lucy had borrowed it again. I kept telling her to get her own; she said she preferred mine because it smelled like me and, after years of wear, it was very soft, if a little bit ratty. I grabbed a sweatshirt instead and made my way to the kitchen; I needed a bucket of tea before I could even contemplate facing this day.

As I came down the hall I could hear noises coming from the kitchen. Pushing open the door, I was greeted by the sight of Jack, wearing my missing dressing gown and not much else. He was pouring hot water into the teapot and he'd laid my little kitchen table ready for breakfast for two. Relief flooded through me; he hadn't left. He was still there, in my kitchen making me breakfast and looking ridiculous. I practically sprinted across the kitchen and threw my arms around his neck.

'Hey, what's all this? Good morning to you too.'

'I woke up and you weren't there,' I rambled. 'I thought you'd gone.' I could feel traitorous tears forming. Jack held me at arm's length and looked deep into my eyes.

'Oh, baby, how could you think that? After yesterday, after everything I said, everything we did—' he gave me a knowing look '—there's no way I'm going anywhere. You have to believe that.' He looked at me imploringly; I couldn't answer, I just wiped away the tears and nodded. He pulled me close and kissed me tenderly.

'That's better. Now, how do you like your eggs?' He moved around my kitchen, making himself very at home, but he did look ridiculous in my fluffy pink dressing gown. It barely covered his very fine arse and only just met at the front; if anyone had walked in they would have been treated to a real eyeful. What about Lucy? I panicked; where was she? I was ashamed to say that I didn't even know if she'd come home last night. I was hoping that she hadn't since there was currently a half-naked man in the kitchen, bending over to look for eggs in the fridge.

'Have you seen Lucy?'

'Not this morning. I heard her come home late last night, but I think she left again soon after. You were very vocal, I seem to recall. Maybe she couldn't handle the noise.' He gave me a wink.

'Oh, God, no. Please don't say she heard us. That would be so embarrassing, for her and for me!' I put my head in my hands and then I heard Jack chuckling.

'You're lying, aren't you? That's not funny, Jack.'

'I couldn't resist. You look beautiful when you're embarrassed.' He turned his attention back to scrambling eggs and I felt little fireworks exploding in my heart at his compliment.

I spotted my phone, on the side by the sink, and went to fetch it. As if by magic a message from Lucy popped up.

> Morning Mum. Don't know if you're still having your little sleepover party but just to say I won't be home until this afternoon. Going out shopping with Becca, be back about 4!

I let out a sigh of relief and sat down at the kitchen table as Jack placed a plate of scrambled eggs in front of me.

'Everything okay?'

'Yes, fine. Lucy isn't coming home until later so...'

'So...?' His face lit up with a wolfish grin.

'Sit down and eat your eggs, you pervert. They look

very nice. It would be a shame to waste all your hard work.' I picked up a forkful and put them in my mouth. I swallowed and made deliberately sexy moaning noises while he stood beside me watching.

'Fuck the eggs!' Jack pulled me from my chair and crushed his mouth against mine. I returned the kiss, as Jack reached past me and swept everything off the table. The crash of plates and cutlery didn't distract either of us from our goal.

'Arms up,' he ordered. I happily complied as he removed my sweatshirt and pyjama top in one easy motion. He made equally light work of my pyjama bottoms and suddenly I was lying naked on my kitchen table. It was surreal: I was naked in my kitchen, about to have yet more mind-bending sex with the most beautiful man I'd ever laid eyes on, and he was looking at me as if I were the sexiest woman on the planet; things like that just didn't happen to me. It made me feel brave; I sat up and untied the belt on the dressing gown he was wearing. He shrugged it off and I gazed at his amazing body one more time.

'Oh, my goodness, you truly are a sight to behold.' It was his turn to look a little sheepish at my overt admiration.

'I like to work out, Abigail. It helps me focus. It's no big deal.' His dark eyes raked up and down my body and the look he gave me made my pulse jump in anticipation. 'Now, that's enough about me. Let's talk about what I'm going to do with you and this delicious body of yours.' He leaned over me and began kissing a trail down my stomach. It felt so good and I was more than happy to lie back and let him continue with his mission. His hand gently traced a path along my thigh and then up between my legs. I raised my head to watch him and he met my gaze, giving me a wicked grin.

'Lie back, baby, just relax.'

Relax? How could I be expected to relax when every nerve in my body was standing to attention? I closed my eyes and murmured my pleasure, but my contented mood was interrupted by the sound of a phone ringing; it was coming from my bedroom. It wasn't mine; it had to be Jack's.

'Jack, wait, your phone, it's your phone.'

'I'm busy. They'll call back if it's important,' he muttered into my stomach and carried on kissing his way down.

'Oh, God, that feels so good,' I murmured. The phone had stopped ringing, thankfully. I returned my focus to Jack's mouth and its ultimate destination, but I was disturbed again by the sound of his phone.

'They really want you, whoever it is,' I said. At least that was what I thought I said; I was finding it hard to get my mouth to form actual words at that moment.

'Damn it!' Jack muttered. He stood and took my hands to pull me back up into a sitting position on the table.

'It's fine, don't worry. You go and answer it while I deal with all this.' I gestured to the discarded breakfast mess that was all over my floor. The phone had stopped ringing but within seconds it started again.

'I'll be back. Don't go anywhere.'

'I'm naked in my kitchen – where am I likely to go?'

He took my face in his hands and gave me a lingering kiss, before he walked away. He hadn't bothered to put my robe back on and I was a tiny bit ashamed to admit that I watched his gorgeous butt all the way down the hall until it disappeared into my room.

Naked cleaning was not a pastime I was comfortable with, so I pulled on my discarded pyjamas before fetching a dustpan and brush from under the sink. I scooped up eggs and broken plates and dropped the whole lot into the bin. I was on my knees wiping the floor with a cloth when Jack came back. I was surprised, and more than a little bit disappointed, to see he was dressed.

'Everything all right?'

'Yeah, well, no. Look, I hate to do this to you, but I have to go.' He couldn't look me in the eye.

'Oh, right. Of course, that's fine.' I didn't know what else to say.

'It's nothing… just a work thing. I'll call you. Okay?' He turned to walk away but then stopped by the door and looked back to me. 'I'm sorry, Abigail.' He looked so sad and my heart sank to my feet.

'It's fine. Don't worry. We'll talk later.' I was aiming for bright and breezy, but I think I fell short. Something had changed but I didn't know what. Jack didn't answer me, he just turned and walked out. I heard the door close softly behind him and I was left holding my dustpan and brush and wondering what the fuck had just had happened.

Chapter 24

'So, he just left?' Liz refilled my wine glass. I'd been sitting at her breakfast bar for the last half an hour, trying to make some sense out of what had happened. Liz frowned as she stirred pasta sauce on her hob.

'Yes, he just left.' I took a sip of my wine. 'He left the room to take a call, when he came back he was dressed and then he left.'

'And he hasn't called?'

'Nope.'

'And it's now seven thirty and you haven't called him?'

'No, I bloody well haven't! And why should I? He walked out on me without a word. I'm not calling him.'

'All right, all right. Sorry I mentioned it. For what it's worth, I think you're right. He should be the one to call you.'

'Thank you.'

Liz went back to stirring her sauce and sipping her wine for a few minutes. Then she said, 'Just tell me again how good the sex was, though.'

'Liz!'

'Oh, go on. Humour this old married lady. How

many times did he make you come?' She sniggered behind her wine glass and I couldn't help smiling.

'I'm not talking about it anymore. It was nice but now it's over. And I'm all right.'

'Are you sure? You do look all right but with you I can never tell. You're very good at hiding things.'

'A skill I must have learned from my mother. Cheers, Mum!' I raised my glass to her. Her lies, about my dad and my brother, were something I was coming to terms with; I might not have agreed with how she'd gone about things, but I thought I was starting to understand her reasons why. Maybe.

'Any more word from that horrible Egan man?' asked Liz.

'No, nothing. He's probably buggered off back to Spain. I do wonder, though…'

'Wonder what?'

'Well, if there is a million pounds that's still unaccounted for, and me and Matt don't have it, then where did it go?'

Liz didn't reply; she switched off the gas under the sauce and went over to the bureau in the corner of her kitchen. She picked up her laptop and brought it over to me, placing it down without saying a word. When the screen sprang to life, I saw the results of a search Liz had been doing; stories about Jack and his business.

'What's all this?' I asked, putting down my glass and scrolling through the pages.

'I did a bit of research. It was something Hector said to me at the party. You remember Hector?'

I cast my mind back to the launch party, to the night Jack had re-entered my life.

'Hector the company lawyer? The old boy who kept staring at my boobs?'

'Yes, that's him. He made some remark about Jack's family and their money. About not being sure where it all came from.'

'Jack's a businessman. He develops computer stuff – he told me so.'

'I know, but how much do you know about him really? He's been out of your life for so many years. I mean, who knows what he's been up to over in America?'

'He's been working, building up his business. I don't see what you're getting at.'

'Just look, here, this article says that Jack's business grew up from nowhere. He's got some very influential clients – they wouldn't just take a punt on a nobody with no backing. Where did he get the kind of money he'd need to start that kind of business in the first place?'

I opened my mouth to answer but realised I couldn't – the truth was, I didn't know. I'd just taken his word for it, about the business, about a lot of things. 'Are you saying that Jack's family have had the missing money all these years?'

'You did say that they disappeared not long after your dad did. It seems a bit of a coincidence, don't you think?'

'Jack knows all about Egan and his threats – if he had the money he would have told me. He wouldn't put me in danger like that.' Would he?

'You're probably right. Forget I mentioned it.' Liz closed the laptop and went back to preparing dinner. 'Do you want linguine or tagliatelle with this sauce?'

'Anything is fine.'

Liz nodded and carried on cooking.

'There's just no way that Jack or his family could have the money. Jack's mum married a really rich bloke – she wouldn't need to keep stolen money.' I took a large mouthful of my wine. My head was spinning – not from the wine, more from everything that had happened. I felt as if I was about to faint.

'Are you all right? You've gone very pale.'

'Could I have some water?' I croaked.

Liz grabbed a glass and filled it. I drank it down in one go and then held the glass out for a refill. Liz duly obliged, then sat on the other side of the kitchen island, looking worried.

'I'm fine now. Thanks for the water. Is it hot in here or is it me?' I flapped the neck of my shirt, trying to waft cool air down my front. My chest felt so tight. What the heck was wrong with me? Liz picked up a newspaper and flapped it in my direction; that was actually more annoying than helpful, so I reached out and held her arm. I stayed like that for a few minutes, holding onto Liz's arm and trying to take deep breaths. Eventually I started to feel better.

'It's fine. I'm fine now.'

'Are you sure?' Liz examined my face closely.

'I'm sure. It's happened a few times in the last couple of weeks. I get this horrible panicky feeling and then I feel faint. The room starts to spin, and I can't stop it.'

'Sounds like an anxiety attack, my darling. It's not surprising, considering everything that's happened recently. It's been very stressful for you.'

'I guess so. I thought I was coping all right with everything but maybe not.'

'It's a lot to come to terms with, all these revelations about your family. As well as everything you're feeling about Jack.'

'He's the least of my worries.'

'Is he? I'd say he's one of the more significant ones.'

'Don't be daft. He's just a bloke. I'm not a fucking teenager, dealing with my first crush,' I snapped.

'No, you're a grown woman who's spent so long protecting herself from the risk of having her heart broken that you don't know how to do anything else. And the fact that all that might be about to change, quite frankly, scares you shitless! Cheers!' Liz downed the rest of her wine in one go and slammed the empty glass down onto the counter. I got the very obvious sense that I'd just been told off.

'I'm sorry, I didn't mean to shout at you, but someone has to get you to see what's going on,' said Liz.

'Thanks.' I went back to sipping my water and Liz returned to her spot by the stove. I didn't know where to take our conversation next. Thankfully I was saved from further awkwardness by the arrival of David, Liz's husband.

'Right, ladies, I've kept out of the kitchen up to this point, but I cannot wait any longer. I'm bloody starving. I need feeding.' He went over to Liz and peered over the pan she was stirring. 'That smells good. When's dinner? Are you staying for dinner, Abby?'

'Of course, she is,' announced Liz. 'Get your fingers out of my sauce and go and lay the table.'

'Yes, sir!' David gave her a little salute, before grabbing cutlery and glasses and moving over to the dining table on the other side of the open-plan kitchen. As I watched the two of them, so familiar and comfortable together, I felt a pang of something like envy. They had each other; even when their kids grew up and left home, they'd still have each other. I took another mouthful of water in an attempt to try and swallow down the sudden lump in my throat; I felt so empty and alone. I discreetly wiped away a rogue tear, praying that no one had seen me, but no such luck. David came and draped his arm across my shoulders.

'Now, what's all this? Why the tears?'

'It's nothing, I'm being stupid.'

'Who's upset you? Do I need to go and rough someone up a bit for you?' He nudged my shoulder.

'No offence, darling husband of mine, but I don't think "roughing" people up is really your thing. You're an accountant, darling.' Liz kissed him on the cheek and David laughed.

'You're probably right. I'll go back to folding napkins, then. Chin up, old girl, things are never as bad as they seem.'

I nodded and wiped away more tears.

'Why don't you just call him?' said Liz, handing me a tissue.

'I don't know what I'd say. Maybe it was just sex, maybe it didn't mean anything.'

'He told you he was in love with you, didn't he?'

'Yes, but—'

'No buts. I don't know him that well, but he doesn't strike me as a man who says things he doesn't mean.'

'Maybe. But I'm not going to call him.'

Liz held up her hands. 'Fine. Let's just get on with our dinner, then, shall we?'

I know I must have answered her, but I can't remember what I said. In fact, I can't remember much of anything about our conversation for the rest of the evening. My mind was elsewhere. Occasionally David and Liz would exchange worried glances when I didn't answer a question they'd asked me, but I wasn't really bothered. I stayed there just long enough to eat the food that Liz had prepared and then I made my excuses and left.

*

I didn't go home after I left Liz's; I drove past my flat and ended up outside my mum's old house instead. It felt like the safest place for me to be right then. Who was I kidding? I was hiding. I needed to be somewhere that Jack couldn't get to me. Jack bloody Chance, with his dreamy smile and awesome body. Jack and his uncanny ability to turn my peaceful existence into a fucking emotional train wreck. God, I felt like such a fool. I'd let my guard down, against my better judgement, and look what had happened.

Letting myself into the house, I was calmed by the silence. The storm raging inside my head was quietened momentarily by an all-enveloping cloud of stillness that was almost physical. I could feel it wrap itself around me and hold me there as I leaned heavily on the door behind me. I breathed in deeply. The once familiar smell of the house had been replaced by a musty, stagnant odour, that reminded me this was no longer a family home. It was just a house that held some furniture and a few memories, and soon it would belong to someone else. I pushed myself away from the door, dropped my bag by the hallstand and walked down the narrow passageway to the kitchen.

I flicked on the light and then stood like a fool, in the middle of the room, unsure of what to do next. You should call Jack, said my inner devil. No, you shouldn't, countered the angel on my shoulder. I spied some empty boxes by the back door; Matt had told me he'd started bringing them over to pack Mum's things in. This was the perfect exercise in procrastination. There was a stack of old newspapers in one of the boxes so I started to carefully wrap each cup and plate, as if they were priceless antiques to be preserved rather than Mum's old chipped everyday china.

Within about half an hour I'd emptied all the crockery cupboards, only leaving out a few stained mugs and the teapot, just in case. I moved across to the tall cupboard she'd used as a pantry and began emptying the contents of that into some black rubbish bags I'd found under the sink. I was like a woman possessed, throwing away packets and tins. Halfway through, when I'd filled a whole bag with food, I stopped and wondered guiltily if I should have been giving this stuff away to neighbours or the nearby food bank, but the idea that I'd have to leave the house to do it soon put an end to any more thoughts like that. I didn't want to go out. I didn't want to see anyone and, more importantly, I didn't want anyone to see me.

I spent another half an hour or so clearing, wrapping and packing boxes. After the larder was empty, save for a lone packet of digestive biscuits and some pasta, I moved over to the drawers by the sink. Opening the first one, I saw cutlery and utensils; I picked them up by the handful and dumped them into a nearby box. The crash they made as they hit the bottom was almost deafening in the quiet of the house, but it was strangely satisfying. I took it as a symbol of progress and moving forward; I was obviously desperate to find some positives in my current situation. Sad but true. The next drawer was the one Mum always referred to as her 'crap' drawer, full of bits and pieces that were essentially just rubbish. Old biros, keys for long-forgotten doors, bits of string of random lengths and fuses; they all languished in the drawer until the day they were needed. That day never came for most of the stuff in there, but it hadn't seemed to bother Mum.

I was tempted to pull the whole thing out and tip the contents, unchecked, into the nearest bin bag but something stopped me – it was an envelope with my name on it, the one that I'd found just after Mum died; the night I'd drunk-dialled Jack and he'd stormed out of my life. I'd thrown it back in the drawer, not wanting to take the chance that it might contain more interesting secrets about my family. I couldn't believe that I'd forgotten about it. Mind you, I had had quite a lot going on. Now there it was again, the stained envelope held shut by sticky tape, with the words 'For Abigail' scrawled on the front. I took it over to the kitchen table and sat down. I tore off the sticky tape and opened it, surprised to find that there were three more envelopes inside. They were all stamped and addressed to me but the writing on them didn't belong to my mum – it was Jack's.

Chapter 25

My hands shook as I held the letters. The postmarks had long since faded but I didn't need them; these were the letters Jack had said he wrote to me after he left. For the last twenty years they'd been sitting in the bottom of this drawer. How had I never seen them before? How many times had I scratched around in this drawer, looking for a pen to write a shopping list or a battery to stick in the plastic kitchen clock that hung above the table?

I tore open the top one on the pile; the date was for a week after Jack left, the numbers written in Jack's childish hand. I wanted to read them in the right order, so I checked the dates on the other two. Opening them, I saw that one was sent three months later, the other only a month. I felt scared; it was all so long ago, what did it really matter what they said? But the perverse part of me, the part that enjoyed torturing itself, took over and I started to read.

> *Dear Abigail,*
>
> *I'm hoping you get this letter soon. I've had to leave. Something to do with Dad's new job at a bank up north. We're*

going to stay with some of Mum's cousins in Glasgow, I think. I'm not supposed to tell you any of this but I don't know why. I've never met any of this side of my family before. I'm a bit scared to be honest. I wish I'd been allowed to come and see you before we left but Mum said I couldn't. She said we didn't have time. She's been really moody for the last few weeks so I didn't argue. But now I wish I had because I know you're going to be worried about me. I'm fine. I don't care what Mum says I'm going to ring and tell you where I am just as soon as I know what our new address and phone number are going to be. I miss you already.

Love Jack xx

I clapped my hand across my mouth to stifle the sob; his childish confusion at being dragged away from his home came across so clearly it made me ache inside. The next letter was dated a month later.

Dear Abigail,

I don't know what's going on. Mum and Dad have both told me that I'm not allowed to get in touch with anyone we used to know but they won't tell me why.

They just keep saying that they'll explain it to me when I get older! I think maybe Dad has done something awful and that's why we've had to move away. Our new flat is nice but I don't fit in here, I want to come home but every time I say something Mum just screams at me to shut up. Dad looks really stressed out, I don't want him to feel bad about all of this so I don't say anything in front of him. I hope you're all right, I really miss you, I wish I could phone you but I'm worried I'm going to ruin everything if I don't do as Mum tells me and stay away. If my dad has done something bad I would hate to drag you and your family into it too. But I want to know that you're okay and that you don't hate me for disappearing. I've included an address at the top this letter so you can just write back and let me know how you are. It's not my address – my new mate from school, Chris, said I could use his so I don't get into trouble for letting on where we are.

Love Jack xx

My heart was breaking, but I couldn't stop now. I

had one letter left; it was dated three months after Jack and his family moved away. This one was short and to the point.

> *When you didn't reply to my letter I sneaked down to the phone box and called your house. Your nan answered and told me that you didn't want to talk to me and that I shouldn't get in touch again. I don't understand. I told you that I didn't want to leave you. It wasn't my fault. Your nan said that you were angry and didn't want me to keep in touch anymore. I'm sorry you feel like that. I don't want to upset you so this will be my last letter unless I hear from you. I never wanted to hurt you, you are my best friend and I will always miss you.*
> *Jack*

'Of course I didn't reply!' I screamed at the letter in my hand. 'I never saw your letters. I never saw anything because I was a stupid fucking child! Stupid! I didn't know anything!' I swept all the letters and envelopes onto the floor and started to cry uncontrollably. I couldn't breathe, I couldn't see, all I could do was feel; the pain of everything that had happened, past and present, was transforming itself into a physical ache that was taking over my entire body. Everything hurt, my lungs were burning, my arms and legs felt as if they were being jabbed with a thousand needles and my brain was trying to force its way out through my eye sockets. I couldn't move from the chair. I gripped the seat until my knuckles turned white, trying to hold on until the tidal wave of pain stopped. Through blurry eyes, I saw a figure running down the hallway towards me and calling my name.

'Fucking hell, Abs, what's going on? Are you all right? Abby, look at me, say something!'

It was my brother; I felt his arms holding me tight.

'Can't... breathe... hurts... won't stop...' I managed. He let me go and grabbed his phone from his pocket.

'I'm calling an ambulance, Abby, I don't know what to do...'

The mention of an ambulance was like a slap in the face; I didn't want an ambulance.

'No, stop, wait... I'll be fine.' I took deep breaths, trying to calm my racing pulse. Matt knelt in front of me and took my hands, helping me get my breath.

'That's it, Abs, good girl, in and out, just like that.'

Gradually my breathing returned to normal and the pain in my body started to subside. Matt brought me a mug of water. 'Here, drink it slowly.'

He looked as white as a sheet. I must have scared him half to death.

'Sorry, I didn't mean to freak you out.'

'I thought you were having a bloody stroke or something! Your face was all twisted up, like you were in agony, and you couldn't focus your eyes properly! Jesus!' He let out a huge sigh and flopped down into the chair opposite. 'Drink,' he ordered and gestured to the mug in my hands. I sipped the water.

'I couldn't seem to stop it. I was in so much pain.'

'What started it off?'

I gestured to the letters on the floor. 'Those.'

'What are they?' he asked, kneeling to pick them up.

'Letters from Jack. He wrote to me after he left but no one ever gave them to me.'

Matt started to read. 'What a fucking mess,' he said, eventually.

'That could be the title of my autobiography, couldn't it?'

'What are you going to do now? You should tell him that you've read these.'

'What for? It's past – no point going over it all now.' I decided it was best I didn't share the fact that Jack had slept with me and then buggered off – there were some things that a big brother didn't need to know.

Matt gave a me a serious look. 'You should talk to Jack, Abby.'

'I know, I know. But not right now. I need time to think.'

Matt nodded and it was then I noticed the fresh bruise below his eye.

'What happened to you?' I leaned closer to get a better look.

'It's nothing, Abs, don't fuss.'

'Who did it?'

'It doesn't matter.'

I reached out to touch his face but he pulled away, wincing in pain.

'Jesus, Matt, what happened?'

'I had a visit from Egan and a couple of his cronies. Nothing I can't handle.'

'This is about that missing money? I thought you said that Egan had dropped all that. He's not stupid enough to think we have that sort of cash.'

Matt shook his head. 'I thought I'd convinced him but apparently not. He must be desperate if he's still hanging about round here. It's a bit of a risk.'

'How do you mean?'

'Technically he's still a wanted man. The police never caught up with him back then, but they could arrest him if they found him here now.'

'Let's go to the police, then. Show them your face, tell them where he is.'

Matt shook his head. 'We can't, Abs. It'll stir up all kinds of stuff that's best left alone. It'll be fine. I'll get it sorted.'

A thought suddenly occurred to me. 'Does he know that he's your real dad?'

'Dunno. I don't think so, but I can't be sure.'

'I don't think he knows. Why would he threaten his own son?' I said.

'Egan used to beat the crap out of his other two boys. Why would he treat me any differently?'

'What are we going to do, then?'

'Nothing. Just leave it alone, Abs. It'll sort itself out eventually.'

'You're not going to do anything stupid, are you?' I asked.

'Me? Nah, not me, Abs. I'm too pretty for prison.'

'Idiot,' I mumbled.

Matt gave me a smile. 'I'm sorry, Abby.'

'Which particular bit are you sorry for?'

'All of it. I'm sorry for all of it.'

'I don't want to fight with you about it. Not today. I don't think I can take much more.'

'Are you all right?' Matt looked concerned.

'I'm fine, just tired, that's all. And there's still so much to do here. Are you going to stay and help me pack up some stuff?'

'Yeah, just gimme a bin bag and tell me what needs doing.' He unravelled a bag from the roll and waited for instructions.

'You can start on the living room. I'm going to finish up in here.'

'And what about those?' Matt pointed to the letters on the table. Without a second thought, I picked them up and threw them in the bag he was holding. Matt raised an eyebrow. 'Really? You're just going to bin 'em?'

'Yep. No point dwelling on the past. Time to move on,' I said, with a certainty I didn't really feel. He left the room and I carried on emptying the cupboards in the kitchen.

I was midway through wiping the shelves in the cupboard under the sink when there was a knock at the front door.

'I'll get it!' hollered Matt.

I was halfway out of the cupboard, my arse stuck in the air, when I heard someone walk into the kitchen.

'Who was it?' I clambered to my feet, expecting to see my brother.

'Hello, Abigail.'

I turned to see Jack, with a look on his face that told me I wasn't going to enjoy the next few minutes.

I wiped my hands on my jeans and attempted to tidy my hair up a bit. 'I thought you'd dropped off the planet,' I said, aiming for cheerful but landing on slightly hysterical. 'Was it something I said?'

He didn't reply so I hurtled on. 'Can I get you a drink? Tea? Oh, but I don't think I have any milk... let me just...' I went to the fridge but his voice stopped me before I could open the door.

'I'm going back to America, Abigail. I have to leave.' His voice was flat and cold.

'Has something happened? Is your mum okay?'

'She's fine... It's not that...' He struggled with the words. 'I'm sorry... I just have to go... I wanted to say goodbye.'

'When will you be back?'

He wouldn't look at me; he kept his gaze firmly fixed on the floor. I didn't need to hear him say it out loud to know what the answer was.

'You're not coming back, are you?' I felt a tightness pulling across my chest. Keep it together, Abby, just breathe.

'I'm so sorry.'

'Stop saying you're sorry!' I yelled. He flinched at my raised voice and when he looked up his eyes were so full of sadness, it made my heart hurt. I reached out towards him, but he backed away.

'I have to go but you have to believe me when I say that I never meant for this to happen. I never meant to hurt you.'

'And yet you're doing it anyway. Please just tell me what's going on.'

He shook his head. 'You deserve so much better than me, Abigail. Take care of yourself.' He turned and walked out of the kitchen; I followed close on his heels, determined to make him talk to me.

'Jack... wait... please.'

He reached for the door but didn't open it. 'It would never have worked,' he said, quietly, without turning around. I couldn't believe my ears; how dared he?

'I don't fucking believe this!' I exclaimed. 'You're using all my excuses against me. You were the one who said I was wrong, you convinced me that we owed it to ourselves to give it a try and now you're throwing my words back in my face!' I lost all control; my first punch landed in the middle of his back but he didn't even flinch, so I started raining puny blows down onto his shoulders. 'You're an arsehole and a coward,' I screamed, 'and I hate you for doing this to me. Why did you have to come back and fuck everything up?' I couldn't stop myself, the rage was so strong, but Jack didn't even turn around.

'Abs, stop! Calm down.' My brother came out of the living room and grabbed me, holding my arms by my sides whilst I shouted. Jack opened the front door and stepped out onto the path. He turned back to me, and I was shocked to see tears in his eyes; shocked but not sad. He didn't deserve my sympathy. I pushed my way out of my brother's grasp and lunged towards the door.

'You don't deserve me, Jack Chance! And I refuse to waste any more time on you. Have a nice fucking life!' I slammed the door so hard that the glass rattled and then leant against it, breathing heavily.

'What the bloody hell just happened?' asked Matt.

'It's nothing.'

'Didn't look like nothing. I thought you two were friends or whatever?'

'So did I. Apparently I was wrong.'

'He's gone, then, has he?'

I nodded, wrapping my arms around myself to ward off the sudden chill I felt. I started to shiver slightly but, to my amazement, I wasn't crying. The tears that had threatened a few moments before had been replaced by a creeping sense of numbness.

'I'm going to pack up Mum's room.' I pushed myself away from the door and started up the stairs. Each step felt as if I were dragging my body through a swamp; my limbs felt like dead weights and my head was swimming.

'Why did you let him walk away if you love him so much?' The question stopped me dead in my tracks.

'It wasn't up to me. He'd already made up his mind that he was leaving. I wasn't about to start begging him to stay.'

'Why is he going?'

'Don't know, don't care. Probably all for the best in the long run.' I turned to face my brother. 'Now, I'm going to finish clearing stuff upstairs. If you want to come and help me that would be lovely, but only if you can manage to keep your trap shut about all of this.' I gave him a look that dared him to argue.

'Fine. After you, then, you stubborn old tart.' He gave me a little bow and walked over to the stairs. I couldn't resist giving him a little peck on the cheek.

'Thanks. I love you, you big idiot. You know that, don't you?'

'Well, I am very loveable,' he said, 'and so are you, in your own weird way.'

'Thanks, I think.'

'Just be kind to yourself, all right?'

'That's all I'm trying to do.'

'Right, then. Let's go and see what sort of rubbish Mum kept in her loft, shall we?'

'Sounds like fun.'

Chapter 26

'Mum!'

Lucy was yelling at me from her bedroom. She was due to leave for university the next day, so she was in there finishing the last of her packing. I didn't immediately drop everything and run to her room because she'd been shouting for my help every ten minutes or so for the previous two hours. Her cries of panic either meant she'd lost something she needed or that she'd remembered something she was supposed to have done before she left. The first few times she'd called for me I'd immediately dropped everything and run to her room, eager to help. I'd stopped doing that after I almost broke my neck tripping on a pile of shoes she'd pulled out of her wardrobe and left by her door.

'Mum!'

'What is it, Lucy?'

'Mum!'

Bloody child! It's not like I'm busy making her farewell dinner or anything, is it? I grumbled. I reached her door and poked my head round it. 'What's up?'

'I can't find Poncho.' She was on her hands and knees, pulling things out from under her bed, and it took me a second to work out what she was on about.

'You mean that manky-looking dragon you used to drag around?' He'd been Lucy's favourite when she was little, I hadn't even realised she still had him. 'I thought we chucked him out ages ago.'

The look of utter disgust she gave me was something akin to the one she used to dish out whenever I tried to get her to eat broccoli when she was little.

'No way! He's here somewhere, I know he is. I need to find him, Mum, it's important.' She was digging through the piles of clothes and books that littered her floor.

'Hold on, hold on. We need a system – all you're doing now is throwing stuff on top of more stuff. You won't find anything like that.' I cleared a small space at the end of her bed.

'Let's fold everything up, put back what you're not taking and then see where we are, all right?' She nodded and then wiped her face with the back of her hand; she was crying.

'We'll find him, don't worry. He'll be here somewhere.' The confidence in my voice was masking the fact that I had a horrible feeling I might have thrown him away. Lucy always refused to get rid of anything, she was such a hoarder when she was young. I'd had to resort to clearing out her room whilst she was at school. Every few months I'd get rid of anything I thought she didn't play with any more. I'd put it into rubbish bags and hide them under my bed. My theory was that if she didn't ask where any of it had gone then she obviously didn't need it, at which point I would sneak the bags out in the weekly rubbish collection. I'm sure it made me sound like an awful mother, but if I hadn't thrown stuff out we would both have become imprisoned in this flat by mounds of dolls' clothes, stuffed toys and old birthday cards. As I sorted through Lucy's things with her I said a silent prayer that Poncho the dragon had managed to escape my monthly cull.

After about twenty minutes of folding clothes into piles and putting shoes back in the bottom of the wardrobe, I'd managed to clear quite a bit of space on the floor and the bed but there was still no sign of Poncho.

'He has to be here, Mum. I have to find him.' Lucy started to cry again and she flopped herself down on the end of her bed. Oh, Christ, perhaps I had slung him out after all?

I sat and surveyed Lucy's room; the posters on the walls had changed over the years, as had the contents of the bookshelves, but I still remembered the little girl's bedroom it used to be. Everything had been pink. I'd managed to get hold of some cheap paint at a car-boot sale, but I hadn't realised quite how pink it was until I'd opened the tin. I'd had to mix it with some white paint that Ted had had lurking around in the yard behind the café. But I'd done it all myself and I'd been so proud of it.

In those days, all I'd been able to afford were curtains from the charity shop and a second-hand chest of drawers that had weighed a bloody ton and taken three of us to get up the stairs. Mum had commented at the time that I wasn't ever going to be able to get it out of the room again, it was so heavy, let alone move it to clean behind it. The idea of not being able to clean behind furniture had driven her nuts but it never really bothered me. I was never what you would call a natural housewife. I'd made the room look quite good, even if I did say so myself, and in my eyes Lucy had deserved to have the prettiest bedroom ever. She had been such a beautiful little girl, inside and out, so happy and helpful. I could still picture her, sitting on her little chair with her stuffed toys lined up on top of the chest of drawers, playing teachers or serving them tea. That was it!

'Lucy, come and help me move these drawers,' I said, scurrying over to the chest. It was wedged in an alcove between the window and the wall and I couldn't see down the side of it or behind it.

'We can't move it, Mum. It's too heavy.'

'Yes, we can, with you on that side and me on this one, we can just jiggle it forward.'

Lucy shrugged but positioned herself on the opposite side just the same.

'I don't think this is going to work, but all right.'

Slowly, with me pulling one side forward then Lucy

doing the same to her side, we gradually rocked the chest about six inches away from the wall.

'Wait, wait, that's enough, I think. Hold on.' I clambered onto the top of the chest and stretched down behind it.

'Careful, Mum, you're gonna rupture yourself. What are you doing?'

'Ha!' I grabbed hold of my prize and pulled it out from behind the drawers.

'Poncho! You found him! Mum, you're a bloody genius. What made you look for him there?'

'You used to line all your toys up on top of this chest and play schools with them. Do you remember?'

'Yes, I do. How did you get wedged down there, then, Poncho?' She brushed dust and cobwebs off her beloved dragon and wiped his face with the hem of her T-shirt.

'Now perhaps you can explain to me what was getting you in such a tizz about finding him?'

Lucy sighed and when she looked at me she had tears in her eyes.

'Hey, what's all this?' I took her in my arms. 'Don't cry. You're going to be fine. You're going to have a great time in Bristol. New friends, new flat.' I reached into my pocket for a tissue and dabbed her eyes gently; it was such a familiar feeling, wiping away her tears and taking care of her. 'You're going to be okay, Lucy, I promise.'

She pulled away from me. 'I know I'm going to be okay – that's not why I'm crying.'

'Then what is it?'

'It's you. I'm crying because I'm worried about you.'

'About me? Why?'

'Because I don't like the idea of leaving you here all on your own. I know you, you'll just work to take your mind off being by yourself. You won't go out, you won't have any fun. You'll spend your time keeping an eye on Uncle Matt, but you won't give yourself a thought.'

'Don't be silly. I'm all right. You don't have to worry.'

'Well, I do worry. I was so happy for you when Jack came back into your life and then he went away. You haven't really explained that to me properly so I still don't get it. Anyone could see he was nuts about you and you lit up like a Christmas tree any time he came near you. What went wrong, Mum?'

I started folding a pile of discarded jumpers on the end of Lucy's bed.

'Nothing went wrong, Lucy. We just realised that whatever was between us was in the past. It was better to leave it there.'

'Better for who? Not for you – since Jack left you've been like a ghost. You go about your day like you always did but you're not really here.'

'I'm fine, Lucy. Please. You don't need to worry about me. My life is not your problem.'

'I know it's not but, bloody hell, Mum, you can't expect me to not be worried about you, stuck here on your own.'

'To be honest, I'm looking forward to some time by myself. I've been thinking about expanding my cake-making business for a while now, and if I don't have to worry about you I'll have the time to do that. The cakes I made for your Auntie Liz's event a few weeks ago were a big hit. I'm thinking I might do a bit more of that.'

Lucy looked at me as if I was making all this up – which I was – but even as I was saying it out loud it didn't sound like such a bad idea. I knew Liz would love to have me helping her with events. Perhaps I'll mention it to her when she gets here for dinner later, I thought. Blimey – the dinner! I stopped folding clothes and headed for the door.

'I need to get the food sorted for tonight or else we'll all be eating takeaway. Are we okay here now? Have I managed to convince you that your old mum isn't going to self-destruct the minute you leave the house?'

'Yeah, we're fine. You go and get on with stuff. I've just got a bit more to do and then I'll come and give you a hand.'

I looked round her room. 'I'm thinking you might have more than just "a bit more to do", my lovely. You get yourself sorted. I can manage dinner.' I kissed her on the cheek and left her to it.

I managed to make it to the kitchen and close the

door behind me before the tears started to fall. You can't do this now, I told myself. You have to be strong for Lucy, so she doesn't worry. I couldn't tell her the truth because I didn't have the words to express just how much I was going to miss her. Tomorrow, that was when I could fall apart; until then I had to go on as if nothing were wrong.

*

I slid the lasagne – Lucy's favourite – into the oven, just in time to hear a knock on my front door. Wiping my hands on a tea towel, I walked down the hall and I could see my brother's outline filling the frosted glass panels in the door. I opened it and saw that he was talking to someone on his phone. He leaned in and kissed me on the cheek, thrusting a bottle of wine into my hands and walking past me, into the living room.

I took the wine into the kitchen and tried to find room for it in my already overstuffed fridge. Why had I made so much food? It looked as if I was catering a party for sixty, not six. Stress – that was my only explanation. When I was stressed, I cooked. Then I ate. My generously proportioned backside was a sure sign that I must have been stressed for years.

'Right, just call me if you hear anything different. Yes, I'm at Abby's flat. No, don't come here, just ring. Right, thanks.' My brother finished his call and stuffed his phone back into his pocket as he came into the kitchen. 'Got any beer, Abs?' He peered into the fridge and then reached in to grab one.

'Oi! Get out of there. You're going to pull everything out and onto the floor. Get your hands away from my croquembouche!' I managed to rescue the toppling plate of choux pastry before he pulled his beer bottle through it.

'Crock on what?'

'It's a French dessert, made of little pastry balls.'

He let out a whistle. 'Wow, sounds posh. It's only us coming tonight, isn't it? No one special that I don't know about, is there?' He wiggled his eyebrows and smirked.

'Drink your beer and stop being so annoying.'

He chuckled as he pulled out a chair and sat at the kitchen table. 'Anything I can do?'

'You can tell me who you were on the phone to just now. Not more leaky plumbing at the gym?'

'No, nothing like that. It was Jimmy. He called me to say that Egan's gone. Back to Spain.'

I was relieved. 'No more ridiculous talk about us being secret millionaires, then?'

'Nope. He'd have to be stupid to think that after coming back here, and even stupider to hang about when he's technically still a wanted man.'

'Thank God for that. The idea of him lurking about somewhere, watching us, was starting to give me the heebie-jeebies.'

'Nah, no need to worry about him. That's all over and done with. He's probably back on his sun lounger in his budgie smugglers, sipping sangria and working on his tan.'

The image of Terry Egan in skin-tight swimwear made me shudder a bit. 'Thanks for that mental picture. Now I need a drink.' Opening the fridge, I pulled out the bottle of wine I'd started whilst I was cooking and poured myself a glass.

'You didn't answer my question,' said Matt.

'What question?'

'Is anyone else coming tonight? Apart from the usual suspects.'

'No. Just you, Flo, Liz and David. Why?'

'All the posh patisserie and the fridge groaning with food and booze. Thought you might have invited someone else.' He gave me a knowing look.

'I haven't invited anyone else. It's just us. That's all I need.'

'You sure?'

I let out an exasperated sigh. 'Look, brother dear, I know what you're getting at. I haven't spoken to Jack and I don't expect I ever will again. But it's all good. I'm fine.' I was saved from having to say any more by a knock at the front door. 'Now go and answer that and stop bloody annoying me.' I turned back to the counter and busied myself with the salad. Soon the flat was filled with the familiar sound of Flo and Liz, bickering.

'I never said you looked cheap. I just remarked on how bright yer lippy was. You know, for a woman your age, Elizabeth.'

'It's Dior, my love. Not some cheap tat off the market,' replied Liz. She appeared in the kitchen doorway first, rolling her eyes at me in dismay. 'Where can I put these, darling? Any room in the fridge?' She brandished two bottles of very expensive champagne at me. 'I need to be very drunk, very soon, if I'm going to be able to cope with an evening in Florence's delectable company.'

'You and me both, love,' said Flo, following her in. 'You all right, Abby? Anything I can do?' She came over and kissed my cheek.

'No, I think everything's under control. The lasagne will be done in about half an hour or so. We've got time for a toast. Go into the other room, Flo. I'll bring these glasses in.' I picked up a tray already laden with champagne flutes.

'Fair enough. But give us a holler if you need anything. Always happy to help, you know me.' She gave Liz a pointed stare and then left the room. Liz mimed strangling her as she walked away and then went back to trying to ram bottles of booze into my fridge. That croquembouche was going to end up on the floor any minute, I just knew it.

'Please, play nice, Liz, just for tonight? For me?'

She stopped reorganising my fridge for a minute and turned to me. 'I'll do my best, but I can't promise anything if she starts. The cheeky cow all but told me I was too old to be wearing red lipstick! I'm not too old, am I, darling?'

'Of course, you're not. We're both in the prime of our lives – the world is our lobster. I've resolved to grab life by the balls and run with it. And bugger what anyone else thinks.' My little speech took even me by surprise but it was true; it was time to make a change.

'Okay, then. Let's get in there and toast the guest of honour. What are we waiting for?'

Liz grabbed a bottle of champagne and I followed her into the living room.

Lucy and Matt were sitting together on the sofa and David, Liz's husband, had just whispered something into Flo's ear that was making her giggle like a schoolgirl. She slapped him playfully on the arm.

'Oh, David, you're a very naughty man,' she said. I was amazed – I think Flo might even have been blushing a bit.

'That bloody woman,' said Liz. 'She can barely tolerate me, but she'll quite happily flirt with my husband. And he's even posher than I am!'

'I think David reminds her of a character from one of those smutty books she's always reading. Perhaps she fancies herself as the innocent scullery maid to his lust-filled lord of the manor?'

Liz shuddered at that idea. 'You're enjoying this, aren't you?'

'No. What makes you say that?' I replied, failing to stifle a giggle.

'You're being very childish, Abby,' Liz huffed at me, striding over to break up Flo and David's burgeoning romance.

As I stood at the doorway, looking around the room at all my family, whether they were blood or not, I was so grateful to have them all in my life, but I found myself wishing that Mum were there. She'd probably have pissed me off within five minutes of arriving, with some comment about my cooking or housekeeping, but at least she'd have been with us. I missed her and that surprised me. We'd barely spoken and we'd seen each other even less, but I'd taken it for granted that she would somehow just always be there; that whatever was wrong with us, I would have the time to fix it. Now she was gone and I couldn't fix a fucking thing. I'd never get the chance to tell her how sorry I was.

And then of course there was Jack, with his gorgeous eyes and declarations of undying affection. I'd let him into my life, against my better judgement, and look what had happened there. I'm such a stupid fool, I chastised myself. I could feel tears stinging my eyes, and I started chewing the inside of my cheek to try and stop them.

'Are you all right Mum?' Lucy appeared at my side, looking concerned.

Pull yourself together, Abigail, tonight's about her, don't spoil it. You can wallow in the stinking pile of crap that is your life another time.

I smiled at her. 'I'm good, love, just waiting for someone to open the champagne.'

'That's my cue!' said David, taking the bottle from Liz and tearing off the foil. He popped the cork and I managed to thrust a glass under the neck of the bottle before the foam hit the carpet.

When everyone had a drink, Matt raised his glass. 'A toast, then. To my beautiful, if a bit high maintenance, niece. Knock 'em dead, Princess.' Short and sweet. He took a sip from his glass and I saw him discreetly wipe away a tear. The big softie was going to miss her almost as much as I was.

After the toasting, and a bit more bickering from Liz and Flo about who should sit where around my makeshift dining table – Flo insisted on sitting next to David and Liz wasn't happy – everyone took their seats. It was a bit of a squeeze but we managed. I brought in the lasagne, accompanied by much clapping and cheering from Lucy, and then everyone dug in. Even the croquembouche dessert managed to make it to the table in one piece. The conversation was flowing, as was the wine, and before long we were five bottles in and feeling very jolly. Flo and Liz appeared to have called a temporary truce and David and Matt were talking football versus rugby.

Lucy picked up her knife and gently tapped her glass, getting everyone's attention. She cleared her throat and then stood up.

'I want to make a toast.'

Everyone duly picked up their glasses and waited.

'To my mum.'

Oh, bugger – I could feel the tears pricking my eyes already and she'd only said three words.

'Mum, you are truly the best mother in the world. You are my hero and my inspiration. You've always been there for me. I've never once felt alone. I've always known that, no matter what happened, or what you had to do, I would be loved and looked after. You're amazing and I love you so much. To Mum!' she declared.

'To Abby!'

I tried to thank her, but I couldn't speak; I was crying so much. In the end I gave up and just pulled Lucy in for the tightest hug I think I'd ever given her and mumbled, 'I love you too,' as best I could into her ear. By the time I let her go everyone at the table was crying unashamedly.

'Fuck me, this is depressing,' said Matt eventually, picking up his napkin and wiping his eyes. 'I need another beer. Anyone want anything?'

'I'll have another glass of wine, if you're asking,' replied Flo. Matt gave me a questioning look and I shrugged.

'More wine coming up.'

I took the opportunity to collect some dirty plates and followed Matt out to the kitchen. He was bending down, looking into the fridge, and I heard him sniffling. I didn't say anything, I didn't want to embarrass him. After a few seconds of 'pretend' searching for the wine – the bottle was right there in front of him – he wiped his eyes with the cuff of his shirt and stood up. I carried on putting plates into the dishwasher.

'Shut up,' he said.

'I never said a word, you old softie.'

He shrugged, and I could tell he was on the verge of crying again. I realised that I hadn't given a thought to how Lucy's departure might affect Matt as much as me. He'd been like another parent rather than an uncle. He'd lived with us, watched her grow up and taught her as much as I had.

'I didn't think it would get to me so much,' he said. 'A couple of times this week I've had to lock myself in my office at the gym just to make sure the lads wouldn't see me crying. It's bloody pathetic.' He sniffed again. I pulled a bit of kitchen paper off the roll on the counter and handed it to him.

'You know, I couldn't have managed any of this without you. As much as Lucy says I made her feel safe and loved, that was only because I had you here to do the same for me. No matter how shitty my situation, and there were plenty of shitty times, I never felt afraid or alone because you were right there with me. I knew you'd never let anything bad happen to me or Lucy.' By the time I'd finished talking, both Matt and I were crying again. I went over and put my arms around him. 'You're going to make a great dad one day. All we need to do is find a woman dumb enough to put up with you.'

'Oi! Cheeky bitch,' he said as he pulled out of my arms. 'How do you know I haven't already found someone?'

'Karen?' I asked, innocently. Inside I was screaming, Not Karen! Anyone but her!

'No, not Karen. I finished things with her just after Mum died. I couldn't listen to that bloody voice anymore.'

'And she was too young for you.'

'Yeah, I know.'

'Who's the new girl? Do I know her?'

'Nah. She's not from around here.'

'When do I get to meet her, then?'

'Soon, maybe. We'll see how it goes.' My brother smiled; this girl, whoever she was, was obviously special.

'I'm happy for you – you deserve someone nice. Just don't fuck it up. That's the best advice I can give you.' I pecked him on the cheek, took the wine bottle, and then went back into the other room. I poured Flo and Liz another glass, before returning to my seat. I was content to just sit back and listen to everyone getting along, until my good mood was shattered by Flo.

'Where's that handsome Yank friend of yours tonight, then, Abby? Couldn't he make it?'

I saw Liz flick a warning glance at Flo, but she didn't catch it.

'I didn't invite him, Flo. We... we're not really friends anymore.'

Flo picked up her glass and gestured at me with it, slopping wine onto the tablecloth.

'That's a shame – he was lovely. Wasn't he, Lucy?'

'Yes, he was. But it's Mum's choice. She doesn't have to be friends with anyone she doesn't want to. Isn't that right, Liz?'

'What? Yes... I mean... no. Definitely. Much easier that way.'

'What happened, then? I thought you two were really getting along. That afternoon you came up to the flat for a coffee.' She snorted out a laugh. 'As if I didn't know what the two of you was really up to. I'm old, not blind.' She chuckled to herself and then drained her glass.

'Now, now, old girl. Let me take that before you drop it.' David gently took Flo's glass from her and placed it out of reach.

'You're so lovely.' Flo patted David's cheek. 'Such a handsome face.' She hiccupped and then burped and for one awful minute I thought she might throw up.

'Is it time to get Flo home, Mum?'

'Probably.'

'Don't worry,' said Matt. 'I'll take her. Come on, Florence, it's time to make a move.'

Matt helped Flo out of her chair and Lucy went to fetch her coat.

'Ooh, where we off to, then, Matt? You taking me somewhere nice?'

Matt shook his head and laughed. 'Yeah, I'm taking you dancing at the club. You ready, girl?'

Flo giggled as she tried to button up her coat. 'Come on, then, young man. Lead the way. Night night, all.' She leaned down and planted a lingering kiss on David's lips before wandering off down the hall.

'I'll be back before you leave tomorrow, Lucy. G'night, all,' said Matt.

By the time we heard the door close, Lucy and I were laughing uncontrollably at David and Liz's shocked expressions.

'I didn't realise she'd drunk so much,' said David. 'Where did she put it all? There's nothing of her!'

'That's our Florence.' I laughed. 'She sits there quietly sipping her wine, until she reaches the point of no return.'

'You're lucky she kept all her clothes on, Uncle David,' said Lucy.

David spluttered out the mouthful of wine he'd just swallowed, and we collapsed into more laughter.

'She's joking, David, you were never in any danger. I thought she was going to keel over completely when

Matt got her out of the chair, though,' I said.

'She probably wanted you to catch her in your arms, my darling,' said Liz, patting David's cheek.

'What can I say, my love? I'm irresistible to women of all ages. It's a curse I have to live with.' He leaned over and kissed her and she smiled.

'Well, hopefully Abby will be able to control herself in your presence whilst you help her with the rest of these dirty plates.' She handed him a stack of crockery as I picked up some empty glasses.

'I'll do my best, David. I don't know how good that is.' I gave him a wink as he followed me into the kitchen.

'That was a lovely dinner, Abby, as always.' He stacked the plates he was holding by the sink and then turned to look at me. 'How are you doing? With everything, I mean?'

'I'm fine, David, really. I'll miss Lucy when she goes, but I'll be all right.'

'No, I meant with everything else. Must be hard for you to hear about it and all that?' He stopped midway when he saw my confused face.

'Oh, bugger... I think I've just put my foot in it, haven't I? Sod it. Liz is going to kill me.'

'What are you talking about, David? Hear about what?'

David shrank back against the counter, looking as if he wanted to climb inside the dishwasher and hide. He couldn't seem to make eye contact with me, so I knew something was up, but before I got a chance to question him further, Liz appeared at the doorway clutching an empty bottle of wine.

'I've come in search of more booze. Please tell me there's more in here somewhere.' She bustled in, apparently oblivious to her husband's discomfort.

'In the fridge,' I said, flatly.

'Fabulous.' She opened the door and retrieved the last bottle of white. 'Corkscrew?'

I went to the drawer by the sink and fetched it for her.

'I'll just leave you girls to it, then, shall I?' mumbled David as he scurried out of the room.

'Disappearing when there's washing-up to be done, my love? Sounds about right.' Liz chuckled. She turned back to me. 'Are you okay? You look very pale.' She placed her hand on my shoulder. 'It's all going to be fine. I'm here, so is Matt, you won't be on your own. Even Florence will be of some help, I'm sure.'

I nodded and turned away, plunging my hands into the hot washing-up water in the sink. 'David thinks he's put his foot in it,' I said, casually, as I swirled the sponge around the plate and covered it with bubbles. Rinsing it under the hot tap, I placed it in the drainer before I started on the next one. Liz had opened the wine and was heading to the door when she turned to answer.

'Put his foot in it? How do you mean?'

'He thinks he's told me something he shouldn't.' I

saw a fleeting nervous look pass across her face.

'It's nothing, my love, we can talk about it tomorrow. Let's just concentrate on having a nice evening. Look, stop that, the washing-up can wait. I have wine.' She raised the bottle, gesturing for me to come back into the other room. 'It's nothing that can't wait, I promise.'

'If it's so insignificant, then why don't you just tell me?'

'Because tonight is supposed to be about Lucy and about you, no one else.' She put the wine back on the kitchen table, grabbed a tea towel and handed it to me.

'Here, dry your hands and come back into the other room. Come and have some fun.'

'Liz, you're worrying me a bit. Please just tell me what David was talking about.'

'I'm going to kill that bloody man! I told him I was going to tell you but just not tonight. Stupid old git goes and opens his massive trap. I've a good mind—'

'Liz, please. What is it?'

'I saw something on the Internet, that's all. You know how I love to look things up on Google.'

I sighed. 'Not more crap about Jack and his shady business past? I told you that none of that could be true. Besides, Egan's gone – Matt told me so tonight. No Egan, no money and that's the end of it. I can't believe you're still—'

'It wasn't about his business. This was personal. It was on one of those celebrity gossip sites.'

I went to speak but she stopped me.

'And that's all it is at this point. It's gossip.'

'About what?' I didn't really have to ask – the only person I knew who was interesting enough to appear on a celebrity gossip site was Jack.

'Jack and Lexie Morgan – according to the website, they're engaged.'

Liz was watching me closely, waiting for me to collapse on the floor in an emotional heap, no doubt. But that wasn't what happened. Did it hurt me to think of them together? Yes. Was I sad that we hadn't been able to find a way for us to make it work? Of course. But despite all that, I was surviving, still able to contemplate some sort of a future for myself beyond me and Jack and what might have been. I took a deep breath and smiled; Liz looked confused for a second, and then relieved.

'Oh, thank God. I thought you were going to lose it for a minute. I need a bloody drink.'

'Me too.'

She grabbed the wine off the table. 'Are you sure you're all right?'

'You know what, I think I am.'

'I fucking love you, Abby Cowan.'

'Right back atcha, babe.' I gave her a reassuring squeeze and we walked, arm in arm, back into the living room.

'What the bloody hell have you two been nattering

about for so long?' asked Lucy.

'The future,' I said as I filled my glass and sat down.

'I'll drink to that,' said Lucy, raising her glass.

Liz was still watching me carefully as she sipped her wine. I mouthed the words 'I'm all right' to her across the table. She winked at me before reaching across to grab some cutlery. 'Right, then, pass me a bloody fork. I need more cake!'

*

Later, after everyone had gone, I was lying in bed when my door opened a crack and I saw Lucy's face peering in.

'Can't sleep?' I asked.

'Nope. Can I get in with you?'

I pulled back the covers and she dived into my bed. She rested her head on my shoulder, and for a few minutes we just lay in that position in silence. When she was little she'd gone through a phase of sneaking into my bed every night, but she hadn't done it for a long time. I'd wake up to be confronted with her little face close to mine, breathing lightly. I hadn't minded really, but all the parenting books had said it shouldn't be encouraged so I'd tried to stop her from doing it; admittedly I hadn't tried *that* hard. To tell you the truth, I'd liked the company and it hadn't been as if I'd needed the space for my vast array of lovers.

'Liz told me about the engagement rumours before she left. I think she thought I should know in case you had some sort of meltdown about it.' She pulled her head out of the crook of my neck and watched me through squinty eyes.

'Are you?' she said. 'Going to have a meltdown, I mean?'

'No, love, no meltdown. It's better this way.'

'I'm not going to pretend I understand – all seems a bit sudden to me – I just wanted to make sure that you're all right with this new development.'

'I'm fine,' I reassured her. She nodded and then went back to lying down. She was quiet for a long time; I thought she'd gone to sleep but I didn't move. I wanted to make this moment last for as long as I could. Then she sat up, suddenly.

'I've got you a present. I was going to give it to you tomorrow, but I've changed my mind. I want to give it to you now.'

'For me? Okay.'

She got up and pulled a small parcel out of the pocket of her dressing gown. She handed it to me with a shy smile on her face. 'It's nothing big, just something that might help you when I'm not here, to give you a cuddle at the end of a crappy day.'

'You're going to make me cry.' The parcel she handed me was wrapped in brown paper and it felt soft. Intrigued, I pulled at the sticky tape. Two big brown plastic eyes and a bright red felt flame, poking out of the end of a green snout, appeared as I unwrapped the paper; it was Poncho the dragon.

'That's why I needed to find him so badly. He was always there for me when I needed him and now I want to leave him here with you. Is that silly? Do you hate it? I can get you some slippers or some chocolates, or both, if you want.' She looked like my little girl again, eagerly handing me over the latest creation she'd made at school, wondering if I really liked it.

'I love it – it's perfect. Thank you.' I pulled my daughter into my arms, and we both started to cry.

'I don't know what I'm going to do without you, Mum, I really don't. What if I hate it there? What if everyone else hates me?' she sobbed.

'That's not possible, Lucy. You're the most beautiful, kind and generous girl I know. You have a magical gift for making everyone around you feel special and once people see that they'll love you as much as I do.'

Lucy wiped her nose on her sleeve.

'Now, you've got a long drive and an early start in the morning. You should try and get some sleep.'

'All right. Night, Mum.' She didn't get out of my bed, she just snuggled down under the covers and I tucked her in tight.

'Night, beautiful.'

I lay beside her and tried to sleep but I couldn't. My mind was too full of questions – none of which I had

418

any satisfactory answers to. Lucy was leaving in the morning – how was I going to cope with that? I didn't know. My business was dying on its arse – how was I going to fix that? I didn't know. Jack was gone but I still didn't really know why – should I call him and demand an explanation? I wasn't sure. I was doing okay, though, wasn't I? I hadn't melted into a puddle of my own tears and refused to go on. No, I'd kept going. What choice did I really have? None as far as I could see. At that moment my life was like a playground roundabout – spinning fast and out of control. I had no choice other than to hang on for dear life until it eventually slowed down.

After half an hour of staring at my bedroom ceiling, questioning practically every choice I'd ever made, I got up and made myself some tea.

Chapter 27

'Mum, Mum, wake up.' Lucy was shaking me gently by the shoulder. I sat up with a start; I must have fallen asleep on the sofa in the living room. I could remember making myself a cup of tea and then going in there to sit down but not much after that.

'Ouch, my bloody neck,' I grumbled, rubbing it to try and loosen the kinks.

'Here, I've made you a fresh one.' She handed me my 'World's Greatest Mum' mug.

'What time is it? What time...? Ow... shit, my neck... I need to get ready.'

'There's plenty of time. Fleur's coming to pick me up at ten and it's only half eight now, don't stress.'

'Okay... well, I still need to get dressed and brush my teeth so I can come down and wave you off.' Getting up from the sofa, still clutching my life-restoring cuppa, I wandered down the hallway to my bedroom. What kind of outfit is suitable for saying goodbye to your only child forever? I mused. Don't be so bloody melodramatic woman. She's going to Bristol, not Mars. Jeans and a T-shirt will suffice. I threw my clothes onto the bed and was just heading to the bathroom when there was a knock on the front door.

'Lucy, will you get that, please?'

'Will do.'

I heard her open the door and speak to whoever was there and then the door closed. I switched on the shower over the bathtub and held my hand under the water as the ancient plumbing in the flat creaked and grumbled to life. Once the water was reasonably warm I stripped off my PJs and climbed under it, letting it flow over my head and into my eyes and ears. I stood there, deaf and blind in the cascading water, for a few minutes until I was shocked by a sudden rush of cold air; Lucy had yanked back the shower curtain.

'Bloody hell, Lucy! What are you doing?' I rubbed the water out of my eyes; some of yesterday's mascara must have leaked in because they started to smart. I shut off the water and reached for a towel. 'I'm trying to have a shower. What's the big panic?'

'This just came, Mum. A messenger brought it. I had to sign for it – it's for me.' She was holding a big white box. I stepped out of the shower and wrapped myself in a towel.

'Who sent it?' The steam had cleared a little and there was no mistaking the familiar Apple logo on top of the white box. What the hell?

'I don't know. I'm going to open it.' She rushed out of the room, with me following behind, down the hall and into the kitchen. She put the box on the table and we both stood for a few seconds just looking at it.

'Well, it's not going to explode if we open it, is it?' she said, slowly lifting the lid. 'Fuck me! It's a brand-new MacBook.'

I had to resist the urge to tell her off for using that kind of language. That ship had sailed long ago.

'Isn't there a card or anything?' I said, examining the box more closely.

'I don't think... no... yes... look, there's one here, tucked inside.' She pulled out a small white envelope with her name written on the front.

'Do you think it might be from Dad?'

'Maybe,' I said, although I was pretty sure it wasn't. Martin wouldn't have been able to get hold of something like that unless he'd stolen it. Oh, Christ, please tell me he hasn't sent our daughter a stolen laptop, I panicked.

'Mum, it's from... it's... blimey... really?' Lucy was staring in amazement at the card in her hand. Impatiently I took it from her since she'd obviously been rendered incapable of coherent speech at that moment. The card was made from thick, expensive-looking paper. It was edged in black and had the initials 'JHC' printed in the top corner. JHC – why was that sending all the alarms in my head haywire? Then I read the message. In a confident, sloping hand it said:

For Lucy, I hope this will be of some use

to you. With much love and luck, Jack Chance.

'Fuck me!' It was my turn to swear. What on earth did he think he was doing?

'This is awesome!' she cried, lifting the thin and gleaming computer from its box. 'Fleur is going to be spitting chips when she sees this!'

'You can't keep it, Lucy. It's too much. He hardly knows you... no... it's wrong. You definitely can't keep it.'

She looked crestfallen. 'What? Why? That's not fair!' The whiney tone of adolescence crept back into her voice for a minute.

'You know we can't accept this, Lucy. It's not right. It must have cost a fortune.'

'But, Mum...'

'No buts, Lucy, it's going back. You can write him a nice little "thanks but no thanks" letter. All right?'

She put the computer back in its box with a petulant, 'Fine,' and then turned and stalked away.

I was so angry. How dared he do something like that? *Like what? Like something so unbelievably kind and generous?* No! It wasn't generous, it was controlling and high-handed. I could have had that little argument with myself all day, but my inner ramblings were interrupted by the ping of my phone in the living room. I could hear Lucy banging about in her room, muttering

swear words under her breath; no doubt cursing her
sheer bad luck at having such a total bitch for a mother.

I found my phone tucked down between the sofa
cushions. I must have dropped it when I fell asleep there.
I swiped the screen and saw that I had a text message.
My stomach started churning as I read.

> I'm sure that right about now you'll be trying to
> decide how best to return my gift but please don't.
> It's a present from an old family friend, nothing
> more. Take the bloody computer Abigail, Lucy
> deserves to have the best. Jack

I stared at his name at the end of the message. How
did he know that I would want to return the gift?
Because he knows you, you bloody idiot. He probably
knows you better than anyone else. I pushed those
thoughts away. He was right, though, Lucy did deserve
to have the best, and it wasn't as if he couldn't afford it,
was it? I took the box to Lucy's room.

'Here,' I said, holding it out to her. 'You're right. It
was a gift meant for you – you should have it. Jack
wants you to have it.' Lucy ran over and grabbed the
box and then grabbed me.

'Thank you, thank you, thank you! Mum, this is
bloody awesome!' She kissed me and ran back to her
bed to open her present. As she pulled out the laptop she
looked up at me for reassurance.

I nodded. 'It's fine, Lucy, really, go ahead.' She

clapped her hands together excitedly and then opened the top of the computer. I decided to leave her to it.

'Don't get sidetracked by your new toy. Are you ready to go when Fleur gets here?'

'Yep, deffo. I'm all sorted. Mum, can you give me Jack's number so I can send him a message to say thanks?'

'Don't worry about it. I'll do that for you. I have a few things I need to say to him myself anyway.'

'Be nice, Mum,' she warned.

'Always.'

I went to my room and sat on the bed; seeing Jack's name had taken all the air out of my sails. I took a few deep breaths and tried to calm my racing pulse. Stop being so ridiculous, I told myself, just send him a quick message to thank him and then that will be the end of it. I composed my reply and then deleted it so many times; everything I wrote came across as either trite or cold. I couldn't seem to make the words convey the right message. Maybe because I didn't know what the right message was. Maybe you should just call him then, said the voice in my head that liked to encourage me to do stupid and pointlessly destructive things. Thankfully, my sensible self kicked in, just in time to help common sense prevail. No phone calls. But I still needed to thank him for the computer. I tried again with a message that I hoped sounded casual but still grateful.

> Lucy says thank you for your generous gift. She's very happy.

I didn't put my name; I figured it was unnecessary. Within seconds the phone pinged with a reply.

> And what about you Abigail? Are you happy?

Why wasn't he asleep? Surely it was the early hours of the morning in the US? I didn't want to start a conversation with him, so I typed back what I hoped was a polite, but terse, response.

> Yes, thank you. Everything's great. Can't talk – just waving Lucy off now.

There, that should do it. *Ping!* Oh, bollocks!

> Tell her I said goodbye and drive safe. I'm glad you let her keep the computer.

> I will. Congrats on your engagement BTW. Hope you and Lexie will be very happy. Bye Jack.

Within seconds the phone started to ring in my hand. I threw it down onto the sofa. I thought about answering it, but I stopped myself. If I really didn't want to have a conversation with him then I didn't have to, did I? My life, my choice. I ignored the phone and walked out of the room.

*

It rang about a dozen times before I eventually switched it off.

'Someone really wants to get hold of you,' said my brother.

'I'm busy.'

Matt raised an eyebrow but said nothing; instead he finished heaving the last of Lucy's things into the back of Fleur's little car. 'Right then, missy, that's you all packed up and ready to go.'

'Thanks, Uncle Matt, couldn't have done it without ya!'

'Too right you couldn't – some of your shit weighs a ton!' He chuckled.

'Maybe I should follow you up,' I said suddenly. 'Help you unload at the other end.'

'I'll be fine, Mum, honestly. It's better this way – can't have you sobbing on the kerb outside the halls of residence, can I? Way too embarrassing.'

'Yeah, don't worry about it. I'm sure we'll find some fit blokes to give us a hand if we need it!' said Fleur, poking her head out of the driver's side window.

'That's what scares me.'

'Stay away from fit blokes, Lucy – they're nothing but trouble. I should know!' said my brother, with a wink. He gave her one last final massive hug. 'Seriously, if anyone gives you any grief, you just let me know.' She nodded and then turned to me.

'You mind how you go, okay? Drive safe.' I said this last bit more to Fleur than to Lucy and she gave me a reassuring wave.

'No sweat! Come on, Lucy, we need to get going.'

Lucy smiled at me and I started to feel the tears pricking my eyes. I began to chew the inside of my cheek, hoping to distract myself.

'Well, that's it, then, I guess. Here I go!'

'It's going to be great, I just know it. Make sure you enjoy every minute, but don't forget to study as well.'

'I will, Mum, I promise. Thank you, for everything.'

I waved off her thanks with a casual, 'It was nothing.' But she was intent on making her point.

'I mean it, Mum. I know what you've sacrificed for me, how hard you had to work to keep us afloat after Dad buggered off, and I want you to know I'm so grateful. You've taught me so much – you've taught me how to work hard and about the kind of woman I want to be. When I grow up I want to be just like you, Mum.'

No amount of cheek-chewing was going to stem the tide of tears that were threatening if she kept talking like that.

'Oh, Lucy, my little girl. When did you get to be so grown up?'

'I learnt from the best.'

That did it; I was done for. 'I didn't want to cry,' I said. 'I wanted you to think I was strong.'

'You are strong, Mum, crying doesn't change that. I love you.'

'I love you too.'

With one last squeeze, she slipped out of my arms and made her way to the car. When she reached the door, she opened it but stopped before she got in.

'Call Jack! Have a life. You don't need to worry about me any more so have some fun for yourself!'

'Go!' I shouted back. She laughed and climbed in. I watched the car as it pulled away and I didn't stop waving until it disappeared round the bend at the end of the road.

'Is it too early for a drink?' asked Matt.

'Nope. Somewhere in the world it's already cocktail hour. That's good enough for me.'

I slipped my arm through my brother's and we walked back to my flat.

Chapter 28

I woke the next morning feeling like crap; I lay there, staring at a crack I'd never noticed in the ceiling. It was weird; I'd been by myself in the flat before but this was different. However alone I'd been then, I'd always been comforted by the fact that I knew Lucy would be home eventually. This was different; I was on my own.

Matt had hung around for a while yesterday but then left. To be honest, I'd been glad. I'd felt as if he was watching me, making sure I wasn't about to collapse into a sobbing, snotty heap on the floor.

I took a deep breath and stretched my arms above my head, mentally taking stock of myself. How did I feel? Was I about to lose the plot? No, I wasn't; there didn't seem to be any sign of an impending mental breakdown. I was going to be fine. That realisation hit me like a smack in the face; it buoyed me up with a feeling of strength that I hadn't felt in a long time.

Pushing back the covers, I swung my legs round and sat on the edge of my bed. The flat was still silent, but it wasn't scary; in fact, it felt strangely liberating. I had no one to answer to – I was free to do whatever I wanted; just needed to figure out what that was. I found myself itching to be on the move, to be doing something, anything. I grabbed my phone from the bedside table and dialled.

'Liz, it's me. Yes, I'm fine. Actually, I'm great. Can you come over? I want to talk to you about something.'

*

An hour later, and Liz and Flo were sitting in the café looking at me as if I'd completely flipped out.

'Are you sure about this, Abby?' Liz asked.

'Totally. I've never been surer of anything.'

Liz and Flo exchanged worried looks but I ignored them and ploughed on.

'This business is dying and if I don't do something soon all I'm going to be left with is a mountain of debt and regrets. This is my chance, our chance—' I gestured to them '—to do something new. To build something that I think could be pretty marvellous. I want to close the café. I want to start a new business, cakes to order, catering for events, weddings, bar mitzvahs, whatever!' I was a little breathless by the time I'd finished my impassioned speech. Flo shifted uncomfortably in her seat.

'I thought you loved this place. You always said you did.'

'I know, but I just think the time has come to make a change. I've kept the café open for so long because it was Lucy's home and because closing it, or changing anything, would have felt like betraying Ted and Rose and what they'd given me. The café was their life and for a long time I've felt like I've just been a caretaker of everything they'd started. I need to make this my business now. I'm sure they'd understand that.'

'Well, I never thought I'd see the day,' Flo said. She pulled a hanky out of her pocket and blew her nose. 'It's the end of an era, that's what it is.'

'I think that's rather the point though, Flo,' said Liz. 'That time has passed. Things are different for Abby now.'

I was grateful that Liz understood but I knew I had to be completely honest with them about the other reasons behind my decision.

'Things have changed for me, that's for sure, but that's only part of it. Everything here, the way it is, reminds me too much of Jack, of being kids here, holding hands under the table by the window.' I sat down opposite Liz and Flo. 'I held onto those memories and I've always thought about them with fondness. I enjoyed imagining what might have been between us but I can't do that anymore. Every time I picture those two stupid kids now all I can see is pain and secrets and a world that conspired to keep them apart. It hurts too much to be reminded of how things were and of what might have been. I need to move on and forget about the past.'

'And does that include me?' asked Flo. 'Am I just a reminder of the past now too?'

'Oh my God, Flo, no!' I leant over and grabbed her hands. 'I didn't mean it like that. You're my right-hand woman. I can't do any of this without you.'

Flo dabbed her eyes with her hanky.

'I need both of you if this is going to work,' I said. Liz and Flo exchanged more wary looks.

'Liz, we always said that we would go into business together. When we were at college we were going to rule the world. We can do that now. You can organise the events and I'll do the catering. You know this makes sense – you love to organise.'

She gave me a sly grin. 'You're right. I do love to boss people around. You were always the better cook anyway. All right, I'm in. Partners?' She held out her hand to me and I took it.

'Partners?' I said, holding my other hand out to Flo. I could see her weighing up her options and I had to admit that for a split second I thought she was going to say no.

'All right, partners it is,' she said, grabbing my hand and shaking it. 'On one condition.' She stared pointedly at Liz. 'I won't be bossed around by anyone. Agreed?'

Liz held Flo's gaze and then smiled as she stuck out her other hand for Flo to shake.

'That's fine by me. But you have to agree to no more snarky comments about my age, my make-up or how posh I am.'

Flo nodded. 'I think I can manage that.'

I let out a relieved breath – this wasn't going to be easy, but it would be worth it.

'Fucking Nora! This calls for champagne, my darling!' exclaimed Liz.

'I don't have any champagne, I'm afraid.'

'Urgh! How awful. Well, that's the first thing we'll have to do in here then – install a wine fridge.'

We spent the next couple of hours drawing up lists of things to do. Between us we managed to come up with a plan that meant we would keep the café open for the next few months, whilst we had our conversion plans drawn up and submitted for official approval. Then it would be all systems go for our new catering company.

'I'm giving you one last chance to change your mind about all this. No pressure,' said Liz, as she put on her coat and made her way to the door, after we'd decided to call it a day for now.

'We won't be upset if you decide this isn't what you want after all,' Flo piped up. I looked around at the café's tired paintwork and chipped Formica counter. I'd loved the place just as it was for more years than I cared to remember but not anymore.

'I'm not going to change my mind. This is all about the future. No matter what happens, it's time for me to start taking some risks.'

'Ooh, this is going to be so exciting.' Flo clapped her

hands together. 'Come on, then, Lizzy, you can give me a lift home.' Flo kissed me on the cheek and wandered out onto the street.

'I hate being called Lizzy,' grumbled Liz, before taking a deep breath and following Flo outside. 'After you, Florence. Mind you don't trip on anything and crack your head now, my dear.'

I listened to the two of them bickering as I locked the door behind them. No – it wasn't going to be easy.

*

After they left, I still felt full of energy and ideas. I went to the kitchen with a plan to experiment with some new cake recipes. It felt good to be so fired up about something for a change. I flicked through my underused collection of recipe books, eventually settling on a delicate chocolate-framboise cake. I'd been meaning to try it for ages but there really wasn't much call for that kind of thing in the café, so I'd never bothered.

I busied myself in the kitchen, weighing out ingredients, reading and rereading the recipe. I was putting the flour back in the store cupboard, when I thought I heard someone rattling the back-door handle. I stopped and waited, but the sound didn't come again. Stop spooking yourself, Abby, put some music on or something. I pulled my phone out of my pocket and tried to switch it on, but nothing happened. Out of battery. I smiled at the memory of Lucy, always telling me off for not keeping the battery topped up. I figured I'd just have to go old school and switch the radio on.

I went to the window ledge and turned on the battered, but reliable, Roberts radio that I kept there. Scanning through the different stations, I finally settled on Classic FM. Music began to play, it sounded familiar although I couldn't place it. I tipped cocoa powder into the bowl of my mixer and watched the whisk go round and round, breathing in the comforting smell of chocolate, as the ingredients mixed together. The music on the radio continued to play, filling the kitchen with its soothing notes that rose and fell like a wave, carrying me along with it. I closed my eyes, enjoying the feeling of getting lost in its lilting phrases. An image of a white rose floating on muddy water flashed through my mind and I snapped my eyes open; the music on the radio, it was the music Jack had played for me that day on the ferry.

I couldn't listen to any more. I switched the mixer on even faster, the sound of the beaters drowning out the music quite nicely, and I watched the soft, swirling mass in the mixing bowl; it was quite hypnotic. The sound of rattling came again, this time from the front of the café. I switched off the machine; someone was knocking on the front window. I made my way towards the door, weaving carefully between tables and chairs in the dark. The knocking had stopped but I checked the bolts at the bottom and the top of the door anyway.

I peered out of the window but I could barely see the street outside; the only working streetlight was doing a pretty piss-poor job of illuminating its surroundings. It's probably just kids, mucking about, I thought, turning back to the kitchen. An image of Egan's smug face popped into my head and made me shiver. He was long gone though – Matt had said so. I was just jumping at shadows.

Maybe it was time to call it a night and go up to the flat, I thought. Bugger the cake. I knew I'd feel safer upstairs. I grabbed my phone, dead battery and all, switched off the radio and the lights, and started up the stairs. I'd barely reached the second step, when I was stopped by the sound of the back-door handle being tried again. Shit – why hadn't I kept my phone charged? The sound came again, more insistent, and then a voice.

'Abigail! Are you in there?'

Relief flooded through me at the sound of Jack's voice. 'Abigail! I know you're in there. Please answer the door.'

I pulled my keys out of my pocket and unlocked the door. Jack stood there looking pissed off and annoyingly sexy. He was dressed in jeans and a navy polo shirt, with a healthy smattering of stubble, and he was wearing those damn glasses again; the ones I'd seen him in the night I'd got topless and crawled onto his lap in the back of his car. Despite all this, though, he looked tired. His eyes were red, his face pale. We stood and stared at each other for a moment. I couldn't quite take in the fact that he was there.

'Is everything all right? You look awful.' Not strictly true – even with pasty skin and tired eyes he was still the most delicious-looking man I'd ever seen.

'Gee, thanks. You certainly know how to make a guy feel good.' He threw me his slightly crooked smile and my heart thumped in my chest.

'I'm sorry, that was rude. I'm just surprised to see you. I thought you were in America.'

'I was. And now I'm here. Can I come in?'

'What for?'

'I need to talk to you. It's important.'

I stepped back and let him in. The kitchen was still in darkness, so I flicked on the overhead light.

'Well? What's so important that you had to fly all the way across the Atlantic to talk to me?' I crossed my arms and stuck out my chin, giving him my best cool stare. I probably looked more like a petulant toddler than a feisty heroine, but what the hell? I had a point to prove; I needed him to see that his leaving hadn't been the end of me. I was still standing, making plans for my future; I didn't need him.

By contrast, he looked unsure of himself, which was strange. I'd only ever seen Jack looking confident and in control; the man in front of me now was different. The hairs on my arms began to prickle and a feeling of foreboding made me shudder.

'What's wrong, Jack? Are you all right?'

He took hold of my arms, forcing me to look at him.

'You have to believe me when I tell you I didn't know anything about all this before. I swear to you, Abigail.'

'Know anything about what? I don't understand.'

'Tell me you believe me. I've never lied to you, Abigail. Never.'

'All right, I believe you.'

He dropped his hands to his sides and slumped down onto a nearby stool.

'It's such a fucking mess. I'm so sorry.' He scrubbed his face with his hands, frustration etching lines across his forehead. 'The phone call I took, the morning after we were together. Do you remember?'

I almost burst out laughing at that question – being abandoned after a night of passion wasn't something a girl and her ego easily forgot.

'Yes, I remember,' I deadpanned.

'The call was from one of my people, an investigator. I'd asked him to check out that Egan guy who was hassling you and Matt. He told me plenty I already knew, about your father and the robbery. But there was something else, something I was pretty sure even you didn't know. I didn't know how to tell you, or even if I should tell you.'

'For Christ's sake, Jack! What are you getting at?'

'My dad got yours locked up, Abigail! He put him

behind bars and left you without a father.'

Now it was my turn to need to sit. I pulled a stool out from under the workbench and sat opposite Jack, our knees almost touching. For a long moment, neither of us spoke. I didn't know what to say. I had a million questions racing around in my head, but I couldn't settle on which one to ask first. Eventually Jack reached across and took my hand, gripping it tightly; my cold fingers just sat limply between his.

'When I came to you that night, at your mum's house, and told you I was leaving, I thought it was for the best. I thought if I left then the past would stay where it belonged, that it wouldn't be able to hurt you anymore. That *I* wouldn't hurt you anymore. And needed to make sure it was true.'

I slipped my hand out of his and sat up straight, gathering my scattered thoughts at last.

'You're jumping too far ahead, Jack. I need you to go back and explain to me why you think it was your dad' fault.'

'Your father and mine were friends. After the robbery, your father confessed everything to mine. He was drunk, full of fear and regret for what he'd done. My father took that information to the police. He got your dad put away.'

'He testified against my dad at his trial?'

Jack shook his head. 'No. Apparently when your dad realised who the police were going to put up as their sta witness, he confessed everything so that my father wouldn't have to stand up in court and give evidence. He spared him that.'

'But how did your investigator find all this out?'

'He didn't. He only gave me the basics; the rest came from my mother.'

Jack's mother, Sally Chance, now married to her second husband and living the life of a trophy wife in Boston.

'Why would she tell you all this now? After all this time?'

Jack looked down at his hands. 'She came by to see me at my apartment and found me passed out drunk. I don't do that sort of thing, Abigail. She was worried.'

I tried to picture Jack drunk, but that image didn't fit the man I knew. That man was strong and in control; he made me feel safe. I'd felt that strength, enough to want to throw caution to the wind and let him into my life. I couldn't reconcile that image with one of him passed out drunk.

'Why were you drunk? What happened?'

Jack flashed me a look of shock. 'Are you fucking kidding me? Why do you think?'

'I... I don't know... I...'

Jack stood up, sending the stool crashing over behind him, and took my face in his hands. 'Because of you, Abigail. I'd had to say goodbye to you. I couldn't stop the pain, so I tried to numb it, but it didn't work.'

441

He looked at me, his beautiful face etched with agony. 'I'm in love with you. You are the love of my life and I knew I couldn't be with you. When I left I was hoping that I'd find out my investigator was wrong, but when I confirmed the story, I knew it meant the end for us. Your dad's disappearance had hurt you so badly, I knew that, and to realise that my family, my father, was responsible for that pain...' He shook his head. 'I didn't want to put you through any more of that. I did what I thought was the best thing. I left so that none of this shit would get raked up again. I had to protect you, and I thought that was the only way.'

I saw tears in his eyes as he moved his face closer to mine. I thought he was going to kiss me but instead he let his hands drop to his sides and he moved across to lean on the counter opposite.

'My mum sobered me up and listened while I told her all about you, about meeting you again. I told her about what I'd learned, the robbery, everything. When I was done she sat me down and filled in the blanks for me. Once she started talking it was like she couldn't stop, like she'd kept it all bottled up for so long.'

'What else did she tell you?' Did I even want to know?

'She told me why we'd moved away so suddenly. Terry Egan wasn't happy about what my dad had done so he started making threats. Dad was worried for our safety, so he spirited us away in the night. That's why they told me I couldn't keep in touch with you or anyone else. It wasn't safe.'

'Your parents must have been so scared, to feel like they had to run away and hide, all because your father chose to do the decent thing.'

Jack looked surprised. 'He put your father in prison, Abigail. You lost your father because of him.'

I took a step towards him. He was so wrong and I needed him to understand that.

'He did what was right, Jack. My dad sealed his own fate the minute he decided to throw in with Egan. He committed a crime – no one forced him to do the things he did. I can't blame your family for any of that. I don't.' It was true; there was no way I could blame anyone but my father for what he did. If anything, Jack's family had suffered just as much as we had. Mr Chance's decision to tell the police what he knew had ended with them fleeing their home in the middle of the night, leaving behind everything and everyone they knew.

'We were just kids, Jack. We're not responsible for the choices our parents made, and I, for one, don't intend to let those choices stop me from moving on with my life. It's over with, it's done. We need to move forward. It's the only way. You need to get on with your life.'

Jack's face was lit with a bright smile. 'Abigail, you are amazing.' He took a step towards me, but I held up my hand.

'Stop. I meant what I said – you have to get on with your life, as I do mine. But not together. That can't happen.' I watched as the smile on Jack's face fell away, to be replaced with confusion.

'You left me, Jack. I trusted you. I gave myself to you, because I thought I could rely on you to be there. For the first time in years I took a chance and it backfired. You left me.'

'Abigail, please, I told you why I did that. I didn't think I had any choice. I wanted to protect you.'

'By making me feel worthless? Like something that could so easily be tossed aside. I trusted you, but you didn't return the favour. You didn't trust me, trust us, enough to tell me the truth. Instead of having some faith in what we were starting to build, you chose to decide what was best and you walked away. I don't know if I can forgive you for that, or if we could ever get past it. What happens the next time things get difficult? Will you just run away again? I can't take that risk.'

'You're wrong. I love you, Abby. I can't breathe without you. I can't think. Leaving you broke me. I wouldn't let anything come between us again. You are everything to me.' He moved closer.

'Stop, Jack, please.'

His hand snaked around my waist, pulling me in to his body. 'I can't just move on with my life and forget about what's between us. Don't ask me to do that.' He leaned down and pressed his lips to my neck and I felt the heat travel all the way down my body. There was no denying the fact that I still wanted him, I wanted him so badly, but he wasn't mine to have. I pushed myself out of his reach.

'There is no chance of a future for us – too much has happened. And I know, somewhere deep down inside, you agree with me. Otherwise you wouldn't be getting married to someone else.'

'This is about Lexie?'

'No,' I shouted, 'this is about me. I'm choosing me.' I walked over to the back door and held it open for him. 'I want you to go now, Jack. There's no point in going over and over the same old crap. We'd just end up right back where we are now.' I wanted him to go, before the tears came, before I lost my resolve. This was the right thing to do; I wasn't prepared to risk my heart again.

'Abigail, please don't do this. You have to listen to me.'

'I don't have to do anything!' I yelled. 'Please just go.'

He stood there, not moving, for what seemed like forever, until he finally walked over to the door. As he stepped past me he turned. 'I know you're not ready to listen to me now, so I'll go. But you need to know one thing. I am not engaged to Lexie. I don't know where that idea came from but it's not true. That's why I flew all the way here, to tell you that I'm not marrying anyone, unless it's you. I love you, Abigail. I always have

445

and I always will. This thing between us isn't over, not by a long way.' He leaned closer and kissed me gently on the lips and then he was gone. I slammed the door shut and then leant against it. My legs were shaking so hard I didn't think I'd make it up the stairs, so I just stood there.

Chapter 29

It took me a while to regain some control over my shaking body. I stood, propped against the door, just absorbing what Jack had told me. He wasn't engaged to Lexie; he wanted to marry me. It had taken everything I had not to fling open the door and chase him down the street. But it didn't matter whether he was engaged or not, I told myself, there was too much in our shared past that was always going to get in our way. We would never be able to get over all that. Would we? No. Yes. Maybe. Bloody hell!

I didn't have the energy to think about it anymore. I was done. I shoved myself away from the door, ready to go upstairs to my flat, but I almost jumped out of my skin when I heard the knock on the door. Jack – had he come back? My good sense did the quickest about-turn ever – of course I wanted to be with him; why was I even questioning it? I flung the door open, ready to throw myself into his arms; that excitement died in my chest when I saw who was standing on my doorstep.

'Well, well, little Abby. You look disappointed to see me.' It was Egan. 'Can I come in?'

He didn't wait for an answer, just shoved past me

and into the café's kitchen. The hairs on the back of my neck started to prickle; this wasn't good.

'What do you want?'

'I think you know what I want, Abby.'

'I don't have your money,' I said. 'Look around you. Does it look like I've got a secret stash of cash?' I would have laughed if I weren't so scared.

Egan looked me up and down. 'Shall I assume you were expecting someone else when I knocked? Perhaps your new rich boyfriend. Or maybe that lovely daughter of yours? Lucy, isn't it? She'll be in Bristol by now, won't she? Settling into her new student flat.' His mention of my daughter made my heart stop; how did he know where she was?

'Leave her out of this, Egan. If you go near my daughter, I swear I will kill you.' My fear turned to fury. Egan just smirked and came closer. I could smell alcohol on his breath and up close his eyes were glassy and unfocussed; he was drunk.

'Now, now, Abby, that's not nice. I came here in good faith, to give you a chance to return what's mine, and this is how you talk to me.' He grabbed my chin, roughly turning my face towards his.

'Your dumb fuck of a brother wasn't any use, so I thought I'd get you to help me persuade him to be a bit more forthcoming.' He held my face so tightly I couldn't look away and his stinking breath made me want to retch. 'Where's the fucking money?' he hissed, spit flying into my face.

'I don't know anything about any money, I've already told you.' It felt as if he was about to crack my jaw, his grip was so tight. 'Please, just let me go.'

He shoved me backwards against the wall and he turned away from me. I decided I had to take my chance and try to get away. I wrenched open the back door into the yard but my path was blocked by a giant arm: one of Egan's men.

'Running away from me? When all I wanted to do was talk? I can't have that, can I? Stupid bitch.' He hissed these last words in my ear and then yanked me around to face him. The last thing I felt was Egan's sovereign ring making agonising contact with my eye socket and then the world disappeared.

*

My head was pounding and I could taste blood in my mouth. The pain was sharp and intense and I reached up to touch the side of my face. When my hand came away it was covered in blood. I tried to focus on where I was. What was I sitting on? I could only see out of one eye, the other one was swollen shut, but I knew I was still in my café. Relief flooded through me; I was still alive and I was still at home, at least for now.

'Wakey, wakey, Abby. Rise and shine.'

Egan's face appeared in front of mine and any relief I

felt instantly left me; I was still in danger and I had to do something about it. *Think, Abby, don't just sit here, think.* I had the upper hand; he needed me if he was going to get what he wanted from my brother.

'Is there something funny, Abby?' he asked.

Was I smiling? I couldn't tell; I couldn't feel my face. I didn't think I'd even be able to get my mouth to make words come out; it felt like a weird out-of-body experience. Egan grabbed me roughly by the arm and shoved me back so my head cracked on the countertop behind me. My whole body screamed with pain.

'It really didn't have to be like this, Abby. All I wanted was what was mine. But you and your brother, so stubborn. Just like your father. He wouldn't do as he was told either. Not until I got a bit more – shall we say? – forceful in my efforts to persuade him.' Egan smiled at the memory and then chuckled to himself. 'He came round in the end though. Just a shame he couldn't seem to get control of his conscience. Spilling his guts to that bloody mate of his.' Egan shook his head.

'Dad was a good man,' I mumbled. 'How did you manage to get him to work for you?'

'Your dad *was* a good man, you're right, and he loved his family. Even that mental bitch of a mother of yours. Mind you, I can't blame him, she was fucking gorgeous.' Egan licked his lips suggestively and I wanted to gag. 'Always fighting, the pair of 'em. Made it very easy for someone to slip in and offer her some comfort.

He waited for a reaction from me and seemed a bit disappointed not to get one. This wasn't news; I knew that she'd slept with him. I also knew she'd regretted it every day for the rest of her life. Egan carried on.

'I found her outside the pub one night, sobbing her little heart out, she was. She'd just found your dad propped up against the bar again – he'd spent all his money on booze and fags and she needed a shoulder to cry on. I did the gentlemanly thing. I took her back to my place, gave her a few drinks to calm her down. But I knew what she really wanted, she didn't have to say it. Sometimes a woman just needs a little push, if you get my drift?'

I could tell Egan was enjoying reliving this memory; it was written all over his disgusting face. I let him carry on. I knew that the longer I let him talk, the more time it would give me to try and figure a way out of this.

Egan's expression darkened. 'She tried to say that I'd forced myself on her, silly cow. But I knew she wanted it as much as I did. It was written all over her face.'

I wanted to cry. Oh, God. Matt! What if Egan tells him? I thought. The truth would destroy him.

'Terry Egan didn't need to force himself on anyone,' he said proudly. 'I had girls falling at my feet. She was gagging for it.' He shrugged off his coat and turned to hang it on the door leading into the café. I saw the gun tucked into the back of his waistband and it hit me: he was going to kill me. No matter what I told him, he was never going to let me walk out of here. I had to keep him talking.

'You never answered the question. How did you make my dad do your dirty work?'

He smiled lazily. 'It wasn't hard. Like I said, the man loved his family. All I did was explain to him the consequences for all of you if he refused to help me out with a little job.'

'You threatened us?'

'Oh, that's such an ugly word, Abby. I just gave him a few options and he picked the right one, eventually.'

'You bastard.'

He shrugged. 'I certainly am. Now, with that in mind, are you going to tell me what I need to know or am I going to have to persuade you some more?' He pulled the gun out of his waistband and placed it on the counter beside him. 'Shall we call your brother?'

I had to keep Matt well away from this man. 'We don't need my brother. Like you said, he's just a dumb fuck – he doesn't know anything.'

Egan's smile grew wider. 'Well, well, look who's all grown up and in charge now.'

'That's right, I am. Do you want to make a deal or not?' I was winging it, hoping for inspiration, and then it hit me; I had a plan.

'I'm listening. What sort of deal did you have in mind?'

I swallowed down my gag reflex and forced a smile.

'It's not the kind of deal that needs an audience.' I threw a glance over to the goon in the corner. 'I think we could come up with something that suits us both if we had a little privacy.'

Egan laughed. 'Like mother, like daughter, eh? I suppose we could help each other out. Shame your face is a bit messed up but then, like I always say, you don't look at the mantelpiece when you're poking the fire.' He looked so pleased with himself at that little joke that I wanted to brain him, but I managed to smile through my gritted teeth.

'Fuck off, then, for a minute, Dave. Abby and I have some business to discuss.' The meathead across the room looked up and nodded, before leaving. Egan made his way across the room towards me, but I stood up before he could get to me.

'You're not going back on your word, are you, Abby?'

'Of course not, but I thought you'd want to see the money first.' I walked towards the door that led into the café. Egan picked up his gun and waved me on in front of him.

'Lead the way.'

I stepped over to the coffee machine; I knew I would only have one chance at this.

'I just need to get the keys to the safe. I keep them under the counter.' I bent over and slid my hands along the shelf, until my fingers landed on their prize. Egan stepped closer, trying to see what I was doing, and I took my chance. I swung the spanner up and into his face, knocking him back against the wall. He dropped the gun and clutched his face with his hands. 'You fucking bitch!'

I lifted the spanner and hit him again, this time catching him on the forearm as he tried to shield himself. Leaping over the counter, I ran towards the front door of the café, wrestling my keys from my pocket. Egan was lying on the floor, groaning and swearing in pain. My fingers shook as I tried to make the keys fit the lock. Egan had managed to stagger to his feet, but he was blinded by the blood on his face. I slid open the bolts on the door and ripped it open just as Egan began crashing across the café towards me. *Run, Abby, run!*

'Abby!' I heard my brother's voice before I saw him; he was running down the street towards me.

'Matt, no! Stay there, he's coming!' I couldn't let Matt near the café; it wasn't safe. He charged towards me and I fell into his arms, trying to stop him from going inside.

'Where is he?' he screamed. 'I'm gonna fucking kill him!' He charged past me and I heard glass breaking. When I looked back, my brother and Egan were on the floor, struggling.

'Matt, stop! He's got a gun!' I stumbled across the floor towards them and then I heard the gun go off. Oh, God, please, not my brother. I can't lose him too.

'Matt!'

I went to him and flung my arms around him; Egan was lying at his feet.

'It's all right, Abs, I'm all right.'

He's fine, he's safe. Everything's going to be all right.

He held me at arm's length; his face was pale. 'Abby?'

I didn't know what was happening; the floor seemed to be moving up towards me. My legs felt weird, tingly, as if I had a bad case of pins and needles. And I was freezing. What was happening to me? I felt a burning pain in my side and then my vision shrank to a pinpoint. From somewhere far away I thought I heard Jack calling my name.

'Jesus Christ! Abigail! Abby, stay with me! Please, Abby, don't leave me.'

<u>Chapter 30</u>

My eyes felt as if they'd been glued together. As I reached up to rub them I felt something sticking out of the back of my hand. After a bit of squinting and blinking, I managed to open them slightly. My left eye felt swollen and then I remembered – Egan. I tried to sit up but everything hurt, as if I'd been kicked down a flight of stairs – twice. There was a needle sticking out of my left hand – that was what I'd felt when I'd tried to rub my eyes – and there was a tube running from it to a bag of clear fluid that was hanging up beside me. The sunlight streaming in through the window made everything look so clean and bright. Hospital – I was alive and in hospital.

I raised my head slightly and saw my brother asleep in a chair in the corner. He had his elbow propped on the arm of the chair and his head was resting awkwardly in his hand. Relief flooded through me at the sight of him; Egan hadn't shot him. But I was sure I'd heard a gun go off. Matt adjusted his position in the chair and as he did his head slipped out of his hand, waking him up. watched him try to find another comfortable position without much success. He looked exhausted. His eyes were ringed with red, as if he'd been crying, and he hadn't shaved. He scrubbed at his face with his hands and looked over to the bed.

'You look like shit,' I muttered. I wasn't sure if he'd heard me – my voice came out as barely a whisper – and then I saw him smile. He jumped out of the chair and came over to the bed.

'I thought you were a goner, Abs. I thought he'd killed you. I was so scared.'

'I'm still here.' I tried to manage a smile, but my face hurt and my mouth felt like a sandpit. 'I need a drink.'

'Bit early for that, don't you think?'

'Don't make me laugh. It hurts.'

He picked up a cup of water and carefully put it to my lips. I sipped it gingerly and then lay back on the pillows. He leant down and gave me a gentle peck on the cheek.

'That's a serious black eye you've got there. And I should know – I've seen enough of 'em at the gym.' He grimaced.

'Can I have a mirror?'

'Um... well...'

'What?'

'The doc said it'll heal but you might get a bit of a shock when you see yourself. It's not permanent – you're going to be fine.'

'I want to see.'

He took out his phone and set the camera so the lens

was facing me. My bruised and bloodied face stared back at me from the little HD screen; I looked like a monster.

'I look like the bloody elephant man!'

'Don't cry. You're going to be fine, I promise.' He put his arm around my shoulders and did his best to hold me close to him, but it was tough with all the tubes and wires. After a few minutes, I managed to gather myself. I was alive; that was all that mattered.

'What happened? The last thing I remember is you outside the café and then you went in after Egan. I heard the gun go off. I thought he'd shot you.'

'You were the one who got shot, Abs, not me. I was struggling to get the gun and it went off... I thought you were dead.'

'It's not your fault. You saved me. If you hadn't been there, outside the café, he would have killed me for sure.'

Matt nodded but I could tell the guilt was weighing heavily on him.

'Why did you come to the café?' I asked, hoping to distract him.

'For a career criminal, Egan's pretty fucking stupid,' he said. 'He'd been down the pub, drinking whisky and bragging about how he was going to pay you a visit. Scotch Jimmy overheard him and he called me when Egan left the bar.'

'Good old Scotch Jimmy. I think I owe him a very

expensive bottle of something. He probably saved my life.'

'I dunno. You looked like you did a pretty good job on your own. You made a right mess of Egan's face. What did you hit him with?'

'A spanner I keep under the counter for fixing the coffee machine.'

Matt let out a whistle. 'Remind me never to ask you to fix anything of mine.' He smiled weakly. 'I don't know what I would have done if he'd... well... you know.' His shoulders sagged.

'I'm all right, you big softie. Really. I'm just happy to be alive.'

'I love you, Abby,' he muttered.

'I know you do. I love you too. How long have I been here?'

'A couple of days. You lost a lot of blood, but the bullet went straight through without hitting anything important. You were lucky.'

'Yeah, funnily enough I'm not feeling that lucky.'

'Well, this news ought to cheer you up, then.' Matt walked over to the window and looked out. 'We found the money.'

'What?'

'The missing million. We found it.'

'Where?'

Matt smiled. 'Scotch Jimmy had it.'

'And he let Egan threaten us for it? Why didn't he say

something?'

'Because he didn't know he had it.'

I was confused. 'How can you not know you have a million pounds? It's not easy to hide.'

'I know. Apparently, Dad came to him just before he turned himself in. He gave him some boxes of stuff to look after, told him it was old photos and papers. Told Jimmy to keep it safe for him. He said he'd be back for it one day.'

'Jimmy never looked in the boxes? Wasn't he ever curious?'

'Probably, for a while. Until he had another drink at least. Jimmy was drunk a lot of the time.' Matt chuckled. 'Dad put the boxes in Jimmy's lock-up but over the years they got buried under whatever job lot of crap he was trying to shift at the time.'

'Bloody hell! There's been a million pounds in cash, just sitting in a lock-up garage under boxes of cheap cigarettes and hooky designer jeans, for twenty years?'

'Yep. Jimmy reckons all the recent drama sparked his memory. The question is – what do we do with it now?'

For a few brief moments I conjured up some happy images of what life might look like if we had that kind of money; so many things I could do for Lucy, for Flo, for my new business. It would be life-changing for all of us.

Penny for 'em?' asked Matt.

I sighed. 'Just imagining myself in my new apartment

complete with views of the River Thames and a twenty-four-hour concierge service.'

'Nice. I was thinking more along the lines of a private jet and a chauffeur, but we can go with your idea.' Matt smiled and we both burst out laughing.

'Ow, stop it. Everything hurts,' I said. 'We can't keep it, Matt. We have to hand it over to the police.'

He nodded. 'I know. Doesn't hurt to dream though, does it? You never know, maybe the bank will give us a reward for returning it?'

'Give a reward to the children of the man who robbed it off them in the first place? I can't see it somehow, can you?'

Matt chuckled. 'Nah. Probably not.'

I lay back on my pillows and looked around the room. 'Am I allowed visitors? Where is everyone?'

'We've all been taking it in turns to sit with you since you were only allowed one person in here at a time.'

'All of you?'

'Yeah. Me, Lucy, Liz and Flo, we've all been here.'

My heart sank a little; I'd obviously been mistaken when I'd heard Jack's voice before I blacked out.

'And Jack,' added my brother. He smirked. 'You were disappointed when I didn't say his name, weren't you?' He wiggled his eyebrows, mocking me.

'No. Maybe. Oh, shut up.'

'He's been here the whole time, Abs. Ordering the nurses about, making sure you got the best treatment.

He refused to leave.'

'Where is he now?'

'Went to get a coffee, I think.'

'He doesn't drink coffee, only tea.' I smiled at the memory. 'I want to see Lucy. Can you call her? In fact, call everyone. I want to see my family.' Grateful tears were sliding down my face. Matt wiped his eyes with the sleeve of his shirt and coughed.

'All right. But first you need a doctor to check you over. Okay?'

I nodded.

*

After I'd been poked and prodded by a team of doctors and nurses, I finally got my wish; I was surrounded by my family. Lucy, Liz and Flo took it in turns to hug me and to cry with me, but they were tears of joy and relief.

'I can't believe this is what happens when I leave you on your own,' said Lucy. 'I know I said you should get out and do things, but this is bloody ridiculous.'

'I know. Sorry. But I'm fine, really.' I wiped the tears away from her face and tried to reassure her 'Everything's all right now. Egan's gone, so no more excitement for me.'

'Oh, darling, don't say that,' interrupted Liz. 'We've got plenty of excitement to look forward to. We just need to keep you away from guns and spanners, that's all.' She gave me a wink and I laughed.

'Ow! That hurts.'

'Take it easy, love. You need to rest. Tell her, Matt.' Flo busied herself adjusting my pillows and straightening my sheets. I placed my hand over hers and she looked at me with watery eyes.

'I'm not going anywhere any time soon, Flo. All right?' She nodded and pulled a hanky out of her sleeve to dab her eyes with.

The room was full of people and flowers and balloons, but there was something missing. Still no sign of Jack. I didn't want to care that he wasn't here, but I did. I saw Matt glance at his watch. 'Visiting time's almost over. We should let Abby get some rest.'

Flo looked surprised. 'No, it ain't, we've got ages.'

Liz and Lucy gave each other frustrated glances and Matt shook his head.

'No, Flo, we have to go *now*.' He emphasised the 'now' in a way that made me suspicious and caused Flo to hastily tuck her hanky back up her sleeve and grab her handbag from the chair. 'Yes... right... we should go. Take care, Abby, I'll see you tomorrow. Ta ta.'

Matt laughed as he came to kiss me goodbye. 'See ya later, sis.'

He walked to the door, holding it open for Liz and Flo, who both gave me a wave as they left.

'What's going on, Lucy?'

She put on her jacket and came over to my bed. 'You

463

deserve only the best, Mum, and that's what I think you've got in your future. If you let yourself have it, that is. You've just got to trust what you're feeling and not be afraid.' She leaned down and kissed me before walking to the door, pulling it open to let someone in – it was Jack. 'You've got nothing to be afraid of, Mum, not anymore,' she said, before closing the door and leaving us alone.

Jack stood by the wall, looking down at the floor, and I knew that Lucy was right: there wasn't anything to be afraid of.

'Matt said you went for a cuppa,' I said, sitting up. Jack looked up at me. 'Where did you go for it? Ceylon?'

The smile that lit up his face was dazzling. In an instant, he was beside me. He didn't speak, just carefully took my hand in his and leaned his forehead against mine. I closed my eyes and relished the feeling of him, this amazing man. I felt his tears splashing onto my cheeks and when I looked up into his eyes, the pain that I saw took my breath away. I reached up and touched his cheek and he turned his face into my palm and kissed it.

'I'm here, Jack, and I'm fine.'

'I thought I'd lost you. When I heard that gun go off, Matt had you in his arms and you looked so pale, so lifeless. I...' He shook his head, trying to get rid of the memory.

'It *was* your voice I heard.' I hadn't dreamt it; he was there.

'I came back. I had something to give you. I pulled up outside the café just as you followed Matt back inside. Then I heard the gun. Why did you do that? Why did you go back inside?'

'Because he's my brother. I wasn't going to leave him.'

'But you could have died. I could have lost you, forever.' His beautiful face was etched with fear and pain. 'You're everything I want in this world, Abigail. I can't lose you. I won't.'

'You still want me? Even though I currently resemble a circus freak?'

'You're mine, Abigail, and I am yours. No matter what. Everything that's happened, everything that may happen, it's nothing compared to the way I feel about you. You are the love of my life.'

'And you are mine. I love you, Jack. I've always loved you.'

He took my face in his hands. 'Damn, I wish I could kiss you right now.'

'You can try.'

He hesitated for a minute before leaning in and kissing me gently on the lips.

'You can kiss me like that any time you want,' I said.

'You're amazing, do you know that?'

'I'm coming round to the idea.' I smiled and he kissed

me again. 'What did you want to give me? You said you came back that night to give me something.'

'I did. I still have it, if you want it. We can wait though, there's no rush, if you're not ready.'

'I'm ready.'

He reached inside his jacket pocket, pulling something out. My heart was pounding as he took my hand. He looked adorably nervous; taking a deep breath, he held out a small box.

'I don't ever want to be without you again. I want you in my life forever. You have my heart. Abigail, will you marry me?' He opened the box and there, nestled in the folds of white silk, was the most beautiful ring I'd ever seen. My eyes filled with tears and I couldn't speak, I just nodded. He took the ring out and slid it onto my finger. It was a perfect fit.

'How did you know my ring size?' I asked, holding up my hand and watching the ring sparkle in the light.

'I know everything there is to know about you, Abigail. You are my world.'

'And you are mine,' I said. 'I love you, Jack. Always.'

Jack was my past, and for a long time that was where we'd been trapped, but not anymore. He wanted to be part of my life and I wanted to be a part of his. We were meant to be together. I've never been more certain of anything in my life.

Epilogue

'If you don't get that tray of canapés out there now, you will find yourself on the sharp end of my very bad mood,' yelled Liz.

The object of her frustration, a young waiter clutching a tray of smoked salmon and cream cheese whirls, blurted out a garbled apology and then fled from the kitchen. I shook my head. 'Your people skills never cease to amaze me.' I turned my attention back to glazing the mini raspberry tartlets on the tray in front of me; I was anxious for everything to be perfect. It was a very important day, after all.

'People are my thing, Abby, what can I say? It's a gift.' She leaned over and grabbed a tartlet, popping it into her mouth before I could stop her.

'Oi! Hands off.' I stepped back and admired my work. The tray of glistening red pastries looked perfect. I handed them to a passing waitress. 'Could you take these for me, please? They need to go on the main table, over by the wall. Thank you.' I glared pointedly at Liz as I spoke. 'See, it doesn't hurt to be polite.'

'You do your thing, I'll do mine. It works better that

467

way – you should know that by now.' She smiled and nudged me with her hip as she passed. She was right, we did have very different ways of working, but after almost a year in business together we'd found an approach that was proving to be a recipe for success. Our catering and event management company was going from strength to strength. After a few quiet weeks at the beginning, which had been a bit scary but expected, the bookings had started coming in thick and fast. Between my food and Liz's contacts, we were booked solid for the next twelve months. Product launches, company events, weddings – you name it, we catered for it.

Building my own business had given me a real sense of accomplishment. I finally felt as if I was in charge of my own destiny. Life wasn't just a series of unfortunate events that happened to me anymore; now I made things happen, I got to choose. The woman of a few months before, the one who'd felt as if she were drowning under the weight of her own past, was gone. I didn't recognise her any longer.

'Abby! We need some more champagne glasses. Where are they?' Flo pushed her way through the kitchen doors, holding an empty tray. 'And what are you doing still in that outfit? You're supposed to have got changed by now.'

'All right, all right. Just checking a few last details,' I replied, pulling off my apron. 'The glasses are in the box by the door. Get someone to help you, though, don't do it on your own. That box is heavy.'

'Stop fussing, I can manage,' Flo said.

'No one is doubting that, my darling,' said Liz, going over to the box of glasses to lend Flo a hand. 'We're just here to assist.'

'Well, that's all right, then. Here, you take the tray. I'm going back out to make sure those bloody waiters are doing their jobs properly. Honestly, I have to follow them around barking orders or else they just stand there looking gormless.'

I shook my head; I knew that wasn't the case. All our staff were very efficient and responsible, but Flo liked to make sure they knew who was boss. She and Liz were remarkably similar in that respect.

'You go get 'em, Flo.' Liz chuckled. Flo bustled back out through the doors.

'Don't encourage her,' I said. 'We'll have a mutiny on our hands.'

'It's fine. They all love her. She's like their surrogate grumpy gran.'

'And what does that make us?' I asked.

'Utterly fabulous, darling, as always. Now, Flo's right, you should get changed. You need to be out there – it's an important day for you. Here.' She tossed me a brown leather holdall. 'Go and change in the loo. It'll be quicker.'

'What about you and Flo? You need to get ready too.'

'All under control. As soon as Flo comes back I'm dragging her away to get changed upstairs. Off you go, then.' She waved me away.

*

As I stood in front of the mirror, I marvelled at the difference twelve months could make. I was wearing the same red velvet dress that Liz had given me on the day that Jack had come back into my life. But not the underwear – nothing could have persuaded me to try and squeeze into those torturous bits of fabric again. Besides, I'd amassed quite a decent collection of nice underwear of my own recently.

I adjusted my cleavage a bit and then pulled the clip out of my hair. It tumbled over my shoulders in dark blonde waves and I grinned – I looked good. Even though I did say so myself. My eyes were shining, and I looked happy and confident and strong. This was the me I'd always known was inside somewhere, but I'd let her get lost. Not any more though. There was a light tap on the door.

'Come in,' I called.

'So this is where you're hiding. Liz sent...' Jack stepped into the room and stopped mid-sentence. 'Jesus, you look amazing. That dress. Is it...?'

'Yes, it's the same one.'

Without another word, Jack strode across the room

and took my mouth in a breath-taking kiss. He pulled me close to him, his hands snaking their way down my back.

'Hey now, stop that. People are out there waiting for us.'

'They can wait. This is much more important.' He began kissing along my jawline and then down my neck.

'Down, boy,' I said, reluctantly pushing him away. 'I need to finish getting ready. You've smudged my lipstick. Here.' I handed him a tissue. 'You've got Dior on your lips.' I turned back to the mirror to re-apply and Jack stood close behind me. I watched as he wiped his mouth and then pocketed the tissue. I raised my eyebrows.

'Souvenir,' he said, grinning. His dark eyes sparkled, and I laughed.

'I love that sound so much,' he said as he placed his arms either side of me, trapping me against the sink. I looked at the reflection of the two of us – the handsome tech millionaire and me – and we looked perfect. Whereas before I'd convinced myself that a man like Jack – gorgeous, confident, sexy as fuck – was too good for me, I'd come to realise that wasn't the case. If anything, it was Jack who was the lucky one; he had me. Strong, sexy and with one heck of a talent in the kitchen, I was a force to be reckoned with. I turned and kissed him gently on the mouth, before ducking under his arm and moving over to the door.

'You do know what you do to me, don't you, Abigail?'

'Of course. And you love it.'

'I love you.'

'I never tire of hearing you say those words. I love you too. Now come on, people are waiting.' I held out my hand and Jack took it and kissed the back of it before we made our way out to the waiting crowd.

*

'I'd like to thank everyone for coming. I want you all to know how happy we are to have you here, sharing our special day.' My brother Matt waited for the applause to die down before continuing his speech.

'Getting married isn't something I ever thought I'd do. But when you meet the one, well, you just know.' Matt wiped away a tear and looked down at his new wife, Sarah, sitting beside him. They looked so in love and it made my heart soar. They'd only been together for about ten months when he'd told me he was getting married and I'd been a bit sceptical. It seemed very quick but then, after I'd seen them together, I knew that Sarah was the one for him. At only five feet two, she was tiny when she stood next to my man mountain of a brother, but she was fierce and fearless, as well as kind, funny and generous of spirit. She was everything my brother didn't even know he needed. And today, on their wedding day, I was so happy for them both that I couldn't stop crying.

After the speeches, and after I'd managed to pull myself together, I sat at the table, surrounded by everyone I cared about.

'I can't believe he's gone and done it. Can you, Mum?'

Lucy and I sipped our champagne and watched my brother and his beautiful new wife glide around the dance floor.

'He looks so happy. I'm so pleased for him. He deserved to find someone lovely,' said Lucy.

'Yes, he did. And what about you?' I gestured to the young man that Lucy had brought to the wedding with her. He was currently deep in conversation with Jack on the other side of the room.

'Toby? He's nice. We have a good time, nothing serious.'

I winced a bit. Try and be cool, I told myself, she's a grown-up. 'As long as you're being careful, that's all I'll say.'

Lucy rolled her eyes and finished her champagne. 'What is Jack saying to him over there?'

'No idea. They're just chatting, I think.'

'Mmm. Well, I'm going to go and rescue him. See you in a bit.' She pecked me on the cheek and walked over to Jack and Toby. Jack said something to her that made her giggle and then he shook Toby's hand and came back to our table.

'Everything all right?' I said.

'I don't like him,' said Jack, matter-of-factly.

'Who?'

'Toby.' He picked up his glass and took a sip. I laughed.

'Why? You've only just met him.'

'He has a handshake like a limp bit of cod and an earring through his eyebrow.'

'So?'

'He's not good enough for her. Simple as that.'

'You're being ridiculous, but it's very sweet nonetheless.'

'I'm not being sweet, Abigail. You have to be careful. Lucy is too good for him.'

'I know, you mentioned that.' His sudden paternal feelings made me smile.

'Don't laugh at me. This is important. Who is this guy anyway?'

'She said they take a few classes together. History of art, I think.'

Jack raised his eyebrows. This was too funny; I couldn't resist winding him up a bit more.

'Maybe you should have one of your security guys check him out? Just to be on the safe side,' I said.

'Do you think? Yeah, maybe…' He reached into his jacket for his phone, but I stopped him.

'Don't you bloody dare! I was joking.'

'Well, I'm not. We need to know, he could be—'

I stopped him mid-sentence by planting a kiss on his lips. 'I love that you want to protect her. It's very sweet. And quite sexy, actually. But she's fine. She's a clever girl – she knows how to look after herself. We just have to trust in her judgement. All right?'

'Okay, fine,' he said. 'Can we go back to the part where you called me sexy?' He gave me a wolfish grin that made me clamp my thighs together.

'Gladly,' I said. I leaned towards him and kissed him hard on the mouth. I felt his growl of pleasure as I ran my hand along his thigh.

'That's disgusting. Behave yourselves.'

Jack pulled back in surprise at the sound of my brother's voice. Matt was grinning like an idiot and Sarah was trying to stifle her giggles behind her hand.

'You two enjoying yourselves? Actually, don't answer that. I don't think I wanna know.'

Sarah slapped my brother's arm. 'Oh, stop it. They're in love. Anyone can see that.'

Matt looked at me and pulled a disgusted face. 'Yuk. That's my little sister.'

'Shut up, you idiot,' I said.

'Abby, thank you so much for organising the catering and everything. It was perfect.' Sarah came over and kissed me on the cheek.

'You're welcome. It was an honour.'

'She's right, Abs. Everything was perfect.' My brother

pulled me in for a hug.

'Jack, are you going to come and drag me around the dance floor for a bit?' Sarah held out her hand and Jack duly stood and took it.

'It would be my pleasure.' He kissed Sarah's hand and gave her a little bow, before pulling her in the direction of the dance floor. She turned back to me and mouthed, 'He's so cute.'

'I reckon it went well. Don't you?' asked Matt.

'It was perfect. Mum and Dad would have been very proud of you.'

'And of you. No way Mum could have criticised your cooking skills today. Your food went down a storm.'

I smiled. 'Nah, she still would have found a way to be critical about something, but that's all right. It was just her way, I guess.'

'Look at you, all grown up and philosophical about everything.'

'Life goes on, Big Brother.'

'It certainly does.' We clinked our glasses together and watched Jack and Sarah doing a very passable Macarena. One by one everyone on the dance floor joined in. My brother finished his drink and then stood up. 'You coming?'

I shook my head. 'Not my thing. You go, show 'em how it's done.' I winked at him.

He loosened his tie and headed for the dance floor, positioning himself at the very front and singing along at the top of his voice. I watched for a bit, amazed to see Flo and Liz dancing arm in arm and giggling like a pair of schoolgirls. Who would have thought it? Lucy and Toby were standing by the edge of the floor, looking on in amazement at all the adults acting like teenagers at a school disco. Matt and Jack might, or might not, have been having some kind of dance-off; it was hard to tell exactly.

I left them all to it and stepped outside, into the cool evening. I walked a bit further away from the marquee that housed the revellers. I made my way down some stone steps in the hotel grounds, and towards a wooden bench that faced a long avenue of apple trees that led to the rose garden. I sat down and admired the fairy lights that twinkled in all the branches, echoing the array of stars on display in the night sky above. I could hear music and laughter – such an amazing sound – and then I heard footsteps on the gravel path behind me. I didn't need to turn round to know who it was; whenever he was near me now I could feel it.

'Was my dancing too painful to watch?'

I turned to see Jack holding two glasses of champagne. He'd taken off his tie, I could see it hanging out of his jacket pocket, and he'd undone the first few buttons on his shirt. He looked practically edible.

'I just fancied a bit of fresh air. It's such a beautiful night.'

Jack came round and sat beside me on the bench. He

put the champagne down on the ground and took both my hands in his. His thumb caressed the engagement ring on my left hand.

'Is it our turn next?' he said, softly.

I reached up and touched his cheek; he turned his face towards my palm and kissed it gently.

'I still can't believe my luck,' he said, 'to have you back in my life after so long. Sometimes I think it's all been a dream and one day I'm going to wake up and you'll be gone again.'

'Me too. But I think there was a kind of inevitability about it all. You were always there, Jack, in my head and in my heart. I'd imagined us together so many times and for so long, I think maybe the universe just decided it owed us one after all the heartache. Does that sound really dumb?'

Jack shook his head. 'No. I know what you mean. I think that's why I could never make a relationship work. I knew you were out there somewhere and I needed to make it back to you. No one else would do; it had to be you.' He leaned closer and kissed me softly on the lips.

'Do you remember you asked me once about where I wanted to go? You said just say the word and you'd take me there.'

'I remember.'

'Take me to a beach, Jack. With white sands and tropical breezes and a clear blue ocean.'

'Right now?' he asked, his eyes glittering in the

moonlight.

'Right now. I want to wear a white bikini and have flowers in my hair. And I want to stand on the water's edge and become your wife. That's what I want. Right now.'

He stood, pulling me with him and holding me close. We kissed until we were both breathless.

'I love you so much,' he said.

'I love you too.' I looked back towards the marquee. 'Now let's get going before they drag us into that conga line.' I gestured to the long line of our nearest and dearest that was snaking its way down the path towards us.

'Good idea,' said Jack, as he took my hand and we ran through the trees and into the rose garden.

Acknowledgements

My first thank you must go to anyone who has bought this book – your support means the world to me, it's what makes all this possible. Thank you to everyone at Aria Fiction for all the love and kindness you have shown me since I joined your publishing family. A special thanks to my lovely editor, Lucy Gilmour, whose unwavering faith and passion in this story gave me the opportunity to fulfil a lifelong dream. Our random conversations about anything and everything, usually not to do with the book, continue to make me smile!

I will be forever grateful to the Romantic Novelist's Association; not just for their amazing New Writer's Scheme, without which I have no doubt I would never have achieved my dream of becoming a published author, but also for the love and support of the Association and its members. The RNA has given me the opportunity to meet some of the most amazing people and their continued support has meant more to me than I say. In particular, Rachel Dove, Julie Stock, Kate Field – you three ladies rock my world! Thank you for everything.

I also need to thank my lovely chums at Red Wine Writer's. Guys, you've spent years listening to me read stuff out loud and your feedback and positive criticism has kept me going throughout this whole journey. A big thank you to Terry Martin, you read the whole thing! An even bigger thank you must surely go then to your poor wife, Liz, who read it twice!! Thanks also to Lisa Hall – you kickstarted this journey for me and I will be forever in your debt.

I didn't need to do masses of research for this book, I'm way too lazy for that, but I was helped tremendously by a few people. Firstly, to Julie Pearce, who shared her many years of nursing experience with me to make sure I got those scenes in hospital just right; to Barry Leban for his insight into prison procedures and to Joanne Clow for her help with my questions about criminal court procedures.

My last lot of thanks go to those people I love most in the world, my family. And I must include two very special women in that group; Lucy and Sonia, you are my 'sisters from other misters' and I love you both so much. Thank you for believing in me and for always being prepared to drink alcohol with me. My love and thanks to my Mum and Dad; I know I've always been the perfect daughter, but this makes me even better doesn't it? To Joanne – that online writing course you bought for me paid off eventually! Love you lots Little Sis!

And last, but by no means least, to my husband and my two amazing children; you are everything. This is all for you.

HELLO FROM ARIA

We hope you enjoyed this book! Let us know, we'd love to hear from you.

We are Aria, a dynamic digital-first fiction imprint from award-winning independent publishers Head of Zeus. At heart, we're avid readers committed to publishing exactly the kind of books we love to read — from romance and sagas to crime, thrillers and historical adventures. Visit us online and discover a community of like-minded fiction fans!

We're also on the look out for tomorrow's superstar authors. So, if you're a budding writer looking for a publisher, we'd love to hear from you. You can submit your book online at ariafiction.com/we-want-read-your-book

You can find us at:
Email: aria@headofzeus.com
Website: www.ariafiction.com
Submissions: www.ariafiction.com/we-want-read-your-book
Facebook: @ariafiction
Twitter: @Aria_Fiction
Instagram: @ariafiction

Printed in Great Britain
by Amazon

64968471R00276